CREDS

The I.R.S. Adventure

Ben Parris

BLUEBERRY
LANE BOOKS

New York

CREDS: The I.R.S. Adventure, A Novel Based on a True Story

This edition was produced by Blueberry Lane Books
Published in the United States of America
Cover art © Copyright 2014, 2015, 2020, and 2022 Blueberry Lane Books

Blueberrylanebooks.com

ISBN: 978-1-942183-03-7

To L.
It couldn't have happened without you

FACTS

Life happens on a need-to-know basis and this is what you need to know. This adventure-in-novel-form is about the enforcement of tax law and the people who undertake that complex task, foibles and all. To paraphrase J.B.S. Haldane and Sir Arthur Stanley Eddington, not only is the IRS stranger than you imagine, it is stranger than you *can* imagine, a system both scarier and more comforting than reports would have you believe. Just like those who wear the uniforms of police, firefighters, emergency services, armed forces, and secret services, there are heroes in the Treasury Department quietly fighting for your rights and way of life at the risk of their own.

The idea of a government collecting taxes of any kind is to provide for the public good and we trust that it generally works that way. I won't say that insisting on paying *higher* taxes is patriotic. That would be asinine. The duty of a government is to create a functional, humane system and administrative framework resulting in the lowest possible burden to its people. Our duty at the personal level is to pay no more than the law requires after taking into consideration any tax-reducing incentives provided by congress. Neither government nor individual actions in these matters have been perfect or ever will be. Our duty to each other, however, is to refrain from forcing our neighbors to pay our taxes for us by not paying them ourselves.

The U.S. Treasury Department in my time consisted of 180,000 employees. My experiences in the particular time and place described might be atypical, although I was not the only one who wanted to treat taxpayers fairly while catching the real bad guys. The less-than-ideal government employees I encountered and described in these pages acted far outside of policy and their training.

As for the civilians described, some people will do anything to get out of paying their taxes, including attempts to destroy the whole system. The story told herein will reveal the nature of the beast in its myriad complications and contradictions. Enlightenment may or may not follow.

Danny "Creds" Shapiro,
Internal Revenue Agent Emeritus

IRS Brooklyn District Management Chart

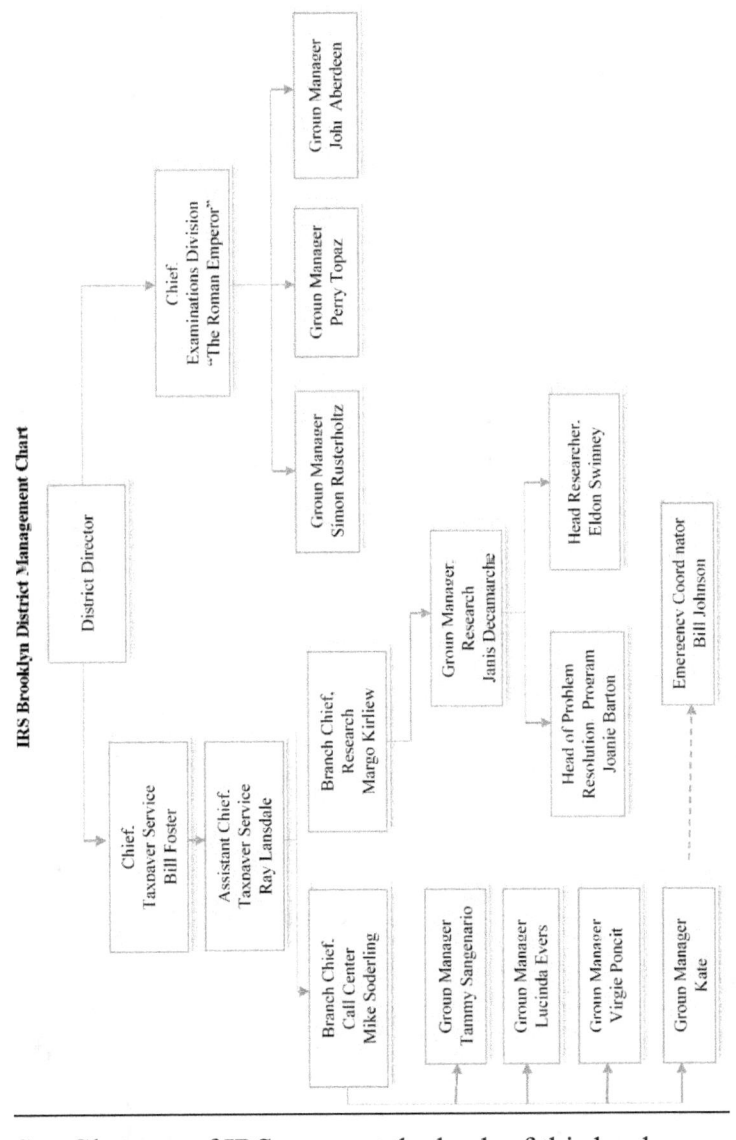

See Glossary of IRS terms at the back of this book.

"That's the damnedest thing I ever saw!
I don't know, it seemed to swoop down at you deliberately!"

–The Birds

AMBUSH: March 27, 1987

Something felt odd about that unseasonably warm March night, and it just didn't sink in with me when it should have. A taxpayer's rep had given me an elliptical warning shortly before I left work. Some nonsense that I would pay for daring to audit the State Senator he defended. I had seen the look in his eyes and should have taken his fury more seriously.

But the D Train lulled me across the trestle with a slow, swaying motion, the lights dimming and rising. When I stepped over the doorway gap to exit, the night air, laden with moisture and ocean salt, seemed to make my heavy briefcase float. I felt I could ignore vague threats from people who relied on intimidation. It was something that came with my job. The gum-spotted platform I walked on masked any incipient worries with a lifetime of familiarity. I looked forward to reuniting with Linda that weekend. To say that our relationship needed work was an understatement. Most of my thoughts were about her. It was not the sort of night where I expected to wage a contest for my life.

1

Like any other evening, I hammered down the stairs for the seven-minute dash from the elevated train line that served Little Russia.

Most of the time I would dodge around the multitudes streaming from the station and see them off to the knish shops and Odessa-style nightclubs that topped off many resident's evenings. Returning from extended office hours when daylight was shortchanged by the season, I saw instead the muted version of Brighton Beach at street level. Suits and ties like mine were few among the blue-collar commuters and further diminished at the ragged tail of rush hour. This spit of land that bordered Coney Island was a beach community most alive in summer. The corner doomsday preacher and street performers like Disco Freddy had no interest in performing for this paltry crowd. They had long since melted into the night.

Behind me, the rail line straddled the length of the avenue like a dragon born of metal and concrete. Ahead, its vertebrae and legs lumbered across the intersection to form a curving canopy, making the darkened stores on the opposing street look as though they had piled under the petrified beast in an east-blowing storm.

From there, I barreled north on Coney Island Avenue past the less popular establishments that abruptly transitioned to residential wood frame shacks. This route would re-join the high rails nearby, tracing along the diagonal street that led to mine. Three blocks from the station, I found the section deserted as if its residents were still in the psychological grip of a bitter cold winter, rather than a pleasant early spring. When people were scarce, even at night, there would usually be pigeons and seagulls scavenging in their wake. Some recent disturbance must have driven every living thing away. A truck going too fast down the street would chase birds easily enough, but that didn't explain why no one was out on the stoops.

Splitting off to Brighton 10th, the side street disappeared into a bend, and once there I waded into a profound darkness that I'd never seen before. Normally the streetlights beamed every fifty yards or so, illuminating a spackle-veined collection of two-storey brick houses on the near side of the street and one-storey stucco homes shouldering the train tracks on the far. In March, the very few trees of Brighton were still shadowy sticks.

As I paused to let my eyes adjust, the uniform blackout struck me as bizarre. There had never been more than one lamp disabled at a time. The moon shone meekly through the overcast like a reflector deep in a tunnel. My normally shiny watch face gave back nothing.

I jogged back out onto Coney Island Avenue to see if the whole city had suddenly gone out in the seconds it took me to turn the corner. There I saw the bright white mercury-vapor lights secure on their high mast poles. Stumped, I took a moment to watch green traffic lights transitioning through yellow to red. Across the wide street, a hodgepodge of incandescent lamps glowed in apartment building windows under which a stray dog knocked over a barrel, and a cat jumped ahead of him for the spoils. Too stubborn to walk the long way, I turned again and proceeded to tackle Brighton 10th in the dark. I considered that neighborhood my back yard and felt territorial about it. Karate lessons, along with the natural reflexes and speed of my twenty-five years, had made me a little too brave.

Past the bend, the gloom was so palpable that I reached out expecting the air to be thick with it and instead found a void empty as space. I had to wait again for my pupils to catch up. In a block or so, where the dim squares behind shaded windows resolved a growing collection of anti-burglar bars, I noticed something else. Thin moonlight glinted off broken glass on the ground, directly under the first light pole.

Now this was a mystery. The massive lens itself had come crashing down. The demolition reminded me of the days when my tough but nutty friend, Jason Ament, used to smash light bulbs in tenement stairwells with the back of his calloused hand. These outdoor coverings, however, were far too thick for Jason to attempt. Too thick even if he were armed with a baseball bat. The only way to break these street lights was for someone to have climbed up, taken the bolts out, and let the whole assembly drop.

Four houses later, shattered glass adorned the foot of the next pole in a confusion of oversized shell and filament. I couldn't help but crouch to examine these fragments, because up close, the chunky shards and their enormous bolts were the light bulb equivalents of elephants laid low.

And there were more of these gargantuan wrecks to come. The loss of illumination was no accident. Each of the city lights had been taken out in an unusually methodical act of vandalism, where the vandals fled into the pitch blackness. Nothing pierced the velvet beyond, so I couldn't see the nature of the trouble ahead, but I was willing to bet that the whole six-block stretch had suffered the same kind of attack.

On the first branching street, the lights had been eliminated as well. I could see the comforting glow of Coney Island Avenue, now a full block away. The contrast reminded me of childhood when the adults stayed up in the bright living room for serious talk while us kids pretended to be asleep in the dark. At each break on my current diagonal route, that beacon of safety would grow more distant. A vandal would have to have scrambled up a very tall ladder or crow's nest at least fifteen times to smash all these lights. Who could have pulled that off? I walked on, puzzling it out, not realizing just yet that there might be more to the circumstances than some deviant's taste for wanton destruction.

As an avid Alfred Hitchcock fan, I considered with a wry smile that maybe the vandals didn't need a ladder. Maybe it was Brighton's missing birds laying an even more sophisticated ambush than they managed in the movie. Nature's revenge. But screeching birds with their talons out was one of poor Linda's phobias, not mine. I wondered what she was doing at this very moment and whether she was thinking of me.

My distraction didn't last. In the stillness, I could hear a chorus of fearless crickets mingled with the low purr of a well-tuned car engine creeping slowly behind me. Possibly looking for an address in the dark, but I didn't like this new element added to the mix. In my neighborhood, with muggings common, you were constantly alert to anyone out of place.

Getting jumped from a passing car that then sped away was the latest crime pattern. Was it part of the assailant's M.O. to make the streets dark in advance so that they couldn't be identified? That approach seemed too sophisticated and risky in itself. Earlier in the day, Yoffe Millstein from work had complained about my overactive imagination. "Danny, Danny, your brain is getting slow. Too much auditing on your mind. Tomorrow's another day to stop the bad guys. If you bring your work home, you bring your troubles home."

Yoffe was one of the few people at work too kind to tag me with the ironic nickname Creds. They called me that because I didn't throw my weight around, didn't flash my credentials at civilians who gave me trouble. Except for that one particular incident that I would never live down.

But I was growing certain that I had more than an irksome nickname to worry about now. In the corner of my eye, I could see the lights of the car trailing behind me, long pale phantoms groping the black gutter. The car had moved closer. Still no other pedestrians on the street. Then the high beams kicked in. It was a legal move when the streetlights were out, but these were no standard issue. They erased the night like floodlights and took in the sidewalks on either side, exposing my exact position. I heard the insistent purring get louder, possibly a block away.

In my business, instinct was the cornerstone of safety. Although my pulse quickened from the near-certainty of attack, I didn't want to betray my awareness of the danger; survival in my neighborhood always depended on some element of counter-surprise. I knew every feature of the triangular section of blocks I called home. If my pursuers didn't, there had to be an advantage in there somewhere.

Moving along, I passed the home of the Mancini's, who used to live on my old block, still occupying the subterranean level they preferred. Their lights were off. They would have drunk themselves unconscious by now, and no amount of door pounding would rouse them. If I knocked at a stranger's door instead, they would either hide or get defensive. It might make them call the cops, but that would be too late to help me. Above the houses and across the street, a train climbed the spine of the dragon and clattered past unconcerned. I realized that practically all the people I knew lived in the houses surrounding mine, four blocks ahead.

The car chasing me rallied and halted like a champion steed that would not be denied. When it wasn't gaining ground, it averaged three miles per hour, matching my pace. The driver must have had to ride the brake the whole way to keep this up. This was no mugging, or else he would have been on me already.

I passed the spot where I had once witnessed a four-year-old girl nearly shot dead by a drugged-up teenager in broad daylight. The little girl's father, a cop, had been keeping an eye on her from the doorway. He tackled the young man who pointed the muzzle at his daughter's head, and then exacted a measure of revenge. Where was that cop now? He worked nights, so he wasn't there.

Soon the pool of light pinned my oversized shadow to the passing houses, held steady, and got the hang of keeping pace with me. I stopped in a pretense of tying my shoe, and glanced over my shoulder so that I could just about see the vehicle: a silhouette of a pick-up truck with some kind of wicked iron cowcatcher hiding the silver of the front bumper and concealing the license plate.

They pulled to a stop. Three solid men filled the small cab, cranking windows down, rattling a large unfolded map, and making noises like they were trying to find an address. I didn't have a chance to pick out any details or distinguish one person from another with the light in my eyes.

Facing forward again, any object outside the wash of light appeared darker than before, a disconcerting landscape of gray on black, painted in muzzy streaks. My briefcase with its burden of confidential papers seemed heavier when I picked it up and continued. There was no opportunity to stash it in some hiding place without them noticing.

The travelers resumed too, holding their pick-up steadily anchored to the rhythm of my legs. Now I was scared by their whole set of tactics. But I would not give in to that feeling while I still had freedom of movement.

If it wasn't a mugging, what was it? Were they from a tax-protest militia group? No, this approach wasn't their style. It wasn't the style of any known threat. Given that the State Senator's papers were in my briefcase, however, it occurred to me that the car at my back might be there to deliver a personal message, and one that I might not walk away from in one piece. Now I wished I had placed a call to Linda before I left the office. If anything happened to me…well, it was best not to think about it. I needed to concentrate on making sure that no calls from me—or about me—would be necessary.

I was already moving at a brisk pace, so I had to bend my knees to a soft jog to find the next gear. It felt good to channel my adrenaline. If and when all those guys got out to confront me, I would have a slim chance. I had been taught, in theory, how to fight several people at once using an open stance with three-hundred-sixty-degree awareness and methodical, practiced moves. If I were face to face with them I would occupy my mind by deciding tactics from the local terrain and each opponent's physical characteristics. I would visualize a combination of blows calculated to punch through my targets, and I would display my confidence with a smile before delivering a full-throated roar. But first I would let them draw nearer because I was especially good at taking weapons and breaking noses. When facing a superior opponent, there was a premium on moving fast and sure. The key to that—and half the time spent training—was learning to believe. I could be scared-as-hell or I could be eager for a fight. I chose the latter.

But when my pursuers' engine revved high, the way it does when the pedal is forced suddenly to the floor, reality cleared away my hopes of calling on my karate training. What remained was the idea that you must always be ready for a tactical retreat. I knew better than to waste time casting my gaze behind me and getting blinded. My fingers fused around the briefcase handle, protecting the case's secrets as long as possible while preserving its use as a weapon of last resort. Adrenaline-crazed, I put one foot in front of the other as if I could outrun a car. I tried to make myself believe it could happen in the same way that a karate master breaks cinder blocks by believing his hand will pass through.

As I ran, time slowed to make way for my last crowded thoughts. I admitted to myself that it had to be the Senator who sent this car. I was the only one who knew about the antique biscuit jar that could bring him down. The pickup's cowcatcher could lift me off my feet, and if it did, the men in the truck would get my notes. If I wasn't alive to tell about it, the Senator's troubles would be over. The idea of dying so young made me light headed. Why did I ever become an IRS agent? Without my Linda I never would have gotten in, probably never have succeeded. As she might have said, who asked me to succeed so well? Yes, I should have called her before I left the office.

As the night filled my laboring lungs, the neighborhood's saltwater air intensified. It stirred memories of those humbling days as a kid, pushing through packed wet sand to meet the immensity of the surf. Moving down the underwater slope and feeling the tug of the ocean clearing away the surrounding grains to leave me on foot-sized plateaus. Then, encountering the sharp band of broken shells, the seaweed lapping my toes as if to salve them, water billowing my suit, and finally the lull of the full current taking charge and brooking no dissent.

The bright lights extinguished, making it darker than ever; there would be no witnesses. The car climbed the curb behind me with a double thump.

I would never see my precious Linda again.

CHAPTER ONE
The Plunge

Linda. Nearly three years earlier, in 1984, Linda and I were coming back from a party on the east end of Long Island. Our on-again-off-again relationship was on the upswing. We had a long night drive home in my dad's fourteen-year-old Ford LTD, rain splattering the windshield, the kind of moody circumstance that allowed her to corner me in a serious conversation that I otherwise would have avoided. I cut off the radio when I heard some pundit speculating that anything America might achieve in the Los Angeles Olympics would be worthless if the Soviets chose to boycott.

Linda cleared her throat. "Danny, now that college is over, what are you going to do with your life?" She used her provocative, sexy voice on me, her way of getting me onto the subject in a non-threatening way.

I looked over to see if she really wanted to know, and also as an excuse just to see the face I cherished. Her black hair framed an alabaster complexion. In a quick look I couldn't spot the couple of premature gray strands on her head, but I knew just where they were. Her innocent face had an evil little smirk. I decided that with her question she was signaling the proprietary nature of our relationship. It wasn't an out-and-out promise, but she had an interest in the rest of my life because she preferred to be a part of it. Secretly in

11

love with her, I reached over and cupped my palm on her thigh.

"You can't do that," she laughed without shying away. "You're driving. Put your hands at ten o'clock and two o'clock, mister." Grabbing me by the wrists, she placed my hands in the appropriate positions for me.

I laughed too. "You love to tease me when I can't do anything about it."

"What? No, I really want to know. What are you doing with your degree?"

Not anxious to confess to my meager career progress, I watched a little rivulet find an independent path down the windshield, way on the side where the wipers couldn't reach. The flood had captured a tiny bug that was fighting all the way. Sometimes it did the impossible, scaling the slick, vertical wall against the tide. More often, it would succumb to exhaustion and pinwheel wherever the current wanted it to go. Before it lost too much ground, I said, "I want to get a job in accounting."

"So?" She meant: So why haven't you done it?

"There are too many accountants out there."

She gave me a long, pensive silence while the rain drummed the hood like so many impatient fingers. Her parents had drilled into her that she needed to marry someone rich, and they specifically warned her that I was a loser. That's what I feared she might be thinking about at moments like this. "Why'd you go into it?" she said.

"Why did I get an accounting degree? My high school guidance counselor said there was a shortage."

"That was stupid," she said, and I glared at her for that remark.

"Don't look at me," she warned lightly. "Look at the road."

I went back to staring into the dark. When I checked on the windshield river, I had to trace it all the way to the corner before finding the bug twirling down that final inch of glass, and disappearing into the wiper well to try its luck there. Linda was smart, fun, strong in the face of her phobias, practical, and above all, compassionate. I owed her a good explanation.

I admitted, "Maybe it was stupid. The point is that no one is advertising for these positions now. I can't even land interviews, let alone a job."

"So what are you going to do with your life in the long run? All you want to do is be an accountant? You're better than that."

"I have plans."

"Tell me." She really did sound like she wanted to know.

Although I couldn't rely on Linda Sobel to stick around, to say that I wanted to please and impress my pear-shaped beauty was an understatement. While Linda was one of many fine-looking women I had dated, she was the one I cared for the most and the only one I continued to see whenever she allowed it in the years since I'd met her. She made no secret of the fact that she only wanted to marry someone with a lot of money. But I saw no clue that she craved a lavish lifestyle. Her words were a perfect echo of what her parents wanted. Four years of her repeating that mantra, while so often at my side, sometimes made me question if she would ever break away from that lie. When we were together, though it was not often enough, there were sparks between us. I could tell that she wanted me, that she would ultimately accept me whatever I would become. Wise or unwise, every time she declared herself free, I came running.

"Ok," I said. "I want to begin with a career in accounting then move through the ranks of the corporate executives. The place could be profit or non-profit, but I prefer if it's in science."

"So you want to be a corporate executive?"

"I've read a lot of business biographies. Did you know that Lee Iacocca started out as an accountant?" I realized too late how defensive that sounded.

"I read that too," said Linda, surprising me, so I gave her the rest of it.

"In accounting you do better if you specialize in taxes," I said. "Lately I'm thinking I want to start at the IRS, where I can really learn from the source. Also they don't pay much, so I think I can stand that better now than later."

"What do you mean, you *want* to start at the IRS? What's the problem?"

I appreciated that Linda didn't complain about the fact that I had started out a gifted physics student before I switched to accounting. Her lack of criticism was part of the reason I knew she was rooting for me in any way possible. When she spoke like this, she was intense but not harsh. More in the mode of a decision-maker who needed all the information. "The job I want is called Revenue Agent," I told her, "but there's a hiring freeze on."

Without a moment's pause, she said, "Get a job in the Treasury Department as a janitor."

"How will that help me?"

"They don't freeze all the jobs. You get in anywhere you can."

"Then what?"

"Then you apply for the Revenue Agent job, stupid." She was smiling. Now that the solution to my stalled career had presented itself, she took my right hand and restored its place on her thigh.

I was dumbfounded. Even though I knew that Linda worked for the City of New York, and that her father was a civil servant too, it never occurred to me that she knew something about this stuff.

She spelled it out slowly for me when she saw I wasn't getting it. "You take any stinking little job they have. Then you apply for the job you want internally. The freeze is only external."

I risked a glance at her. "You mean I can get in, claiming I want one position, and then apply to a different job immediately?"

"Yes."

"The IRS doesn't consider that a scam?"

With a gentle finger to the tip of my chin, she pointed my attention to the road. "Call it whatever you want. That's how it works."

ACCORDING TO THE postings, the only job opening that I qualified for was called Taxpayer Service Representative, or TSR for short. In the dimly lit corridor tucked in Manhattan's 26 Federal Plaza, I read the details with growing horror. In this position, I would be less respected, and not nearly as well compensated as a janitor. The Taxpayer Service Division was, in effect, the complaint department for everyone who paid taxes and owned a telephone. I would be picking up angry calls all day if I were lucky enough to work full days.

According to the posted card in the glass cabinet, becoming a TSR meant that you would be a part-time, seasonal, conditional, and *provisional* employee. TSR's were good for $4.35 per hour. The end of tax season brought no work at all. The conditional aspect meant that you were on a kind of probation for the first year. The ambiguous word "provisional," and the fact that they tacked on yet another qualifier bothered me. I needed to survive long enough to apply for a better job within the system.

A veteran Federal job seeker looking over my shoulder explained the last term to me with sadistic certainty. "If the phone stops ringing, they send you home. If it starts ringing again, they call you back, and you had better be ready to go to work, or else."

I looked at his drawn, nodding face. Surely the practice he described was a long forgotten medieval-period torture that someone had neglected to replace with a twentieth century job description. If I landed the position, then I would have transitioned from an advanced placement physics student to one of innumerable people with a bachelor's degree in accounting, and then to a complaint department clerk. My difficulties with higher math were sinking me.

"The job is hard to get, too," he added.

Any stinking little job they have. Good 'ole pragmatic Linda was going to be proud.

TWO MONTHS LATER, I climbed the steps to the D Train one at a time instead of my usual two, jostled by the flow of humanity. I was going for the TSR job at the IRS. After being introduced to the fifth dimensional land of government forms, where every "yes" answer threw open the door to a sub-schedule, the day had come when I had an appointment for an intelligence quotient test.

Through some alchemical process unknown to me, the more I thought about this IRS work in connection with a possible future with Linda, the more it seemed to matter. And the more effort I put into obtaining this goal, the more I wanted to get value out of it. My frail ego told me that job or no, an IQ test would pin a label on me, and that label might be different from what I had thought about myself until now. I might turn out to be, heaven forbid, average. Linda was anything but average.

Throughout the ride to Manhattan on the D Train, I kept comparing my watch to the information in the letter I pulled out of my pocket: 7:30 am on the dial versus the 9:00 am reporting time, 7:40 am versus 9:00 am, and so forth. My brain and the passage of time didn't mix well. This trifling handicap, known as dyscalculia, affected every manner of calculation. I knew it was crazy of me to want to be any sort of accountant at all.

While I was at it, I also re-read the location: Room 2906, at 26 Federal Plaza. The notice grew soaked and fragile from sweat and refolding. Soon I had no choice but to memorize the appointment in case the paper got worn to a puddle of shreds from my worries.

As early as I got there—at 8:35—I arrived to find a room already filled with my peers. A motley bunch, but quite a few looked very sharp, and those few answered my friendly gaze with the death-wish stares of hungry competition.

I chose a seat the way all good New Yorkers do, measuring off the maximum distance from every beating heart. Many of our city's residents believed it was actually legal to stab someone who strayed an inch closer than he had to, so I took no chances. Although the test hadn't begun, one man nearby hunched over his blank exam paper, squinting back at me with resentful eyes. He probably wore a lead lining in his shirt to seal out x-rays. I didn't have the slightest desire to copy his psychotic answers, whatever they were.

The appointed hour ticked closer. Having been a "be-prepared" Boy Scout, I arrayed my pencils and sharpener on the desk. At the front of the room, the proctor offered what he called "some useful advice." With a voice as charming as a slamming door, he told us, "Fill in the circles and mind your own business. If you cheat on this test, you will be escorted out by armed guards. You will not work for the Federal Government. Not now and not ever."

Welcome to Fed World. I had never cheated on an exam and had no plan to start with this one. I would have to get used to strong warnings that presupposed villainous intent. My hunchbacked friend nearby did not seem the least bit mollified by the strict rules. He looked like he wanted to jump up and warn the authorities about me.

Finally, we were instructed to break the seal on our packets. The intelligence test hit me like nothing I had seen in college, or since. For a lousy job, they had managed to create an exceedingly difficult hurdle. Why, for example, would the IRS want to discover your ability to mentally rotate two-dimensional representations of convoluted three-dimensional magnets? My years in college had left me bloated with useless facts. Why couldn't the IRS ask me about some of those?

Though I had tried to shed awareness of my peripheral vision, this particular set of questions made me glance around at faces to see if anyone else was climbing the walls. No, they were filling answer circles like art majors. You could have balanced a drink on their heads. I had no idea how others could be so confident when I was so unsure. The proctor caught my eye with a sharp look as if he itched to catch a cheater. Since I wasn't cheating, he glared at me in impotent pain, the way the unsuccessful lawyer in the Perry Mason episodes used to look at the defendant while Perry was getting someone else to confess.

I would learn later that the 3-D skill on the test was based on kinesthetic—or physical memory, if you will—and apparently I already had that talent in spades. That's why I learned karate so rapidly. It was compensation for the dyscalculia, I supposed. The actual outcome of the test, however, would keep me on ice for some time.

THE NEXT SEMESTER saw me back in the classroom. Even with my bachelor's degree in accounting, I lacked some supplemental classes required to take the CPA exam. I had previously postponed them, the way I do when something has the potential to go disastrously. Now I arranged to add that burden at night, optimistically allowing for full time day work. My greatest wish was to earn some real money while I was in school. I would need the bankroll to get married. Yet until that blessed manna fell, all I could do was come to school early to watch Brooklyn College build a lily pond behind Whitman Hall, and hope I didn't remain idle enough to see the finish of it.

As it turned out, however, the Japanese goldfish in the pond were beauties.

Nine weeks of miserable unemployment later, while I was sweating the material for an advanced accounting test, an odd-looking letter arrived in the mail. The friendly version of an IRS greeting came with a government-blue logo rather than the Darth Vader black other recipients would see. My trembling hands told me which way my hopes were running. Nonetheless, I made myself wait until I could answer a simple question: Did I want this career move for me or did I really want this for how it might improve my standing with Linda? Tearing ravenously at the corner of the envelope, I decided they were one and the same.

It turned out I had scored high on the IRS I.Q. exam, much better than the cut-off. That surprised me since I had only guessed on most of the math problems. My dyscalculia laid its claim in that realm too.

But there was more information. Seeing the interview date on that page, just nine days hence, brought home the point that my life was in motion.

When I got Linda on the phone and broke the news to her, she didn't reply, "That's wonderful," or "You're brilliant," or "I knew you could do it," as you might expect of a dull and ordinary girlfriend. She said, "Meet me at 75 Maiden Lane after your interview."

Linda's decisiveness and overall mystery could easily have been mistaken for spy training, which I found much more exciting than congratulatory noises. If I hadn't asked why she wanted me at that address, I'm convinced she would not have told me. She said, "Drop your resume in my office in the New York City Housing Development Corporation as a back-up."

My heart was on fire. Not only did I appreciate that she was covering these bases for me, but the idea of possibly working by her side almost wiped everything else from my mind. Of course, "working by her side" was probably a wild exaggeration. Time spent in her proximity was all that counted. It was all coming together.

In real life, though, events don't work out that way.

WITH A HIGH test score in hand, the last step was an "interview" in Brooklyn's downtown IRS where some psycho must disembowel you. I have no recollection today of who conducted the interrogation or why he was so hostile. I would never encounter him in the building again, and that in itself would turn out to be a fitting introduction to a world where nothing was as it seemed.

The man across the desk said, "You know that we fingerprint you, right?"

I was fascinated with his white shirt, pocket protector, and the crew cut he stole from 1960. His features were twisted in permanent disapproval.

"Yes, I read that somewhere. It's not a problem."

"The file on you will stay with the FBI forever, even if you don't get this job. You will never commit a crime and get away with it."

"I didn't intend to," I laughed uneasily, even though he looked deadly serious, or maybe because of it. "Besides, I've already been bonded, so the FBI has my finger prints."

"Why?" he demanded.

"Why was I bonded? I worked one summer for a bank."

"That doesn't get you out of our fingerprint process if that's what you thought!"

"No, I'm fine with it."

"Let me see your passport."

"I don't have one."

"Why not?" he barked.

"I could never afford an overseas trip."

"Ha. You won't be able to afford it now either. Do you know what Interpol is? After the FBI runs your prints, Inspection will investigate you. We'll find out if you really have a passport or not. And we'll know where you've been." The last part he drew out, making the vowels sound ominous.

I smiled gently. *Ok, 1960, whatever you say.* Out loud, I said, "No problem."

His locomotive rolled on. "They'll talk to your friends, family and neighbors."

"All right."

"You know you get audited, right?"

"No, what's that about?"

Now he smiled, satisfied to stick me with something I hadn't anticipated. "The past three years of all applicants' income tax returns get audited. And if they find anything—anything at all—you're out of here and you have to face the consequences."

I said, "I suppose it's only fair. If I'm going to be telling other people what to do, I should be clean myself."

"Don't be a wise guy with me," he shouted. "You come in to Office Audit just like everyone else, no special favors."

People often mistook my naïve sincerity for mocking, but this guy worried me. Nineteen eighty-four was the year George Orwell chose to illustrate our country's transformation into Big Brother. Was this pugilistic interviewer a CIA spook in disguise? Would that kind of heat always come with the job? I tried not to think too much about the sort of things that might scare me away.

I WATCHED THE mailbox constantly, and the Feds ended up delivering a stunner wrapped in another government-blue logo. They'd given me a formal confirmation of my clean background in just three days. That meant they must have started the process long before I met Mr. Scare-Tactic.

I commenced dialing to share the good news. But my on-again, off-again Linda had bad news. She'd been "fixed up" by her mother with a medical student named Wayne Sapperstein. Nothing serious, as it would turn out, yet supposedly a potential union on the right track for her. I had to convince her that she would find my news important before she would see me.

She agreed on the condition that I pick up some Chinese food on the way. To motivate my contribution of culinary treats she spoke Chinese to me, and I loved it. She knew some of the language and I'm guessing she faked the rest.

In another change in her life, she had moved out of her parent's house. Due to her parent's loathing for me, I had never been up to her room when she lived at home. To my surprise, her modest Bay Ridge apartment turned out more practical than girlie. With a clean desk, shelved reference books, and rows of filing cabinets right up to the spice rack, it was a marvel of organization. Linda had perfected the home office thing even before it was fashionable. As yet she had no framed prints on the wall, though her beautiful face was decoration enough for any abode. Mainly I was pleased that there were no pictures of Sapperstein around. That would have chilled it. Maybe she'd invented the guy altogether, in order to motivate me with jealousy. I never knew, but later events supported that theory.

Knowing I could be voracious while eating, she insisted on hearing the news as soon as we spread the Chinese take-out in front of us in a middle-of-the-floor picnic.

"All right, I'll tell you what happened. I got the job."

"Which job?" Linda liked to be very precise sometimes, and liked to tease me too, so I didn't know for sure which she intended.

"The one you suggested in order to get me into the IRS. I'm now a Taxpayer Service Representative, a TSR." I crowed, "I'm part-time, seasonal, provisional, and conditional, baby."

"When do you start?" The concern in her voice caught me by surprise.

"Three and a half weeks from now. Why?"

"Apply for the Revenue Agent's job immediately!"

"Of course I will, but what's the emergency?"

Linda reached for a little white box, popped open a cardboard tab, and examined the fried rice like a professional pork inspector.

"Linda?" I prompted to get her past this attack of nerves.

She corralled a few stray rice grains, while saying, "The transfer could take a while."

"What do you mean it could take a while? I could be stuck there as a TSR? You never said anything about that."

"Everything moves slowly in the Federal Government. Time before they post the announcement; time before they call you; time before the interview; time before you hear something... Don't look at me like that. You've done the right thing. I have faith in you."

I groaned.

CHAPTER TWO
To Have and Have Not

"I'd hate to take a bite out of you. You're a cookie full of arsenic."

—Burt Lancaster, *Sweet Smell of Success*

November 26, 1984

At least the training period provided full time work. I got to see what a whole paycheck looked like at the rate of $4.35 per hour. Since I had been toiling as a foot messenger just to get by, this gave me more money than I had seen in a long time. That largesse, however, didn't keep me from running into the dingy hallway every day to check for new job listings, Linda's warning ringing in my head.

In what would become a long pattern, I found no Revenue Agent posting the first day, not even on the internal listings. Worse yet, Linda told me she wouldn't see me for a while because I needed to take my time and study. Her absence didn't surprise me since she had offered one excuse after another for over three years. We were already deep into the "phone calls only" phase. I had gone through four fruitless, obligatory fix-up dates imposed by friends and family since Linda told me to get into the IRS any way I could. But my feelings for Linda ran deep. Hers for me ran shallow, or so it seemed. She'd said, "I have faith in you," and it sounded like she meant it. I held on to that.

The first day of training began with fifteen of us trainees scrutinizing each other across tables arranged in a U while awaiting someone in authority. Two of my fellows seemed to take a proprietary interest in me. Directly across sat a beefy Latino, mid-thirties, expansive moustache, and eyes that alternately stared owlishly through round wire frames and then disappeared in the glare of the florescent light. The owl's name would turn out to be Hector Chavez.

Next to him, I couldn't miss the bookish, shapely blonde in a mini-skirt, slightly overweight with white stockings on legs that parted in concert with her licking off cherry red lipstick. She had used one of the black markers and blank name cards left by each of our seats. The bold, precise hand identified her as Verna Tucks. Sometimes Verna looked across and winked at me awkwardly as though a false eyelash troubled her. Winking is not all that common an act. Repeating it—as she did in case I didn't get the message—seemed really odd. Her dirty blonde hair actually looked dirty. She simultaneously attracted and repulsed me. I sensed she swung a little off kilter.

As a group, we would spend four highly concentrated weeks together in that room learning about personal income taxes, and sometimes about each other, all day long. The instructor's style weaved drunkenly between a souped-up H & R Block course and the two college courses I had already taken in the subject. I breezed along with my main emphasis

27

on learning how not to be too bored by material I already knew. The intrigue took care of that.

Somewhere during a break on the first day, while I was standing under the Ronald Reagan portrait by the water cooler, Verna came up to me and whispered her first words, "They're watching us."

"They're watching us?" I repeated, trying to draw out the meaning. Most people would have said hello and introduced themselves before launching into a conspiracy theory.

"Verrry carefully," Verna purred. Her eyes widened as she nodded several times to underscore some hidden meaning. Her coated lips mesmerized me. I felt like Burt Lancaster trapped in an old movie. If ever someone smelled like a cookie full of arsenic, it was her.

After looking around for escape routes and finding none to my satisfaction, I said, "The instructors? Yes, I suppose they are."

Verna leaned in closer, ready to paint my ear red. "There's no supposing about it. Watch what you say. They're testing our patriotism."

She spoke in clipped tones, boosting her last bit of wisdom with a verbal click meant to be encouraging. Everything with her came out overdone. I didn't know what to say.

"They like your stuff," she assured me. "I can tell." Another slow nod as she delivered the good news about my stuff. I hadn't seen every old movie classic, but I had heard audio bites like "come up and see me sometime," and Verna had obviously perfected an amalgam of the Lauren Bacall and Mae West voices, if not the moves.

"Okay," I said. "I appreciate that you noticed."

She winked. "Anytime, sport."

You know how to whistle, don't ya?

Verna backed away, still watching me and nodding slowly, glossing her plump lips with her tongue.

You just put your lips together and blow.

To Have and Have Not. Why would someone try to pull off that act in real life? I found it a little bit sexy that she was making the effort, and a great deal creepy that it came off as it did. I wondered if I would have to get used to that combination around there.

When she left, Hector the Owl sidled up nearly as close as the first oddball had gotten, and spoke his first words, "I see you've met Verna. She's strange, yes?" Up close, Hector carried his extra weight well. He wasn't old enough yet to labor on account of it.

"I don't know Verna well enough to say that."

"You know that she is. My name is Hector." I already knew, but I appreciated the relative normalcy of an actual introduction.

"Nice to meet you, Hector. I'm Danny."

"You understand that this whole thing, this training session, is bullshit, right?"

Oh, what now? "How so, Hector?"

He clutched and held my arm to draw me closer to his soft voice as I tried not to cringe. "They get us in here, what, eight hours a day, five days, for four weeks? You're an accountant. Do the math. A hundred and sixty hours and we're gonna know nothing when we come out." Hector knew I was an accountant from the information our instructor had elicited. Or so I hoped.

"I already know the material. I took it in college."

"So did I, at H & R Block. Took the course twice before. But you understand that all of this tax stuff has nothing to do with the job and the politics of the job. In the end, we won't really know shit."

"Uh huh. I guess you're right." Let him be right.

"Think about it."

I felt lucky that he ended the conversation, giving me the opportunity to "think about it," because I didn't know if I could stand any more of these confidential asides.

January 7, 1985

At the end of training, I found myself facing my first productive day at my voluminous Post of Duty, a label that hinted at its paramilitary nature. The workstations that filled it fit together in five parts, looking like pentagon-shaped daisies scattered across a plain. They carried the fresh sawdust smell of new installations. I wondered how a single room could be built so large, or why it would need to be. The center of the floor supported over a hundred of these mini-offices bordered by the larger manager's stations on two sides, a wall on the third, and another zone for higher level employees beyond the fourth side before ending in corner offices. But that wasn't the extent of it. Behind one management boundary and a partition was yet another specialist zone and a public area, all of which were unknown to me at the time.

I told myself my nervousness had no rational basis. Surely the job description, with its bleak elucidation of the working conditions held no further surprises, right? But no, the revelations kept coming.

Within minutes, we learned that we would be tethered to the desk in a virtual chokehold. The TSR could go no further than the 30-inch length of cord that connected their headset to their telephone jack. In this manner, your station constituted your world. A computer faithfully recorded any minutes and seconds of disconnect to ensure that you had no more than a fifteen minute break each morning and afternoon, and a thirty-minute lunch. We were days past the real 1984, as opposed to George Orwell's prophetic novel of the same name. Just what had I gotten myself into?

Trepidation aside, I plugged in and accepted my very first incoming call with these words: "Taxpayer Service, Mr. Shapiro speaking. How can I help you?"

"Is this… Taxpayer Service?" I heard later-middle-age in the man's voice.

"Yes it is."

"Who am I speaking with?"

"I'm Mr. Shapiro," I said.

"Piro? Spell that."

"S-H-A-P-I-R-O."

"What kind of name is that? It's not Italian, it's not Irish…" He said this as though we had met in a supermarket over a leisurely conversation about canned ham. I would have thought that people calling the IRS had pressing issues.

"How can I help you?" I said again.

"I knew a Shapiro once. He was black. Are you black? I suppose it could also be a Jew name..." he offered, waiting for my response. Lucky me. I hit the hillbilly jackpot on my first call and my anger was keeping me from being nervous. I wasn't going to be baited.

"Did you have a question today, sir?"

"Oh yes. Where are you?"

"This office is in Brooklyn."

"How could you be in Brooklyn?"

"That's where we're located, sir."

"Where in Brooklyn?"

"At 35 Tillary Street."

"What is that, Tillary Street? Like Hillary with a "t"?

"Yes."

"What an odd name for a place."

"That's where we are." I could say one thing for this caller. He certainly had easy questions.

"I never heard of it. Are you sure you're there?"

Fortunately, I had a lot of patience. "It's in downtown Brooklyn."

"You can't be in Brooklyn," he said. "I called 516."

"They must have routed your call here, sir."

"I'm going to be in Brooklyn tomorrow."

"All right." Who cared?

"Can I go to this Tillary Street and see you in person?"

Just what I needed. My mental sigh was so loud that I thought he must have heard it. "Well, not me. My job keeps me on the telephone all day. Someone else will help you."

"But I've already gotten used to you. I don't want to start again with someone else."

Wow, now it was getting too weird. Does the caller hate me or like me? I said, "Nonetheless, they don't let me off the phone."

"Can I talk to someone face to face? I have to see what kind of person I'm talking to." *Black, Hispanic, Jewish, other...*

"I'll find out for you. Please hold." Regardless of who I was talking to, I needed to know how the office worked. We had literally been told nothing about the set-up.

Back in school, if you had a question you would raise your hand and wait. Silly me, that's just what I did. It took a while to get someone's attention. The supervisors flitted around to each station like they were making up for a bee shortage in a marigold factory.

The nearest supervisor, the one who approached now, wore ill-fitting clothes over a serious weight problem. Her top was stained in contrast to my low budget business attire, which was at least clean. I thought that her hair was falling out, some of it clinging in batches to her sweater. Then I realized it was cat hair. Unprofessional as she seemed, she qualified as an authority figure. I put on my best smile.

"What the hell do *you* want?" she said.

I got the message right away. I of all people (whatever that meant) should be minding my business. At the age of 23 I had boundless energy, enthusiasm and optimism, so I felt undeterred. No doubt when she found out that I had a legitimate question that our little school had not taught, and I could not have known beforehand, then everything would be fine.

I removed my headset before speaking. "Um, the taxpayer wants to know—"

"Put the taxpayer on hold," she shouted.

"He is on hold," I pointed to the blinking light so she could verify that, which earned me a grudging nod. "The taxpayer wants to know if he can come in here and talk to someone face to face."

"He can go to walk-in," she snapped.

"What's walk-in?"

"Taxpayer Walk-In. Next door."

"Thank you, uh, what's your name, please?"

"My name is Kate. Don't you ever quote me as having said anything. And I'd better not hear you ask the same question twice."

As Hector had warned me on day one, the training had indeed been bullshit inasmuch as they told us nothing about the mechanics of the job, where anything could be found, or what it took to survive. Hector, I concluded, proved smarter than me. A wise owl indeed.

A decade or so earlier, someone had belatedly come up with the new concept that taxpayers were like customers and should be treated accordingly. Someone thought it worth a whole division. So, in 1975 the Taxpayer Service Division emerged. The ten-year period from then till 1985 qualified as a short time by government standards. So far no one had put much thought into the whole arrangement.

A veteran who shared my pentagon daisy leaned back and said to me, "Welcome to the shit storm."

CREDS: THE IRS ADVENTURE

WE HAD OUR fifteen-minute break periods carefully staggered at the POD so as to minimize impact on phone coverage. At the first opportunity, I bolted for the basement, where I had heard that all the IRS publications were stored. By this time, I knew that the IRS printed separate booklets on every subject. These turned out to be a great deal easier than deciphering tax law directly out of the congressionally penned Internal Revenue Code, or from our training material, which was awash in errors. These publications would be an invaluable aid. Since a few other people took their strict fifteen-minute break at the same time, I wanted to get downstairs before the rush. I assumed that everyone wanted to be the best they could be. I was the only one in a rush, though. My journey may have begun with Linda, but the challenge was drawing me in, and my self-respect demanded that I best my competitors.

After some wrangling, an old man in the basement let me collect two of each booklet, every day. I took one set home and kept another in the office. I would fall asleep every night poring over them. I marked the gray pulp with blue and red pen, and yellow highlighter, and amassed separate notes. Then I attached multi-colored tabs to the edges so I could pull them out quickly when a question came up. As the shelves at my station filled, the old man downstairs finally relented and let me take large batches at a time. When that chore became too much for him, his rules fell by the wayside. He let me go into the cage and find them myself while he took a nap.

My studious rummaging revealed that many of the booklets were filed wrong, and missing ones had to be ordered from Virginia. The old man surrendered his telephone so I could make the calls. If a casual observer didn't notice that we never actually spoke, she might have thought that the old fella and me were becoming quite good friends.

While I poked around the dusty stacks for hidden treasure, I ordered a copy of the Taxpayer Service Procedures Manual, a hefty tome that told you how the office was supposed to be run. The lady on the phone said that no one from my district had ever ordered a copy before. I disbelieved her, but I shouldn't have.

IN THE EARLY days of the season, when most taxpayers didn't have their information in hand yet, there could be a minute or two between calls, time I used to study and organize with colored pens, markers and tabs. Soon enough, the inquiries came back-to-back, fast and furious:

I live in Florida and I summer in New York. Where do I file?;

My employee refuses to let me withhold taxes. What do I do?;

How will the changes in the taxability of my Industrial Development Bonds affect my Alternative Minimum Tax?;

Can you tell me if Felix Zworkin is an honest and competent tax preparer?;

I just know my employer is going to refuse to give me a W-2. Can I write my own?

Excellent questions, most of them. But my favorite exchange of all came at the end of my second week:

When I picked up and introduced myself, the latest caller abruptly asked, "Mr. Shapiro, how tall is the IRS office building?"

He didn't sound the least bit distraught. "Why do you want to know that?" I obliged.

He took a deep breath for the sake of timing. "Because when I jump off, I want to make sure I die." He added, "Drum roll, please."

We both laughed at that, and he went on to tell me how annoying our tax forms were. I didn't tell him how miserable I was to be on the other side of it.

In Fritz Lang's 1927 masterpiece film *Metropolis*, our hero, Freder Frederson, finds a harried factory worker with his arms on the hands of a giant clock-like structure. He must move the oversized hands ceaselessly in a complex pattern of positions. A blood curdling alarm will go off if he ever stops. Frederson, the rich son of the owner, who feels guilty for having lived too well up until now, takes over the task from the peon, plugging himself into the monstrous structure, while the jump-suited worker collapses in exhaustion. In Brooklyn's Taxpayer Service, a picture of *Metropolis* should have been on everyone's desk.

Grueling as the work may have been, I took solace in being able to straighten out taxpayer's problems, some of which were caused by the IRS, and some of which, I pointed out occasionally, were caused by the caller himself. The more educated I became, the better I could help. But was I telling everyone the right things? After one particular night of reading the procedures manual until the sun came up, I came in to work and asked one of the bosses, "Who is my

OJI?" The term was Treasury parlance for "On-the-Job Instructor." According to the manual, everyone supposedly had an OJI assigned to them.

I addressed this question to a Group Manager named Tammy Sangenario, considered the friendly one because you could never get in trouble asking her a question. She came across as Marilyn Munster from the old television show, as she resembled the beautiful aberration born amongst a family of monsters. The others in my office weren't all that bad, of course. It was just that she was spectacular. My friend Hector Chavez was lucky enough to work directly for Tammy, and I had the feeling that the sly Dominican had somehow engineered that arrangement.

"We don't have OJI's," said Tammy rather carelessly.

My face must have fallen.

When she registered my disappointment, she reluctantly added, "Oh wait, I guess it would be Ladislav Ras."

"Ras? How come I haven't met him?"

"He's got a hundred people to look after."

"One OJI for a hundred people?"

"Oh, also you have the supervisors who walk around," she said cheerfully. "They're kind of like OJI's."

Oh yes, why didn't I realize that myself? That would include Cat Hair Kate who didn't want to be quoted.

Remembering my recent caller's joke, I said, "Someone could jump off the roof while they're waiting for help."

"What?"

"Just kidding. I heard that somewhere."

"Oh. Good one," she said, humoring me.

I knew the on-the-job-instructor personnel shortage to be a violation of the rules, and I could complain about it, but when Tammy smiled, everything seemed okay. She favored me with a golden one just then.

I LOCATED THE overworked Ladislav Ras after a couple of days. As his legend unraveled, I learned that his scarcity was born not of a surfeit of responsibility, but of a lateness and absence problem due to chronic car troubles. A tall, gangly Czech that had never been Americanized, he insisted on driving an old compact Skoda. It was not one of the stylish ones either. At his height, he had to fold himself into it like a man taking a child's go-cart. I couldn't imagine where he got that car or how he made it street legal. As far as I knew, those toys weren't sold in the United States.

Ladislav announced his nationality with pride and defiance as if he were fully expecting a beating on that account, and would suffer it gladly. The wacky haircut didn't help him fit in either. He looked like the bad end of a cockfight.

Although his expected persecution never came, I felt sorry for him on all counts. He wanted to help, but most of those who might benefit from his advice walked away stymied by his impenetrable accent. Having grown up listening to Slavic variations in Brighton Beach, I devoted ten minutes a day to our talks. He insisted we work over lunch in his car.

Ignoring the cramped space, I asked him what the various sections of the office did. Sometimes he told me, and other times his eyes flashed like those of a caged animal, and I let it go.

I learned everything I could from Ladislav until one Monday morning when I opened his car's orange door to the smell of borscht and climbed onto the broken springs. He held up a hand, swallowed a spoonful, and said, "It's enough."

Enough soup? "What did I do wrong?"

"I've seen your work. I've heard you on the phone." He shook his head. "I should be asking *you* questions, not the other way around."

I was ready to agree with his assessment even though the man owned a Skoda.

WITH NUGGETS OF vicarious wisdom from Tammy and Ladislav, I dived into my work with even more confidence and vigor, certain that all this learning about how the Service works would give me an advantage when I went for my "real job." In the back of my mind, where fantasies are stored and fed, I was still impressing the heck out of Linda. One day her care for me would overcome her parent's ambitions. I fortified my days with a morning peek through the keychain bauble that magnified a view of us on our first date: She in a blue satin dress with faux pearls, leaning close against me. Me with the red beard I had sported that winter, sitting tall at the restaurant table. Both of us with the dreamy smiles of teenagers in a first experience.

Sometime in my second week at the POD, as I stopped to look at that magical image once again, a shrill klaxon went off, loud enough to jar even a seasoned New York City commuter. Through a door that opened into the hallway, I could see crowds of people starting to run. Within our department, all ninety-five TSR's put their taxpayer callers on hold.

"Don't move. Don't touch anything." The resonant voice reached into everyone and stopped us cold. It belonged to Jim Johnson, a big Southern gentleman who looked like he could enforce his firm advice. I was used to his usual slow, calm cadence. Now he sounded commanding.

"What's going on, Jim?"

"We're being evacuated, Mr. Shapiro." I found it odd that this somewhat older man addressed me by my surname as he did—not in the tone of a teacher—but as though he were a respectful subordinate of mine, even though he had seniority and was our emergency coordinator. I guessed it had something to do with his being black and from the south. I had told him not to call me Mr. Shapiro, but he'd laughed it off like that was never an option.

"Why are we being evacuated?" I asked.

"Someone called in a bomb threat. Either for us or the Federal court attached."

"You mean there could be a bomb planted in the building?" Jim looked too relaxed for a man who might be sitting on explosives.

He shrugged. "Could be real, could be fake."

People around us stirred. They had their headsets off but looked towards Jim like they were still tethered, this time to a set of rules.

"Jim, why aren't we leaving?" I asked.

"We have to follow procedures." I was relieved that someone knew the procedures. Jim was just one of the guys until this crisis came up. Here he asserted his long years of experience, which made me grateful. Everyone was listening to our conversation on the edges of their chairs.

"All right, Jim. What do we do?"

"Nothing, Mr. Shapiro."

"Nothing? How could it be nothing?"

"We have to leave everything exactly as it is. The dogs will sniff it out."

"So why aren't we leaving the building?"

"We have to wait while Examinations Division is evacuated. First Field Examinations, then Office Audit."

"But those functions are on the Fourth Floor while we're on the ground floor, closer to the exit." Frantically, I looked at the door I wanted to leave through.

"Yeah, that's right," he said slowly and painfully.

"Shouldn't we logically go first?"

Jim used his sleeve to mop his dark brow. "Yeah, you might think that. But that's not how it is."

This was so frustrating. "All right, then what? Who goes next?"

"Then, you know, Collections, Review, Inspection…" I raised my eyebrows, impressed that he knew the whole structure of the place as well as the pecking order, but I was liking these rules less and less.

"Then us?"

"After Appeals."

"Dammit," I said. Beyond the doorway, taxpayers and personnel kept dashing by to safety. No one had ever declared that all divisions at the IRS were equal. In fact they were decidedly unequal: one more reason that I looked forward to finding a Revenue Agent announcement, a notice that would offer the position for those already in the Service.

42

Revenue Agents were part of the Examinations Division, a group so respected that they saved those lives first, and made no bones about it.

"Do these evacuations happen a lot?" I asked since no one else was chiming in..

Though it didn't show in his voice, perspiration slicked Jim's face faster than he could clear it. "Not so much now, but twice a month in the summer time when people get crazy."

"How many bomb threats turn out to be real bombs?"

He shrugged. "Been fake so far. Odds get better that this one's real."

I reckoned Jim was right. While the chance of an individual coin toss coming up "heads" was fifty-fifty, and the next one doing the same remained just as likely, statistics showed that the average always caught up to half-and-half in the long run.

Some people were waddling around like they had to go to the bathroom and cursing under their breath, unlike me who was cursing out loud. I wondered how long the rule-following discipline would hold.

After some signal I missed, Jim finally gave us the cue to jump. *En masse*, we peeled out of the room just as the bomb-sniffing dogs charged in on taut leashes. Their handlers freed them, and the dogs went searching everywhere. In a last look back, I saw one of the courageous beasts shoulder my chair out of the way as it plowed under my desk. On winged feet, I joined the last people to evacuate the building.

In the park across the street, all of us shuffling around behind the car barriers, I discovered how cold it could be waiting to see if your building blew up. Had anyone really measured how far we needed to retreat for every sort of bomb? Or were we standing at some arbitrary distance? The people around me were strangely quiet, and in the confusion I didn't see anyone I knew. I couldn't even spot Ladislav, my Yoda with a Skoda, whose head would have poked high above the crowd. Feeling isolated, I asked a well-dressed lawyer type, "What are we doing? Who would be crazy enough to bomb a federal building? Or even threaten it?"

He looked at me like I was the crazy one. "Only a fourth of my clients."

"Posse Comitatus?" I asked, referencing the violent tax protester movement we'd been warned about.

Now he laughed bitterly. "That's only one group. You obviously haven't been around here very long."

He got that right.

Eventually, we heard the all-clear signal wailing above downtown's traffic noise, and we slogged back like a band of weary 1940's Britons spared because the Axis had bombed somewhere else that day. Given the relief I felt, I was ready to adopt a stiff upper lip as well as the next guy.

After a run through the metal detectors, and a return to our wing, Hector Chavez slipped something sturdy under my arm and said he wanted to talk to me in the hallway. "No, don't look at it yet," he cautioned, unbuttoning his green jacket in the indoor warmth. He made a point of wearing green from head to toe, as if to remind everyone that he used to be a manager at ALC Global. Maybe he just couldn't afford to replace the wardrobe.

I let him steer me for the moment. Hector and I had something in common. Unlike most people, neither of us were ever sent home when the phones got slow—me because I worked so hard; him because he was the wise old owl that seemed born to the knowledge. With all that, he had a flair for melodrama that made me wary.

"I have to get back on the phone," I reminded him.

"Oh don't worry about that," he said. "The system has no way of knowing when you got back in the building. You're Ashkenazi, right?"

"What are you talking about?"

"There's Ashkenazi and there's Sephardic," he explained patiently. "There's only two kinds." He held up two fingers to make his point. It so happened, I knew what he was talking about. At least on a superficial level. The Sephardim were the Spanish branches of Judaism, and often their appearance and customs reflected their Spanish heritage. The Ashkenazi were Caucasians. I just didn't understand why Hector brought it up. I suspected unsavory reasons. There was a lot of that going around.

"All right, your point is that I don't look Sephardic to you." Naturally, he didn't know about my Cuban cousins, or the Italian side of my family for that matter. "What about it?"

"I'm Dominican."

"From the Dominican Republic," I replied in a clumsy attempt to keep up my end of the conversation while not encouraging him too much.

"In my culture," said Hector, "the life of one person is as valuable as another. Is it the same with yours?"

Then his point came into better focus. He was trying to peg me, but the effort was benign. If I was a light skinned Sephardic, then he figured we were somewhat of the same culture. If I was not, then he wondered what my culture had to say about the day's events. "Okay. You're talking about the bomb evacuation and the pecking order that Jim talked about. Yes, I agree with you. Makes no sense."

"But it does make sense," he insisted. "It starts with the Examinations Division and the Collections Division." He ticked the branches off on his left hand with emphatic assistance from his right hand as if his digits would only cooperate if pried open. "They get saved first because those two bring in the money. Review, Inspection, and Appeals help them keep the money for the government, so they go next."

Wondering what a really bad day at the IRS would be like, I asked, "Where does that leave us, Hector?"

"Taxpayer Service? Expendable. And maybe a little stupid."

Perhaps I needed to start listening to Verna or to Hector after all. I fervently wished I knew which one.

CHAPTER THREE
Objects in the Mirror

"Doesn't scan, does it Norman? But... a lot of shit around
here doesn't."

—Psycho III

The search dogs were gone. My chair had been knocked
over and my desk drawers pulled out. So were everyone
else's. The bomb search had been thorough, and I was
grateful for that. They found nothing. Or they found
something and didn't bother telling us. In any case, we got
the "all clear."

I set everything back in place at my station and sat
heavily, wary of donning my headset and going into
lockdown once again. The 1985 tax season at the IRS had
officially begun. At the rate of pay we were getting, I never
would have guessed we were doing such dangerous work.
Maybe I should have paid closer attention in Threat
Assessment Training.

We would never know whose bomb threat it was, but
we had a list of suspects. In training, the instructors had
made us aware of one salient fact: there were earnest people
with a unique philosophy who wanted us Treasury
Department types dead. Several groups of militants in the

47

country's interior had formed loosely affiliated units mostly called Posse Comitatus. This movement denied their obligation to pay any tax at all. They invoked a patchwork of shifting claims to support this idea. Anyone among them who had an anti-tax notion could toss a theory into the pot. Some of them wanted to believe they had a religious obligation not to pay taxes. They tied it to the idea that "Jews were the spawn of Satan" and "blacks are not humans, but animals in disguise." Members of the group that overlapped Posse—called Aryan Nations—liked to say that the federal government is illegitimate and in the hands of a Zionist conspiracy.

In their minds, it seemed to follow that it was not a criminal activity to use deadly force on those hired by their fellow Americans to enforce the law. In the 1980's, their targets would encompass an ever-expanding circle, attacking IRS agents, police, U.S. Marshalls, anyone anywhere in the process of administration, and potentially anyone else who got in the way.

As I learned, *posse Comitatus* adherents took their name from an 1878 law strengthening local rights. Its name meant "power of the county."

It happened that two years prior to that date, the presidential election of Hayes versus Tilden was disputed due to electoral fraud in four Southern states. The south could concede these states and give the election to Hayes, but the "Rebel States" of the post-Civil War south were furious about the 20,000 occupying troops enforcing the Reconstruction Acts. A deal was made to withdraw the Army from the South in exchange for settling the election. Two years later, the Democrats controlled Congress. They enacted a law called the Posse Comitatus Act intended to prevent the U.S. Army from ever again being used as a domestic police force.

The latter-day group of tax protesters took up the name Posse Comitatus to provide a justification for their pseudo-legal arguments about not having to pay Federal taxes. Their problem was that the law they claimed to rely on had to do with asserting local rights as far as the Army was concerned, but nothing to do with income tax. They didn't care.

They also believed that the old law justified maintaining a militia-type operation in order to counter a possible incursion by federal troops. They liked that the term *posse Comitatus* meant "power of the county," rather than *country*, because the Posse Comitatus group did not want to be subject to federal law and federal taxes, and they wanted their own army. They sought local rights across the board and no national responsibility.

When they were not threatening the lives of IRS agents, they had been known to draw up what they called "common law" liens against individual agents and judges that the militia members came in contact with. These claims went on top of the pile of their documents declaring independence from the United States.

The term for our job at the IRS—tax compliance—was synonymous with enforcement of the law that this group hated most. That put us directly in the line of fire. The courts—and even the IRS' official lingo—utilized the benign-sounding term "tax protester." But they weren't referring to Tea Party activists advocating responsible government and lower tax burdens. This group used the emblems and philosophy of white supremacy and the tax dodge as a path to their vision of Aryan rule.

Since the county level of government was supreme with Posse Comitatus, you might think that there was no one more revered in their circles than the country sheriff. The sheriff would, by definition, be their sole legal authority. Someone has to be an authority, right? But the posse had an out for that too. If the sheriff "refuses to carry out the will of the county's citizens," as defined by the militia:

> **"...he shall be removed by the Posse to the most populated intersection of streets in the township and at high noon be hung by the neck, the body remaining until sundown as an example to those who would subvert the law."**

Posse members practiced survivalism in case they turned out to be wrong about their ability to enforce this. One spectacular illustration would soon be public knowledge and therefore part of what I knew and feared.

ON FEBRUARY 13, 1983, as I donned my jeans and sneakers for a typical morning in the final year of my undergraduate studies in accounting, tax protester Henry Jessup—fifteen hundred miles away—loaded his Ruger Mini-14 rifle and stepped outside to check the scope for clarity and accuracy. His big son Brock, and his friend Leon Higg did the same with theirs. The warrant for Jessup's arrest for tax evasion had put them on alert. Leon squeezed off a single shot into the woods and whooped with joy.

Jessup stared at him. "The hell you doin'?" he asked. They didn't have any time for nonsense.

"Saw a rabbit in my sights."

"Just happened to?"

"Yeah, and I got it."

"All right, then, boy. Good shootin'."

The temperature at that hour of the morning in Bowie, North Dakota would have been round about zero, something the locals were used to coping with when handling firearms. Thinking again, Jessup went back in the house to add a shoulder holster and a .45 caliber pistol to his outfit before shrugging on his coat. Later—at the point where this collection of firearms had turned into murder weapons— Jessup would talk his son into switching clothes with him. Brock was a strapping young man so everything would fit just fine. Meanwhile, Jessup rounded up his wife, Nelda, and they all drove into town where other family and friends joined them for a tax protest meeting in a place called Commons House. Some people mentioned the cold that day, but the most popular complaint was about the government.

"As such," said Jessup when it was his turn to speak, "there is no legit government in Washington D.C. Any money you send them goes straight to communist headquarters."

"And the Feds," his son reminded him from his seat in the gallery. "That's a violation of our rights."

"That's the problem, yes." Public funds pooled from income tax did indeed go partly to federal law enforcement, and the idea of anything but local justice-by-posse was troubling to this crowd. Jessup had held similar views as early as 1967 when he wrote a letter to the IRS stating that he would no longer pay taxes to "the Synagogue of Satan under the 2nd plank of the Communist Manifesto." True to his word, he held out until the result was eight months in prison, followed by release on probation.

"So let's don't send them any of our money. Who here is with me?" cried Jessup. He got back the cheers of nineteen fine people. "Good. Then you'd better be ready to back it up. I sure am."

"Locked and loaded!" yelled a voice in the back.

"Let's give Satan what he deserves," yelled Jessup.

Even when the meeting broke up, there was very little traffic on the dusty streets of Bowie, and not much more on nearby Interstate 94 as it ran past the spur that led to the fifteen-score population. A hundred miles from Fargo and fifty from Bismarck, in the dead of winter, Henry Jessup's part of America must have seemed about as far from government authority as it could get.

Driving off with Jessup that day were his wife Nelda, and his son Brock, as well as rangy Leon Higg and two others who had been in attendance. They headed north out of town and had just rounded a bend when they saw the roadblock with flashing lights and knew what it meant. The illegitimate law was going to try to arrest someone, and Jessup knew there was a warrant out for him. No pauper, Jessup had some success on his 500-acre farm. Since his 1967 offense, he had continued to refuse to pay income taxes even though that act was a parole violation that would put him right back in prison. He stopped the car.

"Gonna back up and go around?" asked Leon, scratching his beard.

"Nope. We're good here."

"Henry Jessup," squawked the marshal with the bullhorn. "The only one we want is you, so I suggest you get out of that car, move away from the innocent bystanders, and give yourself up."

"How'd they know to set up here?" asked Brock.

"Not hard to figure out which way we'd go," said Jessup. "That's why we come prepared. I'm the one trapped *them*."

"Now what?" asked Leon.

Jessup picked up his rifle. "Now we get out and shoot us some rabbits. Hope there are some IRS hares among them."

Jessup, Brock, and Leon emerged carrying their semi-automatic carbines, far superior to anything the authorities carried, and let loose. The barrage was an irresistible wall of lead. Even car doors didn't stop these shells. Four United States marshals from Fargo and Bismarck went down, two dead, two badly wounded, some of the gruesome job done by shrapnel.

Among the litter of bodies, Jessup saw that a Bowie law enforcement officer was down too, eyes open and vacant.

Jessup said to him, "Howdy, Calvin. I'm gonna need your keys." He bent and unhooked them from Calvin's belt, catching a blood smear along the way. He sat in the car and tried to put the keys in, but a set was already in the ignition. "Whoops. I guess this was unnecessary." He tossed the keys back to Calvin.

Turning to his son, he said, "Brock, how would you like a new hat?"

Brock looked petrified. "From him?"

"No, from me. I want you to take our car and drive east wearing my clothes."

"Just east?"

"All the way till they stop you."

"What if they shoot our boy?" asked Nelda with an edge of hysteria.

"They're too stupid to shoot him, you know that."

"Wait," said Leon, "how do we know that Calvin and the others aren't playing possum, bloody as they are?"

"Yeah, could be," said Jessup.

"How about one more shot for each?" Leon raised his gun. "One or two of 'em look like IRS to me."

"No," said Jessup looking with satisfaction at the mangled bodies and feeling magnanimous, "wouldn't be right. Anyone playing possum that well is welcome to it."

Starting out in the squad car and changing rides later, Jessup fled to Arkansas, where he was then sheltered by those with loose affiliations and deep sympathies.

The weather grew warm, and then hot, but he never emerged from his bunker, and must have made his host wonder if he would abuse the hospitality forever.

In June, Jessup's string ran out. A tipster placed him in the provisioned bunker in tiny Smithville, Arkansas. Whatever Jessup may have thought about his course of action in fleeing the law, his circumstances had not improved with time. A local sheriff waited for the S.W.A.T team, and together they formed a tight cordon around the site. The sheriff took a few steps in with his bullhorn and said, "Jessup, we're not leaving without you. You may as well come out."

Right about then, things went terribly wrong for everyone involved. A shot was fired and that triggered a fusillade in every direction. Here the sequence of events was muddy. The sheriff died of bullet wounds. Jessup got caught in an explosion of the massive amount of ammunition his host and fellow conspiracy theorist stored. No one ever knew whose bullet or which other action set off the conflagration.

The following months were not quiet either. Even after Jessup himself was out of the picture, posse strongholds remained, and a new round of conspiracy theories and anti-government grudges were born based on his legend.

While I waited for my first pay check, an IRS Revenue Officer was shot to death, another was shot and paralyzed, and the District Director from Oklahoma was taken hostage. I now knew that the lives of latter-day Klansmen, as well as garden variety criminals, were woven around the world I had stepped into at the IRS. These stories were kept as quiet as possible and no IRS official ever commented on them.

WHEN MY WANDERING thoughts returned to the present day, I remembered what Hector Chavez had said as we returned from the evacuation, *they don't know when you got back in the building.* Hector—always in one of his green suits because he'd worn those when he worked for the shipping company that had an "employee tracking system" just like ours.

Of course, Hector was right because we were disconnected from the system after the anonymous caller spread havoc to kick off the start of our tax season. Well, that excuse would hold for a few minutes. I looked at what Hector had slipped under my arm, a double-sided color cardboard slick. It rattled in my shaking hands. Momma never told us there'd be days like this. I placed the slick flat on my desk while my adrenaline subsided.

On the front of the glossy board, I saw a description that purported to outline my job, the job of a Taxpayer Service Representative. Oddly enough, I had never seen this particular brochure before, and Hector seemed to know I wouldn't have. Judging by the cost of printing such a thing, these boards must have been in short supply. Now I had to puzzle out why Hector gave it to me, the method to his madness, if any.

The board was an odd cross between a technical fact sheet and a recruiting poster. One side of it blazed in fire engine red with white lettering. The description made the TSR job sound rather exciting:

>**When you work for the IRS, you'll encounter daily challenges and opportunities that will build a solid foundation for your future career. You'll enjoy the latest and most sophisticated computer, telecommunications, and data management technology. And with a seasonal or part-time position, you can add this impressive credential to your resume without cramping your style.**

This write-up didn't sound like the government I knew, and so far they hadn't let us anywhere near a computer. They must have spent even more money on the design and comedy writers than they did on the printing. Flipping to the back, it went on to talk about the different starting grades. Strangely enough, the job announcement I answered never said anything about starting at a grade other than GS-4.

In the document I held, it said they made exceptions for "Top Academic Achievement" in college. That sure wasn't me. *C'mon Hector, what's this all about?* On a good day back in high school, my average performance matched that of a handful of geniuses there. But when it came to college classes, if the professor didn't threaten penalties for non-attendance, I usually went to work a job during what should have been class time. To make matters worse, I also tried for a normal social life during what might have been study time. My overall Grade Point Average charted a disappointing 3.4 out of 4.0. Good, I supposed, for someone who didn't attend most classes and just skimmed the textbooks, so what the f—

Then I saw it: The numeral **3.4** stood out in bold on the Job Summary. Astonishingly, the IRS considered an average that was not even halfway from a "B" to an "A," to be "Top Academic Achievement." That lofty plateau merited beginning the job at Government Service Level 5, as opposed to the GS-4 I had been handed.

I looked up, and sure enough, my coworkers were taking their time getting back to work. Was I going to challenge the mistake in my hiring grade? I thought of my job in Taxpayer Service as an apprenticeship toward becoming a field agent. In our era of hiring freezes, that position had to be earned twice over. An improved GS level would help. More importantly, Linda was keeping herself squarely on the sidelines. I needed a win.

The next day, during the morning break, I followed the sign that said "Personnel," and climbed to the third floor. There I found an older section of the building where the short cubicle walls were immovable blocks topped with wood-framed glass, and the central fixture on each desk was an electric typewriter. As with Taxpayer Service, you walked into a sea of buzzing workers and navigated by whatever trouble-avoiding divining rod you carried in your head. Asking as few questions as possible, and going where I was told, I sat down with an advisor, Mr. Clarence Gatling, fully expecting the IRS to follow its own rules in regard to my situation. Fair was fair and I could use the money.

When I explained why I came, Gatling seemed affable enough. Even though his cubicle and desk both had a nameplate suggesting his permanence, he seemed as clueless and complacent as a tourist in Rome. I hoped his laid-back attitude was a good sign, but these things were unpredictable.

"I suppose you brought your transcript with you?" he asked.

"Right here." I handed it over to Gatling. Every tourist needed his guidebook.

"Hmm," he said as he riffled the oversized sheets, too intent to take his eyes off the paper while he reached for his candy bar. "Hmm, you took some interesting courses. Oceanography, The Physics of Musical Sound, Planetary Science, then Philosophy and lots of literature and creative writing, and art history, and you still managed to get an accounting degree with an English minor." I saw a flicker of trouble pass over Gatling's face. For just a moment, he looked at me as if I'd pulled off a bank heist on his watch.

"Yes, because I had studied those other subjects on my own before college, but I came to see you about the grade point average."

"And you say it adds up to at least 3.4?" Gatling said around a mouthful of Three Musketeers. It must have been the candy supply that calmed him because he was back to wondering where the Coliseum was and whether we would go there by bus.

"It does," I said. "Technically my GPA rounds to just above that."

"I don't understand this stuff, so I'll take your word for it."

Bingo. "So you'll adjust my status to GS-5 level?"

He stopped chewing. "You want what now?"

"That's the reason I came in. We went all through this."

"Oh, *that's* what you were talking about?"

"Yes, the IRS made a mistake in my pay scale. I'm a GS-4 when the rules say I should be a GS-5."

"So you want me to bump you ahead?"

"Only to what it was supposed to be."

"And what the hell makes you think you deserve something other people don't have?" Now he was an angry tourist that had been overcharged.

"What do you mean?"

"There's people in that room that go five, ten years before a promotion to GS-5. You think you're smarter and better than them? You think that your zero experience is better than five or ten years of experience? When you walk back into that room, and show your face again who's going to respect you for thinking that?"

I thought of Ladislav Ras who had taught me so much, and how unfair it would be if he earned less than I did. Seeing how this move might trigger a flood of resentment, I said, "No, when you put it that way, I guess not." I believed in authority more than I believed in self-aggrandizement.

"You guess not," Gatling mocked. "Then get your ass out of here." He rose stiffly and pointed the way to the exit.

I did get out of there. Or I tried. Halfway down the long aisle, I felt long fingernails dig into my arm and pull. I staggered into the nearest cubicle and fell against a tangle of blonde hair and a soft body that in turn landed in a chair that we both piled into. Fortunately, this floor had big old swivelers with ample padding and wide metal bases that stopped rolling when they rammed into a solid desk.

"Verna?" I asked.

I knew very well who it was—Verna Tucks, the clumsy hybrid of Mae West and Lauren Bacall that I went through training with. I was just dumbfounded to find her yanking me around.

Once we rearranged ourselves, Verna clucked three times and shook her head. The scary part was that she verbalized the word "cluck" before sinking to a whisper. "I was passing by. I heard everything."

"Everything of what?"

"This is not my first tour of duty with the Feds. I used to work for Air Force administration." She spoke her last three words heavily as though laden with encrypted information that I was never going to guess.

I studied Verna's face, her scarlet lipstick and pasty make-up. She had a couple of years on me so it was likely she worked somewhere else before coming to the IRS. I'd give her that much.

"You're being surveilled," she continued. "Always. And that meeting you just had... was a set-up."

I remembered how Ras said that he'd heard me on the phone. He didn't say he *over*heard me. The phones were probably bugged. But no, this idea of a set-up was too farfetched. And as for Verna, she sold paranoia like she'd gotten it wholesale. I had to figure this out.

Verna had leaned close to me when she said it, but she stayed there, and I admit I still felt a little aroused from when we collided.

She must have noticed that because she purred, "Just so you know, I'm cleared for takeoff... and landing." The Air Force thing. Her eyebrows jumped and she licked her lips but overshot them like a cat trying to get at distant crumbs.

"Sure," I said, as though uncertain what she meant. "Listen. To be smart, we'd better split up before we go back to work."

Her eyes flashed in alarm. "That's right." She took off in one direction while I made my way straight back to work by the same route that had taken me to this hall of mirrors.

Gatling had really convinced me that I was being ridiculous. I was no longer certain of that. Or of anything. It was strange the way Gatling changed his attitude so quickly and spun me around like a shooting gallery duck. As I made my way back to my division, the only thing I was sure of was that Hector hadn't sent me upstairs to be embarrassed. However badly his suggestion turned out, he had tried to get me a raise. It should have worked if things made any sense around here. There was my dilemma again. Should I keep listening to sensible Hector, who was a little too perfect, or start paying attention to crazy Verna?

DEEP INTO THE next week, I had shaken off my suspicions from the Gatling incident by burying myself in my work and studies. That was easy to do. There was so much of it.

Everyone I spoke to on a daily basis on our phone lines was incensed. That was how it felt. Those who called the IRS during tax season were pumped with stress and distress. Some petitioners just wanted a particular form, and none of those were ready yet. Others were in deep trouble, with desperation leading them to dark places. I'd get one of each of those calls followed by a complex tax question followed by someone who had failed their anger management class. If their problems were of their own making, I would tell them how it happened. If it was more likely the fault of the IRS, I would help expedite their claims. Most cases, however, were not so clear on the face of things.

As I was eyeing the clock for my first break, wondering how long I could keep up working by day and going to grad school at night, an unfamiliar face appeared above me, surmounting the low cubicle wall.

"Put the taxpayer on hold," she said crisply. Backlit and halo-wreathed by the fluorescent lights, she looked rather dreamlike. She may as well have said, *"Do you know how long you've been in the hospital?"*

"Sure," I said, taking care of it swiftly, "who are you?"
"QA."

"Your name is Cue-ay?" I wasn't trying to be a wise-ass. As far as I knew, there was no such terminology in the early 1980s.

"Quality Assurance," she clarified.

Ah Quality *Control*. That explained it. The interruption was because of something I'd said on the phone or did in the office. Some complaint. I said, "I've never seen you before."

"You're not supposed to. We monitor your telephone calls from a remote location. You're not even supposed to know who we are."

We? The trouble must be even worse than I thought. Whatever I did had flushed management out of hiding. Two more people had gathered around my station, these looking down at me like otherworldly interns in an operating theater. One was a sage gray Irishman, the other an eraser head. I'd never seen the movie by that name but he had the hair about right. With their bemused and curious expressions, I wondered if abduction by aliens felt like this. "Who are the rest of you?" I asked.

"QA," said eraser head, confirming their species with a slow blink.

By now my manager, Lucinda Evers, had joined them. The mysterious gathering looked like serious trouble to me: manager-with-a-complaint times four. *You're not even supposed to know who we are.* All because I wanted a raise?

"When did you take Phase Two training?" demanded the round-faced stranger. Their leader?

"You mean Phase One," I corrected her.

"No, I *know* what I mean when I say it. When did you take Phase Two training?"

63

"I don't know what you're talking about. I'm a new hire, just three weeks out of Phase One."

The alien doctors in human guise looked at each other as though they could share thoughts with a mental communion. Round Face said, "Then why are you answering Phase II questions?"

If they were worried about the taxpayer remaining on hold so long, they gave no sign of it.

"I have no idea what Phase I and Phase II questions are," I said defensively. "I just answer when I know the answer and write up a referral to Technical when I don't."

"How can you answer so many questions?" said the Irishman.

"I took tax in school," I shrugged. "Maybe I'm the only one in this department with an accounting degree."

"You just may be," said their leader, withdrawing. "You just may be."

The inexplicable visitation concluded, their intrusive probes stowed, I was allowed to go back to work. But this new wrinkle in my status made me want to take another run at the grade promotion. At the next break, I kept hold of my resolve and charged back up to the third floor, into the sea of Old World desks. First, I made sure Verna Tucks wasn't around, and then I went back to Gatling's cubicle. Only I couldn't find it because the spot was empty. Both wall and desk nameplates were gone, with nothing left but the typewriter and the industrial strength swivel chair.

Moving one space to the right, I called out, "I'm looking for Mr. Gatling."

The occupant, a woman I'd seen there the previous week, said, "Don't know him."

"Clarence Gatling?"

She shook her head. No eye contact from her.

The man at the desk to the left of Gatling's old position was looking at me, though, as if he could not look away. He'd been there last week as well. I repeated, "Clarence Gatling?"

"Never heard of him," he said through gritted teeth.

"You never heard of the person who sat next to you last week?" I was getting loud. In the meantime, I noticed a scrap wedged between the wall and the IBM electric. It was part of a Three Musketeers wrapper.

Before I could shout again, someone way down the row took note of me. Leaning into the aisle, he called out, "He's been reassigned."

"Where?"

"Maybe Atlanta."

I glanced back at Gatling's former neighbor, the man. He shrugged. "Like I said, I never heard of him."

That meeting that you had was a set-up.

At what level was it a set-up, though? And why? Softly, I said, "Score one for Verna." But I wasn't happy about it, and I was sure it was never Hector's idea.

OURS WAS NOT a coffee office. That pleasure, like all other amenities, was *verboten* in the giant, brand new room. I understood why. Management didn't want coffee spilled anywhere and they didn't want employees gossiping around a coffee pot every morning. A red tinge from the high narrow windows offered the only evidence that the sun ever set or rose in Taxland. There were no other jobs to be had in an accounting or tax environment, so here I stayed.

When I sat down at my desk, Lucinda stared at me from her station like the canary that had swallowed the cat and then used the cat's claw for a toothpick.

Finally, I said, "What?"

Coming over to perch her slender form on the edge of my desk, she sprinkled a few answers on me. According to her, this QA department not only found me to be answering what seemed to them a remarkable number of questions correctly, but further decided I knew procedures exceedingly well, which completed the illusion that I had worked there a long time. They were impressed too that I gave cheerful service with an eye to public relations, something they rarely saw.

"You're gooooood," Lucinda crooned in summary, the only sort of compliment she uttered to anyone.

"What does that mean?"

In answer, she hauled over a sloppy two-foot high stack of paper: action requests and inquiry referrals of every kind, each form printed in a different color ink. Riffling through them quickly, I could find none that were filled out in my handwriting, which was a relief.

"This is one day's work in my group," she said. "In the mornings, you'll be on the phone as usual. In the afternoons, you'll be reviewing the group's paper. Or vice versa. However you want to manage it."

"Good deal." I tried to be as cool as her, but I was thunderstruck by the sea change, and it probably showed. "Is this because of the visit from QA?"

"Partly," she said with a secret smile. That was as much

of an answer as I was ever going to get. I was learning that we in the Taxpayer Service Division were not a talky bunch. Management fed on secrets the way whales gorged on plankton.

Doing the paperwork meant that I would take all of the forms submitted by my group, and "pass, fail, or perfect them." *Perfect* meant fix. For anything amiss—a "fail,"—I would find the originator and teach him or her to do it right for next time. Fully authorized to approach the staff at any time, I would be the one asking them to put the taxpayer on hold as we chatted.

My rapid ascension should have caused tension, I thought, but it turned out that the group welcomed my explanations and assistance. While anxious to see how other people stacked up to me in terms of the quality of their work, I also knew that getting away from the phone conveyed huge benefits. No matter how good you might be at deflecting trouble, the work took its toll. I did not look a gift job in the mouth by asking my boss why she couldn't do her own paperwork.

Within days I was able to work the stack so quickly that Lucinda ended up lending me out to other Group Managers for the same purpose, no doubt for deals struck and horses traded. No finger got lifted in that office without pressing a political lever.

So here I was, not good enough to get GS-5 status but the only one so far chosen to be an unofficial assistant manager. Little did I know, I needed all the confidence I could get because the first threat to my job lurked right around the corner.

<u>Late February, 1985</u>

Terrance Chat was the invisible man. Coming and going as he pleased, whispering honey and bile in manager's ears, no one knew what level he occupied. Suitless and tieless, he looked like a civilian even while he enjoyed the unencumbered movement of upper management. I had noticed his shadowy presence lately, sowing smiles and scandal along management row, but we had never met.

One day, Lucinda corralled me and introduced the two of us by name; his was pronounced "shot." She told me, "You're going to be on special assignment," and left me to his mercy.

"Let's go get some privacy," said Terrance, deepening the mystery. "Come into my office."

"Alright," I said, wondering why he thought we lacked privacy, and why confidentiality was needed. I thought his office would at least provide a clue as to his station within the Service. We ventured into the noisy hallway, and when I saw he was going no further, I stopped to face him. He resembled the actor Sidney Poitier without the extra height, though he looked just as serious.

"There is no office, is there?" I asked.

"Shapiro," he said, "they tell me you are very smart."

"Thank you. Who is 'they'?"

"It ain't no thing, who said what. I checked you out. I know it for myself." His accent told me he'd transferred in from Atlanta within the past couple of years. Maybe Baton Rouge before that.

"Well, anyway, it's nice to meet you, Mr. Chat." I took care to pronounce his name correctly.

"Yeah, yeah, save all that bullshit. You'll find out later if it was nice to have met me. If you don't do a good job for me—if you fuck up—then you will fuck *me* up. Then you're going to be very sorry."

This marked the first time I heard someone at manager-level speak like that in this Federal island on a Brooklyn sea. Good old straightforward profanity. Somehow it made him more real than the people who fit into legitimate categories, which is to say clearly distinguishable ones.

"What is this about?"

Softly, he said, "The Undeliverable Refund Project."

For some reason, Terrance the Shadow, standing in a hallway, had the ability to pass me vaguely defined assignments that came from the misty mountains on high. "Is that code for something?"

"It's no joke," he assured me, ignoring the crowds of flowing people in the hall. "This is serious shit, and we're in trouble."

Terrance explained that if a refund was sent out and returned to us in the mail, the law required the IRS to do a certain amount of research and find out where that missing person went.

The concept of us hunting people down to give them their refunds was news to me. What the "research" consisted of, I had no idea. Every IRS division in the country was failing in its responsibility to some extent. For some reason, the Brooklyn District, consisting of 12 million taxpayers, including Long Island, was three years behind, and I had two months to cobble together a way to catch them up, and then "institutionalize the plan."

"Terrance," I pleaded, "I don't have any reason to believe I can come in off the street, wipe out backlogs, and institutionalize plans."

Terrance stared a hole through me and went on staring as though having a profound experience. "Do you know the Division Chief, Bill Foster?"

"I've seen him in here. What about it?"

"You know you look like him?"

"That's what everyone says." I hoped my looking like Foster wasn't being mistaken for an actual qualification.

"Anyway," said Chat, "I told the Division Chief that I would get the job done for him because Dan Shapiro can do this job."

"What? Why would you tell him a thing like that?"

"Because you can."

"I don't know anything about refund handling. I wouldn't know where to start."

"You're smart. You'll think of a way."

"I have to clear up a three-year backlog all by myself?"

"Of course not," he shook his head. "You gotta come up with a new method by yourself. Once you have the method, I can give you a crew of fifteen to work the job."

"My crew would be off the phones all day?" That advantage would make the task a hair less crazy.

"Pull whoever you trust, but you gotta rotate five at a time. That way, all the managers will cooperate. Except for Virgie."

"Virgie Poncit?" I'd caught the name before, and even spotted her a couple of times. She had looked pleasant enough to me. "Why would she be a problem?"

"C'mon," he said with a tilt of his head. "I'll show you how to hit the DMV, stuff like that."

I released a breath I didn't realize I was holding, relieved that he actually planned to show me something, whatever "hit" the DMV meant.

With his face washed green by the glow of the cathode ray tube in the computer screen, Terrance revealed some of the ways the IRS tracked people down. Since the postmaster didn't have the answers in these cases, we queried the Department of Motor Vehicles first, then the county clerks, the courts, the FBI, and even Interpol. Yes, even international criminals had to get their refunds. Anywhere someone might pop on radar. Through an avalanche of coded commands, we were tied into every other government agency with seamless cooperation. The methods were actually very effective. That scared me because if the Feds could peer under every rock, and they were three years behind anyway, then what were they doing wrong? What could I possibly teach this dancing elephant that it didn't already know?

Terrance said, "I'll let you study this awhile and then I'll come back. Just remember what I said: If you fuck this up, I'll make sure you fall further than I ever do."

As I said, I liked Terrance. He came across as emphatic and sincere without the need to put his finger in your face. Even so, the repeated warning began to get to me. To make it clear I didn't need to hear it again, I said, "I have no intention of fucking up, sir."

He scrutinized me to see if I was being straight with him. Then he stalked off.

From a safe distance, Hector Chavez watched him go, mouthed a silent three count, and then sidled up to me. "I heard you're taking on the Undeliverable Refund Project."

"How did you hear that? I just found out about it myself."

"Way to go, Danny. *Mazeltov.*"

He sounded sincere so I said, "Thank you...I think."

Then he fixed me with a cynical eye. "You know it's bullshit, right?"

I sighed. "All right, Hector. Tell me how it's bullshit."

"That project is an old stinker that's burned everyone it touched. If you somehow do well, Terrance takes all the credit. If you mess up, you get all the blame. And there's nothing you can do that the IRS hasn't already tried, so you can't help but mess up. I wouldn't want to be in your shoes." As he said the last part, he tapped me softly on the lapel like he was shedding cigarette ash.

"You're saying that because you weren't picked for this," I called after him.

"No, they picked me first. That's how come I know so much about it... I turned it down."

Hector was always a step ahead of me. Why didn't I think of turning the job down?

AS THE LATE sun cast our busy shadows on the east wall, I assembled my first team of five from the most senior of floor staffers who ranged from age forty to a feisty seventy-eight. They were game for anything, the sort of people who just looked for interesting challenges, especially the old man. My first step was to recreate the way the URP was currently run. I had to see the process in action to know what might be wrong with it. My crew sat in a row, materials close to hand, and began at my signal to duplicate the mess we were in. Their task was to work the old way, tapping into other agencies, and then stuffing envelopes with inquiries to anyone who was not in our web.

Like a gambling house with an Eye-In-the-Sky, upper management always knew when a big event was going down. On cue, Division Chief Bill Foster came from his second-floor office, glanced at my old soldiers, and patted me on the back wordlessly on his way past. That was the first time he'd ever done that, and there was no comfort to be had since the gesture seemed to fall halfway between encouragement and condolence.

Foster struck me as a very young man to occupy the position he did. Both of us that day were wearing polyester powder-blue business suits, stood the same height, a little hunched in the shoulders, and enjoyed approximately the same trim fitness level, he a bit more filled out in maturity. We each had the same darkish hair and haircut, and occasionally slipped the same tortoise shell aviator glasses over our blunt boxer-type noses. All a match, except that in two months he would still be the Division Chief, while I might be unemployed due to my stupidity in taking on an assignment no one could do.

Lucinda slinked over to me in a zesty and mischievous mood, "You know that you and Bill are like twins?"

"I see that, yes." I also saw that for some reason Lucinda was trying to show me she was on a first name basis with the boss. Even if that easy camaraderie were real, a manager at the IRS wouldn't normally bandy the boss' first name with a subordinate.

"Bill is really concerned about this project you took on."

"You think?" I heard it more clearly in her tone this time, the buttery implication that she was close to the Division Chief, as though she had mingled with him in a social setting. There were rumors that she'd married someone up the chain of command.

Lucinda had perfected the evil smile, which she shared with me now as she added, "I wouldn't want to be you."

I said, "No, there are one too many of me already."

CHAPTER FOUR
Into The Gutter

"Some people can read War and Peace and come away
thinking it's a simple adventure story. Others can read the
ingredients on a chewing gum wrapper and unlock the
secrets of the universe."

—*Superman*

Terrance wasn't kidding about the Division Chief
watching closely that winter. My doppelganger appeared in
our demesne more often now, hovering about like a
battleship off the coast of a troubled country that might have
to be kept in line with an artillery barrage. From that
distance there would be no more patting me on the back
unless it was with shrapnel. I imagined him retiring to his
war room and grabbing a shuffleboard cue stick to update his
scale model with the troop movements he'd observed.

My team's war room turned out to be the Square
Orange, my name for Ladislav Ras' compact Skoda. He had
been the first enthusiast to volunteer for my effort. Upon my
initial return to the parking lot retreat, the car seat gave a
shuddering twang as another of its springs surrendered to old
age. The compressed padding released the smell of pungent
beet juice it had absorbed and refined over the years. I
commented, "This thing is smaller than I remember. Or
maybe your hair is bigger."

Lad, as I now called him, took in the remark stoically as someone might take birthday punches to the arm. "If you want to plan anything at the IRS, you do it away from the microphones."

"So everyone keeps telling me. I'm going to need you to run some numbers on my teams, maybe even take over a shift if I get called away."

"Anything you need. What do I have to know?"

"Every standard procedure to get refunds into the right hands."

With a smile, he asked, "Do I get to use the stopwatch?"

"I borrowed that stopwatch from you, Lad."

"And what is the result so far?"

The watch was necessary because I had already begun to train my five-person test group and time each task, such as taking an "address unknown" envelope off the stack and checking whether that person had gone into the military. The output times varied greatly, producing a mix of idling bottlenecks. Worse yet, computer searches didn't provide the answer for everything. Too much of our work involved sending requests to previous employers and "last known associates," which made the resolution iffy. Trying not to sound discouraging, I said, "I need to see uniformity and lower averages." Based on our abysmal results, I could see how the overall job would take too long and sink us another three years behind.

"How much can efficiency help?"

"Not enough," I admitted. "Even at its best, the existing plan is unworkable."

"So we need another tool and we don't have one."

"Yes. Do you want to bail out?"

"No, I trust you, Danny. Plus, I can't bail out. It's my car."

I laughed, glad that Lad had a sense of humor. He was going to need it.

When we got back, I thought Lucinda was going to reprimand me for my freewheeling use of time. Instead, she folded her hands under her chin and mocked, "Fill me in on your secret meeting. Please, please, please." She must have thought I would work better if I lived in a soap opera.

Each day, her silky-voiced running commentary told me I was flirting with danger at every turn. The show was fun and spicy from where she sat. She even brought in popcorn one day. In truth, she was making sure that I was directly associated with the likely train wreck, not her. If I chose to go beyond her reach and take orders from the big boys, she was going to plant her stocking feet on the coffee table and laugh at my folly. But if I knew one trick that might save me, the idea was to remain more methodical than the average bear.

When I felt confident I had absorbed and passed along the full range of hunting skills to my team, I made a hallway appointment with the invisible man in hopes of glimpsing the existing PERT chart before I tried to fix anything. According to Terrance, the public hallway was the only place in the building that wasn't bugged. I wasn't yet cynical enough to believe that, though I played along.

Once we were in the public section, I made my request.

"What's a PERT chart?" he said without a trace of guile.

"Your CPM chart? A diagram?" The chart would tell me how the project's workflow was arranged. There had to have been a huge error in that planning document for things to have gone so wrong.

He shook his head.

"Performance Evaluation Review Technique?"

He stared.

"Your Critical Path Method for the Undeliverable Refund Project? The managerial accounting plan?"

"We don't have none of that," he said, already moving away, and now calling out to me. "Whatever that is, you'll have to work without it."

The dark clouds parted and a slow smile traversed my lips. They had been doing all the procedural grunt work without the benefit of a work flow plan? None at all? This was the break that would spoil Lucinda's fun. I could devise such a chart and set out a shingle that said, "Wizard."

Ducking back into the big room, I set Lad free, grabbed my briefcase, and together we headed out to the Square Orange.

"New development," I told him as soon as we were in the car. "They haven't been using managerial accounting on this task."

He thought I'd gone over the edge. "You're worried about accounting now?"

"It's not number crunching. It's a tool to manage the job. Have you ever heard of Polaris?"

Lad's brow furrowed in consternation. "Of course. The United States' H-bomb from the 1960's. We had them in my country too."

"Not like ours. The way we built the delivery system was more important to us than the bomb itself. Sapolsky called it 'a computerized planning, scheduling and control device,' and it took years off the project."

"Who is Sapolsky?"

"Doesn't matter. It conquers repetitive tasks, bottlenecks and interruptions."

"For anything?"

"Any complex task. Rips through them like a savage beast. Here, look." I started sketching out sheets of small, numbered circles connected by a latticework of labeled arrows and letters.

When I was done doodling, Lad said, "Looks like chemistry." And it did, now that he mentioned it. The picture resembled a complex molecular structure.

"These nodes and routes represent our required milestones and activities with maximum and minimum time spans. Out of this diagram, the critical path itself and the surrounding slack time will sparkle like a diamond in coal."

"I hate chemistry," said Lad. "Or whatever this is."

"Then think of it as cinema. I can determine how the flaws in our process could be eliminated by rearranging the steps like a movie filmed out of sequence and reshuffled in the editing room."

"If you say so."

"I do."

"Isn't that the sort of thing they use computers for?"

"Yes. The catch is that I don't actually have industrial software. Our budget for this work is zero."

"Doesn't that make *you* the software?"

79

"Right, the way Alan Turing and his team did it before computer programming language was invented."

"And stuff like that works?"

"I don't know. It has to be good enough. I don't want to lose my job if this project fails."

As for Terrance himself, his rare appearances were for the apparent purpose of a schmooze-fest with the mostly female managers. He'd ask me how I was doing as an afterthought. Or so it seemed. By distracting them with his charm, the managers almost forgot that he stole some of their best people, and had me do the same. When the time came to choose the rest of my crew, I made a list of the most promising of the newcomers whom I knew from their paperwork, and they already saw me as a boss. If I tapped the resources of group managers Lucinda, Tammy, Kate, Dawn, and Virgie, that meant I could draw a total of three from each to get my fifteen. The staffers I pre-screened were all-too-happy at the prospect of getting a respite from the phones, so they cooperated enthusiastically.

I had my fifteen lined up at computer terminals and was all ready to call out, "Action" when the infamous Virgie Poncit, who Terrance had warned me about, said, "No."

"No?"

"Put my people back on the telephones."

"Why?"

"You can't have any of my people. Ever. Again."

I couldn't believe she would sink me just like that, when I had the solution all worked out. Trying to make sure it didn't sound like pleading, I reminded her, "I gave you advance notice, Virgie."

"I said, no."

"I haven't taken any more of your people than anyone else's."

"No."

"You're going to have to stop saying no."

Virgie considered the challenge for a moment and said, "Forget it. You can't have any of my people."

I sighed. For this conversation, Virgie had enough of her buttons open to show a mountain of cleavage. A very attractive woman, she used it as well as she knew how. It was easy to be mesmerized, but you couldn't let the body fool you. Her tactic hid a sucker punch.

She complained, "You know why? Because you never worked for me. You worked for everyone else."

"I didn't—"

"The paperwork that you did for them. The supervision."

"Oh," I groaned. Now I got it. When they set up my assistant manager gig, they left her out of the rotation. That was reason enough for her to go after me...though she might have had another reason. I do remember something in my early studies about a queen with a magic mirror trying to ensure she remained the "fairest one of all."

Fortunately, Virgie didn't have the resources of a fairy tale queen. By reputation, what she lacked in brains, she tried to make up for in hair pulling and cat scratching. She didn't play nice, and in turn, her peers didn't share with her. Virgie's trick of heel dragging when it came to my project seemed a feeble attempt at global retribution, even though I was an innocent bystander in her feuds.

I continued, "The decision about who we helped was Lucinda's choice. Not mine."

"Then take double from Lucinda's people," she said. "Payback's a bitch and so am I."

"This is not Lucinda's project. It's Assistant Chief Lansdale's project. Would you like his contact information?"

"I have it," she said indignantly.

"Well Art Landsdale told me to give you a message if you insisted on hearing it."

"And what is that?"

"He said, 'When Virgie gives you shit—and she will—tell her that she has no choice, and give her my phone number.'" I had his card, and I dropped it on her desk. Her wide-open mouth was all the satisfaction I needed.

Once these nasty personnel details were settled, I covered the out-of-sequence tasks by cross-training my crew in every step so that each of my people would be interchangeable. I still went to school at night, and still spent part of the evening in self-study of advanced income tax rules. Although Virgie did not interfere again, she stared daggers at me as we worked.

I didn't care about how the politics of jealousy played into it. If the IRS did one thing right, it was promulgating internal methods and procedures across the county. That meant that if they were not doing something in Brooklyn, they were probably not doing it anywhere. So, refunds were a national problem that would now have a national solution. Not only was my method working, but its success would ensure that it lived on. More importantly, that I would live on.

To be on the safe side—because things seemed too

perfect to be true—I quietly asked Terrance, "No offense, but are you sure we're really doing what the brass wants?"

"Meaning what?" asked Terrance.

"I mean, the old system was terribly backed up for a long time."

"What about it?"

"How do we know that state of affairs wasn't a matter of policy?"

"What policy?"

He was making this question difficult, and I couldn't believe I hadn't considered this scenario sooner. I remembered what Hector said. *This project is an old stinker that's burned everyone it touched.* I bit the bullet, and said what I was thinking. "How do we know that the IRS wasn't perfectly happy to keep money from people who were hard to find anyway?"

"Oh that," he laughed. "Yeah, you're right, they weren't feeling it that much. But Congress got hold of the stats and roasted the commissioner. Now he got religion. So, if you're asking if it's okay to do a great job, it's like I told you in the first place. Finish it like you were going to."

"Right. Got it."

I was relieved that Terrance's straightforward instructions did not waver in the face of a possible success. Towards the end though, circumstances changed in the most frightening way.

Virgie began to smile at me as though she'd thought of something that would help her get even. I brandished a two-handed sign of the cross with left and right index fingers, improvised proof against vampires, and I swear she shrunk back and hissed. Or possibly neither of those things happened. I would deal with her retribution when it came. How bad and how prolonged could her vengeance be? I had no idea, so I slunk back to work.

As Foster and Terrance orbited, my team and I ripped through the old obstacles. Unlike the Polaris project, we weren't doing rocket science. We were finding people who had dropped off the grid and mailing checks to them. Nothing could explode on the landing pad.

To my relief, my little refund factory made a breakthrough. Everyone in the effort knew how to pick up pieces of the puzzle and form them into the components we needed upstream and downstream of the workflow. In short, they were able to follow my blueprint. With each team member productive at all times, the bottlenecks vanished and we pared three-years-worth of work to four weeks in a dazzling flash of un-governmental efficiency. I was at the end of a successful journey, and that sort of initiative should be rewarded, right?

Wrong.

Virgie was not my only problem. When Lucinda asked me to write up my accomplishments for the file, Terrance was at my shoulder, telling me he wanted to see my notes first. During my blissful bee-working interval, I had banished any thoughts from my head that said, "Things are going too smoothly." Now I focused on another thing I was good at, which was writing reports. After all, I was still a diligent grad student at this time.

My report laid out the adventure step by step, omitting only Terrance's methods for greasing the wheels, which I never fully understood anyway. I drew up neat circle templates to formalize my diagrams.

When I was done with my documentation, I found out that a refund project, much like Polaris, could indeed explode on the landing pad if not handled like political nitroglycerin. Standing in the hallway with the general public rushing around us, Terrance shook his head. "The way you wrote this looks like you did everything and I did nothing."

"That's pretty much the way it was, though," I reminded him. "As I mentioned in the report, you taught me everything I knew about the old way the project was done. Then you checked in once a week, but you didn't give me any input or participate in any direct way. I didn't fault you for it on paper." At the moment, Terrance held the title of "Undeliverable Refunds Project Coordinator." I wondered what his job consisted of other than asking me for updates.

"I know that, but it can't look that way."

I briefly admired his honesty until I realized where it came from. Any challenge to his version of events could put a cloud over his career. Not wanting that to happen to me either, I said in exasperation, "How *can* it look?"

Terrance stared at me, biting his lip. "Alright, here's how it will go down. You give me all the credit, call yourself a helper or something, and I'll give you the best advice you could ever have."

"Advice?"

"Yeah, the good stuff."

"Such as?"

"Such as this: You are going to be The Man around here. You're already well on your way."

"So… what's the advice?"

"The best way to gain power is to take it."

"From someone else?"

"Not like that. You see how I just come and go as I please, do whatever I want, give the manager a kiss and just slide right in beside her?" In that year, all the group managers in our branch were women.

"I've noticed, yes."

"I don't have any right to do those things. I do them. You act 'as if,' and it becomes real."

"That explains a lot," I said diplomatically. Then again, he looked like Sidney Poitier.

While I saw value in his suggestion and filed it away for later, nothing was becoming real for me just yet, unless you counted *Realpolitik*. I needed someone to ground me and I knew just who to consult.

Lad drooped a little but he and his hair were unmistakable. His mild greeting, while never reassuring, was at least familiar. We walked out to the parking lot and he stopped within the barren confines of two white lines. No car. A bad omen if I ever saw one.

"Where's the Skoda?" I asked.

"It's in the shop."

"Huh, okay." A little uncomfortable in the car-less vacuum, and with our extreme height difference when he wasn't folded up, I proceeded anyway. "You did a terrific job, Lad, everything that had to be done. You'll be commended in my report."

"I'm sorry," he replied.

86

"Sorry about what?" He already knew I'd been screwed?

"You know what. Where do you think you are? This is the IRS. It's his word against yours if you choose to fight him, but some good will come of this."

"*His* word? You mean Terrance."

"Yes," confirmed Lad.

I was still a beat behind. "What do you mean, 'some good will come of this'?"

"Even if you say nothing at all in your own favor in that report, you will at least get a little credit. But in my opinion, it's best to work hard and not to fight."

Lad was an unusual Slav, I thought, not all that toughened by his old country's system. A good man, though. The IRS must have worn him down. Now I asked myself again why I was doing this. Yes, for Linda, and yes to become a field agent. But why did I want to head out into the wider world and put myself in harm's way?

The answer, for better or for worse, was that I had an ingrained sense of duty. I came from generations of soldiers. In my father's case, as a military policeman, it was law enforcement too. The army had turned me down for having flat feet.

In a world where many of those who were well off were always looking to shift their tax burden to their poorer neighbor, someone had to bring a little fairness into our system. It took a young, strong back to bear the weight, and as usual I had no idea what my action would cost, but I was in all the way.

In "correcting" my report, I wasn't chump enough to label myself a "helper" as Terrance had requested. Nonetheless, after a flurry of negotiated changes, a greatly watered down version of my accomplishments ended up in the file and Terrance was delighted. Bill Foster did not return to pat me on the back. Any celebrations surrounding my miracle must have been quiet ones. Apparently, all I accomplished was "not fucking up." Even that claim would soon be debated.

Hector Chavez, the Wise Owl, came by and thumped me on the shoulder, genially adding four little words: "I told you so."

I KNEW THAT something important had changed when I saw Lad, the man with his ear to the ground, the tall, Chech version of Sancho Panza, approach me, beaming with triumph.

I put the taxpayer on hold and asked him the news.

"That will be your last call."

"Last of the day?"

"Last ever as an underling. When Lucinda comes down from her meeting upstairs, she's going to tell you that you have full time supervisory work."

"Are you sure?"

"I guarantee it." He sounded proud.

"But why?"

"The IRS is desperately in need of better management. They can't afford to keep you on the front line a moment longer."

It turned out he was right about the shift. If nothing else, I seemed to have bought a permanent ticket off the chain gang. With the refund project successfully concluded, no matter how busy it got at the height of the tax season, Lucinda had me spend most of the day on quality review and the rest on her paperwork.

The quality review detail I performed was a Group Manager's quality review, quite apart from the work of the super-secret Quality Assurance Section. When she called me up, I sat at Lucinda's oversized station and listened in on telephone conversations between our Taxpayer Service Representatives and the taxpayers. I could interrupt at any time to offer advice, and sometimes I did. The usual reaction from the TSR's was, "I'm sure glad you were listening because I was about to pull my hair out." The taxpayer who had called would say much the same thing to me.

Unlike the policy in most non-government customer service call centers, group managers were not allowed to refuse to take over the phone call if a taxpayer initiated the request for a supervisor. The callers who got "bumped up" were the most rankled taxpayers of all. They were either too angry to listen to reason or too frustrated because they had been mishandled earlier. These next-level requests brought out both righteous anger, and occasional insane, bomb-threat anger; the kind of calls that customer service managers at every company have nightmares over. At the IRS I'd witnessed our leaders having a number of "daymares" too.

Most managers did not follow the rules; they ran and hid from tough situations. Being a competent phone rep myself with a genuine desire to help, and a shield of naiveté, irate callers didn't frighten me in the least. I saw the big picture in taking over the call, a honeymoon period of ninety seconds just for being someone different than the person they were originally speaking to. If something went sour and that taxpayer then asked to speak to my supervisor higher up, I would theoretically have to put Lucinda on the phone, and she in turn would have to put Branch Chief Mike Soderling on the phone, but neither of those transfers ever happened. The buck stopped at my desk every time.

My status did not remain unique for long. Over at Tammy Sangenario's station, the enigmatic Hector Chavez soon led a separate life doing much the same thing I did. Hector and I would come to be known as a pair of *wunderkinder,* the like of which this relatively new division had never seen. Given that success, it became *de rigeur* to pull the best people from the ranks and put them in assistant manager roles.

While I was riding high, I should have stopped to review the laws of physics, and recall that every action has an equal and opposite reaction. The scientific approach would have been better than flying like Icarus into the feather-melting arms of the sun. The sun, in this case, was named Virgie Poncit.

CHAPTER FIVE
False Label

"What we have here is a failure to communicate."

—*Cool Hand Luke*

April 19, 1985

In a process that cycled all through tax season, the army of one hundred hired with me swelled to its capacity as things got busy, and shrank as the machine wound down. All the while, people were fired, quit, or were omitted from the roster while a very few like me, got their hours boosted permanently. Once we were past the mid-April filing deadline, however, we experienced a sudden drop in personnel. By late April, a handful of us rattled in the giant room of vacated pentapods, wondering fitfully what came next.

When I crossed to and from my station on April 19th, the fourth day of settling dust, I drew surreptitious pity glances from the group managers. My position was far from secure. No matter what it said on paper, no one on the second floor actually believed that Terrance Chat had reached into his hat and come up with the Performance Evaluation Review Technique, or the Critical Path Method, or whatever you wanted to call it. Upper management quietly gave me the credit. They simply forgot to tell me that. Perhaps more self-confidence would have helped. I was missing something for sure. If I had been certain that my efforts were well known but underappreciated, maybe some of my decisions that followed would have been different.

Here's what actually happened, based on what I pieced together later: Some people that I knew slightly, such as the Division Chief, and others up and down the chain whom I would not meet until years afterward, had a major meeting about me in the executive conference room. It seemed my work on the Undeliverable Refund Project had saved an endangered backside or two. I was smart, they ceded, but they'd known that since the IQ test. On the downside, I had failed Gatling's test by allowing him to talk me out of my rightful grade level, the GS-5. That had been a test after all, a "set-up" as Verna called it. In my favor, I had stood up to Virgie Poncit, shifting the personnel I needed with no hesitation.

I learned later that a healthy debate raged on the subject of my future career. I would even one day see the legal pad with my name on it where someone had scrawled across, "NO MANAGEMENT POTENTIAL," with a double underscore. Maybe they were saving the assessment for a glass case in the Smithsonian. By the time the Assistant District Director struck the gavel, the majority conclusion was that my allowing Terrance to take all the credit for my accomplishments meant that I had washed out. A true Treasury Department warrior, they said, would have sliced off Terrance's balls and given him a fiery Viking funeral before suffering the humiliation of a report like the one I submitted. Therefore, they were going to allow another agency to recruit me, one that had more use for my demonstrated talents or could perhaps train me not to be such a fool. If the visitor waiting in the hall would have me, I was going to be traded away like last year's baseball player minus the financial incentive.

Here's what *I* thought happened: No one talked about me, no one cared, and an avalanche of weird, inexplicable things followed. For instance, this:

Lucinda came to my desk and said, "Mark your calendar. First thing Monday you're in computer class." My heart sank. I wanted to continue being a supervisor, not get re-trained as if my computer skills were not good. Where would they send me after that?

"What did I do wrong?"

She gave me a wicked smile. "Nothing."

My favorite circumstance—being punished for nothing at all. "I took computer studies in school," I hedged. "What level is this?"

"Special."

I didn't like being taken out of action, but spoiling Lucinda's fun, or even trying to pry more information from her, wasn't healthy. Class was conducted in a part of the basement I had not seen before, and the other "students" were nine stooges I did not recognize and would never see again. The syllabus called for a four-week course in personal computing led by a Mr. Dodd. I could describe him in detail for you, but that information is classified.

Personal computing was in its infancy, and for our purposes we were each given an enormous "portable computer" built into a suitcase on wheels. I wasn't happy acquiring that burden in addition to the suitcase of textbooks I lugged daily for night school.

On the first day of class, Dodd emphasized that the computer world was a small one where its denizens stuck together, and that was certainly true at that time. As an undergrad, every time I met one of its practitioners, It irritated me no end that they hid their simple programming tricks like magicians in order to keep their club small and exclusive. In their snobbery they held that you had to be referred by someone on the inside in order to join the field without opposition.

Without invoking a ceremony, Dodd implied that those who succeeded here would be inducted into a kind of underground brotherhood that went even deeper than that of ordinary programmers. My curiosity about computers had already been dampened. Shouldn't someone have consulted me before yanking me off my career path?

Even with Dodd's hint of a clandestine purpose afoot, the class seemed routine and boring with its uninspired content. Until the day Dodd ordered me to stay after class.

As the others cleared out, I wondered how I had gotten singled out so quickly. I really wanted to get back to work on my chosen career track, not be entangled in all this nonsense. Locking the door first, and turning on some music that was mostly static, the instructor held up a floppy disk. He said, "Do you know what this is?" With a broad smile, he handed it to me to let me study the label.

It read, "Anti-viral."

"No idea," I shrugged. "Should I?"

He accepted it back and inserted it in one of the machines with a click. "Don't worry. It's pretty much a false label anyway. This is a utility—actually, a beta program."

False label? Dodd came off as sincere and helpful in his murky, underground sort of way. He looked like a smiling fireplug. I thought the intrigue was all in his head. There were actually four disks in the set, and he offered them out like a lure. "Take them with you," he urged. "Study them."

Wary now, I paused, deep in thought. They wanted to eat into my personal time? It was one thing if I chose to do that and another to be ordered. Could I say no?

"At home," he added meaningfully, in case I didn't get it. "And make sure you're alone."

This occasion was not like Terrance leaving me to study the computer access to our sister agencies. This time I didn't know what the assignment was or whether it was even authorized. Why would I need to be alone? Anxious to see what I had, I closed the hard shell over the computer, set the suitcase on the floor and extended the long handle. I discovered that it was made to accommodate a briefcase like mine riding on top. They fit together so that both handles interlocked, and I hurried home. Once there, I made sure I had privacy, and set up the computer as I had done in class.

When the program booted up, Dodd's "utility" unfurled the waving image of a skull and crossbones on a black flag and announced that this was the "Pirate's Toolkit." For a moment it was hard to take that image and the cartoon icons seriously. Then I saw the suite of functions: the first was an anti-viral (whatever that meant), the second a general maintenance package. The third was represented by a mask icon, and this must have been the secret part, tools that could remove copy protection from commercial programs, and engage in other mischief that sounded suspiciously like hacking. Hacking was something I'd heard of because an acquaintance of mine boasted he had gotten into the computer system at Brooklyn College and given himself the perfect grades he could never earn. Why would the IRS need me to have that capability? I wondered. In those days I did not know there was such a thing as "white hat" hacking. I hadn't thought about it much.

The next morning, Dodd told me there was someone he would like me to meet, and then disappeared. "The man waiting in the hallway," as I've called him, was tall and wore a dark suit, such as a funeral attendee would wear. He led me into a bare room, which he locked us into. He showed me credentials that said, "NSA"—in fine print underneath, the National Security Agency—and informed me that, "Your DC knows I'm here," using our abbreviation for Division Chief.

"Here for what?"

"We're just chatting." He smiled like a model in a catalog, pleasant and calm.

"Chatting about what?" I demanded.

"What did you think of it?"

"Think of what?"

"About the disk."

"The one I took home? It disturbed me."

He didn't ask why, but smiled vacuously, waiting for me to elaborate. That was when I should have realized why there were excessive levels of "quality assurance" in our division without all that much quality, and why we had gone through such rigorous testing without all that much feedback. As I would learn later, other agencies were allowed to monitor our activities in order to cherry pick which employees they wanted to offer "alternative opportunities." If you didn't get such an offer, you would never know of these clandestine provisions.

This was my open door to Hacking School. I had never heard of the National Security Agency or their specialty in intercepting signals intelligence and the need for cryptanalysts. Or in this case, their need for "white hat" hackers. But getting served up to an interagency raiding party left a bad taste in my mouth. Besides, by then I had my heart set on being a Revenue Agent. Though I was still technically a "part-time, temporary, seasonal provisional," an extraordinarily vulnerable position, I gladly gave back the Pirate's Toolkit and said it wasn't for me. Then, mysteriously, the so-called four-week computer class was over on Day Three with a terse comment from the NSA guy, "Don't discuss this."

When I got upstairs, I was feeling inexplicably bereft. Had I made a horrible decision by stubbornly sticking to the plan I'd worked out with Linda? Even though I didn't know that my management path was considered blocked, I had the disturbing sense that I could end up with no career at all.

Then the marvelous Tammy Sangenario beckoned me over.

"Tell me some good news," I urged.

"You're getting promoted to Permanent," she said with one of her golden smiles.

"How do you know?"

"Just apply and you'll have it."

That was the only time I'd heard her sound impatient with one of my questions, yet she spoke the truth. The timing was no coincidence. The moment the permanency paperwork was done, Tammy directed me to the Big Carrot, the Revenue Agent posting I had been waiting for. Since I supposedly had no future in management, and had turned down an interagency transfer, Taxpayer Service was steering me clean out of their Division. No guarantees—nothing promised this time—but they were pushing.

As they say in Heaven, when a door closes, a window opens. Sometimes Treasury advises: Go jump out that window.

<u>May Day, 1985</u>

Shifting to the Examinations Division was what I wanted, right? It should have been good even though I was being pushed there instead of going on my own accord. I should have been holding steady until the transfer came through. When I thought I finally knew where I stood, however, the ground shifted under me with a mudslide of events that only Fate could have devised. Fate in collusion with the IRS. This was May 1st.

I dressed to the sound of the morning news where the reporters pointed out that half a world away in the Soviet Union, they were celebrating the old European holiday, May Day, as a militarized "Labor Day." What used to be a pagan festival with a Maypole dance—and an occasion that now supposedly celebrated workers—became for them a gross display of their military might, with missiles in place of Macy's floats. By now I was glad that we had in Ronald

Reagan, a president who stood up to them without starting a war. They were scary times nonetheless.

As I locked the door on the way out of my house, I found a single piece of mail with a blue Treasury Department logo on it. No postmark, as though someone other than a mail carrier had delivered. It contained news about my application to be an Internal Revenue Agent, a confirmation statement of my eligibility. An overall evaluation of me placed my score at 86. Whatever that meant, it gave me *entre* to an interview and a head start on winning the position.

Finally eligible to make the attempt, and cautiously optimistic, I tucked the notice into a pocket close to my chest and thought of Linda, who kept me going. She seemed so distant just now and I wished I had more definite news for her. The actual interview could be a painfully long way off. I had never blamed her for letting her parents keep us apart. Some young women still felt very much at the mercy of their parents, but the latest separation felt endless.

I headed for Brighton Beach Avenue's elevated track, the metal dragon, as I called it. With my mind already spinning with the good news, I came face to face with Verna Tucks as we were both making a dash for the moving D Train from the lower staircase. I was impressed by the fresh blue pinstripes that peeked from her collar. Unlike the bargain clothes we federal underlings usually wore, she was turned out with military precision and wrapped in a smart woolen coat against the unseasonably cool day. I think I said something nice about it but I don't remember her reacting.

We were lucky enough to squeeze into the only seats in the car, one of the little side benches, a polite proximity considering that neither of us seemed to have anything to say. Since I wasn't looking for her approbation, I kept my uncertain job news to myself.

It seemed remarkable that she was so sad and jumpy when I thought about the steady hand she must have applied that morning to her immaculate hair and make-up. She did not seem in the mood to yank me into an alcove and speak of conspiracies. In fact, I didn't mind sitting snug up against the lovely Verna as long she made no clumsy attempts to snare me. Up close and silent, and looking her best, while stop after stop jostled her blonde hair onto my shoulder, it made me wonder at my strict decision to keep my distance. At that age, part of me argued that crazy women were the most interesting. You can guess which part.

We sat in tense silence that lasted long enough to take us downtown while I tried to think of what I would say in my upcoming Revenue Agent interview. I refrained from any sudden moves with Verna, and I thought that would be that. One stop before the end, however, she burst out, "I can't take it anymore."

I looked over, startled to see her face drenched in silent tears that were still flowing. "What happened? What's the matter?"

"The job is so hard, so much harder than I thought possible," she said without a trace of the phony Mae West voice.

"You can do it, Verna. You have the brains, the talent, and the right attitude." I did think she had those qualities if you scraped beneath her paranoia and general weirdness.

She smiled a little at the praise, but not for long. "I'm not like you. You're in management."

I laughed. "I'm not in management. Not officially."

"Officially or unofficially you're in management. You've got what it takes. I don't." Even as one of the smartest in our ranks, Ms. Tucks had not been a participant in the assistant manager program.

I took a deep breath, partly to give myself time to think. "You have to define your own success," I told her. "It's not all about comparison."

"I'm a disgrace. I have to leave the Service." So that explained her outfit. She must have been an opera enthusiast. All dressed up for her Swan Song.

Even though Verna was thoroughly eccentric, I felt bad about her feeling driven to quit, which made me grope for something to give her a reason to stay. I didn't know she had already given notice. I said, "I'll miss you if you go."

She slowly—and with a strange look—turned her head to face me, and then sat ramrod straight. That comment switched something in her. "Mr. Shapiro, I salute you." Thankfully she didn't literally do it. "You are the bulwark against the forces that are trying to tear this county apart." Her lower lip trembled and her eyes were a scary reflection of things I couldn't see. Poor Verna, I thought, she's offering up the worst psychobabble yet. *I'm the bulwark?* In her humility she had seemed like a regular person, but that moment had fled.

It must have been hard for her to break down in public while trying to retain the formality her unusual mind demanded. In fairness, she liked me, and we all say ridiculous things to the opposite sex that would sound uncharacteristic of normal human beings when recounted later. Plus, Verna had turned out to be correct about a few things. The thing with Gatling for instance. I reminded myself that Verna was a lovely young woman, who I probably wouldn't encounter again. She was trying to do what was right, and I wished her the best. I realized now that I would genuinely miss her because she was part of the Treasury Department's quilt. Just because I already had a woman that I cherished didn't give me the right to be uncharitable.

It was in fact, Verna's last day, which she would spend in the elaborate exit dance that was our fate, but she should have stuck around for the irony. When I got to the POD and reached the manager's desk, I found Lucinda to be the second devastated woman of the day.

I said, "You don't look so good, Luce."

She said, "Don't worry about it, Danny. You don't work for me anymore." To the untrained eye her demeanor would probably seem cool, but before she broke, I heard the quaver of someone trying to tough it out. "Starting this morning, you're working for Virgie Poncit."

Virgie hid a sucker punch. And there it was.

While Lucinda sounded bitter and resigned, the bile in her voice was not half as much as mine would have shown if I had managed to speak. I had spurned the NSA, and here was the Big Stick that went with the Big Carrot. Virgie was the fate I must endure for every moment I delayed getting out of the division. Faced with this turn of events, I imagined I might be leaving the Service even before Verna did.

I READ THE paperwork on my orders to report to Virgie Poncit, hopelessly trying to find a technical error. You could get out of a parking ticket that way, so why not harsher penalties like this? At the top, it said May 1, also known as "May Day," which I now recalled was not only a Euro holiday but also a term for the international call for distress.

Hector, who naturally knew what was going on, caught me staring at Virgie from a distance, and noticed my hesitation to approach her. Virgie was the sort of blue eyed, black haired woman you might find in Istanbul. I admitted to myself that I was developing a strange, mild attraction to her. Hatred is a kind of passion.

Hector said softly in my ear, "Butter Face."

"What are you talking about?" I whispered back.

"Everything is good about her but her face. She has tits that could poke your eyes out. In your case, I'm sure that's what she's aiming for." He slipped something in my pocket—"just in case"—then he pushed the back of my shoulder. "Go get her, sport."

As I trudged along that trajectory, I wondered what Virgie might do with her lingering frustration over the Undeliverable Refunds Project. Would she see things as benignly as I did and realize the lack of choices I had faced, or would it now be her time for a fully proactive retribution?

"Welcome to my group," said Virgie with a wry smile. "I had to pull some strings to reel you in."

"You wanted me that badly? What did you have in mind?"

"Here's your phone schedule," she said with wicked good cheer.

A phone schedule? I scanned at the paper. She had me directly answering calls wall-to-wall. No management work. I admit that I cringed a little. The phone work was supposed to be a thing of the past.

I faced her bright smile with a forced one of my own. "You really want me on the telephones, Virgie? Why would you waste me there when I've been on special assignments and supervisory duty?"

"Because that's your real job, not all this running around disrupting the manager's work forces. We'll see how smart you are now. You did some tricks to get such good stats back when you were on the phone in Lucinda's group. I'm going to find out what your tricks were, and when I do, you'll be sorry."

That ended my speculation over whether or not she had hard feelings. By the end of her speech her smile disintegrated and she sounded a bit teary. I was beginning to think I had a bad effect on women. Contrary to what Hector had said in his fit of pique, I thought Virgie's face was pretty good.

"Virgie," I said, "let me show you something." Without asking permission, I came around the high desk, Terrance-like, and slid into the chair next to her. Up close, I got a full dose of her best attributes and had to force myself to ignore them. To counter her spite, I was just going to be friendly and firm.

I swiveled her status monitor so that we could both see it. "Of your five employees, you've got three idle right now, here, here, and here. You haven't put any of them on a break even though the phones aren't ringing. Later they'll be on breaks when you really need them. I would fix things like that if you gave me a chance. Now look at your average call time and look at the individual calls taking place at this moment." I tapped the screen. "You've got one that's been going on for over twenty minutes. Instead of talking to me, you should be breaking in on that call to find out how to speed it up." From what I'd heard, Virgie did not have the technical capability to understand much of the encoded data in front of her before I explained it.

She looked at me blankly, so I continued. "Virgie, I'm going to let you in on a secret. The reason your group has the highest idle time, the longest calling time, and the worst stats overall in the entire district is that the most successful managers each have someone who works their quality problems all day, and you don't. Tammy has Hector, Kate has Paul, Dawn has Wayne, and Lucinda had me. Now *you* have me, and I'm the best. This is your chance to beat Lucinda if you want. Don't throw it away."

Virgie glared at me with suspicion, afraid of being outsmarted. "We'll try having you on the phone for half the day, and half off."

"Good enough," I said. Maybe it would be.

Stepping away from her, I fished in my pocket to see what Hector had dropped in there "just in case." I thought the joke would be that it was a condom, but, no, it was a document outlining the international procedure for a distress call:

MAYDAY, MAYDAY, MAYDAY; [NAME OF STATION ADDRESSED]; CALL SIGN; NATURE OF EMERGENCY; PILOT'S INTENTIONS OR REQUESTS; LAST KNOWN POSITION; FUEL REMAINING IN MINUTES; NUMBER OF SOULS ON BOARD.

Any portion, it explained, could be omitted for expediency. I would have to remember that.

THE MAYDAY DISTRESS call would wait. I rejoined the chain gang long enough to baffle Virgie with my telephone skills. This time around I was even better than before. To her chagrin, I achieved still shorter average call times, and got more kudos from QA. I became the person to whom the QA team listened in order to learn the "Model Way." They were vocal about it, and the points I was racking up frustrated Virgie no end.

She had not yet relinquished the idea of getting even. Far from it. Instead of shredding my paperwork after I filled a taxpayer's request, as standard procedure would have it, she marked most of my work "erroneous," and locked it in a drawer. She documented endless fictitious conferences with me in which she told me why I was "wrong." But she didn't put the hammer down. She seemed to be hoarding all of this paper for the End of Days, or maybe for the day I might cross her.

In contrast to my golden status, every so often Virgie got called on the carpet for taxpayer telephone complaints that had slipped past her to the Branch Chief. These were taxpayers who were not satisfied with Virgie's answers. I'd been watching her sweat for weeks. One day, when she came shuffling out of Mike Soderling's office with a bowed head and hunched up arms, the boss still yelling over her shoulder, I sweetened the pot. As before, I pulled up a chair to join her when she regained her station. Now pliant, she let me gently take the twisted paper clip out of her sweaty hands, and stroke a stray bit of dirt out of her tousled hair, before I said, "Virgie, make me a permanent supervisor with no phone schedule, and I'll take all your irate phone calls off your hands."

She narrowed her eyes and drew back. "Why would you do that for me? I haven't done anything for you." Her voice was hoarse as though she'd been weeping.

"I'm doing it for myself," I said. "To me it's better than being in the trenches."

That clinched it. She gave in with only a sniffle, and I reciprocated as promised by saving her from future visits to the woodshed. She did not, however, surrender her "X" file on me.

Once I was free to roam again, Hector, who had an opinion for everything, edged up to me and asked, "How did Virgie ever get to be a manager?" We were observing her from a distance as she did frustrated battle with her computer, slapping the side of the monitor repeatedly.

"I guess you're going to tell me."

Hector beckoned me close, and spoke softly under his moustache, "I'll tell you how. Virgie is doing the flat-back fandango. That nasty bitch is fucking somebody, or did at one time."

His vehemence and word choice surprised me. Some bitterness there. I replied, "No, that's not it. If you want to learn anything here, you can't look at a person's shortcomings. Every Group Manager in the POD got to where they got because they each had one or more skills."

Hector, up to the challenge, ticked them off on his fingers, "Let's see. Tammy is a genius, Lucinda's husband is a Branch Chief, Kate has no other life, so she can concentrate on this. Virgie..." He took a deep breath. "Virgie is a stupid bitch. I give up, what's Virgie's talent?" He showed me a rare grin.

"Virgie," I said, matching his drama with a long pause, "is a gutter fighter."

CHAPTER SIX
The Dregs

"If there's anything in life you want, go and get it. Don't wait
for anybody to give it to you."

–Peyton Place

<u>Summer, 1985</u>

Even in the throes of my semi-management
compromise, I still couldn't believe I was under Virgie
Poncit's thumb. My fate was the employment equivalent of
being an alcohol-free, smoke-free vegetarian struck down by
heat lightning. Irony reigned.

To balance the cosmic scales, the sparkling Tammy
became my not-so-secret guardian angel, an activity that had
to have been sanctioned by the higher-ups in order to work.
Slowly, I was rebuilding my capital with upper management.

In mid-May, with no date set for my interview, Tammy
was green-lighted to throw me a pity bone in the form of a
status promotion wherein my sick days and holidays were
going to be paid ones. I sorely needed it. I didn't have that
perk to begin with because the Federal reward system was a
roast beef sliced thin. Tammy was now the third group
manager I'd met who had a set of strings to pull, and I tried
not to ask questions about how she managed to bestow the
advantage on me.

I actually learned of my new benefit one morning when I saw Virgie gazing at me in contemplation while she crushed an envelope in her left hand. I waltzed over, pleased to think that I might be the cause of her ambivalence. It beat the alternatives.

With calm assurance, she said to me, "I heard you were getting a bump up to WAE."

"That gives me my sick days and holidays?"

"Yes, and I informed personnel that you don't deserve it."

I laughed, predicting, "And that got you nowhere." My own experience with the Personnel Department revealed to me the impossibility of challenging a *fait accompli*.

She frowned. "Then I complained to management."

"Of course you did. And they told you to shut up."

"No," she admitted softly. "They weren't that nice about it."

I never knew what genie Virgie had petitioned to convey me into her clutches, but she had obviously burned up all of her wishes with that first whopper. Her play at this juncture was to cause me some temporary anxiety. It didn't work.

"Great story, Virgie. Very entertaining and educational. I'll take that envelope now."

Clutching it tighter as I grabbed one end, she said, "How did you know?"

"I think we're developing a personal connection that allows me to read your mind. It's the power of love."

That suggestion made her flustered, and in her fluster, she let go. I didn't count that as a winning round. It was too easy, and the prize too small. There was only reward I ever wanted.

December 31, 1979

Linda. I was eighteen the first time I saw her. It was at a New Year's Eve's party, at the house of a schoolmate on Long Island's ritzy North Shore. Somehow I'd mingled my way through each of the party rooms and missed running into her in all of them.

My friend's mother stumbled towards me, clearly tipsy. I hadn't expected her at a teen party, but it was her house after all. She adjusted my collar as she spoke to me and I just thought she was doing her mom thing even though it came with a weird smile, which I chalked up to the alcohol.

"Have you ever been on a yacht, Danny?" she asked.

I admitted I hadn't.

"You could be on mine tonight."

Frances was an attractive woman upon whom the bit of extra weight she carried landed on all the right curves. She was pleasant enough company. We stepped out coatless into the chilly night, and the nippy air made us run to the shelter of her status symbol at the end of a long dock. This was a cruising yacht well over fifty feet long, the kind with a whole apartment inside for long trips, a vessel that would have easily set the average person's salary back twelve years.

We boarded, and Frances decided to get right to showing me the area below decks. The choice of direction was up to her, I supposed. It was her yacht after all.

Providing very little in the way of tour guidance, she giggled and playfully pushed me from one end to the other until there was no place else to go. By then she had me up against a bulkhead or something nautical like that. I would happily share what she said if it were more than a series of guttural sounds against my neck.

New Year's was understood to be an occasion where people drank quite a bit. I needed to drive myself home, so my plan was to have one beer early in the evening and let it wear off. I'd done that. Perhaps if we'd both been roaring drunk, Frances and I would have gone together like peanut butter and jelly. I'll never know.

The little bit of rough sea at dockside must have been throwing her for a loop because every time I tried to steady her, she fell towards me again, the last time knocking me onto a couch. I had literally been a Boy Scout just a couple of years earlier and I was absolutely certain that any action with my friend's inebriated mom would constitute "taking advantage." I told the rich lady "thanks, but no," and made sure she experienced no mishap on the return trip to her house.

It was against the backdrop of this little adventure that I reentered the central room, and there—for the very first time—was Linda. Everything went silent and my vision tunneled. A poet's feast of raven hair, alabaster skin, piercing blue eyes and a pink dress that cascaded around her. It was like being struck in the face with a volume by Carl Sandberg.

Belatedly, I noticed that my vision of perfection had a boyfriend. With his expensive suit and finely chiseled features, he looked nothing like me, which was a bad sign. I probably should have seen him sooner. Their involvement was hard to miss as they linked arms to sip their red wine in a classic European gesture.

This woman could obviously have anyone she wanted, and I was convinced right down to my Brooklyn roots that I wasn't her type. I didn't have very long to think on that topic though. Just when it seemed the two of them had achieved romantic nirvana, he vomited through his beard and onto the floor and then followed up by diving into the pile and taking an impromptu nap. The next events kept me frozen with wonder. Without asking for help, Linda somehow got him onto the couch and found a blanket with which to cover him. I rediscovered my feet when she ducked into the kitchen. I heard her say, "Where are the paper towels?"

With brutal efficiency, shouldering other eager men out of the way, I made sure I was the first to find and supply her with what she'd requested. That was when I learned her first name and little more.

"He can't hold his liquor," she explained without my asking.

Linda went back out and wiped the floor without a word of complaint. Luckily the covering was not a rug. Angelic was the only word that could describe such behavior as hers. I mean, no other girl her age would do that in a home that had its own housekeeper, would they? If I were a woman I sure wouldn't.

To review, she was the most ravishing woman I'd ever seen. She was sophisticated, and already taken, I was not her type, and she was too good for my less-virtuous caboose anyway.

In some small hour of the evening, a group of us said our goodbyes. Linda hopped in her car, one of those vast 1970's models that reminded me of Frances and her yacht. Since she was boxed in by other cars, I wondered why she bothered attempting to get out. I was certain that in a moment she would ask for my assistance, and I would guide her to safety. A chance to help her might salve my evening's disappointment, at least a little bit.

With the kind of skill I'd only seen from the most exceptional professional drivers, this teenager extricated herself in a flurry of deft maneuvers and peeled out at top speed as if that was the only speed she knew.

Linda was an extraordinary woman in every way. The halo I envisioned on her head that night never left her. But as I stood in the dark admiring the asphalt her tires had touched, I thought there wasn't the slightest chance I would ever be with her. After all, we'd barely met.

BY AN ASTOUNDING coincidence, I saw her again just two weeks later in the Catskills, and she was alone. Grossinger's Resort was a winter break rite-of-passage for college freshmen, the singles event of a lifetime. Anyone dumb enough to bring a date would know better than to leave them alone for even a second in the enormous lounge with the dim lights and the mood music.

Up until now, the more I liked a woman, the more shy and incapable I would become. Linda was different. I would never be more certain of anything in my life than the fact that I needed to be with her. It transcended all of my shortcomings and tore my rulebook into bite-sized pieces I could chew at leisure. I asked her if she had come with her boyfriend, the one I'd seen on New Year's Day.

"Ronan? That was our first date and our last."

First date? That made her benevolence toward him even more amazing. "What happened?"

"He wanted me to go with him to Connecticut for the weekend."

"After a date like that? I hope you said no and put a curse on his descendants."

She laughed. "I should go back and do that."

So, meeting her there wasn't such an odd coincidence after all. She simply went where singles go. The first time I'd encountered her, I had my little outing with Frances to thank, and now it was winter break. Timing was everything. Anita Ward was singing "Ring My Bell," and I asked Linda, "Would you like to dance?"

She would, and she did. Both of us had apparently had lessons in some very energetic disco moves. Outside of the silver screen, I'd never seen a couple dance as the room stopped and watched. We were that couple, tearing up the floor. After a while, they played Pink Floyd's "Hey You," which counted as an intimate song, and other couples floated back to the checkered squares in the middle. I felt my heart beat even faster when I held Linda close. We were an ideal height match for her to lay her head on my shoulder and give me a nose full of her floral perfume. Maybe she was tired, to rest her head like that, but I supposed I must be doing well. Considering that one thing leads to another, I looked forward to the possibility of an even-better evening ahead.

As we stepped up on the side platform following a second slow number, I saw the big round shoulders and straight sandy hair of my friend, Ari Vascombe. Or rather Ari saw us, and drew our attention by knocking everyone over to get close. Damn him for ruining the momentum.

"Who is this?" he asked with wonder.

I introduced Linda to him. She reached out to shake his extended hand, but then she drew back, clutched her head, and screamed as though she'd seen a monster. Without a word, she ran off, dodging pell-mell around the minglers in the direction of the exit. I ran after her to see what was the matter, but I had one hell of a time keeping up. She kept disappearing from sight and popping out again as I tore through the crowd in her wake.

The chase ended in what I supposed was her room, and I caught the door before it slammed shut. Instead of throwing me out, she curled up in a ball in the far corner, behind her suitcase. Her whimpering was pitiful, and I crouched down next to her.

"What happened, Linda?"

"I saw an aura. A bad one." I knew that for some people these were a rare consequence of migraines.

"Hallucination," I supplied.

"The image of him was worse than the pain."

"Does this happen often?"

"It happens too much. Go away."

"Why?"

"You don't want someone like me."

"Of course I do." I was distressed to see this abrupt transformation, but it didn't make a bit of difference. Gently, I turned her enough so that we were face to face.

"I'm also afraid of roadkill, spiders, snakes, needles, and bridges," she said through her tears.

"As much as this?"

"Sometimes more," she sobbed.

Yet I noticed she had no fear of men, dancing, or fast cars. Her determination to face life boldly, given a list of phobias like hers—hell, her ability to leave the house at all under those circumstances made her better than anyone I knew. "Forget all that. You're doing great."

She hugged me and cried it out, the two of us scrunched up on the floor while I stroked her hair. After a while, she pulled it together, told me how much she appreciated the support, and we agreed to meet up later. I gravitated toward women in distress, especially when they found courage.

At a classic Grossinger's dinner of white fish and white wine, we immortalized our first day together with a photo I still carry in my wallet. She was still a bit fragile, but you would never know it from her big smile as she pressed close to me. We topped it off with our first kiss and began our staccato relationship. By the time I was in my fifth year of fighting to stay in her life, I was more in love than ever, and more lost. In matters of love, however, I had a strong sense of destiny, and destiny loved to bat me around.

June 18, 1985

Virgie Poncit, fashionably dressed in a low summer neckline, worked at her desk singing "Live and Let Die," an inauspicious way for your boss to begin a day, but appropriate conditions from which to launch the next and most significant phase of my career derailment.

It happened to be the day of my Big Interview, an event that poised me on the edge of the future that Linda and I had planned for so long. Linda had not set the bar unreasonably high. Since I refused to become a doctor, as her parents wanted, a solid livelihood was in order. I didn't think that staying in Taxpayer Service counted as a profession. It certainly didn't pay anything.

Now I had to watch the clock closely to combat my dyscalculia. Clearing a buffer zone usually helped. Since Tammy had wisely counseled me to be half an hour early, I rose promptly and told Virgie that I intended to head up to the second floor.

Virgie said, "No. Your interview is half an hour from now. It doesn't take that long to get to the second floor."

In a bull-headed mood, I said, "I know that. I'm going anyway, just in case." She didn't consent, but I kept walking. Damn the torpedoes, as Admiral Farragut proclaimed when he ran the minefield.

I'm not actually sure if he lived through that.

It took a minute for me to lope to the second floor and nine minutes for the gatekeeper to put her phone call on hold and ask why I was sitting there. I wasn't certain she was speaking to me as she assiduously checked her nail polish.

"I'm still a few minutes early," I told her, "but I would appreciate if you would let the interviewers know I'm available in case they wanted to start sooner." I thought my request sounded sufficiently diplomatic.

"They know you're here," she said.

I couldn't tease any meaning from her flat tone of voice so I didn't know whether that meant there was a hidden camera, or she had pressed a concealed button, or that the interviewers considered it unthinkable that I would be late. At the IRS, any of those things could easily be true. If I weren't such a sappy optimist, I might have considered the more obvious alternative that a flat tone means, "I don't care."

As she engaged her caller with a run-through of her weekend activities, I got down to the important business of making sure the magazines on the coffee table were in their best possible order. Having noted the twenty-minute mark, I split the difference for another ten before trying to regain the gatekeeper's attention.

She waved me off angrily and went back to a telephone conversation that made her giggle and loop the cord around her finger.

I ran out of things to do and that led me to think about the fact that only five people in my district were going to be hired in this round. Though I didn't know how many applicants there were, the chances sounded slight. At one minute before the appointed hour, I said, "Can you try again, please?"

Sighing with enough wind to power a tuba, she said, "Fine." She dialed, paused, and shrugged. "I can't get them on the phone."

"Can you leave a message for them?"

"No, I already hung up! I told you—they know you're here. If they wanted you, they would have let me know."

Each of us was starting to piss the other one off so I chilled out. She finally got them on the phone ten minutes late and then waved me along with alacrity.

Three dark suited men were lined up at a folding table. One fragile chair sat across from them and I took it.

"You're late," said the tall one in the center. He pushed his square glasses up to his squinty eyes and made a note. The other two nodded.

"I'm not late," I said mildly. "I arrived half an hour early, and I've been waiting to be called up to the interview."

"You're late and you're a liar," he rejoined.

"Just please check with the reception desk and we can clear all this up."

"We don't have to do that."

I swallowed and said, "Check with my manager then. She wasn't very happy that I left for the interview early." *You could also check the well-arranged magazines in the waiting room.*

"What kind of a name is Shapiro?"

"Just a name."

"You're a Jew, right?"

I repositioned the legs of my spindly chair and asked, "What are you getting at, Mr. –?"

"Walter Bach. Nothing at all. We just want to know who we're talking to."

"I see." I ignored the jibes and did the best I could through the rest of the interview, hoping the inappropriate demeanor, including the last remark, was a test like so many I had seen. Field agents need to be tough, right? And never thin-skinned. I was determined to always be one of those and never be the other.

As far as the genuine interview questions went, they ran me through some hypothetical situations that I thought I did well on. But once they'd established that I was late and a Jew, the rest of it was a blur. The last thing the lead interviewer said to me as I walked out the door was, "Enjoy Hollywood." And at this point he finally laughed.

<u>August 1, 1985</u>

Each interview subject for a Revenue Agent position earned a numeric score based on their measurable qualifications plus an average of the three interviewers' opinions. Then the numeric score was suppressed while the relative ranking was published. I was ranked number nine for Revenue Agent, which, although not many were interviewed, was considered high. Only the top seven were hired in this round. I told myself that at least Bach laughed at the end, which left open the possibility that the hazing I'd gotten during the interview was a joke. But no. Another notice sat behind the first, an explanation that regardless of my rank, I had been automatically disqualified for being late to the interview. I was devastated to find out they weren't just testing me.

Wondering if I could prove the role those Jew remarks had played in this fiasco, I naturally called our Equal Employee Opportunity Office for advice. I asked whether EEOC should be my first stop or whether it was more appropriate to go through my union representative initially.

Penny McKendricks, who would turn out to be the whole EEOC department, asked, "Why, have you been there yet?"

"I haven't."

"Good," she confirmed. "You're required to meet with me before you can meet with the union." She consulted her calendar and gave me an appointment a month and a day later.

AT THE APPOINTED time, McKendricks, an older woman with a bright scarf covering her V-neck seemed very excited to see me. I took her natural ebullience as a good sign, and filled her in on the delays leading up to my appearance in the interview room.

"That's hilarious," she cackled. "The girl who was doing her nails should be fired."

When I got to the part about how my interview opened, asking me about the origin of my name, she smiled broadly. "Really? They said that, huh?"

I thought I heard amusement rather than incredulity, but I answered, "Yes, really."

I told her the finale, and she said, "I love it. 'Enjoy Hollywood.' I get it, too—because the Jews control Hollywood."

"Yes, that's what I thought he was saying."

"I think they discriminated against you. They really did."

I nodded. "What's the next step then?"

"Nothing," she said with a smirk.

"Why?"

"There's nothing in the law that says you can't discriminate against a Jew," she laughed and her shoulders shook with undisguised glee.

I got to my feet, not willing to let her enjoy her ridicule any longer. Looking back, a cell phone video would have been great just then, but they hadn't been invented yet. I went straight from her office to that of my union rep, who was not far.

The man who lodged across the hall from EEOC, Ellis Koalaman, was well-meaning and hapless. I think he was pudgy from inaction. I was about to find out, and not for the last time, that the Treasury Union was the country's weakest representative body.

"Yeah, what happened?" he asked.

My story was a longer one now, thanks to McKendricks.

"Dammit," he fumed, and his hands went up to his loose wavy hair. "They outmaneuvered us again."

"What does that mean?"

"It's not August 31st. It's September 1st."

"Meaning what?"

"You have to see your union rep within thirty days. This is thirty-one."

"So, what can you do?"

"It's too late for me to do anything," Koalaman moaned, throwing his hands higher this time.

"If she's cheating, why can't you backdate the paperwork for our appointment?"

"Because you legally have to see her first. Agreeing to see her thirty-one days after your job notification means you waived your right to take it up with the union. If you'd seen me first, I would have told you so."

I wasn't in the mood to sort out the paradox of his last remark. The way I read the situation at the time, the woman who'd helped slam the door on Linda and I was a sociopath, part of the four percent of our society born without a conscience. Since Taxpayer Service Division had failed to push me over to Examinations Division, I had no idea how to salvage my career now.

I REMEMBER IT as a cool, delightful morning for summertime. Two seagulls were fighting over a bit of trash in the street. Early for work, I walked the long way and was treated to the sight of a flashy yellow Cadillac as it turned the corner. With its extra chrome providing a blinding flash, it pulled up in front of the best house in the neighborhood, a description that wasn't saying much about the property but for some fancy brickwork. Only one family within an eight-block radius of my house—these folks who owned a fish cannery—could clearly be described as middle class or better. Why they wanted to live among us poor slobs was a bit of a mystery, but if the aim was to hide from IRS scrutiny, it was a smart move.

Jaime Rollins, the daughter, emerged from her house in a bulky rabbit fur coat, skimpy sequined hot pants, fishnet stockings and high heels. They must have been too high for her to walk properly because she seemed to have slipped and fallen into a vat of clown makeup. The gentleman caller at the wheel had a nice leopard fur hat, a purple suit and some very large jewelry. I was glad that our country had not yet lost all of its worthy traditions.

Jaime and I were well-acquainted, since we had gone to grade school together. With a wave, I cheerfully tried to get her attention. Perhaps her friend would give me a lift. Jaime was concentrating on walking, and she donned a large pair of dark glasses just then. Maybe not a coincidence.

I didn't really have to ask about her situation, though. Hers wasn't a complicated story. I knew the first part and could guess the last.

Daughter had been cut off from her allowance but not driven out.

Daughter hated Mummy and Daddy.

Daughter had become a "bad dresser" to humiliate them.

She wasn't the only bad dresser in our neighborhood, though. She drove off, and I wished her well as I continued toward the train. On my commute, Jaime's financial misfire reminded me of my own money troubles. The IRS was shorting my pay, plain and simple. The hours in my pay stub did not match the master sheet and the rate of pay was wrong too. Was it my government or one of my bosses messing me up? Either way made sense, so I could take my pick. As per the rules that such matters were questioned only on a Monday, I had set up a conference with Virgie to ensure that my current pay scale was on tap in the computer.

Virgie looked lovely that day, reminding me of a top-heavy Venus de Milo. I knew she would be interested in my plight. She may have even had something to do with it.

When I filled her in and showed her the documentation, she said, "I don't care if they never pay you."

I smiled and told her sweetly, "You look pretty today… and every day." Unlike my neighbor, Jaime, I had resolved never to be a prostitute, but hey, you never know.

Virgie studied me and said, "Go to hell."

Feigning confusion, I asked, "Do they pay better there?"

"What?"

"Virgie, we both know you're going to fix this."

"I don't know anything."

As promising as that remark was, I replied, "If you don't do it, the next time a taxpayer asks for a manager, you're going to have to actually be a manager."

Virgie was horrified at the idea of going back to doing her job without me covering for her. "This will be straightened out in two weeks," she promised. "Your back pay could take a month. Here's my callback list."

I took it gladly. Once she was preoccupied with the task at hand, Hector of Green Gables steered me to a neutral corner.

"Nice suit," I commented. He must have had a closet full of them.

"Thank you. You had fun just now, yes?"

"A little," I admitted.

"It wears off fast though, doesn't it? Begging for scraps at Virgie's table is no way to live."

He was right. Disappointed by my losing streak, my incipient career as a prostitute stymied, I began going on outside interviews again. I conceded that maybe the IRS was not my fate after all.

CREDS: THE IRS ADVENTURE

<u>September 12, 1985</u>

On an ordinary Thursday, I opened my mail looking for tangible results from my recent job hunting. The morning discussion on the tube was about how the Persian Gulf War between Iraq and Iran was nearing its fifth year and just getting uglier. A CNN commentator was saying, "Let them wipe each other out."

When I saw the audit notice with my name on it, I forgot all about the Middle East. I had honestly thought my employers had neglected the ritual cleansing that they claimed every employee was supposed to go through. Before I discounted it completely, I had even begun to wonder if Mr. 1960 had only used the mention as a scare tactic. One thing I knew was that even if I quit my job now, this audit was going forward. I shut off the television just as the other commentator said, "It can only be good for us."

There were two divisions at the IRS dealing with audits. One encompassed the sophisticated ranks of business auditors doing fieldwork, which I had been aiming to join, and the other existed to deal with relatively defenseless wage earners like me. The latter was simply known as Office Audit. There was so little to audit in my young life that I needed no preparation time, which was why I hadn't minded the requirement in the first place. Now that I knew firsthand how senseless some of my fellow employees could be, I grew mightily apprehensive.

On the fateful day, I went up to the Third Floor with my skinny folders containing copies of my returns and the meager documentation that went with them. I told the receptionist I had an appointment with C. Vandacoro. Then I sat and waited with everyone else but it didn't take long. The auditor, who I would have pegged as a professional wrestler, seemed eager to see me as she barreled through the door.

Her office was nearby, and once we were seated, we sat staring at each other for a moment. I think she was catching her breath.

I rummaged briefly in the folders, drew out the years in question and set them in a fan fold on the auditor's desk. She didn't touch them.

"I hear you're on an R.A. track," she began, referring to the Revenue Agent position I sought and had hoped to seek again before I grew discouraged.

"Yes, that's true."

Without pause, she blurted, "The bastards didn't take me. Why do you want to become one of them?"

It didn't require awesome investigative skills on my part to deduce that this particular office auditor was bitter about not being a field agent. What do you say to a question like hers? She shouldn't have known so much about me, but you get used to that sort of thing when working for the IRS. I shrugged and shook my head.

Wounded by my tepid reaction to her passion, she said, "Well maybe I'll stop your career right here. All I have to do is tell management that you're a cheater and you won't even be able to keep the job you have now."

This audit wasn't the ritual cleansing I'd expected. It was more like the Japanese art of seppuku with a rusty blade. I would find out later that the stock in trade for many office auditors was immediate and overwhelming force as opposed to scholarly deliberation over matters of tax law and actual facts. Some of them knew absolutely nothing and desperately depended on taxpayers rolling over in docile futility. If someone could be startled into a confession, hacks like her were happy to save the effort.

"Have you actually seen my tax returns?" I asked.

"I have the originals."

"Then you know there's nothing to see."

"Or did you hide it all?"

If C. Vandacoro had wanted to advance her career in a smart way, she could have dazzled the up-and-coming ranks like myself with a show of professionalism. If her employee-audit subjects got promoted, they would speak well of her as tough but fair, perhaps even field agent material. She chose instead the route of bitterness. She had no idea that I was close to quitting the IRS, and I didn't feel like telling her.

I asked, "Do you have anything serious to say?"

"I'm going to make an adjustment!"

"Of what?"

"Missing income."

I was certainly missing income, but not in the way that she thought. I sat up straighter now. I don't know what Treasury was thinking when they scheduled the audit so long after my hiring. I was no longer the average taxpayer. Due to the experience I had acquired at the IRS, this office audit tyrant was no match for me.

I stood and told her, "No, you're not. You're wasting my time." This is the kind of thing I say when I'm going on pure instinct—things that would seem inadvisable in a more rational setting. Before she could think of anything else to say, I continued, "You've got absolutely nothing. We're done here."

She was speechless for the moment, so I couldn't wait. Going bluff for bluff, when I walked out the door, mine won.

Not to downplay my victory, but being a pauper was a very nearly bulletproof position. On top of that, I was fairly sure that a non-employee could not have pulled off such a coup. If I was doing a public service message, I'd say, "Don't try this at home, kids."

In retrospect, if I had done anything that day, it was simply standing up to a playground bully. Gaining a sense of what I could do felt great. What's more, it renewed my determination to stick around. My career was something I wanted every bit as much for myself as well as for Linda.

That jibed with what Hector said. He hadn't been advising me to step off when he told me that gobbling Virgie's table scraps were no way to live. He was advising me to step up.

And step up I would.

CHAPTER SEVEN
Restricted Area

"Why me? Why does it want me?"

—Sarah Conner, *Terminator*

THE INDIAN SUMMER heat and humidity at the foot of Manhattan was banished when I crossed the threshold of Brooklyn's Taxpayer Service. Surprise, surprise. We had real air conditioning. As if to prove the change in policy, my forehead dried rapidly in the cool air. First time that ever happened. I set down my briefcase and made sure I collected a greedy breath.

This relief seemed scant compensation for what happened next. At nine AM, our telephone lines lit up and burned with the tax problems of twelve million citizens, reminding us that the heat was still out there and would find its way in. Big Jim Johnson waded into this summer glory like a lifeguard scooping up two drowners at a time. Ladislav Ras, who stuck up like a shoreline reed as he chattered away on the phone, gave me a mini-salute that looked like a swiveling duck at his brow. I gave the voluptuous Virgie Poncit a wink, and she rolled her eyes. She liked watching me in battle. I was sure of it.

My screen's stats gave me the volume, and it seemed to me that four hundred inquiries an hour was an unusual number of calls for mid-Summer, considering that we weren't near any tax milestone date. But then again, I had worked in Taxland for less than a year. How would I know what summer was supposed to be like? I supervised my side of the room. Hector Chavez, resplendent in green, covered the other. He looked more comfortable in this environment than I did. *But I'm not a Lifer here*, I reminded myself, *I'm a Mover*. It was time for me to move and not think too much.

As I was making my rounds at the pentapods, making sure that my group didn't get overwrought from the traffic, a strange man—hair high, angular features, and bug-intensity gray eyes—collided with me and pushed past. I knew a hundred and thirty people who toiled there, but this solid-chested gent was a new one. Though I had paused to make way for him just before the moment of impact, he actually snarled, "Watch where you're going."

Then I did watch. I observed him carefully as he navigated the mammoth room. With all the obstacles he had to circle, it looked as if he was taking evasive action. In the distance, he finally disappeared in a spot where he shouldn't have been able to vanish. I squinted at the mysterious portable wall panels that had arisen at the far side of our cavernous workplace. Was there a doorway along there? Distracted as I had been by getting audited recently, I had no time to investigate the new construction. I might have been more interested had I realized that the hidden corner harbored something entirely new in the world.

I tried to return to the battle by responding to the frantic wave of a hand in the trenches, when our division chief, Bill Foster, turned up next. He blocked my way by stopping expectantly in front of me. Once again, we matched each other right down to the suit, his a scant one-size bigger. At that distance I wasn't sure which of us was which. But that might have been wishful thinking.

"Danny," said Foster, "How's it going?"

"It's a hornet's nest in here. I'm trying to—"

"You're in a new training class."

I grunted at the pain of gritting my teeth. "I'm a little extremely busy."

"It's over here." The boss moved on with a rallying wave of his arm, and I had no choice but to follow. Together we traced the same pentapod labyrinth that Bug Eye had taken before he vanished behind the wall. Apparently, I would be next. Now the mystery zone had my full attention.

Foster led me as far as the barrier in front of the sign that read, "Restricted Area. Do not enter." The next panel's posting said, "DANGER" inside of a red triangle with a lightning bolt icon. It was beginning to remind me of the time I had visited a nuclear power plant and my radiation card ran "a little high."

Foster said, "Wait here," and he fetched out the man I'd just encountered.

"Danny, this is Martin Cowler."

Cowler snorted and folded his arms. Faced with the complication of a three-way social engagement, he couldn't meet my gaze.

Foster glanced at him uneasily and said to me, "He built the machine you'll be working on." Then the chief made for strategic high ground, muttering something about having a lot of work to do.

Pale and unsmiling, Cowler trained his gray bug eyes on me and glared.

Cravenly anxious to deflect his ire to other innocent parties, I asked, "Where is everyone else in this training class?"

"Doesn't matter." Martin pointed at me. "*You* will teach what I tell you to everyone else. I don't want to go through this again." The revulsion with which he said "you" implied that his instant dislike of me was deepening by the moment, and the idea of mingling with "everyone else" made him shudder.

"Okay," I said amiably. "They never tell me what's going to happen, so that could just as well be right."

"Oh, I *know* I'm right. Don't think you ever have to tell me when I'm right."

"Modest" Martin Cowler, as I would dub him, carried himself with the assurance of a master electrical engineer, always weighing people and things on the scale of his broad knowledge of how nature worked. He didn't suffer fools, and in the age of Mr. T, everyone Martin met was a fool.

Without further ceremony, he ushered me into the zone that had been requisitioned for the mystery project. The machine I found there might have swallowed two giant-sized living room entertainment cabinets arranged end-on-end. I mean, it might have actually ingested them. If this was a computer of some kind, there was nothing else to explain its size. Not to offend its maker, I checked surreptitiously to see if it said "Univac" on its backside. Some of the earliest computers ever made were on a par with this megalith.

"What do you call this thing, Mr. Cowler?"

"This 'thing,' as you call it, is a damn sight more important than your ass. It's Teletax."

"And Teletax does what?"

"It talks to people." This he was proud of.

"How?"

"It understands what they say, and gives them what they want."

"Does it really?" I asked with fascination.

I examined the behemoth with new respect, wondering where it kept its voice box. Notwithstanding my aversion to professional programmers, I'd always been morbidly fascinated with the rise of the machine, how rapidly technology was infiltrating our lives. In a burst of either coincidence or prophecy, the movie *Terminator* had come out the year before. It predicted that we would very soon be dominated by a product of the Department of Defense, a self-aware artificial intelligence system called Skynet. In the movie, as soon as the fictional Skynet was activated, it felt discomfited by people and got rid of as many of them as possible.

Looking at the crude form in front of us, it occurred to me that reality's version of disaster might not, in fact, begin with the Department of Defense, but at the IRS. Suddenly I understood why the air in our division had been tuned to Goldilocks perfection. It wasn't for the benefit of the human beings in the room.

Cowler fired up the future with a toggle switch, and we got right to work. So, what did our home version of Skynet do? This first automated telephone information system in the United States was designed to serve up harmless, prepackaged recordings when given verbal commands by incoming callers. Cowler walked me through a few of the machine's number-keyed prompts and the theory of how to elicit them manually. At the moment, he held back from the audio demonstration itself.

Of course, voice recognition and data retrieval are not self-awareness. It's not even artificial intelligence. I wasn't yet sure of what we had here. But it was a step toward shuffling humans out of the picture. Thursday, September 20, 1985 had the distinction of being the day mankind decided to stop talking to each other so much and start talking to computers. Cowler called it "Implementation Day," a phrase that sounded way too much like *Terminator*'s Judgment Day. I shivered, considering that this first beast needed someone to hold its metallic claw. And that would be yours truly.

Cowler removed himself from my presence with all haste, and that was fine with me. Between him and Teletax, I felt like my thinking had already become robotic. I sat down at the vast console and looked forward to working through the documentation and testing the switches without the Wizard of Oz pressed so closely behind the curtain. But that mercy didn't quite materialize. Only minutes later, some component fizzled, and I had to run and summon Modest Martin.

"Something is stuck," I told him.

"You're stuck?" he asked dangerously.

"No, the machine is."

Fit to rival a gale force wind, he bellowed, "It's not the machine. It's the operator."

Wiping his spit from my eye, I said, "That's good. I was afraid you were going to take the glitch personally."

"I told you, it's not the machine." Somehow his eyes bulged out further than they had before and his hands clutched and released.

I took note of his short fuse for future reference, realizing why the Mr. T of the engineering world was not allowed to speak to anyone other than me. He wasn't a people person. I said, "Well, it's not working, and you might want to check it out or nothing else is going to happen today."

Clutch and release. Clutch and release.

While he did his finger exercises, I snuck back to the land of the living, amazed at the short commute. Johnson and Ras each gave me a nod.

Virgie was laboring over our group schedule, busy with her eraser nub, then abandoning the worn one, and casting about for another. As I approached her, she said, "Where've you been?"

"Kidnapped. And if you value me at all you'll think of a reason why I can't go back to the other side of the room with Martin Cowler."

She put her head down and went back to work. "Ask the kidnappers to chop off a finger so I know you're still alive."

"Good one, Virg," I smiled. "But since I'm still here, I'll give you the finger right now."

Before I could accomplish that, Cowler, apparently finished with his work under the hood, emerged to find me again. "Go back in there," he said.

"What was wrong?"

137

"Needed a part," he acknowledged under his breath. "Don't break it again."

During the next hour of testing the components, I worried that I had caught some sort of punishment assignment. Otherwise, why me, a non-engineer playing engineer's assistant?

Cowler returned periodically, prodding me to check all the individual components, much the way NASA must have checked the first Space Shuttle before its maiden voyage. If there were rockets on the computer's underside it would explain Cowler's other excursions to check the cloud cover and lightning forecast. At times like this, I pictured Linda and I owning a lakeside house in the country, a serene spot where we would teach the kids to swim. It didn't have to be that scenario exactly but I pined for a transfer to something easier than the Treasury Department's most intense office. I'd seen a job opening for a special sub-division that dealt only with exempt organizations and employee pensions. This niche was a popular choice among field agents whose ambition had cooled. How much trouble could I get into in a backwater like that? Not much, I decided. That job was looking good right about now.

Finally, Cowler finished attaching a trunk of our telephone system to Teletax. Or was it vice versa? A new light came on, along with a signal tone. Communications at last! We were connected to the world.

I said, "Now we get to the good stuff, yes? The interactive part of the show, right?"

Cowler turned a sullen cheek.

I observed, "You're awfully quiet for someone who's about to make history with your brainchild."

Instead of answering, Modest Martin nodded at me to don the second headset, and then he hit the call button to open the line to ACD traffic.

A call came through and the first taxpayer to ever call a machine asked his question live. There should have been a line of cameras and reporters behind us to record the momentous event.

The machine said nothing.

Cowler did nothing in response.

After long moments of silence punctuated by the caller repeating a lonely "hello?" our chief engineer hit a recorded response button and then cut the ACD feed so that no one else could get through.

"Huh," said I. "That's it?"

Although Cowler sagged with disappointment, I noticed that he hadn't been surprised that the voice commands did not work. If he already knew about the problem, though, why was this supposed to be Implementation Day and not a troubleshooting session? I wondered if Modest Martin remembered the old television show about an irksome talking horse named Mr. Ed, who spoke to no one except its owner, Wilbur. The horse actually delighted in embarrassing him by pulling pranks and then playing dumb in front of strangers. The circumstances led them to blame Mr. Ed's owner. Like the beleaguered Wilbur, Martin seemed to have gotten used to the abuse.

I almost asked him about the TV show, but then Cowler's day-long anxiety attack suddenly began to make more sense in a queasy-pit-of-the-stomach sort of way. It was as if he knew about this major flaw and he'd already given up.

"Get your people ready," he said.

"For what?" I asked. But it was obvious, wasn't it? I was fairly certain that this real-life failure was not caused by sitcom-style whimsy. Our digitized horse really could not talk. It was missing hardware or software or both. That would mean that Martin and his machine were sitting on a much bigger, and considerably more embarrassing secret than a single faltering part. If I was right, then our tax information system wasn't anywhere near ready to work. It wasn't Judgment Day, then. More like Misjudgment Day, featuring Skynet Junior. If my crew was being called in to man the machine, we were about to go into a premature launch and cover-up.

I made my way to the Division Chief's office to get some answers, and he was reposing idly behind his desk as though expecting me at that very moment. Yes, there were cameras on the work floor and probably a small monitor facing the boss.

"I take it you want an explanation?" he asked calmly.

"I do."

Foster took a hefty old stapler into his hands to help ponder the matter. "You saw how many calls are flooding in down there. And you know how many answers we're getting wrong. The commissioner is leaning on us to divert some of the call flow to automation with standard responses that will always be right. The rest of it will still be up to us."

"And at the same time, it's meant to reduce our manpower."

"Yes," he agreed.

"Automation was supposed to happen this year…"

"Yes."

"And yet the system hasn't been invented yet."

"Yes."

I felt like I was doing too much of the talking and was beginning to wonder who was briefing who here. One might surmise that the DC's job description had a lot to do with maximizing deniability. By and by, however, I got my explanation.

Cowler's system, touted to the news media as a fully automated wonder of the twentieth century's ninth decade, was in fact a *semi*-automated smoke and mirrors machine. No one in the general public was supposed to know the difference. The scheme was for human beings to make up the gap between what Teletax *could* do and what it *should* do. Specifically, its operators were meant to pretend that we were the machine's voice recognition software without revealing the arrangement.

Imagine if you were using an Excel spreadsheet, and it could do some of the required calculations, but once in a while you had to pull out a pencil and paper to help it out, then punch the intermediate numbers back in before it could continue. That was the preposterous state of Teletax at its inception. The IRS bought technology that wasn't finished, and put it in service as if it were. You would think the American taxpayer deserved better than that. Then again, Americans were demanding accurate answers to their tax questions, and that goal was the bottom line.

It was in this great hour of need that Foster informed me I was the implementation manager, not Martin. Foster said, "It's up to you and your ability to make this work."

"You mean to make it appear that it works in order to avoid a huge scandal."

"Yes," he admitted softly. "That last part."

Foster was an able administrator who worked with what he had while saying remarkably little in his own words. I'd hate anyone to think I didn't appreciate the elegance of his approach.

Of course, if Teletax's human handlers ever went AWOL from their humble place at the computer's side, that misstep would blow a neat hole in the deception. After a bit more chatting with the boss, I found out that my first order of business as "Implementation Manager" was to figure out how many people it took to feed the beast 24/7, and to ride roughshod over any other managers that got in its way.

"What's the damage?" Foster asked. "How many are we talking?"

"I have to pull out and train a minimum of eight people to start."

"Why?" he wondered.

"Three eight-hour shifts, and breaks for each."

"That's six," he pointed out. "Six people that will be absent from our regular phone lines." He sounded regretful.

"No, we have to allow some leeway for lateness, sick days and vacations. Eight is the least. Twelve would be safest. And by the way, Teletax is very chatty when you press the right buttons for it. The call times will increase, not decrease."

"Do it," he said. "Eight people, ten people—whatever it takes. Once we start, that machine can never go down, even for one minute."

"Yes, sir," I agreed cheerfully. Who says automation takes away jobs?

In what I thought was a natural next step, I went to enlist the help of Hector Chavez on Monday morning, saying, "Would you like to be *co*-Implementation Manager? It's a big resume builder."

In my ear, he said, "Not me. I warned you. You have no one to blame for this but yourself."

"How's that?" I didn't remember being warned about this one.

"The technical skills you showed off." He thumped me on the chest. "The champion of undeliverable refunds is now champion of unusable computers. I want no part of that."

My usual sidekick, Ladislav Ras, turned out to be unusually reticent about the project as well, if the vigorous shake of his head was any guide. Therefore, it was up to me alone to spread the pain of the manpower loss around. I knew I had to get the toughest opposition over with first: the inevitable objections of my former manager. Lucinda. She was already looking at me funny, so I headed straight over.

She pretended to be working. "Luce?" I said.

"Uh uh, no." She put down her pen. "I know what you want."

News traveled fast. Her look of distress and alarm at the idea of pulling her people off the busy phones told me all I needed to know. Now that I no longer worked for Lucinda, she was not okay with sacrificing her people to operate a special project, even one as dear to upper management as Teletax.

"You know it wasn't my idea to go work for Virgie," I explained.

"Nonetheless, you do work there and you don't work here."

Luce wasn't one to make threats, so I wouldn't hear one now, but when she went cold as a lizard like that, I knew there would be trouble down the road. She obviously thought I was too cozy with the attractive she-devil that all the other managers were at odds with. That was the heart of the matter. Well, I was a big boy now, and I knew what upper management expected of me, so I would brook no dissent even when it came to Lucinda. It seemed there was no doing a job at the IRS without turning a few good eggs into enemy omelets.

"Here's a deal for you," I told her. "I need two people from each group. They'll be your choice, and I only need one right now. If you step up and give me the first one before anyone else in this room does, your second one may never be needed, if you get what I mean."

I met her eyes and nodded solemnly so that she knew I wasn't kidding about any of it.

With her mouth set in a tight line, she said, "Take Bret."

"Yes, ma'am." Although I knew Bret to be the weakest member of the herd and probably should have rejected him, I lost no time pulling him from the phones. Modest Martin and I reconvened for Test Number Two, set as soon as I had trained Lucinda's employee, which took about an hour. We plopped a headset on the kid and said, "Go."

"Wait, what do I say again?" Bret asked.

Forestalling Cowler's reaction, I explained, "You don't say *anything*. Ever. That's why there's no mic on your headset. You listen to the caller, read the chart, and press the corresponding button. But first hit the one that says 'ACD' on it to get started. Good?"

"All right." His tentative finger found its way to the ACD button, and a waiting caller was drawn from the busy lines immediately, whereupon Teletax came alive. Its clear, robotic female voice spaced the words so that they could not be mistaken, and grouped them for dramatic effect: "Welcome... to our automated... tax... system,"—and provided a series of options.

When it was time to make a selection, the caller seemed unsure it was his turn to speak. I heard a muffled woman in the background on the caller's end say, "What's happening?"

"It's a recording, honey."

"It asked you a question, though, Bobby. I think you're supposed to answer it."

"How?"

"I don't know. You wanted to know how tax status worked. Ask it about that."

When the man spoke again, he sounded like he'd been prodded out of a dream, "Can you hear me in there? How do I take Head of Household?" That was one of the options.

The silence that followed went on for too long while Bret searched the chart for that choice and its code. Excited by finding it, he fumbled the chart to the floor, and then panicked and hit some random numbers to get a recording going. An awful mistake.

"You've chosen... married filing separately," the robotic voice declared, and Teletax began the long spiel on that topic in its deliberate and infuriating way, "You can choose married filing separately as your filing status... if you are... married."

"No, I didn't choose that," the caller fumed, "That's wrong. Give me the other one." No one had ever "spoken" to a recording before, and it clearly scared this man. The movies about out-of-control robots had scared everyone. "Give me head of household," he tried again with growing angst.

"...when you file separately, you are not responsible for..."

"Please! Stop it. That's not what I wanted. Head of household."

"...on a separate return," the recording droned on, "report only your own... income... and expenses."

"No! Who's in there?" Now he was on the edge of hysteria. "Shut up. I'll kill you. I'll kill everyone in your office."

The woman again: "Honey, calm down."

"No, I mean it!"

"Don't—" she said.

Cowler cut the feed dead, and I pressed on Bret's shoulder to keep him in his seat as he tried to rise. Through my fingertips, I felt him tremble. "Unlike the regular phones," I assured him softly, "this duty is completely anonymous. No caller knows who you are."

"The guy said everyone," Bret whined. "That he would kill *everyone*."

"We get empty threats like that all the time. He didn't mean it."

"I heard him say he means it!" Bret was struggling to pop up.

I said, "Martin, can you trace that call?"

"No." He'd stated a simple fact.

"Martin, are you sure?" I took a step back and pointed to Bret, hoping that Martin would get the message that Bret needed some reassurance to settle him down.

"I'm sure," Cowler said, as unmindful of the situation as before.

"Well, you might want to acquire that capability. And fast."

THE NEWS OF our first public mishap spread quickly around the office. I knew there were going to be consequences. Lucinda, who had provided the victim, was chewing her lips, trying to stay calm while I offered my apologies. I had no problem admitting fault for what happened on my watch, and doing all the talking. Virgie, just three stations away, could see what was happening between us, and she was fist pumping with joy.

Replenishing my breath, but running out of patience, I said, "Please speak to me, Lucinda."

In answer, Lucinda abandoned her station and stalked out the door.

Watching Lucinda intently until she was gone, Virgie pranced like the Best in Show at the Westminster Kennel Club. And the way she looked at me, the dance step wasn't the only animal quality she'd acquired. She grabbed me by the elbow as though she were a blind woman that required my assistance to cross the street. It may not have looked coercive to the naked eye, but her fingernails dug in hard.

"You seem excited. What's going on?" I asked.

"I need your help getting something in the supply room. Right now."

"Right now, Virg?" While I could see that the sexual tension was boiling over, I didn't know how far she was going to take this.

"This can't wait," she said as she drove me forward at a near run. I was pretty sure she'd pierced my suit jacket.

"Keep looking for the vein," I said, "I haven't had my blood drawn in a while."

She didn't seem to hear me. We did the necessary zigzag across the room in record time, ignoring a plethora of pleas from our charges to answer their incessant questions. I think that half of them just wanted to query me about the Teletax farce and whether we really had a computer as dumb as the usual personnel. Feeling like half of a besieged celebrity couple, I let Virgie lead me to a door I'd never taken note of. She had a key out and in a moment we were inside and she had the lights ablaze.

Although the door seemed to be the type that relocked automatically, and it clicked hard when Virgie slammed it, she blocked it off with a wood frame corkboard propped snug under the knob.

"Oh, this is where they keep the supply cabinet, huh?" I teased. "Are we here for more pencil erasers?"

Even with everything warehoused inside, the space looked bigger than most hotel rooms. Nice and new, like everything else in Taxpayer Service. I didn't have a chance to get a proper look around once Virgie shoved me onto my back across a low box. My flailing arms knocked a few things down and I suspect they must have been hazardous materials because Virgie had the presence of mind to protect me with her own body. At that point our legs entangled so that I seemed to be wearing the plaid skirt as much as she was, and her lightweight summer blouse deposited her breasts close to my face. Her body's alignment with mine was superb, and certainly put her in a position to know how I felt about all this. It slowly dawned on me that maybe the thought of her boy messing with her main rival, Lucinda, was an aphrodisiac to her. As if to confirm my theory, she sealed her lips to mine.

Her mouth was hungry, savage. Her breath hot on my face. As she pulled back to rapidly unbutton my shirt, I said, "Just to be clear, what was it you wanted in here?"

She looked at me like I was crazy. "I want that finger you promised me, and everything else."

This was going to be a problem. Whatever talents I may have had in my mid-20's, extraordinary power to resist an aggressive beautiful woman on top of me was not one of them.

CHAPTER EIGHT
Clashes

"We all go a little mad sometimes."

—Norman Bates, *Psycho*

When we were done, Virgie had no covers to hide beneath, so I saw everything under the same strong light that favored our workstations. I liked what I saw, including the impression that she seemed to have gone through a helluva fight and come out smiling. Her hair and business attire looked problematic though, and so did mine, I supposed.

I was grateful that we were on cardboard with packing material under it because if we gave the same performance on an old wooden crate we could have really gotten hurt. I scanned around at all the parcels and the loose items that had somehow cycled back to the supply room, including a loose pile of nameplates of former employees. Mindlessly scanning the discards, I recognized a few from the recent tax season. Though I checked carefully for them, "Poncit," and "Shapiro" weren't there yet.

"Did we just get mugged and our hotel room trashed?" I asked.

Virgie's smile faded. I was back to rubbing her the wrong way.

"The top of our bed has a dent in it," I reported further as we dressed hastily, "and while the muggers were at it, they stole our bathroom."

"You look like shit," she countered.

"That's why I was concerned about our one-star accommodations. It was your job to check the travel guide."

"Shut up." She lent me her mirror to comb my hair while she located her panties. I was glad I didn't have to borrow her big pink brush. A young man in the 1980s was never without some grooming tools. I could have filed my nails just then if I'd been so inclined. It would have looked cool, as if supply room trysts were my normal fare. I had a feeling that if we didn't get moving, though, Teletax was going to reveal its secret robot arms and legs, and barge in after us.

While I was musing, Virgie had managed to get herself together faster than I did. "What's this?" she asked. "Yours?"

"What?" She had my keychain in her hand. Specifically the part with the single-slide viewer attached. "Don't look at that." I warned her.

"How does this work?"

"It shows you a picture of exactly what you don't want to see at the moment," I said miserably.

She put the small end to her eye and tipped the other side to the light. Then she rotated the image of Linda and me so that it was right-side-up for her.

"I'm sorry," I said, reaching out for the viewer.

Virgie cupped a proprietary hand over it as though she meant to keep it. "No, it's okay," she said bitterly. "Your girlfriend who didn't satisfy you can go fuck my husband who never touches me and the four of us will be even."

I wanted to tell her, *It's not like that. Linda and I are just getting some space*, but that sounded lame in my head, like something I wished was true.

I didn't know where to go from here. When Virgie first threw me across that box and wanted to have her way with me, why hadn't I just told her that I heard someone else trying to get into the room for a set of emergency pencils? That, of course, was easy to say now that my manager was showing a lot less skin and all of our bad ideas had already been tested.

I took my keychain back from her and our hands rubbed, mine tingling from post-coital sensitivity. The way she looked at me, we might have ravaged each other all over again if I had lacked a healthy dose of shame. Instead, we sat down to put our lost shoes back on. Just one shoe in her case.

"Are the two of you serious?" she asked, checking the heel. "You and this girl?"

Instead of diving into that pit of snakes, I wrapped sharply on the side of our box with three quick knocks— giving her a start—cupped my hand over my mouth, and said, "This is your government. You have one minute to finish up in there or we're coming in to collect a recreation fee."

"Fuck you."

They say that the figurative version of that phrase is easier to endure right after you've had the literal, but as Implementation Manager, I can tell you they don't compare favorably.

WHEN I REENTERED Taxland, I found that my encounter with its wicked and amorous queen had left me in an altered state, a sense of disconnectedness not unlike the effect reputedly produced by a sensory deprivation tank. The idea was to get cut off from the exterior world to experience a rich and perplexing interior life.

I was roundly confused when Ladislav said, "Everyone is talking about you."

"They heard about us already?" Virg and I?

"I'm sorry I didn't get involved."

"I'm not into that anyway," I replied. Lad looked vexed, but he was used to me being stupid. Rather than following up on my quasi-confession, he politely continued, "How much trouble are you in with Teletax?"

"Oh the Bret thing. *That's* what you're talking about."

"They're saying you didn't train him well."

My extracurricular activities hadn't given me much time to think about that question, and they may have been clouding my judgment still, because I replied, "Mistakes are relative. All I have to do is make a much bigger one so that the first is forgotten."

"How can I help?"

"Free me up so I can go do that."

"Okay."

Okay. No questions asked. Good ol' Lad.

It was time to get a little smarter and get out from under this nonsense. Implementing my next step, I trained Lad in how to run Teletax, and put him in charge of training everyone else. Then, following the precept of *ask*

forgiveness, not permission, I went to have a little talk with
Cowler to square the arrangement.

Until now, Modest Martin hadn't shown any
embarrassment at all about his own role in the debacle, but I
found him hiding behind a computer screen, melancholy
with data inebriation.

"I told them in the beginning," Cowler wailed. He
looked miserable, and I wasn't sure he knew I was there.

"Told who?"

He looked at me. "The higher ups. I warned them that
the technology wouldn't be ready on their timeline."

"What did they say?"

"They didn't listen. Obviously! Now I don't care what
happens next."

"Then you won't care if I have Ladislav Ras do the
training instead of me doing it."

"Hold on, hold on. You can't do that."

"I just did. I'm authorized to handle Teletax as I see fit,
and that's how I see fit. If I'm going to be Implementation
Manger, I have to take a step back to manage it right."

"You're on your own then."

"Always was."

Funny thing, though, the guy who claimed he didn't
care, stuck around, as though he was sure that Frankenstein's
monster would not dare destroy its own creator. While he
didn't literally gawk over my shoulder, he fairly haunted the
Brooklyn POD at one of the empty manager stations,
diddling with the computer in what I hoped were simulations
that would provide a fix for Teletax sooner rather than never.

I pulled all the team members I wanted and told them to
report to Lad. Before I set him loose, though, I clued him in

that the toughest nut to crack was going to be the public, who weren't used to an automated system. As I'd already learned, people didn't expect this wacky idea of asking them to either "speak" their choice or "enter" a number. What kind of fool would hit buttons on their phone when they were already in the middle of a phone call?

Lad's whole team needed to know, in case they hadn't heard the rumors yet, that our computer didn't recognize speech, or any kind of sound, and our human operator did not understand the tones punched in when they heard them. In setting up this system, the IRS had managed to approximate the three wise monkeys of Buddhist legend who would "See, Hear, and Speak No Evil" by blocking out their senses. The original sensory deprivation tank. Our computer couldn't see or hear, and in this case, "Speak No Evil," was about hiding the truth.

Since I had chosen people who liked an operation cloaked in secrecy better than their lives on the phones, I determined that we pioneers were going to be okay anyway. Remember, I was one of those monkeys.

BY THE END of the week, I had my eight recruits in regular rotation. Things had changed, both for better and for worse. For one thing, Cowler had finally found a way to derail the machine when we made a mistake, and put it on a new track. That action was now part of the training, but we had already lost a trainee, due to attrition.

As I was spot-checking the new replacement, Antonio, I heard the caller on his line blurt out, "—the fuck is wrong with this thing? I want to speak to a real, live person. Wake up and get a damn human being on the line!"

"What's the matter?" I asked Antonio as he dithered. "Just give him the recording he wants."

"He didn't ask for a number in the first place," Antonio complained to me nervously, with one of his shirttails hanging out. "He didn't make any choice. And he's mad now, and I can't speak to him. What do I do?"

Though Teletax seemed to provoke a great deal of hostility, callers like this one were downright endearing compared to the man who wanted to kill us all. Every situation was different though. In this case, I had an idea of how to utilize Cowler's latest advance. I said, "Pick something for him."

"Like what?"

"Anything at random."

"You mean… make a mistake on purpose?"

"Yes."

Antonio tried one. The robotic voice pieced together, "You chose… to listen to information about… refunds."

The caller rejoined, "No, I didn't… I called about the Child Care Credit."

I nodded my permission, Antonio hit him up with the right one, and we had ourselves a believer. Cowler had done something right this time. At the end, the caller even said, "Thank you."

Yes, talk to the wonderful machine (or whatever you think it is), be sincere, and it will give you what you want. This was smooth sailing compared to before, and it took us through most of September before it blew up.

Thursday, September 26, 1985

"Shapiro!"

"Yes?" I had been passing by just two feet away from him, on my way to a routine check on Teletax, when Soderling shouted.

The Branch Chief grabbed my hand and slapped a paper into my palm. "Here's where you're going now. You're proctoring the test."

"What test?"

"The thing. The test. You know!"

"I don't know."

"At 201 Varrick, whatever test they give over there. It might be the IQ test for TSR's or whatever. They asked for a manager. You're it."

I stood up a little straighter. Here it was nine months after I began work, and I was routinely being thought of as a manager and assigned as one, even by the BC. Presiding over a test I had taken scarcely a year earlier felt like I had come full circle fast. Soderling would never have picked me if he didn't think I could perform without wreaking havoc on his career.

As though reading my mind he said, "When you leave this office representing me, I expect absolutely nothing to go wrong."

"Yes, of course, sir. Has it ever?"

His scowl indicated that he regretted choosing me already.

Two Hundred One Varick Street was a new location for me, but an old one for the borough of Manhattan. You could

157

feel the weight of history in its marbled corridors. You could smell it in the burnt, recycled dust everywhere. All those who entered one of its ancient rooms ran for the windows and discovered that they were scaled shut. You only found more dust there, piled up and yearning to escape. The testing room filled with a new set of wannabees, making the air even closer.

There were two of us proctors, each armed with a set of instructions and a checklist, both of which I had studied on the train. Although my fellow in this endeavor, Kathy, was a real time-in-grade manager, she insisted, "You'll have to take over because I didn't know what to do."

I recalled the last time I'd met a dumb but experienced manager, and I wondered if I was about to be dragged into a supply closet. I gave Kathy a chance to do just that but she merely sat back and watched me. So I was completely at liberty to make all the decisions, and perhaps all the mistakes, by myself. No matter. I had the checklist to follow. I re-read it as we did the job:

1. *Make sure there is one booklet for each participant.* Check.
2. *The booklets are sequentially numbered.* Check.
3. *The booklets are distributed in their sequential order.* Check.
4. *The test commences precisely at 9 am.* Check.

Finally, we knuckled down to work on item 5: *Participants are to be closely monitored at all times.* I saw a bit of shiftiness out there among our test takers, all of it understandable in the circumstances. The room was quiet but for the rasping chorus of lungs trying to reject the worn out air. Without window shades, there was plenty of sun, too. The sea of sweat brought a fetid humidity all its own.

Adverse conditions were a certainty for an IRS test. Heat like this, or inadequate lighting, were your only alternatives. That prerequisite may as well have been on the checklist: *Suffering enough?* They were. And me too.

With all of that, our little soiree seemed under control. Although I had never proctored a test before, the IRS, through its great foresight in providing me with the right tools, had managed to make even the most irritating process appear routine. People, for the most part, are remarkably docile and cooperative in official situations without any prompting. When you add debilitating heat and humidity, they lack the fight to cause trouble. Or so I tried to believe. In point of fact, my criminology class as an undergrad had informed me of just the opposite. So had real life: heat increases misbehavior. For me, it also causes daydreaming.

The potential for trouble reminded me of a sweltering day when Linda and I were returning from a date at Jones Beach, and were driving along Brooklyn's Belt Parkway. My memory of the day was as clear as if it were happening in front of me. As usual, Linda looked amazing, especially in a tank top. Then again, anyone who is deeply in love wonders at his luck in finding such a stunning person. I never doubted our long-term pending nuptials.

"Don't be alarmed," I said, "but we're going to miss our exit."

"Why?"

"The traffic in the right lane is too tight. I'm signaling, but no one is making way."

"I'll help. I'll guide you over."

"I'd rather you didn't. I don't mind getting out late. I'll just take the streets back to your house."

"No, this is easy. It's good to go... now." Linda, aggressive minx that she was, yanked the wheel for me as she spoke, sliding us into the next lane.

Linda, I reminded myself, was an expert driver. The only thing she didn't know was that the view from the passenger seat was a different perspective than she was used to. She learned that lesson when we heard the crunchy thud and felt the shudder of impact. I sucked air through my teeth. From the moment of contact, I struggled to keep the car from slipping out of control. I concentrated on evening it out and guiding us to the side of the road, where we stopped.

The car we'd hit—a tan wagon—had pulled off twenty yards back. Four Hispanic weightlifters piled out.

"It wasn't your fault," Linda assured me as we exited. "They sped up."

We took our first look at these guys and practically hugged the car for dear life.

I didn't tell Linda whose fault I thought it was, but I did say, "Please let me do all the talking."

"Why?"

"Their shirts are off."

"So?"

"So you can see how big and muscular they are. I'm not going to tell them it was their fault."

"It was though. You signaled. They should have let us pass."

"Quiet. They're coming."

The widest man made his way up to me. The other three stood behind him with their arms crossed.

"He's the driver," said Linda. "I waved at him to let you in, the bastard."

"He can hear you," I whispered fiercely. "Let me do all the talking."

"You hit us," said the man.

"You hit *us*," Linda countered. I hoped he would ignore her, and at first he did a nice job pretending not to hear.

"Let's exchange information first," I said to him. He had no problem with that part. His license identified him as "Mateo Vasquez."

Linda read it with me and sensed that I was caving in, but we were of two minds to begin with. "Don't let him get away with it," said Linda mustering the defiance with which she faced all of life. She really believed in what she said. Most of the time, her attitude made me proud. Now it had me worried.

I edged to the side to block Mateo's view of her. "Mateo, it was my fault and I'm very sorry. How much do you think it will cost to fix it?"

"Six hundred dollars, and we don't want nothin' on insurance so we'll take it the hard way."

I surveyed his group and they all seemed in agreement with Mateo's sentiment. I had the feeling that their attitude might be because of something we'd said. I told him, "You won't do that because you don't have to worry about insurance companies. I'll mail you a check for that exact amount."

"Maybe it costs more," he said with a hint of threat in his voice.

"You show me the bill and I'll pay anything up to six hundred fifty dollars." No use appearing too soft.

"You better. Or we will come looking for you."

I didn't like the sound of that. I wasn't entirely sure that my bank account held six hundred dollars at the moment, let alone more.

"Fuck him," Linda shouted. "Don't send him any check. Let him learn how to drive." Speaking of not appearing too soft, that was Linda's Brooklyn-style negotiation, but it was misplaced with this bunch.

"I'll kill you," Mateo said as he advanced toward her with the rest of his crew.

I stepped between her and Mateo again, and put my right palm up. "Don't speak to her." I played to his *machismo*. "Why would you even try to speak to a woman under these circumstances?"

I was taller than him, so he had to stretch to the side to see her again while he contemplated my question. "She insulted me."

Yes, she had insulted him. Repeatedly, if anyone was counting. While I was certain I could take the big man one-on-one, there was a limit to what my karate could do to protect us against the whole group. I was terrified, in fact, but he and the others would only get near Linda over my dead body. "So what if she insulted you," I said, all puffed up now. "You're talking to me, and I said it's my fault, and that I'm sorry and going to pay for it. That's not good enough for you?"

In answer, he stepped forward so that my hand met the sold muscle of his chest and I had to strain against his insistent push. His heart was not beating at nearly the rapid pace of mine.

While he was in a thinking mood, I told him, "*Es una mujer*. Do you know what kind of a man fights a woman? A *maricón*, that's who. *Pero un hombre con corazón...nunca!*"

He looked at me with new respect, even through his uncertainty in the face of my poor Spanish, and I repeated more clearly, "*Nunca!*"

"She insulted me in front of my friends," Mateo recalled.

"Do you want your friends to think you are a *maricón*? If you do, then fight her, and make a fool of yourself. But you do that after you fight me."

He took a long measuring look at us both, and I saw the shame coloring his face. As he turned to head for his car, leading his crew away, he reminded me, "The check, *señor*, or I come looking for you..."

"No problem." I was a tough guy when I had to be, and a bomb defuser the rest of the time.

SOMEONE CLEARED THEIR throat noisily.

"They're done," said manager Kathy, trying to bring me back to the Varick Street hotbox.

"What?"

"The test is finally over."

Hmm. Back in Dust Bunny Hell. Right. I consulted the last item on our checklist: *All booklets and answer sheets are collected.* We had our test takers pass them forward. Kathy swung into action, sifting through the booklets as they piled onto our desk at the front of the room.

Kathy cleared her throat to get my attention. "Booklet number 17 is missing," she announced hesitantly, looking to me for guidance. In hindsight I think she knew that there had been trouble in this venue before. Hence her nervousness from the start. A government test had much better resale value than a football game ticket. Copies could be sold over and over again.

"Missing? Are you sure?" I asked her.

"Absolutely sure."

That only meant one thing. The notion of this day being routine just bit us on the rear. Soderling wasn't going to like this.

After that, things happened too quickly for me to think about them all that much. Though I was turned in Kathy's direction, my peripheral vision registered furtive movement. I swung toward the door in time to see three people bolt through. "Stop," I shouted in a voice that reminded me of my days as a ninth grade hall monitor. "Everyone back in the room. We're not done yet."

The three in the hallway, all young men, looked at each other frozen in uncertainty, and then broke into an even faster run. I sprinted past them, humbling them with my speed, and then squared off in front of them. "Step inside, gentlemen, please."

Again, they stopped and turned to look at each other. Having gained a tacit agreement from the others, the one in front swung a fist at me. Perhaps he was not as humbled as I thought. My reflexes were my best feature. Before I knew it,

I had intercepted him at the forearm and swept it away with an inside upper block. My other arm flashed out and struck him in the middle of his face, sending him backward to the floor. The hand he used to cover up sported red ribbons between each finger.

"You broke my nose," he remonstrated miserably.

Meanwhile, Kathy was nowhere to be seen. Holding down the fort somewhere else, I supposed. Working unencumbered was always better in these situations, I told myself. That way there was no need to defend her against them, though I didn't fear these three as much as the four weightlifters I'd faced down before.

"Step inside," I repeated, "unless you all want to be arrested." I took an educated guess that they were going to be arrested anyway before we were through, but the threat worked. They retreated into the room with the rest, and I asked everyone to find the seats they'd had before.

The boys from the hall claimed they couldn't remember exactly where they sat, and they managed to convince some others trying to sit down that no one could know for sure where anyone had been.

With the seating order scrambled, Kathy and I would not be able to match the owner of Booklet 17 to the face that went with it. The government was too cheap to let anyone write their names on the booklets. They had to be reusable. Nevertheless, I had the full group sit still. As our test takers settled down to hard core grumbling, I flashed on the terrible notion that Kathy and I could have made a mistake in counting, but I had no basis for that worry, so I plowed on.

"Raise your hands if you turned in a test," I said. Everyone raised their hands. One hand had blood on it, which I took as a sign of guilt since he was the one who had tried to hit me. I turned to Kathy at her insistence and she whispered, "Someone is lying."

"Yes. Get security," I whispered back, and she took off, only too happy to get out of there. I hovered near the doorway so that no one could get past me again. To the class, I said, "Do me a favor, please. I want everyone to look under and around their seats to see if they can find a test that didn't make it to the front of the room."

I watched them search on, around, and under the seats. Some even patted themselves down for good measure. One of them had to have been making a quality fake show of it. One by one, the test takers shrugged and regained their seats to see what I would do next. Someone said, "I have to leave," and a few others agreed that they had to go too.

"Be patient," I told them with an edge to my voice. "This isn't school." I was sure that this suspect pool could be detained for a few minutes without violating their rights. Hyped up as I was by the recent altercation, I would just as easily hand off responsibility to any authority who came next or handle it myself if need be.

Armed security arrived at that very moment, ushered in by Kathy. The trio of fugitives I had retrieved from the hall saw the uniforms, jumped up, and scattered. The guy who had taken a swing at me ran, of all places, to the sealed windows. First he tried mightily to open one. Next, he tried to crash through it, producing an ugly thump. His head left a stain on the thick, reinforced glass. He teetered in a brief pause and then he fell backward into the room. Test Booklet 17 stuck up out of the top of his pants.

With the security men confident that all was under control as they took charge of their prisoner, the other two miscreants tried to rush us. One of them slammed into manager Kathy. In my concern for her, I was caught off guard when the guy with the broken nose hit me in a wild shot at the top of my head, and then grappled me. He was no longer trying to get away; only trying to get revenge.

We were too close to box each other so I put my leg behind him and shoved him across and down. The other guy had gotten his shirt caught on Kathy's decorative waist belt. He was smacking her repeatedly, probably thinking she had grabbed him and wouldn't let go. I brought my hands together rapidly against the sides of his head and popped both of his ears. That settled him down fast.

When I turned around, the first guy was in handcuffs complaining, "Hey man, we were just trying to sell it." I doubted that any of these nitwits did well on the IQ test.

I was composed after the incident. Kathy was freaked out and weeping. It didn't completely surprise me that someone would attack a woman. But, as I'd told Mateo—a man "with heart" would never do that. They way I'd used the Spanish phrase "un hombre," the literal word "man" meant "a *respected* man," as opposed to no sort of man at all, and "heart" meant "bravery" rather than "cowardice." I won't translate the other word I'd used to sway him.

"Why didn't you do anything when those guys attacked us?" I asked the guard who stayed.

"We didn't expect any trouble. We were coming anyway for a different reason."

"Why?"

"You have an urgent message."

"*All* of you were coming anyway? Don't you have anything better to do?"

He shrugged.

I extended my hand for this message, but he left me hanging. "There's an emergency at your office."

"My POD?" I asked.

"I don't know. Brooklyn. They said you have to get back there immediately."

"Fine," I sighed, wondering whether the Batman ever had to fight two sets of villains in a single episode. Surely it happened in the movie version. "All right. Have Alfred bring the limo."

The guard blinked a couple of times, too straight to realize I was kidding and too dim to come up with a response.

I didn't see the pattern yet, but it would happen that all of the worst trouble would brew when I was away from the office for any length of time. When Alfred failed to arrive promptly with the limo, I relented and took the subway.

The entrance to my building was closed with a line of yellow police tape, and the security detail shifted nervously at my approach. A smarter man would have used that daunting sign as an excuse to go home. I showed my ID and told them I'd been called to an emergency and they waved me through, eager to resolve whatever was happening inside.

The Walk-In area was surrounded by an inner ring of men in blue and an outer ring of division personnel. The usual visitors had been removed.

I picked Hector out of the crowd and asked him, "What's going on? Who's in there?"

"Head of Household is on a rampage."

"Are you kidding me?"

"That's what they're calling the gunman. He says he wanted to know how to claim Head of Household and Teletax gave him Married Filing Separately."

"The guy from a month ago?"

He nodded.

"Why? What set him off today?"

"I don't know. Off his meds? They got him trapped in the Garden Maze." The Garden Maze was what we called the high-walled, soundproofed waiting line passage that was meant to ensure private communications but also crowd control. Each padded panel was a moveable wall braced by crosswise feet. The collection of them were divided into different colored sections that began in blue and culminated in red near the front of the line where people were about to get their questions answered.

"I knew he was upset, but I didn't think he was crazy. What do they want with me?" I asked Hector. "Don't they get hold of the distraught man's wife and mother for these things?"

"They're coming," Hector calmly assured me. "Meanwhile the bosses want someone to join the negotiators and talk tax with the guy."

"You could have done that."

Ben Parris

"That would have meant *me* volunteering."

"I didn't volunteer either."

He studied me. "Have you looked in the mirror? Your jacket is torn and your forehead is bleeding. They needed someone crazy to go in there, and you look the part."

Our courthouse police were doing much better than the guardsmen I'd just left at Varick Street. Soderling took charge of me for the next five yards and then handed me off to a Lieutenant Joseph.

"Are you Shapiro?" the officer asked.

"I am."

"Come in here." He sounded worried.

When I got to the hot zone, the lieutenant's men were calling out to HH, "No one tried to trick you, sir. Teletax is just a machine."

"That's another lie," the gunman called out, his voice raw from yelling. "I'll shoot the next person that lies to me or tries to fool me."

On that sanguine note, Joseph said quietly, "Talk to him, Shapiro. He refuses to give his name, but—"

"I don't want his name. Head of Household is good enough." It would be funny, I thought, if the aggrieved party turned out to be Mateo again. I already knew how to deal with him. "Does he have hostages?"

"Thank God, no."

"How do you know?"

"He chased everyone out."

"Are your men in the same area with him?"

"No, they're just around the bend. Head of Household is by himself in red section."

170

I put a finger to my lips so that Lieutenant Joseph wouldn't inadvertently broadcast what I was about to do. The aluminum frame walls were soundproof only after a couple layers of zigzagging. More importantly, they weren't bulletproof at all. So being the next person to lie to our gunman—as I surely would be in his eyes if we got into a discussion about robotic voices—didn't seem like a good idea at all. I had what I thought was a more pragmatic approach.

I went to the opposite side of the wall from where he was supposed to be. The lieutenant vigorously motioned me to come back, while he mouthed, "too close." I held up one finger to indicate it would take a second. Then every policeman who was standing there waved frantically for my return. Ignoring them, I bent down and rotated the crosswise feet at each interval in their metal sockets so that they were nearly parallel with the wall sections in the gunman's vicinity. That way they could provide no lateral support. "Head of Household?" I called out to be sure that he was standing where I needed him to be.

"Who are you?"

I kicked the red section panel high and in the middle. The sections began to fall, an effect that rippled on down the line as each hinge pulled on its adjacent panel. The falling wall flattened on him. When I saw no movement, I pulled the pin to release the side hinges to give the police access. "He's all yours."

The cops moved in. Lieutenant Joseph said to me, "I didn't know we could do that with the walls." Four of them heaved the corners of the wall frame up and out of the way while all the rest trained their guns where he would appear in the center. Head of Household was stunned. He had lost his weapon.

As they hauled the man away, he looked eyes with mine, and I would never forget his savage and giddy stare, like Napoleon wacked silly with a shovel. This wasn't Mateo, or anyone like him. Good thing I didn't try to reason with him.

When we were back to our section, my hands wet and shaking in the aftermath, Hector said, "You haven't cleaned yourself up yet. How many fights were you in today?"

"That man is out of his mind," I muttered.

"HH?" he asked, handing me a wet towel.

I looked at Hector. "They can't blame me for this, can they? I solved the problem."

Hector laughed. "Oh, is that why you pushed the wall over? Nice try. They can't *not* blame you for this."

"How do you figure?"

He held up two fingers to represent this situation and picked off the two alternatives one at a time. "Everything that happens here is either someone's glory or someone's fault. When something goes wrong, who are they going to blame for this one? The District Director? No. My money's on you."

CHAPTER NINE
Nicknames and Bad Girls

"You sonuvabitch, do you know who I am?"

—Moe Green, *The Godfather*

<u>Monday, October 7, 1985</u>

The first time it happened, I hadn't a clue what was going on. As had become my habit, I was crisscrossing the floor of taxpayer service, stamping on brush fires. There wasn't a moment I was not importuned. I found that if I kept myself accessible, the problems that began in the pentapods did not escalate to the long desks with the monitors. To retain my sense of normalcy, I located the comely Virgie and winked at her. She ducked her head in embarrassment. That's when Antonio, who was on a break at the time, came to me and said, "There's a cop at the door."

"At the door? Why doesn't he come in?" From what I'd seen, all law enforcement came and went as they pleased around here.

"I don't know."

"Well, what did he say?"

"He said he needs some help."

"That doesn't tell me anything."

"Do you want me to go ask him again?"

"No, I'll go."

At the side door, I found a uniformed cop behind a nervous smile and a pile of papers he clutched to his chest. He said, "I know I'm supposed to be on the regular line, but I have a tax problem and I was wondering…"

I had always been a straight arrow and a fan of law enforcement. Even though I was developing mixed feelings about some of my fellow feds and their life on the government teat, I maintained respect for the New York City Police Department. Those guys put themselves in harm's way every day in direct action to keep the rest of us safe, and had nowhere near the layers of insulation that many of us had. I found his discomfort disturbing.

I said, "Hey, don't worry about it. Come around here whenever you need to."

"You sure?"

"I don't want cops tied up waiting on the line. You need to get your asses back to work."

He laughed and flipped me a card that said PBA on it with the current year and a nice picture of a shield next to the words spelled out—Patrolman's Benevolent Association. It looked like that was his union ID card and couldn't imagine why he would want it in my possession.

"What's this for?" I asked.

"It's for when you need something from me or, uh, someone else."

"What would I need?"

"A favor."

"In return for what? I haven't done anything for you."

"You did. You let me skip the line."

I shrugged, guessing he had more than one of these cards to hand out. Apparently, it wasn't an ID card after all.

Unable to imagine circumventing the system for any reason, I thanked him and tucked the card in my pocket to be polite. Then I let him ask his tax questions about who was supposed to pay the tax on a gift, and he was happy. His parting remark was, "Regards to Bonnie and Clyde."

Bonnie and Clyde were of course, the famed husband and wife duo known for their crime spree during the Great Depression. Highly glamorized, sensationalized, and always ready for mayhem, they were only twenty-five and twenty-six when they faced their final gun battle. My PBA friend here was actually referring to the IRS's own Mitzi and Noel Cunning. The Cunnings looked even younger than me and were the biggest stars of the Examination Division, given all the arrests they were responsible for. An astonishing number of taxpayers had tried to bribe them in exchange for reducing their tax assessments. When they were solicited at the outset, Mitzi and Noel would go back for a second round of discussions and each wear a wire to get the bribery attempts on tape. The tactic usually worked.

That left the division with a mystery as to why other agents were not reporting bribery attempts at the same rate as the Cunnings. Whenever the taxpayer's guilt was discussed within their circle of admirers, however, something passed between the husband and wife that they didn't share with anyone else in the discussion. Their secret glances reflected their love but it also looked like they were up to no good. Despite the ironic nickname, we all thought our in-house Bonnie and Clyde were harmless—mischievous in the throes of their youth, given the great time they were having.

I'd met Mr. and Mrs. Cunning once and was disappointed. I asked Noel if we could get together and talk about how best to get into the Examinations Division. He just looked me over and said, "Stay in school, kid."

Mitzi was a little nicer, though I could see her feeling at home perched on the fender of a 1934 Ford with a cigar and a machine gun. She didn't offer me any support for my quest either. So it was mildly irritating to hear those two referenced at a point when my visitor and I were getting along so well. As I've said, the implication in mentioning them was usually that the rest of the revenue agents must be taking bribes instead of reporting the people who offered them. But the uniformed cop didn't look malicious when he said it, and I wasn't a revenue agent at this point, so I didn't take the reference too personally.

The officer that visited me must have been a feeler, someone checking to get a better sense of who I was, because not a day later came Lieutenant Joseph, once tepid, now a great fan of mine since the HH incident. At the side door, declining to enter, he said, "Hey thanks for helping out my guys. Sorry I couldn't talk sooner."

I felt a small rectangle of cardboard in my palm as we shook hands. Another PBA card, I supposed.

"No problem, lieutenant."

"You did okay on the Head of Household thing."

"Thanks." Not a lot of people knew that. In the days before cell phone cameras and the Internet, any self-respecting government agency with secrets to protect could keep a lid on things even if they happened in front of outsiders. No one was hurt, and no reporters got wind of it. I could still be thrown under the bus, but none of the Teletax program's problems, if any developed, had to be aired in public, and that was the way everyone wanted it.

"Two more okay?" He stepped aside and sure enough there were two uniforms in the hall behind him, hats in hand, so to speak. It suddenly struck me: *that's* why the first cop was so nervous. He wasn't asking just for himself and Joseph. He was there for a huge favor—a whole new rule that no cops wait in line.

"Yes, why not?" I replied. I still thought it was a good idea.

I soon had such a good collection of unnecessary cards that I mostly misplaced. The rest I kept only because I failed to clean out my jackets on a regular basis. I even had my eyeglass case in an inside pocket with the eyeglasses I neglected to wear.

Directly after the Teletax dustup, I officially began the training that my superiors imagined I had taken the previous year. As predicted, Phase II was a snoozefest for me, telling me everything I had learned on my own or knew from school. Worse yet, the break times and lunch periods were long enough to go out and get into trouble.

The alternative for lunch, which was the other good reason not to stick around, was the IRS cafeteria. I slummed there the first day. The Dungeon, as we called it, was not a humming social network. Anyone who suffered the visit to its dimly lit warrens would realize that the place wasn't about memorable food either. Since it was convenient for visiting dignitaries who were starving and had no time to go anywhere else, you could meet someone of influence once a year. Or maybe just someone to hook up with.

On the job, I looked after a large number of employees with tremendous success. In that same office, sloppy, spontaneous sex with the wrong woman seemed to be a roaring business with me as well. But in the romantic department I remained a pure novice. I hadn't planned anything, but as soon as I saw the woman sitting by herself, I thought that maybe I could reel in Linda if only I had more relationship experience. Gayle Shriner, an avid sports fan who didn't mind cafeteria food, became the first woman I'd ever picked up easily.

I came up to her and said, "Excuse me, Ma'am, I'm with the restaurant. I'm afraid we don't allow dining alone in this establishment."

She smiled. "Perhaps if you join me, I'll be off the hook."

She was off the hook, all right. I sat down thinking it was my charm that made her want me, but it turned out I was her rebound guy. Plunking me straight into the boyfriend role, she chatted away about her problems, which unfortunately included her tedious work as an administrative assistant. "Not a secretary," she emphasized.

I said, "The IRS has been the first to stop calling people secretaries, and I think they only did that because the Secretary of State complained."

She laughed at that poor excuse for a joke, which was another sign that it was too easy. I was not on the verge of achieving better relationship experience. Her next vocalized thought was how awful her ex was, the ultimate giveaway regarding her state of mind. I didn't listen much after that, which may explain why I found out too late that she was a Mets fan.

The trouble with knowing Linda was that no one compared well with her, so Gayle was easily outclassed. Gayle was average rather than smart, beautiful without being distinctive, and came off whiny when she wanted to sound rebellious. Worse yet, she didn't really understand her chosen obsession of baseball. The fetish was something she'd wrapped around her shoulders in order to meet men. Linda, on the other hand, was too independent to alter her interests to suit a suitor. For me, Gayle was a placeholder that I wasn't too enthusiastic about.

So after two sports-related nosebleed dates that did not include my beloved Yankees, it was Gayle Shriner I was avoiding at the outdoor Fulton Mall on a beautiful October day. That, plus it was about time to pick up the contact lenses I had ordered two weeks earlier.

I'd already run into a couple of reps and other IRS types from my office trolling about in pairs on extended hooky breaks. That reminded me that in our line of work it was easy to fall prey to gossip so I used my walking time to review how I would justify my conceit of ordering contact lenses if anyone asked me. From what I'd seen of personnel in the examinations division, I had the impression that contact lenses would make me a better candidate for any field agent job. Glasses, which I hated wearing anyway, were the final touch in the ensemble that made me look so much like the Taxpayer Service Division Chief. TPS wasn't the big action branch.

Besides, a man of action, unburdened by glasses, can't get shot through the lens like Moe Greene in the Godfather. That was a helluva sight. Mario Puzo's masterpiece wasn't among our training films, but maybe I fixated on the image because he was a Jewish mobster, with smart-guy glasses. Put it all together and I thought I had a pretty solid case for buying contacts, right?

When I got to the enclosed portion of the mall, I didn't see the clerk from the last time I was there, which made me uneasy. I had already been through the whole rigmarole of the eye exam, the sales pitch, and the purchase, which they made me pay for in full. Now when I went to pick up the finished product, the new clerk said, "We don't do astigmatism contact lenses. Get something else. Get some more eyeglasses."

"What are you talking about? We're past that already. I'm here to pick up my contact lenses."

"We don't have them."

"Apparently you do. You must because you guys took my order for them and told me to come back in two weeks. Here's the slip." He refused to look at it.

"That was a mistake, whoever set that up." He didn't budge.

"You're the ones who discovered my condition. Why didn't you tell me that you can't make lenses for me before you took my payment?"

He shrugged. "Like I said. It was a mistake. We're not responsible."

"Then refund my money."

"Can't."

"Let's have this conversation with your manager."

He obliged.

I ran through it again with the manager, a small, middle-aged man who never looked me in the eye as he huddled over a catalog. He pointed behind him to a sign that said, "No refunds."

"That's 'No refunds' if you don't like the merchandise. I didn't get any merchandise." I couldn't believe I was having this conversation, trying to convince a chain store manager of basic business law.

"Doesn't matter. The policy is very clear. No refunds. Store credit only."

Since he was not the least bit surprised that someone had taken my order for a service they didn't do, it left me with the distinct impression that they intentionally took all orders no matter what. They just made sure they had your money pinned down. I said, "I don't want to buy from thieves."

"Then you get nothing. Get out or I'll call the police."

That sounded like a good idea to me. There were plenty of police on the Mall that I could return to the store with.

I was in luck. The moment I stepped out, I could see it from a half block away, a swatch of blue uniform strobing with the passage of the crowd. He seemed to be holding station so I hurried over to catch him before he moved on. I found a cheerful "girl-watcher," pale enough and young enough to have spent the summer as a cadet at the academy, and explained to him, "I was robbed."

"Where?"

"In a store."

"By who?"

"The store."

"Did you speak to the manager?"

"He was in on it. He took my money and gave me nothing."

"Do you have a receipt?"

"Yes."

"Okay, whatever happened in your dealings with a store, that's a civil matter." The young man said it like an awkwardly memorized line, making all of his previous questions superfluous.

"Why tie up the courts when the three of us could talk it out in a minute?"

"I'm not allowed to. Good luck with it, though." He fled the scene, as they say in police jargon. This officer was "friendly," and "neighborhood," but clearly not Spiderman. Not a hero, in other words. He must have felt extra guilty about it though if he was willing to walk away and surrender his skirt surveillance. I had a feeling that his "hands-off" approach to stores would only be repeated if I found another cop like him.

My PBA cards. Now that I had a sense of what they were for, what had I done with them? Does the dry cleaner put them back in the suit pockets? I wondered. He probably keeps them for himself.

With plenty of debris in my pockets, I located and rejected several well-laminated cards with nice pictures of badges. The one I was looking for proved a little harder to spot since it wasn't an actual PBA card. It was a gold-stamped business card and I couldn't believe my luck finding it in that particular jacket, but I did. With the card in hand, I found myself one of the shiny new public phones that went with the mall and leveled the standard gypsy curse at it over the fact that these were no longer enclosed in sound shielding booths.

Lieutenant Joseph came on the line, listened to me explain my problem through the babbling of the crowds and asked, "Can you wait ten minutes?"

Wait ten minutes? I couldn't believe he would show up for me at all. I had never done anything like this before, calling in a favor. Bemused, I said, "Sure."

In my relief, the ten minutes moved fast. I met him outside, and we plunged into the eyeglass store together. The manager went popeyed at the sight of the two of us, but recovered quickly, no doubt remembering that he had PBA cards of his own. When the lieutenant suggested nicely that the store manager return my money, the guy would not listen to him either. He went no further.

Joseph steered me from the sunlit front of the store to a relatively dark corner and said quietly, "I gave it a shot, but it's a civil matter. He doesn't have to listen to my advice." There was that damned phrase again about a civil matter.

"Stolen money is a criminal matter before it's a civil matter," I countered, also holding my voice down, "the same as in a mugging."

"A store is different in the eyes of the law."

"It's a bait and switch fraud though. That's a crime. You have a division for it."

"Refunds versus store credit? His word against yours for less than a thousand bucks? We don't want those in the squad," he acknowledged. "Anyway, you should have flashed your creds in the first place."

"Creds?"

"Your credentials. All the guys in your office do it to get out of a jam or before they find themselves in one."

"I'm not a field agent. Technically speaking, I don't carry credentials." What did he expect me to do? Threaten to destroy the store in an audit? I might as well be Moe Greene if I did things like that.

"Your ID then. Anything that says IRS on it is impressive enough. Do it now while you still can. But wait until after I leave."

This was a well-intentioned, bad piece of advice if I'd ever heard one. I was sorry I had troubled him. In my hoarsest Don Corleone imitation I said, "Society imposes insults that must be borne." This passage from *The Godfather* continued by pointing out that the humble man, if he keeps his eyes open, can one day get revenge on the most powerful. In my case, it just meant I would take my chances in small claims court.

The lieutenant's eye twitched as though he was stoically enduring some pain. I couldn't tell if he disapproved of the quote or just thought I was an oddball. "Suit yourself."

When he began to move away, I noticed that my old boss Lucinda happened to be in the store, standing there listening to us, not three feet away. My face felt hot, which made it even worse. If the lieutenant had seen her, he must have mistakenly figured it did no harm for her to hear it since we were all on the same team.

As I stared at her, and she at me, she casually reached into her purse and removed a candy bar, which she proceeded to tear open, nip into, and nosh intently with her eyes wide. "Mm, mm, mmm," she said, "Refund versus store credit. You're dealing with some tough issues here. I can see why you want to be a revenue agent. You'll learn how to clear that shit up. Joseph gave you the best advice though. Flashing your creds would have worked."

"Don't repeat this to anyone, Luce."

"Me?" She took a bigger bite and waved the peeled back candy bar in the negative while its nougat filling made for a languid chew of pure innocence.

"Yes, you."

I spent the rest of the day in my Phase II training class wishing I had hung around in safety with Gayle Shriner instead of venturing out to get caught in an embarrassing situation in front of someone who was pissed off at me. Gayle didn't care whether I looked slick enough to be a revenue agent or not. I had the feeling that she might as easily set my eyeglasses on the chair across from her, along with a ballpark hotdog, and talk to them about her no-good ex-boyfriend all day. The more I thought about it, the more I began to root for her to get it over with and reunite with her ex already because I sure wasn't making any headway with her myself.

And this thing with Lucinda wasn't over, of course. At the top of the very next morning, I was back in my training class. A young beanpole of a man braced himself in the doorway and all the unfocused gazes that had been on the lecture turned to him. "Um, I was told that there's a manager in this class somewhere?" His voice cracked on the word manager so I could tell he was incredulous about this anomaly.

The instructor took an exasperated walk to the center of the room and drooped her finger over my head as though no one were more annoyed with my masquerade than she.

"I'm not a manager," I said. "You don't want me."

"Daniel Shapiro?" asked the boy.

I had to acknowledge that.

"You're the one they want."

Had this been one of my college classes, I would have been grateful to escape. But at the IRS, you never knew what you might be pulled into. The messenger conveyed me to a small second floor room with Assistant Division Chief Ray Lansdale at the head of a long conference table, and only one empty seat, which was next to Lucinda. "I saved it for you," she whispered sweetly as I settled in.

I nodded discreetly at a couple of other people I recognized and some of them acknowledged me.

"How nice of you to join us," the ADC said to me in the sour tone reserved for those who spoil meetings with their tardiness. "You wanna shut up now?"

I spotted Hector sitting uneasy among the group of managers. If he suspected trouble, so did I.

Still monitoring me with suspicion, Lansdale continued, "As I was saying, it's all hands on deck going into the fall. First we have the extension filers, and then we prepare for next season like never before. Our strategy will be utterly different from last tax season."

I wondered what distinguished last tax season from all the others. If I didn't know that, I wouldn't know how to make the following one "utterly different."

Lansdale stepped over to face me squarely, and looking only at me, said, "Who wants to volunteer to come in on Sunday?"

In the spirit of what I hoped was his deadpan jocularity, I said, "That sounds like a terrible idea, sir."

"Chavez is doing it," he offered as though this were incentive.

From the corner, I heard Hector inquire, "I am?"

"Well," he said to Hector matter-of-factly, "you may want to do it since Shapiro is doing it."

I considered echoing "I am?" but there is such a thing as being too cute, especially since one of the bosses thought he was making me an offer I couldn't refuse. Lansdale was stiff on the outside, and wacky on the inside. When I met Senator Al Gore a few years later, I realized that the two men were cut from the same bolt of Tennessee cloth. "May I ask what is happening on Sunday?"

"No, you may not, but I will tell you anyway. It's PBS."

"Are they doing a documentary on us?"

"No," he said drily. "Every so often the Public Broadcasting Service requests IRS personnel to go on their program and answer questions from the public."

True, but not at this time of year, I said to myself. So it was a lie. Or maybe I was too paranoid.

"It's a chance," he said pointedly, "to show them a different side of the IRS. How helpful we can be."

"Will I be on camera?"

"No."

That was better. Trying to work in front of television cameras was the one thing that scared me. "All right then." I thought this Sunday bullshit was the whole reason I'd been maneuvered into this meeting, but Lansdale wasn't finished.

"This season we're going to select real On-the-Job-Instructors and ensure that the next crop of TSR's is properly trained."

He didn't look at me this time, and I was relieved.

Someone asked, "What would that involve?"

"Well," said the ADC, "we have a couple of options, don't we? You all could start transforming this place into more of a corporate environment, or," he paused dramatically, "you could be like Danny 'Creds' Shapiro over here and tackle the really big issues... like how to get contact lenses."

All eyes shifted to me as the group laughed. I tried not to redden and make it worse, but the set-up had taken me completely by surprise, including the fact that they called me to the meeting late on purpose. The twin realizations that everyone in the room had talked about this before I came in, and that the tag was going to have permanency, were the real zingers.

I scrutinized my nearest neighbor, Lucinda, who betrayed no reaction in front of the group. As if she wasn't the one who had fed the story to Lansdale to humiliate me. That was how Danny "Creds" Shapiro joined the club of tall guys named Shorty, shy guys named Tiger, and arrogant guys named Modest Martin. I had to be a good sport about it or I would be cringing my whole life.

Having delivered his *coup de grâce*, Lansdale strolled to the door, swung it open, and turned his back, signaling that the meeting was over. People began to file out.

Before the room was empty, Luce linked arms with me so I couldn't shy away. Gently as a lover at first, but building to a bitter crescendo, she whispered in my ear, "Instead of worrying about your creds, why didn't you just solve all your problems by finding an employee in the store that hates me? Then you could go fuck them. You're so good at that."

That remark settled the question, in case I'd been wondering, as to whether Luce had gotten wind of certain activities involving Virgie and me, and also the question of who had told the ADC about the contact lens fiasco. I had to admit I was aroused to have inspired such passion in Luce. I had never thought of her in a sexual way and until now I didn't think that she saw me that way either. Rather intemperately, I fed her pique by replying, "I was afraid you'd forgotten me."

Of course Lucinda was no Linda, and I was done with office flings. I had the real thing out there waiting for me to make the right move. Somewhere or somehow. I was fond of pointing out that Linda Sobel had her parents' objections about me to overcome. But if I were to be honest, the truth was more likely to have been the opposite. Her daddy hated me and that's probably why she and I were so passionate when we got together. Anger from any direction was a powerful aphrodisiac.

Support for that particular theory could easily be found in the day Linda took me home by surprise, a sudden idea she'd gotten that we should swim in her parents' pool. As we were walking through the kitchen on our way to the back door, I warned her, "Your parents hate me."

She did not deny that.

I asked, "Are you sure they're not home?"

"They're not."

"And they're not going to arrive while we're here?"

"They're visiting my sister," she said bitterly, as though such a trip were proof that they would never return.

Ah, her sister. Sheila was the comparison sister who lived only to set the standards Linda could never achieve. She was the good girl that hung around the hospital looking for doctors to marry just as her parents had prescribed. Medical billing was her cover job for these ambitions and it worked like gangbusters. This other beautiful daughter got scooped up fast. As smart as Linda was, I could not believe that as an adult she'd let herself be so consumed by her parent's age-old "why can't you be more like your sister?" spiel.

We let the back door shut, and the lovely Linda and I got into the water fast. I was content to allow the matter of her sibling rest, but when I splashed her I sensed Linda hadn't forgotten the angst that fueled her. She retaliated by dragging my head under the waterline where she could trap my face in her cleavage. Her fury had either made her inhumanly strong or me very compliant. In the warm summer waters, it did not take long before Linda was talking dirty to me and we started working out her family issues rather vigorously under a glorious open sky. I had never had sex outside, protected only by a risky low-walled enclosure, as we had here, or done it in weightless comfort with the benefit of pliant swimsuits. This encounter was even better than having highly charged make-up sex since she was still mad and I wasn't the one she was mad at. Did I mention that we were having sex? Me and the person I would love forever? It was blowing my barely post-teen mind.

That's why I was particularly devastated when her father started yelling obscenities out the second floor window. We froze in our passionate embrace, separating only our lips. How much had he seen? How much could the rippling waters hide from his distance? The way Linda held me close, never easing her grip, meant that we had arrived at the same idea at the same moment. We had not yet gotten around to taking the bathing suits completely off and it seemed we were enmeshed in a dirty dancing sort of hug, yet if we pulled apart, her father could then be absolutely sure of our level of intimacy. So we wouldn't do that.

"How is your father's eyesight?" I managed to whisper.

"Good, but not perfect," was her unencouraging reply.

We dared not move all through the angry conversation between Linda and her father. It was nothing short of bizarre that I remained inside of her while Mr. Sobel admonished his daughter for being home instead of having visited her sister's house with them. At the same time, the three of us pretended that his apoplectic shouting had nothing to do with Linda and me fornicating right in front of him. I sweated profusely in the forbidden, conflicted rush I was feeling, and I hoped that he took my perspiration for pool water. Linda, on the other hand, began to get comfortable and seemed quite pleased with our flimsy deception. Towards the end of their argument, she had some fun with me, laughing and trying to push us apart while I continued to hold tight because certain youthful equipment of mine had sustained its vigor.

As I've said, I had little experience with normal relationships. Fortified with these pleasant and mortifying memories, I left Lansdale's meeting room and finished out the day's Phase II training class. Then I returned to my regular desk in the division and did a few hours of work there. When I got home, my message machine was blinking. I hit the button.

It was a call from Linda.

CHAPTER TEN
Couples Poker

"Listen to them; children of the night.
What music they make!"

—*Dracula* (1931)

As a rule, I don't accept calls that float out of a dream or arise from a waking trick of my subconscious, but I played this one back a few times to serve as an audible pinch, and it seemed solid. Linda's voice asking me to ring her back was sweet with the timbre of a woman calling a man for a favor. I made a point of never erasing her previous message until she called again. I was in no rush to clear the tape even then.

My mouth went dry at the thought of calling her back and possibly messing up. I inhaled a cup of water and then gulped another as I reviewed the possibilities. One, this was the first call of the rest of our lives together. Two, the neighbor's cobra had escaped and gotten into the house. Three, she had misplaced the television listings and wanted to know what was on. Four, she meant to start seeing me again but I would say something to blow it. The longer I thought about it, the more I was talking myself into some bad things and would never come anywhere near guessing the situation correctly in my current state of mind.

To fend off total paralysis, I rehearsed dialing. In those days, all phones became an open line with a dial tone as soon as you picked them up. Therefore, I had to dial with one hand on the spring-loaded cradle so that the call didn't go through before I was ready. Then I rehearsed having actual words come out of my mouth. I exercised my vocal cords until I no longer sounded like a child, and then gave it a few more tries until I no longer wheezed like a breathless marathon runner. The only thing that actually got me moving was the fear that I'd wait so long to call her back that she would say, "never mind." What had possessed me to stay late at work when I didn't have to?

I released the cradle and allowed the open dial tone to mock me for an eternal few seconds. Before it could drive me to further hysterics, I pressed the keys.

She grabbed the call in half a ring. "Hello?"

"Hi." Despite all of my practice, my greeting came out rather infantile and generally needy. I wondered if there were vitamins for that.

"What's going on?" she asked.

"I'm calling you back."

"I called *you*?" Her sense of humor. I liked it and she knew that. It actually centered me.

"Everything okay?" I asked her.

"Your brother is a lawyer, right?"

"Oh no, what happened?" I played along.

"Nothing. This guy in my office today. Really every day. He smokes at the desk right across from me. I can't get him to stop, the bastard."

"He's breaking the law," I sympathized.

"Right? Which one though? I want to tell him the municipal section of it."

"It's hard to say. He's violating six penal codes, not to mention the law of the jungle."

She laughed. "Can I take out a restraining order?"

"Being a lawyer's brother doesn't equip me with that information. I mean, coming up with the statute number, not about the restraining order. Do you want my brother's telephone number?"

"No."

"He wouldn't mind talking to you, give you a legal thing or two to say."

"No."

"Should I ask him for advice on this?"

"No, forget it." There it was. In my effort to ferret her out, I'd triggered the dreaded "never mind."

I swallowed, and asked, "Is that all?"

"Yes."

We said our goodbyes. Mine sounded sad to me, and I imagined hers did too, as did her "yes" answer just preceding that. I was about to hang up when it hit me. How could I turn so stupid in so short a space of time? This was a woman I knew so well that I had guessed the digits she picked for her voicemail code based on an old TV show that I assumed she'd once watched. I would never invade her privacy of course, but for fun I had asked her if I was right that the code was "54" and she was mortified at my little trick. She said she would change it immediately and I told her what she intended to change it to next. She made me promise to stop figuring her out on pain of being cut off completely.

The point was that I knew her intimately, knew the harmonics of her voice. She hadn't called me about a smoker. Nothing like that daunted her. Why would I give up now when she obviously needed to talk to me?

I said, "Wait. Are you still there?"

"Yes."

"You didn't call me about a legal matter."

"No…no, I didn't."

"Do you mind telling me why you called? I really miss you."

She took a deep breath and said, "I had dinner with Gayle Shriner tonight."

It was my turn for a deep breath, a sharp one. "Tonight? How do you know her?"

"I don't. I didn't. I heard you were seeing her. She's cute."

"Heard from who?"

"People talk. Doesn't matter." *People talk?* For a moment I thought she was going to call me Creds. People talked about that one too. How closely tied in was she to my office?

I said, "You hunted her down."

"Phone book."

"This is someone I only saw twice."

"Then you waited a while and she called you. You planned a third date."

"Wow." The exclamation was all I could muster. She really did pump someone for information. I should have been mad, yet I felt a thrill coursing through me that she cared enough to do that.

"That part I got from her."

"You talked about me?" Of course they talked about me. That was the point.

"I told her that you didn't want to see her, that you had no interest in someone like her whatsoever."

"Someone that's cute, you mean?"

"I told her it was over. It never really began."

"Why would you do that?" But I had a very good idea how jealousy worked.

"I know you, Danny, and now that I've met her, I know she's not your type."

"You didn't know that before you met her. So why did you meet up with her?"

"You deny that she's not your type?"

"She isn't."

"So good. I did you a favor."

"What did Gayle say about it?"

"She understood. She said she was thinking of going back to her old boyfriend anyway."

"You want me." I may have been crazy to feel this way, but what Linda had done made me love her even more.

"What?" she asked with a nervous laugh. "No, what does that even mean, 'I want you?'" she asked. "We're not together. I'm just being protective of a friend. If she was right for you, she wouldn't have given up so easily and I would have said *mazel tov* to you both."

"You're making good, logical sense," I teased her. "Are you sure you're a woman?"

"Ha, ha, ha," she said humorlessly, but I smelled victory. If she didn't want to admit it, that was fine. Although I was mostly awkward with women, I rose above that quickly when I felt solid ground under my feet. However long the special feeling we shared had lain

197

dormant, her extraordinary act of jealousy confirmed it would never abandon us.

I said, "Did you pay for Gayle's dinner?"

"Of course."

"Then I owe you dinner this weekend. Tomorrow night, in fact." It had to be Saturday because I had committed to work on Sunday.

"Huh," she said. "I guess you do." I could hear her smiling.

THE SAME NIGHT that Linda and I made this breakthrough in our relationship, and about the same time we were making our dinner plans, State Senator Blaine Clarkeson did a barefoot walk through his Virginia home, getting everything ready for bed. He settled himself down with a cigarette and a bottle of beer. Then he remembered to open the sliding doors to the veranda per his wife's instructions regarding cigarettes. A cool breeze stirred the living room.

"Honey," said his wife, Adrianne, when she saw the Dos Equis in his hand, "why are you going to bed so early?"

He gave her a kiss in response and said, "I'm going to the Beltway to see some people in the A.M."

"Oh really? Because whenever you kiss me before answering, I get the impression you're taking a moment to get your story straight."

He laughed nervously. He really did intend to go into D.C. in the morning so that he could make contacts that would one day help him rise to more than a state senator. But the real reason he wanted an early bed was because he was going to get a call shortly after six a.m. from their maid telling him that their house in upstate New York had been burglarized some time before she arrived there. She would also say that the power was out. If she was smart, she'd ask him if he wanted her to call the police from a neighbor's place. He would say yes of course. Then she would be the one to initiate the police report. The authorities in Felton would call him immediately to tell him what happened and he didn't want to be groggy and possibly say the wrong thing when he spoke to them.

Right about now, the "moving" company that he had engaged would be setting the place up to resemble a break-in, and they would temporarily remove his valuables. He had every confidence they would bring them back intact because the favor he'd done for them in Albany was going to net them much more money than the burglary scam would bring him. That was always the way of it. The bribe to him had to be smaller than the prize his constituents were seeking or they would never bite. In this case the bribe consisted only of labor and a modest risk. He'd left the alarm off in order to idiot-proof their task. His own reward would come to him in the form of a greatly inflated refund from the U.S. Treasury.

The staged break-in had worked the first time he'd done it, and Senator Clarkeson was sure it would work the second. Easy as downing a bottle of beer. Besides, if the movers got sloppy, his enforcer, Brinkman, would break that bottle and show them the edge of it.

"Find something to do without me tomorrow," he told Adrianne. "You don't want to be here. I'm going to be very busy."

THE NEXT NIGHT with Linda, I enjoyed the sort of doubt-free confidence that cut through all of her fears and encouraged her to respond in kind. We had our specialty, Chinese food, and it wasn't on her living room carpet this time. There were waiters and waitresses, tables and even hurricane lamps with flames tumbling brightly in the semi-darkness. Choy's Szechuan was a classy place, unlike the ones that consisted of a ten square foot waiting area for takeout, which we more commonly frequented. I had money in my pocket to pay for it too. Outside, a hard rain fell, but it only brought us closer together. Remembering the good results at her swimming pool, I splashed her with my umbrella before we sat. She gave me a quick kiss, a ruffle of my hair, and said, "Down boy."

We did the two-dish sharing thing. Linda insisted on ordering something I'd never had, and feeding me pieces of fish with her chopsticks. The very fact that we could get so comfortable with each other after so long was a vindication of what I'd been feeling all along.

The waitress, tagged as "Sue," rushed over and told us, "Not allowed."

I said to Linda, "See, I told you I'm not allowed to eat fish."

Sue interjected, "No, this, what you're doing, feed eating." Good name for it. "This feed to each other, no good."

"But I don't know how to use chopsticks. She does, so she helps me. We're only trying to act like civilized people."

"No, no, no, family place." Sue swiped an expansive hand at the tables with parents and their children. Apparently, she'd seen our actions as the start of intimate behavior. One thing leads to another, right?

"We're okay now," I said, raising my chopsticks so she could see them in my ham fist. "I'm going to learn." I was a good tipper, but Sue didn't know that.

The moment the waitress turned her back, Linda smeared my chin with duck sauce and said, "Now you have something on your chin. I can't believe what a slob you are."

I took my cloth napkin, soaked it in my water glass, and dabbed at my nose. "Did I get it?"

"No," she said, gesturing with her sticks. "Over there, on your other chin."

I dabbed at the wrong side of my face.

Saying, "Let me get that for you," Linda leaned across to me and licked my face. Boy, Sue the waitress was right. One thing really did lead to another.

"Did you get it, Lindy?" I asked.

"Yes."

"What did it taste like?"

"See for yourself."

It was duck sauce all right, and it tasted even better on her tongue. Stretching across the table was difficult so I came around to sit on her side for my second helping. "We should do this all the time."

Linda said, "Stop that. This is a family place." But she didn't chase me back.

"You're my family."

"There's something wrong with you."

I gave an exaggerated sigh. "I know. I like troublemakers."

"When have I made trouble?"

"How's your smoker?"

"My what?"

"The guy from your office, and the epic legal battle that got us back together."

"Oh that," she acknowledged with a smile.

I kissed her while my hands found one of hers. Thus engaged, I stroked the inside of her palm with my middle finger.

She slapped my hand and said, "I'm going to have to take out a restraining order on you at this table."

I laughed.

Our waitress Sue returned in a huffy mood and demanded to know what we were doing.

I told her, "I just realized we're waiting for two business people to join us, and neither of them likes this side of the table where we're sitting. We discussed it at length and left the other side open. It's a business decision."

Sue looked dubious but didn't know what to say to that. She had to move on when another patron flagged her down.

I remarked to Linda, "With all this trouble, no wonder we usually do take-out."

"How's the IRS?" she asked.

"Oh that," I said. "Where did my food go?"

"Other side of the table."

I said, "Right," and reached across to reclaim my plate and tea cup. "Yeah, I think they like me at the IRS. I've gone to full time with benefits and gotten some special management assignments that worked out well."

"That's fantastic. I knew you could do it. Is anyone out to get you?" she asked as she also went back to eating.

"Why do you say that? Out to get me?" I hadn't told her about the bomb threats or the Head of Household incident.

"I work in government. There's plenty of jealousy over someone like you. Do you have enemies yet?"

I poured a drop of tea and blew on it. Thinking of Virgie and Lucinda, two people I really shouldn't bring up, I lied, "No."

With a gulp of sticky rice, Linda assured me, "You will."

SENATOR CLARKESON HAD timed his vacation to end on the day after the break-in at his house. He and Adrianne arrived in Felton at night but the electricity had been restored, as per his instructions. He stood outside of the car and admired the lights beaming from his house on the hill, a traditional style home with five gables and a two-story family room marked by the high window over the entrance. His next abode would be a true mansion, which he had already picked out. Everything was going the way he'd planned.

"C'mon, Blaine" said Adrianne, "It's chilly. Let's get inside."

"Right. Leave the bags. Alma can get them. Earn her money for a change."

"Are you blaming Alma for the trouble now? It's not her fault there was a break-in before she got here."

"Even if she were here, she would have slept through it," he grumbled. He had to keep up a good front.

"We pay her little enough."

"Whatever."

They proceeded up the hill together. When they came close to the door, Adrianne pulled on his arm and said, "Wait, Blaine, are you sure it's safe for us to sleep here tonight?"

She was making him impatient. "Yes, Adrianne. The burglars are gone. They got everything of value. Why shouldn't it be safe?"

"I mean, they got right through our security."

"So?"

"Two years in a row…?" She was looking at him dead sober, not scared of burglars at all. She had it figured out. Or suspected.

"Shut up. Just shut up, okay? It's none of your business."

He pushed her in first, roughly, shut the door behind them, and reset the alarm. He saw no need to inspect the place for damages or to keep up any other pretense now, so he went straight to his office to open his mail. Once inside, he closed the inner door. The junk mail had already been removed—Alma had taken care of it—so that each item in the remaining mail pile was addressed, "The Honorable" on the envelope. Inside they all began, "Dear Senator."

In Washington, Clarkeson was called "State" Senator to distinguish between himself and U.S. Senators. In his home state he enjoyed the honorific of simply being called Senator. Since so many people were politically ignorant about the difference and didn't know the names of their federal government representatives anyway, the ambiguity managed to confuse them into giving him much higher honors and perks than he deserved. By age forty-two he was not doing badly. Clarkeson absolutely adored the patronage system and knew how to make the best of it. Feeling tired, and satisfied with himself, he set the mail down and went for the cigarette and beer, popping the bottle cap at a side table. Tomorrow he'd have plenty of time to read it all on a relaxing Sunday, and be well rested in time for work Monday morning.

Before he could fill both hands, he saw one last letter pinned under the stapler. He'd almost missed it. Why had that stupid Alma put it on the other side of his desk? When he reached for this one, his finger caught on a half-ejected staple and it pricked him. He cursed and tossed the stapler toward the closest wall where it chipped the paint and landed in a garbage pail. "Shit." As he sucked on his finger, he saw that the envelope was actually an old one turned over with a new piece of paper sticking out of it. He recognized his own powder blue stationery, and pulled the sheet. "What the hell?"

It said, "DON'T FORGET WHAT WE DID FOR YOU."

"The stupid bastards," he raged. "That's what they call discreet? Why didn't they just leave a signed confession for the police to find?" Thank God the police didn't look in his office after he told them that only the basement was robbed. And how the hell did these cheap hoods have the gall to throw the obligation in his face anyway?

In a fit, he shoved everything off the desk until all he had left was the phone. "Nobody fucks with me." Then he got his Marlboro pack and Dos Equis, and sat down. He took a deep breath, pulled a sip of beer, and dialed his enforcer, Brinkman.

THE WAY THEY had Taxpayer Service locked up on Sundays, I had to enter through the Garden Maze. From there, I had a chore to sort my way through before arriving at the pentapod room.

The IRS on a Sunday held acres of empty desks touched only by blue hints of sunlight from the far window. I could hear a couple of voices ahead of me under the single lit bank. Not a bright echoing sound but one deadened by the padded walls. Spooky. I felt like running around and turning all the switches on to at least get the normal lighting back. What was I doing here? This PBS thing that Lansdale had hooked me into came off as suspicious. Or I had developed a suspicious nature. Either way, I'd looked it up. Once I checked, I didn't expect to receive too many phone calls at this so-called IRS event. No one at T.V. Guide seemed to know about it. That could be a mistake, but if it didn't appear in T.V. Guide, the show would have zero ratings.

When I finally completed the transit, there stood Hector, as I suspected, along with Lad, and a guy named Wayne Patton, who had also been assisting managers. Facing them with her back to me was a high-class stranger with an hourglass figure. If she was a stranger, though, why did she resemble someone I knew? I was tired from my night with Linda, and I guess it was making me slow. The golden hair on blue pinstripes reminded me of the last time I saw...

Verna? Verna being sociable? When Lad, Hector and Wayne greeted me, the woman turned to reveal a thinner Verna Tucks, refreshed and looking prosperous.

"Wow, Verna. You look great." I struggled to keep my surprise from hurting her feelings.

"Hello, Mr. Shapiro."

Coming from most people I knew, using my surname would be a cold greeting. From her, it was just right. I hugged her and gave her my cheek but she managed to land her kiss half on the corner of my mouth. Some women are adept at that, and I didn't mind it either.

"You got a job somewhere?"

"Here." She wiped her lipstick off me.

"In another division?"

"No, here. I got my old job. They convinced me to take a leave of absence and then come back."

"I didn't know there was such a thing." Though I couldn't get a read on her, I said, "I'm glad you're back, and here on a Sunday."

"So am I," she said in a carefully modulated, professional tone. The extra day's labor appealed to her work ethic. For once she didn't say a word about any conspiracies, and I wondered if that was simply because conspiracies went without saying. I would miss that part of Verna if she was done with it.

Lansdale appeared. He broke us up with his two lifted hands like he was chasing off geese, and gave me a stiff nod.

"Anyone else coming?" I asked him.

He shook his head. "It's you five today."

So I was joined in this task by Hector, Wayne, Lad, and Verna Tucks: most of the conspicuous achievers club. I wondered idly why our group was so small. There had to be at least another five people who would have done an excellent job. My suspicious nature mused that four of us were under the scope, while Lad, who had already been around for several years, was thrown in as a distraction.

Oddly, Lansdale and the other supervisors sat us as far apart as possible, in different desks from our usual ones, claiming that it had something to do with which stations were switched on in the computer system on weekends.

They utilized the entire department, putting the nearest person approximately ten yards away from me. Since that arrangement made no sense, I assumed they actually didn't want us to be distracted by each other, or communicate in any way.

Lansdale ran the show, so I told him, "I just want to go get my reference books from my station."

"No. You won't need them."

Why the heck wouldn't I need them? Weren't we supposed to give out the most correct answers possible? And couldn't we do that best with reference material? *Not if they're testing you*, the old Verna would have said.

When the preparations were done, big Chief Foster and ADC Lansdale introduced us to the head of Quality Assurance, the head of PRP, and the research manager. I had already encountered the first, and had heard of the other two. No sooner did we all clasp hands than the management group scurried off to the restricted area behind the wall, from which I believed they would be monitoring us. The station was a good twenty-five yards from my spot. It reminded me of the way a doctor or a dentist runs away when administering an X-ray, to avoid the exposure. Or more aptly, I feared, the swift retreat of military scientists from a test site just before setting off an experimental bomb.

But really, why all these VIP's to monitor so few of us? It made sense that someone from PRP was represented on a day like this. The Problem Resolutions Program was the fast track for old and complicated problems. So, yes, if I were someone with a long-running problem, I'd be anxious to air my grievance in this forum. But having the rest of them preside over this event didn't make sense. The research manager, Eldon Swinney, also known as "El Don," was the most mysterious of all. For a reasonably thin man, his face was well rounded, like a giant thumb. Though I'd had no direct contact with him yet, he had studied me with intensity and contempt during the set-up phase. If someone had built the bomb this crew was setting off, it would've been him.

Together they represented nearly one brass button for each of us, or eighty percent coverage instead of the usual three to five percent coverage. And that was only counting the people who they allowed us to see. I knew there was always a man-behind-the-curtain as well. And why did they have to clear the room so quickly? Presumably to catch the very first calls to listen in on.

If this was a PBS thing, there must have also been call screeners deciding what got through. Right? We, or I at least, got a number of softballs to start. Plus, there were long gaps between each call, giving me an unaccustomed chance to rest.

Not half an hour into the program, Lansdale trotted out in a hurry. He had tape recorders for each of us and a stack of audiotapes. To me he said, "The phones aren't ringing that much. In between, I'd like you to play back these tapes."

"Play them back, why? What's on them?"

"Recorded messages from taxpayers ordering forms after hours. Get their contact information and what they want onto the order form. If the order sounds unreasonable, use your discretion."

This was the first I had seen of the procedure, a very simple one by itself. With all possible forms listed, you had only to circle the item and write the number requested. I found it surprising that someone at his level was handing out the sort of assignment usually doled out by the lower levels, but I couldn't say that.

Instead, I asked, "And why are we doing this now?"

"It's a backlog."

"Hmm, okay, no problem." I certainly didn't want to sit around doing nothing during those gaps. Why not find out what this little chore was like? Naturally, many people on tape spoke too fast and there was a lot of rewinding to be done. Then there were a good number who did not speak clearly. I rewound as much as necessary to be certain I got their orders right. For each person who didn't receive their forms, it was sure to generate a complaint call later and we needed as few of those as possible.

After a little while, the head of PRP popped out, a long-necked woman with an apologetic smile. This was getting weirder by the moment. She hurried to cover the distance to me. I couldn't remember her name. Joanie?

"Hi," she said to me with breathless enthusiasm, as if we were old friends and these get-togethers were our weekend routine.

"Yes, hi," I replied. *I'll have both a hamburger and a hot dog, please. I like them from the hot part of the grill if your hubby doesn't mind.*

But there were no refreshments. She said, "I've got some backlogged letters here that really need answering. They're technical questions." *What the hell was going on now? How could old letters really need answering in the middle of a public event?*

"Thank you for having confidence in me," I said diplomatically in hopes of dissuading her from piling it on. "Mr. Lansdale was out here a little while ago and he assigned me some tapes and forms to do."

"Yes, I know. Keep doing those, and also do these. Don't seal the envelopes. We'll do that."

You mean to say you will read all my responses before sending them out. I should hope so.

But they weren't challenging at all. What surprised me was how simple most of the questions were that got referred to Technical. I chose to make a reject pile for those the referring TSR should have been able to handle on their own.

Even as I worked the phones, filled forms requests, and answered technical questions, my mind worked feverishly on the central puzzle: What were we really doing here? By now I was halfway certain that the calls were faked. And once I allowed that possibility, another suspicion sneaked up on me regarding our invisible brass—perhaps they were the ones making the calls. If so, that would be truly bizarre.

I tried to see if I could recognize a disguised voice among the callers. Now that I was thinking along those lines, the voices did begin to sound familiar. It seemed absurd. Was I sinking into complete paranoia? I would not expect our band of VIP's to personally engage in an elaborate charade. The calls seemed fairly realistic but something I couldn't put my finger on marked them as not quite real. When I had processed enough calls, I had the nagging sense that the percentages were off, that there were too many of certain types of calls and not enough of the others. There were too many irate calls, for instance. One particularly annoying caller who accused me of being an "IRS shill," had trouble saying the letter "L," just the way our Division Chief spoke. I had to ask him to repeat his insult. A few calls later, someone with a different sounding voice had the same speech affliction. How crazy was that? Why would Chief Foster make prank calls to the IRS? In his own division no less?

These were dangerous thoughts. If we were being tested, I might stop treating the calls as real. Was I supposed to be especially nice to the Division Chief? Could I really go along with the farce of pretending he didn't know the answers to the questions he posed? Was all this second guessing throwing off my response time?

As my mind swirled, Joanie reappeared to collect my work from all over my desk, and I was surprised to see how large a pile it made. Moving with consistent alacrity, she took the blank forms too. I asked her, "Am I done with that part?"

"The whole event is over."

"So early?" I asked. "Is PBS happy with us?"

She narrowed her eyes. "Who?"

When Lansdale came to pick up the tape recorder, I asked him, "How did I do?"

He paused and screwed up his face as if weighing a great question in a mental catalogue of debates through history, and then he said, "You were okay."

El Don passed by in the background, caught my eye, and shook his head, "no," as though giving me a second opinion.

On my way out, Hector steered me to the side with his usual conspiratorial urgency. "The ACD doesn't work that way"

"What way?"

"At GBJ International we could have had people sit anywhere they wanted." He was referring to the computerized telephone routing system we had in common with his old shipping company. He meant that there was no need for us to sit so far apart.

"Yes, I suspected that; I don't know as much about Automatic Call Distribution systems as you do, but there were other clues."

Hector nodded thoughtfully. "They were testing us."

"You could have tipped me off sooner."

"I thought you'd figure it out."

"Yes, I did at some point." It hit me that Lad was not a wild card. He was there for comparison. Every scientific experiment has its control element, its measuring rod, so to speak.

With a little smile, Hector asked, "Was it the caller with the speech impediment that confirmed it for you?"

213

"You got it," I laughed.

After that, Hector Chavez and I would be given a very special job, one that had never existed before. Lad, Verna, and Wayne were sent back to work, and no one spoke of the Public Broadcast Service again.

ON MONDAY MORNING, FBI special agent Monroe Eastman received an alert on his terminal. It showed him a police report filed for a break-in at State Senator Blaine Clarkeson's Felton home. Eastman knew he could not discuss his suspicions about this information with his boss over interoffice mail, so he trudged down the hall and rapped on the door that read Tanglewood.

"Yes?"

Just inside the door, Eastman asked, "The Clarkeson break-in. Was that us?" Eastman was no kid, but new on the case and fresh out of training. He wasn't quite sure what the FBI might or might not do.

"Don't worry," said Tanglewood, "you would have been informed if we had done that." Tanglewood was thick in the waist, past his prime, and still roguishly handsome. With that face, Eastman couldn't tell if he was telling the truth or not.

"A real break-in then?"

"Not even. No, he's full of shit. We have it all on video from our surveillance on him. They used an unmarked truck at three in the morning, cut the electric to the alarm. In and out fast. These were obviously people that Clarkeson hired."

Eastman liked that Tanglewood never spoke like a cop, saying, "We *like* him for this." The FBI had time to make certain, and not go on hunches. Any speculation on a suspect's guilt—those you liked for a crime—was kept to yourself. Eastman asked, "Why do you figure it was staged?"

"He pulled this same crap last year," Tanglewood laughed. "He's out of town, maid comes in to find the place ransacked, blah, blah, blah. He thinks we're all stupid."

"Two years in a row? What for?"

"Tax dodge. A big theft is deductible. Great for us."

"Ohh, excellent. I know what that means. Now we contact the IRS to nail him for a two-year fraud." As a special agent, Eastman had arrest power and he was eager to use it.

"That step's going to be a while. We have to wait until he files."

"We'll have to get it assigned to the right guy at the IRS, too. We have anyone in the controlling district?"

"No one right now. Besides, whoever catches it, it does us no good if they know where it came from."

"Why not?"

"Because there's a lot of information we don't want to share with the IRS, such as our methods, our evidence, and why we didn't tell them there was a tax violation sooner. I want this absolutely insulated."

"Then I guess it can't be anyone in the senator's district."

"Obviously not, and we need a fearless Boy Scout type, someone sharp who's not intimidated by authority and not afraid of threats."

"Anyone on tap?"

"Maybe. We're already monitoring some IRS people now for down the road. In the meantime, we have a mountain of other things to follow up on. By the time it all comes together we'll have this crooked pol in a pincer."

Eastman stood in the doorway, still thinking about what kind of unfortunate deskman would catch it over at the Treasury Department. He reviewed what he'd seen in the Clarkeson file. The Senator came from Staten Island and had some juvenile assaults sealed up in the records. As an adult, he'd run a moderately successful cab company with a questionable insurance record, before going into politics. Twice, his opponents coincidentally got mugged and beaten up right after they announced their candidacy. Nowadays he was heavy into collecting bribes, had a zest for life, and liked to try a little of everything. "Is this Blaine Clarkeson dangerous?"

"You mean like a street thug?" asked Tanglewood. "Yeah, maybe."

CHAPTER ELEVEN
Enemies List

"Who are you to refuse my sugar? Who are you to refuse me anything?"

—Doctor Zhivago

On day six of my work week, when my head was deep in Virgie's paperwork, I heard someone with a faded Tennessee accent say, "Finish what you're doing and come upstairs." The speaker rested a pale knuckle on my desk. I followed the arm up and confirmed that it belonged to Ray Lansdale.

"Am I in trouble?"

"No," he said with an amused smile as he turned around.

I waited a respectable time and then went on after him.

In his office, he said without preamble, "You and Hector are to write a training course."

Resisting the urge to mimic him with, "We *'are to'*?" I asked, "On what?"

"On what you do." He crossed his arms. I'd once seen a street-fair chicken that supposedly did math with a lot of scratching and pecking. Lansdale was one of those. He had obviously been taking ass-covering lessons from his boss, Foster.

Trying to climb into the same feed trough with the ADC, I said, "I'm going to need you to parse that statement for me."

"You're going to teach new hires how the IRS works, procedurally, and how to present themselves on the phones. Everything you and Hector know. Everything but the tax law itself."

"That's a serious undertaking. When does this have to happen?"

"Immediately. Let me see the outline on Monday."

"*This* Monday?"

"Yes."

"And the training starts when?"

"This Monday, and the two of you will be in charge of it. You have today, Saturday, and Sunday to work on this." So generous.

"Am I still in charge of Teletax?" I hoped not.

"You are still in charge of Teletax. I don't want to hear about any resistance from the group managers on any of your assignments. Just deal with them."

"On the training, shouldn't Ladislav Ras be doing this, or at least joining us?"

Lansdale gave me an exasperated, "C'mon." When I didn't know how to reply to his sudden informality, he added, "No, he shouldn't."

"Swinney?"

"Not him either."

I wasn't going to get an explanation. Instead of a weekend of Linda and me, it was going to be a weekend of Hector and me. At least between the two of us *wunderkinder* we had three days of creation ahead.

Back downstairs, I sought out my Dominican friend. He was handing off some paperwork to Tammy Sangenario and pointing out a salient point or two while she nodded dutifully, but he was always anxious to confer with me. He could tell that I needed to talk, and in a few moments, we had our conference.

"I like that lady," he said of Tammy.

"I do too." When I had his full attention, I asked, "Did you speak to Lansdale yet?"

He shrugged. "We're supposed to train the new hires in IRS procedures."

"Right. After we create the training ourselves."

Patiently, Hector explained, "There's been no training program in this department for its whole ten-year existence. There's a reason for that."

I was excited at the challenge. "I think that between the two of us, we can create it."

"I don't put anything on paper. No exceptions."

"But that's our assignment. Otherwise it's just me."

"I don't do that," said Hector.

To clarify, at the risk of sounding dense, and because I was getting pissed off, I asked, "Don't do what?"

"Writing. That's your thing, not mine."

"Did you tell Lansdale you're not going to do this?"

He looked uncharacteristically sheepish for once, but he said, "I am going to do this training course. I'll do my input in the classroom."

I didn't like that reply very much, but I didn't see myself getting anywhere if I pushed it. That weekend, I jerry-rigged a training course outline complete with a starter set of overhead transparencies. All it took was blood, sweat, and tears. The tears were a product of my completely wrecked weekend on top of the previous half-wrecked weekend. I marveled that I did this with no help from Hector Chavez except that I made him examine the outline on Monday morning before I ferried it up to Lansdale. Hector had nothing to add or subtract, which was good, and then Lansdale approved my outline on the spot. He wanted to see the detailed version in a month. That same day, I immersed myself in a combination of seasoning new hires and supporting the Teletax deception. We still needed to pretend that the behemoth listened to people and responded. But as long as all of us people and machines were giving out good information, my conscience would not scream gory murder.

While I was in the training room, Eldon Swinney slipped in quietly and propped up the wall with his arms crossed. Unlike anyone in the building, he wore a black tweed jacket, cut long, with elbow patches. Even though I didn't really know him, I introduced our head of research to the recruits in glowing terms as a standard "for us all to aspire to," and I invited him to speak. He declined, and continued to monitor me from the side. I refrained from saying anything controversial but noticed that the next five minutes of his simmering anger was beginning to distract the class. What was with him?

I said, "Eldon, please jump in at any time if I'm mistaken about what I'm teaching here. I don't want to give anyone the wrong information."

At that he shook his head and left, making me wish I'd said something like that sooner.

When Hector came to relieve me, I popped out of the training room to make sure the rest of my responsibilities were going swimmingly. I had Lad overseeing the day-to-day of Teletax but the midday shift change happened to be Lucinda's turn to contribute staff, and acquisition of personnel had to remain my province if any of the group managers balked. I had no expectation of Lad standing up to her.

Lad warned me, "I have our emergency staff on Teletax."

"Lucinda's people were a no-show?"

"Yes, and I asked her why."

"Did she answer?"

"Yes, but I don't get it." His eyebrows were riding high. "What does it mean, this word, 'sacrosanct' in regard to her people? Is it French or English? It doesn't sound good."

I didn't have time for any nonsense. I supposed that Lucinda was testing how distracted I would be with my new responsibilities in training. As it turned out, I was not distracted in a way that was good for her.

She manned her station as usual, watching call times on her monitor with a wispy smile.

"Luce," I said softly, with a patience I didn't feel, "you have to release my people now." *Let my people go.* I was positively Mosaic about it.

"*Your* people?"

"Yes, that's why I had you sign off on the schedule. At the appointed times, some of your usual staffers are not in your control. I'm doing you the courtesy of not approaching

221

them and giving them orders directly. That courtesy will end abruptly in the next ten seconds."

Without leaving her seat or altering her icy glare at me, she shouted the names of two employees. When they looked up, she yelled, "Teletax!" The appointed ones scrambled to their feet and bolted for the back of the room.

To me Lucinda said, "I hope you know what you're doing."

I replied, "I do," but I didn't. Employees of the IRS hear a great variety of threats leveled at them, and most, no matter their source, are crude. Lucinda could have schooled every one of our detractors in the art of how to deliver a veiled warning. Her craft was as refined as it got, safely quotable because the hint of harm was all in the way she said it. I had a feeling that her revenge would be equally as classy—so stealthy, and served so frigid, that I'd never see it coming.

In retrospect I was probably not the nice guy I thought I was. If I were, then why did my list of enemies keep growing? Virgie and Lucinda were kind enough to take turns hating me. El Don, meanwhile, was building some kind of grudge I couldn't fathom. If he could snipe at me out of nowhere, how many others had me lined up in their sights?

CURT BRINKMAN LOCATED the weedy gravel walkway of Multiman Movers at the very end of the road in a quiet industrial park. He had briefly considered dressing down that morning for what might turn out to be a messy stop at these offices. Dressing down wasn't in his nature, so he compromised by getting out of the car wearing his usual

$800 suit and leaving the most delicate jewelry out of his ensemble. To keep things cleaner, he decided that his pistol could stay in the glovebox too. The kid wasn't worth a bullet.

Blaine Clarkeson's lawyer was known to the company he visited, and came off as respectable, so he had no problem getting buzzed in at the odd hour. Once inside, he located the sole occupant, a man too young to be ensconced behind the expensive desk in the honcho's chair.

Multiman Movers Unlimited of Felton, New York was at its core a family business, but nothing to do with Clarkeson's family. The younger son, Kyle Pennant, had not been as good as he thought at high school football. He'd earned the nickname "Bouncer" from flying at a three hundred pounder and then flying backward just as quickly. He'd messed up completely at college due to a severe wandering attention problem and questions about some women on campus that had been drugged and taken advantage of in their stupor. Now he worked for his father, who'd managed to bail him out. Around here, Kyle was just called Junior.

"My father's not here," Junior warned his visitor.

"I know that." Brinkman had made it his business to know the schedule over at Multiman, and he'd waited as long as it took for circumstances to align, which was two long weeks with Clarkeson demanding revenge. He knew that Kyle was in the middle of a month of lonely Saturday morning office work as punishment for getting caught stealing a female customer's underwear. Letting the disgust he felt creep into his voice, Brinkman snarled, "It's you I was looking for, Junior." Brinkman came at Junior fast, brandishing the rumpled powder blue stationery of the Honorable Blaine Clarkeson in his fist.

Junior focused more quickly than usual, but fumbled to get the gun out of the drawer while also trying to stand up. By that time, Brinkman was very close, and the terrified Junior couldn't situate his palm on the grip.

Brinkman slapped the pistol out of his grasp, and pinned Junior to the wall by his neck. The paper was interposed between Brinkman's ring hand and Junior's flesh.

"That's your handwriting on this paper, Kyle."

"I can't see it," he gurgled, "but so what?"

"This is the paper you left in the senator's house after the robbery. That's evidence that the police can use to hang all of us and it's in your handwriting."

"Sorry, I guess."

"You're going to eat it."

"What? No!"

As a former football player and current furniture mover, Junior must have felt fairly good about his physical prowess. Add to that, Brinkman was forty, and Junior was twenty-eight. Therefore, Junior made a serious attempt to remove Brinkman's tightening chokehold by pounding and pulling at the cabled arm that held him. But Brinkman was a workout king, much larger than Junior under his tailored suit and able to do some things that other lawyers in his specialty couldn't. In circumstances such as these, he had no need to hire muscle who could later testify about the reasons Brinkman engaged them on Clarkeson's behalf. He was his own muscle.

Brinkman yanked one of Junior's hands away from his arm, and when Junior held up that hand defensively, Brinkman interlocked his fingers with Junior's in the manner of a dance partner. Without breaking eye contact, he twisted his grip a hundred and eighty degrees clockwise and bent Junior's hand back slowly so that he could count off three distinct and sickening pops. Junior made a mewling sound.

"You have two more fingers on that hand," the lawyer calculated as he released Junior's neck. "Now you chew up this stationery and swallow."

The fistful of paper came at Junior's mouth and he had the choice of opening up or getting his teeth bashed. He opened wide and let Brinkman mash it against his tongue. As tears coated his face, he ground the evidence down with the slow progress of a cow compacting hay. When it was small enough, he swallowed hard and showed Mr. Brinkman his empty mouth.

Brinkman said, "Good job."

Then Junior wailed, "You broke my fingers. How are you going to explain that to my father?"

"With the truth. His son was careless on a very important job, and it resulted in an accident. Maybe that will remind Mr. Pennant that the moving business is dangerous."

MY NEW-HIRE TRAINING program was going great. Every morning I completed and revised more sections based on the live results of the previous day. That's what I was doing when Lansdale stopped in front of me without saying hello. Peremptorily, he dropped a rubber-banded package of papers on my desk, and said, "Fix this."

Ray Lansdale was some kind of a genius hiding a passion inside, and most of the time he could also come off as very stiff. The way he dropped the bundle in front of me, I would have thought it made him sick.

"What is it?" I asked. "Fix it how?"

"It's the Taxpayer Service Division Manual. It needs editing. Mark it up. Make any changes you want."

Any changes I want??? "Wait a minute," I said as he was walking away. "What if I want to introduce a new procedure?"

"That's the point. It's not the grammar that needs fixing."

Extraordinary. This was the Manual that everyone in the country used. The manual that every Taxpayer Service Division Chief had to abide by. And now I was making the rules? This was my chance to bring more fairness to the system. When I was on the phone, I was just one person trying to avail people of their rights rather than burying them in confusion.

I saw that Lansdale—or someone—had already made a few notes in pencil and abandoned the effort. It occurred to me that the rules governing service complaints and appeals were already worked out and didn't need my tampering. It truly was the way the IRS went about their business that had people climbing the walls. I could now call for real customer service in our division. Theoretically, if management didn't want me promoting fairness and passing along my methods, they wouldn't have put me on the job. But I'd been wrong about such things before.

More to the point, these extra assignments came with a monumental downside. They were keeping me from Linda at a time when our relationship needed to be solidified. Linda was well aware of this danger too. She threatened to come down to my office and apply for a job just so she could see me. I had half a mind to let her.

While I drifted in contemplation, I must have looked unusually idle. Verna sauntered by and said, "Is there anything I can do to assist you, Mr. Shapiro?"

I stood and said, "Thank you for the offer, Ms. Tucks. There may be. I'll take your suggestion under advisement."

She smiled broadly and continued on her way.

Virgie sidled up next to me the way Hector always did, and hung near my shoulder. It startled the hell out of me when she whispered, "Is that your new piece of ass now?" She was mad we'd never had any follow-up sex. All I wanted was Linda, and in fact I was with her again, but here I was caught in the crossfire of my mistakes.

I should not have replied immediately—probably not at all—but I was thinking that the Witch of Taxland looked awful today whereas Verna had come up smoking hot and was more professional than ever. "Why, were the two of you switched at birth?" Luckily that came out pretty cryptic and Virgie declined to answer that.

In the days to come, I laid out the small, loose pages of the division manual with the care I would have given to an archeological find. But then I read the document with new eyes, and saw that some of the procedures defied common sense. As I shrugged off my trepidation, my red felt-tip pen flowed over the manual until it looked like someone had laid a drop cloth under a Civil War battlefield. In a show of Treasury Department alchemy some clerk would go type my amendment up, and the Government Printing Office would send official copies to HQ in Virginia. Hard to believe. But it wasn't as if anyone actually read the book, did they?

By the time I finished, it was late November and I was close to the moment of truth regarding a promotion I'd applied for. When Virgie beckoned me over, I had a feeling I knew why. As my manager, it was Virgie's responsibility to complete the Job Element Appraisal in response to my application for the Specialist position, a moment that was no doubt fraught with conflict for her. My ascent to that milestone would mean two things to Madam Virgie: One, that she would lose me to another group immediately, and two, that I could potentially be promoted above her, which she would find awkward to say the least. And we *still* hadn't had any follow-up sex. I was determined to keep that from happening. If Virgie planned to be as predictable as I expected, she would do everything in her power to scuttle my chances.

She laid her handwritten evaluation of me on the desk and said, "Read it in front of me. You have to sign it."

"I could walk away and sign it too," I offered absently as I scanned the two-page grid. When I saw how badly she'd gone overboard, I determined it would be better to stay and discuss it with her in the cause of mutual entertainment.

I cleared my throat in an effort to distract from my wry smile. She had decided to award me unrealistic ratings in every element, some scores as low as a 2. I wouldn't attack her decisions all at once, but some of it…

"Virgie, I couldn't help but notice the number you gave me in the category of Procedural Instruction."

"I gave you a four."

"...out of five."

"No one is perfect."

"Do you have any new procedures for me that I don't know about?"

"No," she said warily.

"Then that's a five." I wrote this down.

"What do you mean?"

"Aside from the fact that I was authorized to re-write the procedures? I would bet anything that you've never read the manual and have no idea whether I'm following the old procedures, my new ones, or none at all."

"You can't give yourself a score."

"In my response I can. Next matter: why did you complain that I don't have WAR skills?" Those were a set of secret codes, the central tools of the very job I had recently applied for, and she knew that.

"Because you were never trained in them."

"Right, because that's not part of my job in your group. It shouldn't have appeared on the evaluation at all, yet you show it as a critical element of my current work."

She shrugged. "If you can't teach WAR to me, what good are you?" She was being goofier than usual.

"You don't need to know the program either!" I reminded her. "It's not even legal for you to know it. This appraisal is all going to have to be revised."

"What do you mean? What are you writing down?"

"My notes for the rebuttal." I had the right to submit a rebuttal to any and all of her evaluation. It was a lot of work but it would be great fun. As it turned out, my superiors actually read things like that. Also, she wasn't the only person evaluating me and comparing data. The walls had ears and also a pen.

She leaned forward, anxious to see what I was writing. "What if my review stands up to your rebuttal?"

"Oh, then you'll be totally destroyed."

"What do you mean?"

"If I was doing great under other managers and terribly under you, then who do you think looks bad? They'll say they gave you a chance to shine with my support and you killed the Golden Goose."

She stared at me and bit her lip in a way I couldn't read. Self-pity? Calculation? Horniness? All three? Truthfully, the last option was always something I hoped for in a woman's stare, so I may have been reading into it against my better judgment.

Finally, she said in a silken voice, "You want to earn a better appraisal, don't you?" There it was.

"I don't need you to change it. I just explained why."

"It would save you a lot of trouble though." Trouble that she had caused in the first place.

I moved close enough to tell it to her dainty little ear. "I don't need you, sweetie. I'll take care of this on my own."

She grabbed my lapel to hold me in place as I tried to retreat. "Danny, I need to talk to you in private."

"Been there and done that, love." I especially resented that our former intimacy, however brief, and all of the ways I'd improved her group's performance, did not keep her from trying to hurt or extort me. I hoped she didn't hear the regret in my voice, but I had to stay strong. Now that Linda was back in the picture, I didn't want to risk our relationship by going another round with Virgie or anyone else.

"What can I do then?" she asked.

"Play it straight for once. Retrace your steps and do an honest evaluation. Save yourself a lot of trouble."

"No."

Rather than walk it back, she fell into a pout as deep as any ensorcelled fairytale slumber. By choosing not to change the evaluation, she'd made the unwise decision to test me. One thrust from her. One parry with my mighty pen. This contest saddened me a little. I suppose it wasn't right to think that I could change her.

In the days that followed, no one gave me any feedback on the situation, but coming events would tell me whether this gambit of hers had blown up in her beautiful face or mine.

AS THE YEAR 1985 drew to a close, I saw the biggest knot of employees since Head of Household mounted his rampage. This time they seemed focused on the wall between manager stations. When I got over there, I found a strange assortment of upper and lower ranks jostling like wildebeests at an African watering hole, which was not unlike the crowds at off-track betting. Wayne Patton slinked away from the wall like he'd been slapped by it. He explained to me, "The promotion list is up for our district."

That's what this was about? How long did it take to read a list? Too long, it seemed.

I got in there and jostled with the best of them, catching some unfriendly stares along the way. Patton dove back in with me to watch my reaction.

Only two names in our POD showed a positive result. Wayne Patton's and mine. We had each been promoted to Taxpayer Service Specialist. I'd applied at the behest of Tammy Sangenario and knew nothing about it except that beginning on Monday, instead of being called a TSR, I'd be a TSS. I gathered that this change of initials was a big deal because of the dark and ominous looks directed at us from those who did not climb the ladder. Why then were we getting that same look from our mysterious back office maven, Eldon Swinney? This gaze was subtly different from the way he usually sized me up, a notch more intense. He leaned against the doorway to the research section in casual alertness like a gunslinger waiting for me to draw first. Why did El Don care if Patton and I got promoted? He was already a TSS, and the established kingpin of the realm. As if to prove it, he struck up a match and started a cigarette, never taking his eyes off us. Eldon was the only one in the building allowed to smoke indoors.

"Why is he staring at us like that, Danny?" said Patton, who drooped even more than the last time I looked at him.

"I was wondering the same thing, Wayne. What'd you do to cheese him off?"

"Me?" He sounded petrified.

"Relax, just kidding."

"I think I'm going to give it back," said Wayne.

"Give what back?"

"The promotion."

"Are you crazy?"

"I don't want to be despised, especially by him." It occurred to me then that I hardly knew Wayne Patton, and I wasn't sure who did. Unsurprisingly, no one ever asked this timid gentleman if he were related to the general by the same name.

"Aren't you thirty years old and have a family to support? Or am I thinking of someone else whose wife is going to murder him?"

"No, you're right," said Wayne sadly. "I'm just not good with pressure."

"Then you won't be good with the alternative. Why don't you keep the new job and see if you can get used to it?" Hell, I needed someone to take the heat with me.

"Maybe you're right."

"Of course I'm right."

Tammy came bouncing up. "Congratulations, guys."

"Thank you," I said for both of us. "Now what does it mean?"

"The end of your captivity with Virgie."

"Where am I going?"

"Out of her group at least. Virgie has…let's say…fallen out of favor. She's been asked to take a leave of absence."

"Wow, that's… sudden. Is she ever coming back?"

"No one knows. You didn't hear the news from me." She pulled me clear of Patton, and spoke softly, "I have a job opening for you."

"Didn't we just do that? The result posted on the wall?"

"This is in Examinations."

"Oh."

"Now you can apply for a job as a Revenue Agent from a more impressive position."

This revelation elicited from me a bigger, "Oh." Nothing happened in a vacuum. Everything in our world was connected and consequential in some way.

"Yes, oh."

"More to the point, thank you. I owe you everything."

She waved off that exaggeration but seemed to appreciate my flattery.

Then I said, "What does El Don want from me?"

She turned towards the research section, saw him there, and turned back to me. "He's an asshole. Now get to work. You're working for me and also covering Virgie's group on alternating days starting today."

Now I'd get to see if working for Tammy was the treat that I thought it was. I headed for my appointed territory and saw Hector approaching from the other way.

"Your turn to cover Virgie's group tomorrow," I told Hector as we passed in the aisle.

He stopped me with a friendly punch in the arm. "I never got a chance to congratulate you."

"For what?"

Hector flashed what looked like a victory sign. "That's twice now you fucked Virgie." He obviously considered the second time to be her forced leave of absence, but I was grateful he didn't endeavor to describe either of these instances. Both events were pretty messy.

"I'm not proud of it," I said.

He shrugged. "I would be."

I wasn't as sure as Hector was that everything was coming up roses. Way across the deep field we called our POD, over the heads of the rank and file who were nodding and peaceful like plains grasses, El Don's cigarette was all ash, and still he stared at me in rapt contemplation.

At length, he started ambling toward me, back in gunfighter mode.

I awaited him stoically, wishing I had a long coat and a tumbleweed-strength wind.

When the research chief arrived, he tossed a pile of rubber-banded papers over the railing of the manager's desk next to me. The bundle caught my attention, covered as it was in red felt tip pen, in my handwriting.

"I read this," he said with a grim smile, finally taking the filter from his mouth and tossing that at the desk too. "It was good."

SPECIAL AGENT EASTMAN was just back from a conference in Chicago—a total waste of time. He was about to unlock his desk when he got called to Tanglewood's office. He went down the hall and felt a little rush when he noticed Katie Spindel's name on the work board even though it was just a wooden block placed in the column "available for cases." There were only two other names there since very few people called attention to themselves this way and usually they were first-month agents. He continued to the boss' office and rapped on the open door frame when he got there.

Tanglewood came around the desk and urged him out of the doorway so that he could peek out into the hall before shutting the door. He seemed eager to spill some news, and by the look on his face, it was hilarious.

"What's going on?" asked Eastman.

"Multiman Movers must have messed up big time on their job for Clarkeson."

"How's that?"

"You've been missing all the fun," he laughed. "We got the camera feed from their office before the original was destroyed. A warrant let us tap their surveillance cameras. We couldn't see everything, but we know Brinkman went to see that pervert Kyle Pennant when he was all by his lonesome. Junior ran out of there weeping."

"Weeping?"

"Yes, with his hand wrapped in toilet paper. He's out getting some broken bones set right now." Tanglewood was enjoying this too much. "Want to watch the tape?" He picked up a remote control.

"Maybe later. Should we pick up Brinkman for the assault or have the cops pick him up?"

"Absolutely not."

"To which one?" asked Eastman.

"We do neither," Tanglewood replied, tossing the remote in a drawer and slamming it too hard. "We're at least a year away from the multiple count indictment that Clarkeson and Brinkman deserve."

Was there something wrong with being concerned about public safety? "Have you seen this gargantuan Brinkman? You may not care about Kyle Junior, but don't you think that pretty soon this goon's going to hurt someone that doesn't need hurting?"

"Never happen. We'll shut down the show the moment they plan anything really bad."

I hope we know how to keep track of it that well, thought Eastman. *I'm not sure we're that precise.*

"Do we really have the personnel to keep track? Have you considered adding Katie Spindel to the task force?"

Tanglewood narrowed his eyes. "She say something?"

"Not at all. I just feel like I took her spot and we need more eyes on this."

"Don't let her say that," he replied at high volume. "No one has a spot. You put your best people on your best jobs." Then he sighed, adding, "Anyway, she'll be on it regardless when the probe expands."

Eastman thought he heard a note of regret.

"Take these." The boss handed him some files without explanation, as though in punishment for being obtuse. Was it? As Eastman took a moment to look them over, he mentally replayed the moments since he entered the office. Tanglewood's exuberance had quickly given way to irritation that Eastman didn't seem to share his excitement about the turmoil in Clarkeson's camp. His boss was right to look for cracks in his enemy's armor, but the abrupt change in demeanor worried Eastman that Tanglewood was brittle, wounded by some previous trauma. Despite Eastman's continued reservations about how they were handling Brinkman, he didn't want to be the one to rip the bandage off.

CHAPTER TWELVE
Unraveled

"The battle's finished. The jungle wins."

—*Asphalt Jungle*

Monday, January 6, 1986 (Tax Season)

Disaster was fast approaching and I never saw it coming. Yes, I saw certain difficulties ahead, clashes and ugliness, battles and attendant scars, trash littering the road to my destination. Never a collapse of everything I held sacred. As my little niece would say with a shrug, "All gone! Oh well."

When January dawned feisty and bitter, formal training sessions were kaput. Up until then, our top-level, gold leaf policy regarding preparation could best be described as, "Olly olly oxen free, ready or not, here I come." This year I hoped to improve upon that formula. Some regions of the world still recognize the more ancient version of the call out, "All ye, all ye, in-come free," but we would never say something that sounded like "income free" at the IRS.

In the spirit of this playful season, Lansdale called, "Heads up," and tossed me a key to the storeroom, which I caught overhand. I remembered how Virgie and I had used her copy, and I hoped his intentions were not the same as hers. Just in case, I kept a close watch on him as he went away, and then I proceeded to the supply room alone to do my inventory.

CREDS: THE IRS ADVENTURE

Our dented landmark was gone, but I found some brand new treasures. Voluminous boxes of internal forms, Package X's bundled with all of the external forms, blue and red pens, and sundry desk fixtures. I'd only spanned a single tax season myself, but that was enough to know how valuable this stuff was considered when the fur was flying. Now I was the sole quartermaster.

Or maybe Hector Chavez had a key as well. He kept his cards hidden. Hector and I were now the official On-the-Job Instructors. I was actually the program head. Ladislav Ras was my official assistant. As filing season 1986 dawned in the New York Metropolitan Area, the public would be served by seven "old timers"—the remainder of the Class of '85 as we called ourselves, including Verna Tucks and Wayne Patton—not to mention five super-old timers who had taken up positions on the telephones as retirement jobs, plus one hundred new hires who were essentially in my care. I should have been riding high.

When I emerged from the supply room, I noticed a young man named Warren who did a daily stagger to and from his desk. When he grabbed the wall to steady himself, I could see that the skin of his hands wore the purple that comes from chronic inebriation. Even when he wasn't speaking, an open sewer of soured Jack Daniels made its escape through his pores. I traced another line of that odor and found the bottles filling a drawer in his desk. As he grew increasingly dysfunctional in the following weeks—amazing he lasted that long—I had no choice but to give him the two counseling sessions that paved the road to the exit. He was barely awake for them.

How many whelps would survive this year? Certainly not surly ones like this. Yet I felt as though firing people would be bad karma so I tried to counsel his errant ass into shape.

Tammy Sangenario, bless her soul, did not doubt my judgment when I explained the situation to her. In fact, Warren's behavior did not surprise her. She said, "You're required to have more than one warning conference with him before he's let go. Then write him up and I'll send him packing."

Who would have thought you could fire someone from the government? Having Tammy as my new manager was like living on one of the lower branches of Heaven. But since Tammy ultimately acted on my recommendation and Warren ended up losing the job, I figured there was one strike of karma against me.

Strike two was a smart young man who didn't want to pick up the phone at all.

Strike three, an adorable older woman, was the interesting one. Sadie Greenwich picked up her first call and said, "Hello, hello, 1040 speaking."

"That's a live call," I reminded her. "People can hear you."

She said proudly, "I know."

At first, the only theory that made sense to me was that Sadie had a great sense of humor coupled with some horrendous judgment that made her think she could say goofy things on a government line. Naturally, I ordered her not to do that. When I listened to her for an extended period, and she brought out the puppet theater voices representing various other government forms performing a play, it was clear to me that she was marvelously off her rocker.

So I chased my responsibilities hither and yon, stopping only once to ask Hector, "What did I do to deserve this?"

He said, "There's a quote from the Bible. You sow the wind; you reap the whirlwind, and the IRS sucks wind."

I intended to look up this bit of scripture later, but I was fairly sure he had added the last part.

Tax season was indeed a whirlwind, draining every last scrap of energy you owned. Even tax practitioners outside of government quailed at the thought. I dropped the axe on each of our horror shows and Tammy carted off the heads. How she stayed so cheerful while dealing with our most disruptive employees I never knew. Having to terminate jobs was a fresh and painful experience for me. Fortunately, those three were the extent of it. Three others, who were lesser evils, left us of their own accord. I kept all their nameplates in a small pile in my desk drawer to remind me that these were real people, their loss the ugly cost of quality customer service.

So out of one hundred souls hired, we had our choice of ninety-four for the season and beyond. Everyone who remained qualified to work next year, which was the best record in a history where virtually none survived. The New York press benignly neglected us, and I shined as a manager that winter. Alas, they say that it's not the fall from a great height that kills you. It's the sudden stop for pizza at the end.

The happy pandemonium kept its flavor until one day in the beginning of March. As I waded through a swarm of inquiries from the first year employees, Tammy snaked her arm under mine and tugged me gently away from the crowd.

Thus linked, we strolled like a debutante and her date going to cotillion. A couple of the new hires stood as we neared them, tried to assess the situation, and melted back, puzzled.

I said, "So far I like where this is going, Tammy. You can rest your head on my shoulder when you feel the urge. We can fly to Vegas in the morning…or not."

She smiled and said, "We're just taking a walk. You're being transferred to another branch." We were close enough for her to feel my pulse rate increase. Apparently she wanted to make sure I didn't escape.

"Another branch of Taxpayer Service? How is it I've never heard of that?"

"It's in formation."

"Oh." Since she was one of the few people who revealed things to me, albeit belatedly, a lot of my conversation with her included that sort of, "Oh." To that, I added, "When will this happen?"

"As of Monday you will have a new job, a new manager, and new hours." She was still bright and chipper.

"Who will be the head of OJI's then?"

"That position will be inherited by Hector."

The lower branches of Heaven were temporary ones. I missed Tammy already, and I wondered how this move would impact my career. No one ever let you know if these capricious shifts were up, lateral, or down.

I said, "Tammy, I don't know about this. We're waltzing towards Research, where our paperwork goes to die."

Smiling at my joke, she swatted my arm and said, "It doesn't go to die. It gets processed."

"Like old horses get processed. There's a cartoon picture of a cow on those plastic bottles, as though glue is made of milk, but I know better."

"Shut up," she said. "We're almost there."

"Fine. Just let me know when I have to start behaving myself."

"I already hit you as a signal."

"That's what that was? I thought you'd spotted a horsefly."

She gave me a punch in the ribs with her tiny fist as we went through the door.

"What are we doing right now?" I asked her.

"You're meeting your new branch chief. This will be a good thing."

"Do I get to keep my assistant?"

"No. Shut up."

We went through a door and Tammy said, "Danny Shapiro, this is our new Branch Chief, Margo Kirliew."

Margo Kirliew was on her feet, a stunningly beautiful fortyish military type with penetrating brown eyes, her face framed by auburn hair in an attractive above-the-ears cut. I had the impression she was taller than me, although levels of respect have always colored my perception of height, and I had instant respect for this woman. I knew that all career moves were fraught with danger, but Margo's radiant and competent smile registered with me as genuine.

Once the introductions were secured, Tammy faded a few steps backward.

I said, "Are you going out for a pass?"

"I'm leaving you two to get acquainted."

I followed Margo to her office, a temporary space carved out of our division boundaries with a doorless section of Garden Maze wall. Framed by a bright yellow panel, she said, "It's an honor to finally meet you."

Since Ms. Kirliew was the new branch chief, that should have been my line. "Whom do you mean?" I asked politely.

She laughed and said, "I know everything you've ever done here and it's magnificent."

Magnificent? I couldn't recall having heard a compliment inside of this building since Lucinda said I was, "good." The IRS had put me through my paces in a manner that only government can do. In a place where information flow went only one way, feedback had been minimal. Now here was someone I had never even glimpsed, saying such bizarre things about me, that I experienced a mental disconnect. "I'm sure you've mistaken me for someone else."

She kept her powerful smile. "The assistant manager program, the URP, Teletax, PBS, the TPS training program, the procedures manual, and the OJI program."

I wiped my forehead and said, "That stat list makes for one hell of a boring baseball card."

She laughed again and it was a beautiful laugh. "I know your voice from hundreds of hours of telephone calls, and your writing style from dozens of letters."

So she was one of the people I always suspected was behind the scenes. As much as I wanted to like Margo, her knowledge of me was the fruit of a staggering harvest of spying.

I sat down, uninvited, and she watched me process the information. At the end of all the testing, all the prodding and poking, here was the denouement. Like the most ridiculed part of an old action movie, where someone steps out from the shadows. *Congratulations, Bond, you found my lair.*

Yet it has to be that way. Sooner or later those who study you have to meet you face to face. They have to interact with you in order to fully understand you. The last and best test of all. Only she didn't really have the hang of the Goldfinger role because she capped it off with, "Someday you'll be Division Chief... It would be an honor if I could work for you."

Okay, that was creepy. How could *she* end up working for *me*? Was she another Verna Tucks?

I reminded myself that this was my boss talking. No, my boss's boss. I looked at her to see what she meant by it. She was bursting with pride, on the edge of tears, clearly humbled. I shook my head. Maybe you had to be there for all those months on the other side of the spyglass to understand this. I didn't get it. Plus it was hard to enjoy this approbation on any level because this was also the part of the Bond movie where something terrible was about to be done to our hero.

Do you expect me to talk?

No, Mr. Bond, I expect you to die.

On cue—no doubt because he could hear everything around the corner—El Don slinked in, attempting to go unnoticed, the same tactic he'd employed during my training class. I still had excellent peripheral vision, so I turned his way to show him he wasn't fooling me.

Margo said, "Before I break down any further, I'd better introduce you to Eldon Swinney."

As I've said, Eldon looked as though his features had been imprinted on a giant thumb emerging from a suit. It struck me that his face appeared to be perpetually hitching a ride.

I shook his limp hand, saying, "We've sort of met before."

In a thick voice, he ordered, "Let's go. We have a lot to talk about."

We went off into another set of dividers that weaved on until I couldn't figure out where we were. Most of the long florescent bulbs in the ceiling were dark or twitchy. People at the IRS were forever taking me for walks in pursuit of private discussions, as if there were any such thing as private in that building. Why did I feel like begrudging El Don the same opportunity? Well for one thing, he appeared to be screwing up the courage to say something I wouldn't like.

"Are you here to train me?" I asked, in order to draw him out.

"Something like that."

"Are we in the training area now?" He'd actually led me to a brutish war surplus desk that was supposed to be mine now, snugged nose to nose against his. They'd been nice enough to move my nameplate here. We didn't sit though, so I had the feeling that this meeting was intended as a fleeting encounter.

"Listen Creds," he hissed. "You're a Bush Leaguer in the Big Leagues now."

"Meaning what?"

"I'm the tech guy around here, not you." He went for a cigarette and planted it in his mouth while he struck a match. "I don't know how or when, but I will get you fired, and it will be soon."

I've mentioned that the IRS often bore a striking resemblance to the U.S. Army. I wanted to ask Eldon if he was the sort of army man who liked to travel to new places, meet interesting people, and then kill them. But contrary to popular opinion, I don't antagonize anyone until it's necessary. Besides, I like when people are straightforward.

ON THE MAGIC Monday that I was to start my new job, I rattled in on a quiet post-rush hour train and reported for work near high noon braced for the next set of surprises. Taking no chances with my reticence, Tammy once again led me across to the far end of the enormous hollow space we called home, and introduced me to my immediate manager, Janis Decamarche.

Tall, slim Janis gave me the up-and-down appraisal a mother gives a little boy who claims he has dressed himself warmly enough to go outdoors. "He'll do." Then she realized how that sounded and gave me a little smile and a laugh.

The funny thing was that Janis-with-the-motherly-instinct was an Erin Brockovich type, a startling dresser with a killer bod and a brilliant mind fit to revolutionize project management. It had leaked that some were comparing me to her, as well as to Chief Foster, and I didn't know what to make of that. Killer bod maybe. I did not consider myself as smart as either of them and had no desire to don a leather skirt.

Such were the circumstances where I began to work the "night shift," which in fact combined day and night by reaching from noon to nine. I would go along with this new schedule for a while and then try to squirm my way out of it. Keeping this up for too long would make seeing Linda near impossible.

Inconveniences and El Don's threats notwithstanding, I did get excited every time another curtain was drawn back. Here I finally had my look at our mysterious data retrieval system. Ironically dubbed WAR, for Write And Respond, this was the most ingenious cryptology masterpiece ever invented in peacetime. But considering it had been set in place the year of the Vietnam War's end, perhaps its name was no coincidence at all.

At the outset, all I saw was a screen full of flying numbers. Since I was learning the system together with a couple of people who had transferred in from another office, I examined their faces to see if they were as bewildered as I felt. "How do you get past the screen saver to the work screen?" I asked Janis as I hit the space bar a couple of times.

"You don't," said Janis. "What you see is what you get."

"You mean, that's not a screensaver?"

In WAR, every line and condition having to do with a tax return had its own numeric code, so that all you would ever see was a rain of falling green numerals on a dark backdrop much like in The Matrix, a tale of unreality yet to come. The story the symbols told came in scrambled "paragraphs" so that only someone who was both a system expert and a tax compliance expert had a shot at understanding what they glimpsed. That dual requirement described the entire staff of our department. The order of the "words" was random like a shattered wall of hieroglyphics, and there were other fascinating security elements I will withhold from description. Rumor had it that this wondrous programming came courtesy of our partners at the NSA, and it was obvious that this design was what had rendered all hacking attempts futile. If anyone slipped past the firewall, they would never comprehend what they were looking at, and no single employee, including Janis, understood the whole picture.

Adding to the general security arrangements, Janis warned us of the number one prohibition, "Do not ever enter the names of politicians and other famous people."

"Why not?" asked a young lady named Monique who thought it was sexy to play provocative and dumb.

"Because they're specially flagged," explained Janis. "If you were to try to access such information, an alarm wired to our Inspection office would sound, and you would be surrounded by our in-house SWAT Team." In those days the IRS was serious about violations of the Hatch Act and anything else to do with privacy.

With an impish grin, Monique said, "I'm gonna do it when y'all are not around."

I told her, "Don't even joke about that," because by this time I knew enough about the IRS to understand that the SWAT Team boast could be true. I also knew that if you accessed anything that wasn't tied to a specific request as part of an assignment, your digital footprints were all over it. Treasury was way ahead of the world on this one.

"Is your name really Creds?" Monique asked.

DURING MY JANIS Decamarche days, I had the challenge of learning WAR while answering technical letters and fending off the objections of Eldon Swinney. He was ostensibly training me in answering inquiries, but all his work consisted of telling me I was wrong about anything I happened to say. When you got to know him, Eldon Swinney was more than a thumb. He was like Lewis Carroll's dope-smoking Caterpillar; either creature would languidly contradict you all day long.

Janis never interfered with Eldon's game, but I liked her nonetheless. My new manager turned out to be a supremely competent one. When Janis snapped instructions at us, they were always clear and sensible orders, and she did it while juggling her domestic situation long-distance, which was a divorce proceeding in Florida. I couldn't help but overhear the frequent heated phone calls on that subject. It surprised me, because I could not imagine what kind of man, once wed to her, would choose to divorce her or put himself in a position where she wanted a divorce.

Though I paid close attention, I was not at all confident in my WAR skills. The time came when I made a mistake, and any mistakes in this department carried consequences. Part of Janis's success as a manager came because she was such a powerful leader by example. She was not the sort of person you wanted to let down, so her withering criticism, when it finally came my way, was all the more devastating.

The fact was that dumb-act Monique was taking to this secret code business and I was not. I had misread the screen one day, taken some incorrect action I still didn't understand, and there was no denying it, so naturally I said, "I'm sorry, but it's all your fault, Janis."

"*My* fault? How?"

"Because" I said, "how am I supposed to concentrate on my job when my manager is so beautiful?" With her powerful maternal instinct and all, Janis was a supremely sexy woman. These were the days when you could sometimes compliment a coworker without paranoia setting in. Even the way I did it, you had to be sure first that the attention would be welcomed if you wanted to say it to your boss and live.

She must have liked me because in answer she turned her head away in modesty, and in the one-quarter profile left to me I could still discern that she was smiling.

"Wow," I observed. "You're blushing." She hadn't been, but when I said that, she did.

Scanning the interior of our complex she said, "I think you need a break. Cover the phones."

Tax season had not ended. Everyone was expected to pitch in, so my third job was my old job: supervising the pentapods when things got hot. I saw a man whose clothes came exclusively from the big and tall shops. He was near the center, gaining his feet and gesticulating wildly. He was probably the reason Janis wanted to deploy me to that area. The people I'd trained were not such a handful as this one. Ted Solis, however, had transferred in from another district to cover a shortage.

As I made my way over, he picked up a heavy book and slammed it on the desk. I said, "Ted, calm down."

"But Mr. Shapiro, this taxpayer—"

"I'd like you to sit."

He opened his mouth, and I stared up at him until he sat.

Ted was smart enough to advance, but we all felt that there was something unidentifiably wrong with him, some inappropriateness to his comments and actions. To say the least, he did not project the public face the IRS wanted. A very imposing man who kept himself neat, he would start out friendly and then say something vaguely threatening. He made friends quickly and lost them almost as fast.

He belonged to Lucinda, and that brought me to her desk when I saw him up and pacing again. Business was business whether she and I had resolved all our issues or not.

"Luce, you need to let Ted go."

She looked at me squarely. "Uh uh."

"You know you'll have to fire him sooner or later."

She studied me carefully and said, "Unless it's Teletax on your mind, you have no say in what I do with my employees."

"Think about making an exception," I advised as I left her, "because spite is a thing that backfires."

Since I was still in a supervisory position, and unable to get rid of him, I couldn't entirely avoid the man. I went back and warned Ted, "Behave yourself."

Impotent rage boiled in his eyes and I prayed he knew how to *stay* impotent. This was one big boy I hoped never to fight.

Then Janis crossed the room and Ted sat up like a Scottish Deerhound. This was a performance I'd seen before. Every day Ted would put the taxpayer on hold, jump from his seat, and engage Janis in eager and inane conversation, flogging some question he already knew the answer to. She would try to say something to satisfy him. Then after he switched the topic to movies or current events, she would remind him that he was keeping his callers waiting too long.

When he got hold of her this afternoon, I was busy taking over a call nearby. I heard her say, "It's enough already, Ted. You need to speak to your own manager and not me."

"Yes, ma'am. One more question."

"I'll get Luce's attention for you."

"No!"

He touched her shoulder and she broke away from him, nearly on the run.

Afraid that Ted was becoming a full-blown office stalker, I hustled over there and told him, "Don't ever touch anyone. Do you understand?"

He lowered his head and said, "I didn't mean to, Mr. Shapiro."

Then I caught up with Janis and said, "I'm sorry that happened."

"It's not your fault." It shocked me that she was trembling.

"I'll keep a better watch on him," I promised.

But apparently I didn't. We of the WAR program all worked later shifts than the pentapod room did. Ted must have hidden in the bathroom when his coworkers left at five pm that day. I had the honor of sitting in on an absorbing problem resolution session in the distant section where that work was performed. That was why I didn't see him creeping up on the workspace I'd vacated.

We all had our heads down and Joanie from PRP was pecking away, "unscrewing the screw-ups," as she called it. She was a Decader, with the full ten years' experience and a serious head on her shoulders. Her usual apologetic smile was replaced by intense consternation. "Look at this," she said. "Collections took this guy's house away."

"So?" said Monique. "Happens every day."

"Yeah, but I just found the problem. He never owed us any money."

Without hesitation, Monique came back with, "Fuck him if he can't take a joke." Joanie laughed nervously. Gallows humor abounded in this unit. The IRS was Byzantium all over again. The Treasury Department's responsibility to keep tax information secure made for a necessarily difficult and complex approach to customer service. When it came to keeping data from leaking, the Byzantine system worked. In every other respect, it turned mistakes into disasters. A handful of people like Joanie and Monique—and I'm sorry to say, that included me—served the millions in our area utilizing the scarcely decipherable WAR program.

When Joanie and Monique finally exited through a door on their side of our section, they left me with some of their easier cases to work. I sighed and tried not to become one of screw-ups Joanie despised. I must have closed two or three cases before I got distracted. Though the acoustics were forever muddled due to the distant and complex

254

configuration of our office, I heard a woman down the hall and on the far side of the divider say, "What are you doing here?" It might have been Janis. I wouldn't have heard her at all if the place had not been mostly empty by now.

I could make out a man's voice in response saying, "Lucinda sent me back to invite you to her party at her house." That might have been Ted, but I thought it must be my imagination.

"A party? Are you sure you got that right?" She might have said the name of the person she was talking to, but I didn't catch it. Higher pitched sounds like a woman's voice do not survive around corners as well as the long wavelengths of men's voices.

"I'm going to drive you over there," he asserted.

"I'm not sure I want to go."

"You have to."

She replied, "Is there something I can do to...*help*?"

The way that last word was emphasized got me moving. I walked to the divider, peered around it and saw Ted in front of Janis, who was edging back. Ted must have caught her surreptitious plea too because his demeanor changed.

"I love you!" he proclaimed to Janis.

"That's nice," she said, backing away. She couldn't keep the quaver out of her voice.

"And I want to lick your shoes!"

"What did you just say to me?"

"Just the bottoms!" As she continued her retreat, he begged, "Oh please." Her look of disgust seemed to fuel his urgency. He shouted, "Please, please, please, I need to do it or I'll die."

Why was the room so damn big? I was on the run and still more than fifteen yards away.

Janis turned her back to him and took a few steps. "I'll just call Lucinda to let her know I'm coming to the party." She got to a desk telephone and managed to punch in some numbers. Our push button phones were much faster than the rotary ones in other departments.

"No!" Ted roared. He came from behind, yanked the receiver from her and wrapped the telephone cord around her neck. The coils stretched and then bit into her skin. She worked her fingers under the band but he immediately bent her with a knee to the small of her back to increase the pressure. Her eyes grew wide in panic.

My *sensei* had taught me to have a plan of attack for every person and every situation even if I only had seconds to formulate it. *Thought and then action.* I thought to grab Ted by the hair and punch him in the kidneys until he let go, and that's what I did. Like most of us in those days, he had a lot of hair product in his black mop so it was hard to hold on.

It seemed fortunate that he released her on the first punch, but he turned on me as though he had given Part Two of this whole scenario some thought. Maybe he was angry at the frequent reprimands I'd given him or maybe I was simply the only obstacle between him and Janis. In any case he came up swinging the telephone at my jaw. He had a terrific grip on it because these heavy old phones had a finger well for the user to curl their grip under and move it whenever necessary. Since his movements had been concealed by his body I didn't see the first half of his swing.

I got my forearm up only to share part of the impact. Being hit in two places felt like the worst of both worlds.

The bell inside the phone clanged as they did when jarred. Or maybe that sound was my head. The good thing about being hit in the jaw though is that you don't feel the floor coming up at you after that.

If I was out, it was only for a second. From my strategic position on my back, I could see Janis' feet running away and hear Ted howling in rage. I kicked up at the side of his knee and got him twisting away from me as I rose and claimed one of his arms. He squirmed out of it when his shirt tore, but I quickly grabbed the other.

Once I had a firm grip, the one arm was all I needed. I pinned it behind his back and wrenched it upward. In the heat of battle, I hadn't noticed the approach of our security forces who tapped me on the shoulder, and took hold of him less gently. They very much wanted him to eat the metal edging on the rug and I wasn't in the mood to stop them.

I had a feeling that good old Luce was going to take a hit for this, considering that she was his manager. She'd be pissed at my involvement, which would require my testimony in court, and I would have to watch my back twice as much as usual.

In a far corner, I caught up with Janis who was still teary eyed and casting around blindly until I gave her a tissue that she promptly used.

"Are you all right?"

She shook her head, "no."

"Do you need an ambulance?"

She shook her head again and sought my embrace. "I'm good. It's fine now," she said in a voice muffled by my shoulder. But she didn't let go of my waist. In time, she closed her eyes, relaxed and her breathing grew steadier, though she hiccupped once in a while. A few curious night stragglers who had followed us, saw the situation, and moved along. If it were no more than an emotional breakdown, I would have given her some space, but considering that she had locked her fingers at my back, I stood by in case she needed anything.

After a quiet interval, she said, "Thank you. Come out into the hall. I want to show you something."

Uh, oh. I sensed we were going from the jealousy aphrodisiac to the danger aphrodisiac.

The broad thoroughfare was empty in the late hour. We tread carefully on a floor shiny from the post-traffic clean up. She led me to a closet, and I stopped and said, "I don't know about this, Janis."

"Come on," she urged. "Middle management gives the janitor a few bucks to stash this stuff for a special occasion. We all know about it." She unlocked and swung open the door.

"A mop in a bucket?"

She smiled and led me in, getting the bulb lit with a pull chain and setting a privacy latch. Much of the closet was taken up by an enormous floor waxer, which we had to step around. The shelving held cleansers and industrial sized packages of off-brand paper towels. She reached past these to move a sliding panel and pull out a bottle of scotch and two glasses.

The accommodations were nothing like Chez Supply Room, but I had to admit that the company was outstanding. She poured two fingers for each of us and said in a toast, "Here's to not getting choked to death."

I sipped, took some more, and said, "This is good. How do you keep the janitor from drinking it all?"

"Shut up."

"I've been told that by a lot of women."

Gripping my collar, she pressed her mouth hard against mine. Having been a Boy Scout, I recognized some of what she was doing. She could have tied a clove hitch, a reef knot or even a fisherman's bend with that tongue of hers. What she accomplished with her lips and mine was nowhere in the scout handbook.

This was the free-love-generation hangover—the last gasp—and everyone was trying to mix metaphors and squeeze out the final drop. Had this been five years earlier, we would have skipped the closet and done it on the desk. In fact, with all the office "romances" I knew about, I was surprised we didn't bump into anyone in there. If I wasn't under a restriction to be quiet, I would have asked her if she had it reserved.

When Janis advanced to loosening my tie, she had some difficulty with my trendy knit fabric, which gave me time to come to my senses.

"Okay, okay," I said. "Stop. You are fantastic, Janis, and I'm intensely attracted to you, but I'm with somebody."

"Oh." There was that word, "oh" again, this time sounding like a wounded steam pipe. Wow, did that make me feel bad. By degrees, she relented, letting her shoulders droop and then her hands. Finally she sagged against me and said, "I understand."

Even though I was the one who had stopped her, I very nearly changed my mind. I hugged her briefly and kissed her forehead, more to cool myself down than anything else.

"One more drink?" she asked, searching my face for that kindness.

"Yes. A short one. Then I should go."

We had that other drink in slow sips and comfortable silence. The rest of her staff had gone home so there was no one to miss us back in the big room. Finally, she said, "The DD thinks you could be the Division Chief in five years." She was happy for me. "He wants you to learn something in every department and then go on to bigger and better things."

So Margo was not completely off base when she'd told me much the same. The trajectory didn't seem that quick considering that five years was more than a fifth of my life, yet I knew it would be an incredibly brief ascent as careers went.

Finishing my drink, I said, "The district director has spent too much time in janitorial closets reaching behind the paper towels."

Janis smiled, but left it at that, and began to put everything away.

When I left her to that task, and lifted the latch to leave, my timing was terrible. I've criticized our staff's habitual lack of preparation, yet the truth is that none of us is ever prepared for what life can throw down. I swung the door open to the public hallway, which should have remained deserted until the morning.

The good news was that Linda had found a way to visit me at work. She even looked happy for a moment. The bad news was me.

"Danny!"

My reply was less zesty, more guilt laden, and more of a sound than a word.

She smelled the liquor on my breath, saw that my tie was ajar, my hair mussed. Janis emerged from behind me and completed the picture for a horrified Linda.

I pleaded, "Linda, it's not what it looks like."

Her features were crushed down by incredulity and betrayal.

"It's less than it looks like," I amended. "Much less."

Her hand went to her mouth and she twirled away.

I heard myself braying the hound dog's lament, "I can explain."

Linda moved stiffly away from me as though she'd forgotten how to walk—paused long enough for me to hope she might turn back—and then ran.

I glanced back at Janis, remembering that she was my boss, and she mouthed, "Go."

I ran after Linda, straightening my tie and smoothing my hair to erase the reminders should I happen to catch up with her. Because of the late hour, she had found a spot right in front of the building. I barely snatched my hand back from the door handle when she tore out of there.

AFTER A HORRIBLE night of no sleep and unanswered phone calls to Linda, the next morning at work I staggered in and saw something on my desk that froze the remains of my heart: a copy of a letter I had sent to a taxpayer with something stapled to it.

The letter had been in my locked drawer.

No document stayed out at night at the IRS; it couldn't. Of course it was almost noon, because that was when my shift began. Someone had all morning to cause mischief. Things didn't come out of locked drawers by themselves, and the suspect list in this department was small.

Before the hubbub of the previous day, my new branch chief had pronounced me a graduate of the stifling tutelage of Eldon Swinney, but caterpillar man was apparently not finished with me yet. Certain that this violation was his handiwork, I opened the envelope to see which letter he'd pounced on. The taxpayer had written to the IRS asking if he had to report last year's New York State income tax refund on his Federal return. A common question. The previous year he'd taken an itemized deduction for state tax. I had researched both year's data on his returns and replied to him that no, he "should not report the entire refund." What a relief it must be to get a letter from the IRS like that.

After coming in early and digging up the copy of my letter, Eldon had apparently written a new letter to the taxpayer telling him to "disregard" what I had written. For my benefit, Eldon was kind enough to staple his "correction" to my papers along with a copy of a reprimand and a write up addressed to Margo. The write up advised that I be fired. It said that I'd purposely ignored his advice and sent out "false information that cost the government money."

Contrary to his complaint, he hadn't given me any advice on this subject, and I didn't need any. I knew how the law worked. What was this prick up to? Next to this little package was a pink phone message slip asking me to report to the Branch Chief immediately. My temples pounded to the beat of my pulse.

He was wrong. Now I read each of these papers over again with a surge of joy building inside me, something I thought I would never feel again. This crisis would actually show the boss that I knew what I was talking about, and El Don did not. I grabbed my Internal Revenue Code off the desk and flipped it open to one of a hundred paper-clipped pages: the one about state tax refunds in IRC Section 111. I read it more carefully than I'd ever done.

Oh yes, the Mad Caterpillar was going down. He had made the biggest mistake of all time. But that didn't make sense after all his seasoning. How could an expert like him be so foolish? Where was the trap, if there was one?

The answer came when I had my audience with the Branch Chief. My mind was a tennis match, sallying between my imminent triumph and my disaster with Linda. Still, if something was going right, maybe miracles could happen and I could be reunited with her.

Margo Kirliew's hair was in disarray and her suit rumpled. Her eyes were rimmed in red as she cried, "I've never been so disappointed in my life."

She must have really liked Eldon, I thought. I dropped my smile quickly. Best not to gloat. Or at least try to keep it to myself.

"Eldon has been here since the very beginning," she continued.

"All good things must come to an end," I said. Uh oh, too glib.

She fixed me a deadly stare. "I knew you two didn't get along, but to throw away a brilliant career like that just to get one up on someone?"

"I'm sorry," I told her, "but Eldon made his bed." Again I felt the nagging worry about how he could be so foolish. It didn't make sense to me that I was right and a research manager who was fully a decade my senior was wrong. Where was the trap?

"Don't say another word," Margo sobbed. "Just give me your resignation."

CHAPTER THIRTEEN
Creds Shapiro Lives Here

"The Caterpillar took the hookah out of its mouth and yawned once or twice, and shook itself. Then it got down off the mushroom, and crawled away in the grass, merely remarking as it went, 'One side will make you grow taller, and the other side will make you grow shorter.'"

—Lewis Carroll, *Alice in Wonderland*

My jaw dropped in an effort to catch up with my plummeting stomach.

"*My* resignation?" Branch Chief Margo Kirliew had me on the carpet in the Research Section, and not in a good way. In fact, she'd just demanded a form of ritual suicide over something she considered a major error. The loss of everything I'd worked for professionally, as she cornered me in her temporary office of bright colors and bad lighting, came only one day after I had scuttled the trust of the woman I loved. Linda.

"Yes, yours, Mr. Shapiro." Margo extended her palm as though she wanted me to inscribe my sins on the flat of her narrow hand.

"When you mentioned a brilliant career being thrown away, I thought you were talking about El Don's career."

Oops. I accidentally used Swinney's secret nickname. That mistake wrote another layer of pain on Margo's face. "Eldon," I amended, "is the one who made the error. I thought you read the taxpayer's letter and my reply."

"I did," she said pointedly. The branch chief was an intense woman, and her eyes were drilling into me now.

I had to be very careful here not to insult her intelligence. A sickening seed of doubt was taking hold. Could I still be right even when both expert Eldon and the manager I most respected thought I was mistaken? On such a fundamental issue?? "Margo," I pursued softly, "I did nothing wrong."

"You were my favorite, but at this point your intentions don't matter," she said with a hard swallow. She obviously thought that my intentions were to wage a scorched-Earth battle with my rival no matter what the consequences to her department. There is no greater anger than that of a refined fan who realizes that the object of their admiration is actually a clueless Philistine.

Idly, I pictured the reception I'd get if I carried this dispute to our useless union. There I'd find Ellis Koalaman with a sincere pout, swearing, "Jinkies! This one's got me flummoxed." Any facet of union business had him in aw-shucks mode. As I measured the droop in Margo's frown, I suddenly felt the weight of the Internal Revenue Code book in my hand, and said, "I'm right, though. I have the proof of it here."

Margo scrabbled for that thread. "Really?"

"Yes!" I flipped the book open. My copy was thicker than most, bristling with paper clips throughout. "It's the

Tax Benefit Rule under IRC Section 111. This taxpayer's itemized list barely scraped past standard."

"Does that matter?"

"Yes. He hardly got any benefit from throwing in his state tax. Taxing him on his whole refund would be the same as wiping out some of his standard deduction from the previous year. The Code does not allow that."

"You're sure?"

"Absolutely sure." The comfort I felt, which was not nearly as absolute as I claimed, rose from the fact that Margo did not seem to be versed in what I considered a basic pillar of law. That meant she hadn't taken it into consideration, and now had a reason to listen. I explained the rule again to her, this time with hypothetical numbers.

"Write it up," she said thoughtfully, "and be very specific about how the Code operates."

"Thank you."

"I want to see the Yellow Brick Road with every trail that leads to it. And I'd better find the Wizard of Oz at the end."

Margo was a fair woman, her stunning eyes restive with a glimmer of hope. Most bosses would have had me back on the D-train by now, nursing a kick in the butt for severance. Any woman who shared my love of old movies had to be okay. "Aye aye, Dorothy," I said, smiling at the challenge, and thinking I had a shot at redemption.

"FUBAR," HECTOR ASSURED me in the kindest way possible. "That's what you are, Danny." As much as we resembled a branch of the army, there were a lot more ladies around at the IRS, so with us the term meant *Fouled* Up Beyond All Recognition, as opposed to the version with the other popular "F" word. "You think this is just about being fired, don't you?"

"Isn't it?"

"No. Treasury could take a bite out of your ass like you wouldn't believe. They already brought Virgie back from leave."

"What's that got to do with me?"

"When one person's fortune goes down, another's goes up, and the two of you are linked."

Hector Chavez, the only one secure enough to dare come into contact with my tainted hide, was sitting on the edge of my desk in Research, guarding me with his arms crossed. In his green suit, he made a stout sentinel. But the fact was that Eldon was keeping his distance from me, either by Margo's design or by his own choice. And the Caterpillar must have been content either way because he too would have realized I was FUBAR.

"You know I'm right, though?"

"You're expendable, Danny, so if I were you, I'd rather be lucky than right. That guy you trained, Marshall Colotine, is almost as smart as you are. They'll replace you with him in a heartbeat. You'll need to be the luckiest dog in the world to get out of this one."

"I'll work on that."

He sat with me a bit longer as the morning wore on. After watching all of our denizens take the long route around my central section, Hector came to the conclusion that they were going to let me toil in peace that day. He hadn't arrived at any new suggestions, so he left me to the solitary task.

I caught no other assignment. Under the terms of my suspension, my station in the research group was provisional, furnished only with a deep hole and a small shovel. It wasn't until my pen started moving that I realized how fiercely complex it was to illuminate a counter-intuitive benevolence tucked into a corner of the IRC's voracious maw. None of my assertions that the government should get less money, not more, could be completed without endless cross-references from the material I had arrayed stacked around me like defensive walls.

For my part, I had complete faith in my ability to understand this part of the Code, and considerably less faith in disillusioning management about something they thought they understood in the first place. While it was Congress that wrote the law, I was putting myself in the position of the messenger that my superiors would most like to shoot. No wonder Margo was wary. But I had the elegant choice of traveling this path or turning back toward the firing squad.

Above me the balky florescent bulb twitched and darkened. The swatch of natural light that bounced in from a distant window to my desk looked strangely out of place in Taxland, and I took the anomaly as a sign that vindication in this arena would eventually lead back to Linda.

By the time I was done, the weak spot of sunlight had traversed the entire bulk of my WWII desk and lit a corner of the giant shredding machine where my former coworkers would soon line up to retire the day's business. My work had grown to the proportions of a sizeable seminar, if not an entire white paper on Section 111 and the history of Congress' deliberations on the subject of refunds.

At last, I gathered the heap and ventured over to Margo, who was busy with the paperwork for my release from public service. The gloomy task had turned her from sanguine to sullen. Without quite meeting my gaze, she pointed to the part of her desk where my pile of paper needed to sit in abeyance.

I still had no other assignment to work on, and I wasn't one to mangle paper clips into unlikely shapes while waiting. I read over my extra copy of the report in order to see which part the boss might be up to. Knowing that would hint at when she might be done. Since no one summoned me, I went on to study a few tax topics I'd never seen before, staying on track by pretending there were interesting parts and hitting these with a red felt-tipped pen. After a while of that, I went on to make a dozen sketches in ink. That was how I knew that her review was taking way too long. In the time Margo Kirliew took to read my notes, I could have defrosted a large holiday turkey and put it through Phase I training. But I had a feeling there would be no celebratory meal at the end of my ordeal whether the turkeys were educated or not.

By now I had convinced myself that I had written a masterpiece that spoke for itself. To keep up my spirits, I tried to picture her consulting with a few other people, double checking my source material, nodding and smiling all the way, and occasionally laughing with relief to the point of shedding a tear. But the chief of my branch was not joyful when she called me in again. Her stylish clothes had a camping trip slept-in look as though she'd spent a rainy night under the stars in a leaky tent and fought off a bear attack in the morning.

"Sit," she said.

One of her two guest chairs had been wrestled out of our Walk-In waiting room. Some genius had ordered thin orange padding for the cushion, which had the psychological effect of enraging our civilian visitors, but this design flaw was balanced with a massive clunky wooden base that no average person could ever lift in anger. If, however, some mountain of a man with a grudge came bustling in, he'd be a giant with a formidable missile. The other chair in Margo's space was stolen from Personnel, the type of love seat that Verna Tucks and I had once shared when one of us fell on the other. It was an unwieldy one too, but well-padded and I liked the memories. That's where I settled down and waited while Margo stared off into space as though she'd forgotten I was there. She was going to lose someone today, one way or the other.

Here was the problem that she no doubt wrestled with: Congress made the laws, and as part of the executive branch, the IRS was sworn to faithfully enforce them, either way they cut. But the IRS had its own set of lawyers who formulated the government's position, which favored the collection of more revenue. My interpretation of the law ate into their revenue. And their motto in response to handing out breaks was, "I don't think so."

Some would say that it was my job to realize that I worked for the government and should keep my mouth shut. I hadn't. My horizons at the time were too narrow for me to realize that there was much more at stake than the fate of me, Eldon, and one individual's refund.

While Margo sat traumatized, I began to wonder if I could sneak my dismissal paperwork out of her hand, slip off my shoes, and pad silently over to the shredder with it. Losing information to get out of trouble was the unwritten rule of the IRS. I was also considering walking out and getting on with my day, when she croaked, "I can't talk about what's going to happen to Eldon."

So far so good.

She cleared her throat, which was obviously wrung to exhaustion by the repeated swing of her emotions during the hours she'd sunk into the investigation. Not to mention her fight with the bear.

Nevertheless, I detected a grave note in her cadence and suddenly felt sorry for our chief researcher. The man who looked like a thumb sticking out of a suit had no life but this one, ten years of being in a unique position in the Service. I only wanted to be left in peace, not to see someone else destroyed. In my naiveté I had thought that Eldon would get into deep enough water that if he had any of his further criticism of me, he wouldn't be able to swim out. I didn't realize that we were engaged in a winner-take-all joust.

"He doesn't deserve to be fired," I blurted, as if I had a say in his disposition.

Her eyes flashed with anger. "He recommended we fire you and rescind your pension for sending false information to the taxpayer. Now we know that *he's* the one guilty of that offense."

That news sent a shiver through me, but I said, "It's only one person misinformed. I can clear up the confusion with a single phone call."

She shook her head sadly. "Eldon also broke into your locked drawer and left taxpayer information unattended on the open desk near a walk-in area. Our options are that he could be prosecuted for disclosure, for damaging government property, or brought up on any combination of charges." She paused for a self pat-down as though looking for a pack of cigarettes, and looked bereft as people do when they remember they've quit smoking. "Or he could be allowed to resign," she added, as though that icy dagger was another thing she'd just remembered.

Disclosure was the most chilling word in the Treasury Department dictionary. I actually shuddered when she said it. It meant the illegal exposure of taxpayer data, and it applied equally whether you knew or *should* have known what you were doing. According to our training manuals, disclosure could earn you one to five years in the pokey because of the other charges they would inevitably pile on. I knew better than to defend anyone against that cardinal sin, so I nodded to show that I'd heard. In fact, I'd heard an awful lot from someone who "couldn't talk about what was going to happen."

She waved me away. I took a deep breath and stood. As I left, Margo said one more thing, barely audible, which sounded like, "I'm sorry." If that was it, she must have been talking to her mom in Heaven because I know they don't teach anyone to apologize to subordinates in IRS manager school.

The next day, Ladislav Ras, the man who had been both my former mentor and protégé, shuffled to my desk sheepishly with a lame joke that he "only just found the sign that said 'Creds' Shapiro lives here."

I told him that he owed me some favors on account of that, and the new obligation made him feel less of a traitor.

Most of the employees I knew were not permitted to enter our section for security purposes, so they could not make amends. But neither had I seen them gloating. Crowding behind Lad, Hector stopped by and said, "Amazing. You un-FUBAR'd yourself." He pressed a bottle of red wine into my hands while whispering, "Grab a manager and celebrate."

I was too astonished at the turn of events to respond.

I saw "El Don" one final time as he packed his personal belongings, including the obligatory indoor potted plant waving from an open cardboard box. He removed his tie and threw it in the box with the plant. I found the moment surreal.

"You set me up," he said with flat certainty as he examined the bottle of red on my desk with its glossy blue ribbon tied into a bow.

I almost laughed at the absurd notion. "You give me too much credit, Eldon. I could never have engineered that sequence of events."

"No, I admire it." After a long pause to study his shoes, he said, "I'm supposed to apologize to you as one of their conditions of dropping the prosecution against me."

"Save it. I'll tell them you did."

He gave an almost imperceptible nod.

That pass was the only kindness I could offer him. He was a major league player that had choked. No one wants to see that.

Eldon did an about-face, arms full, and exited through the partition gap; his face hitched a ride, and he was off. What a waste of a smart thumb.

Then I realized that the Caterpillar had left me with the miserable task of calling back the taxpayer in receipt of two conflicting advice letters, the second of which told him to ignore the first. In this third response, I would be asking him to ignore the second letter from someone who had cited himself as my manager while I—the first chump who responded—now claimed to be the ultimate authority. Any civilian facing such a contradictory mess would be within his rights to ask for an upper executive if not a psychologist. We'd be lucky if he didn't call the news outlets.

Margo emerged to stare wistfully into the space where Eldon had been. She had washed her face and brushed out her hair. "Did he give you any trouble?"

"No." I looked at the bottle of wine and I looked at her, a marvelous older woman whose intense brown eyes were beginning to perk up again. But I despised wine, and the only woman I wanted was Linda.

When Margo went back to her office, I called my answering machine at home to check whether Linda had responded to any of my calls. There was one message, and it was from my best friend Bobby Bowman. He said, "I heard that you and Linda Sobel had a big blow up. Sorry to hear that. Do you mind if I...er...do you mind if I ask her out?"

Although my job was preserved, my life was a long way from being un-FUBAR'd.

SPECIAL AGENT MONROE Eastman set a brown bag on his desk and fished out a hot, covered coffee and a block of opaque waxed paper, which he promptly tore open because his mouth was already watering.

"Do not eat that sandwich," said Boyd Van Dejong at his shoulder. "It will kill you."

The FBI was in turmoil. Agents were crammed two to a desk due to renovations in the lower Manhattan Federal Building, so the recently-thin Boyd and his endless food-critic opinions had to be tolerated.

"No," Eastman explained patiently, "it's pastrami on rye. I have it once a month, and it's great."

"If you decrease the amount of fat in your diet, your palate will readjust. You can't readjust now because you've had that twice this month." Thin or not, Boyd still reminded Eastman of Oliver Hardy from the old films.

"I'm not going to drop it," he said around a mouthful. "I'll have it more often, because sharing a desk with you makes me nervous. Where do you get all this weird information?"

"I'm investigating Dr. Dean Ornish, the heart specialist."

"Never heard of him. What'd he do?"

"Nothing, it's not a case."

"So why do the research?"

"I have interests," said Boyd. "You don't."

"You research for a hobby, and I play tennis."

"And the last time you did that was when?"

"Point taken," Eastman acknowledged as he took a hearty bite of the forbidden food. "I guess visiting the deli is my only interest. That and the sport called none-of-your-business."

Tanglewood strolled down the line, selectively pointing to his people, saying, "Meeting, meeting, meeting, meeting." At first he said it one time per person. Then he droned on like a metronome as he squeezed through the passage.

"C'mon," said Boyd pulling at Eastman's elbow. "The boss just saved you from yourself."

"Fuck him and fuck you," Eastman said cheerfully as he took his last New York wolf bites to finish, and drowned them in coffee.

The crew jammed together in the makeshift conference room, eight men and one woman. An assembly scrambled whenever the Blaine Clarkeson case heated up. Eastman knew that there had been a development and there would be some bullshit reason why he didn't know about it before this. Then again, the FBI was meticulous, seeking to control every element, so the new issue could easily be a peripheral one.

Tanglewood pointed at him and said, "What are you doing here, Eastman? You're off the case."

"Good."

He started to get up, but Tanglewood said, "Just kidding. Out of all these temporaries, you are the only permanent on this task force." He waited for Eastman to express gratitude, but when none was forthcoming, he continued, "We're here because we have an issue before us regarding Agent S, the top candidate to be our unwitting asset at Treasury."

"What's the issue?" asked Eastman before anyone else could.

"S stood up for himself against an office rival on a point of law, and it set off a chain reaction that his bosses thought might cost the IRS a fortune."

"What's considered a fortune in his department?" asked Eastman.

"Maybe a hundred million dollar mistake."

"Wait, how is that?"

"It's complicated, but apparently the rival's advice to taxpayers in the district had resulted in a massive national overcharge that Agent S uncovered. Upper management was pulling their hair out trying to calculate how many people would ask for refunds if they found out the truth. The regional director wanted to put both employees in jail for exposing Treasury's greed."

"Past tense, right? So who intervened?"

"The decision on how to spin the issue to cause the least damage went all the way up to the commissioner..." Tanglewood paused to stare at the loose wires that dangled between the missing tiles as though the potential refunds involved might be hidden in this very ceiling. "...So much money to be gained or lost."

Eastman couldn't help but ask, "What happened?"

"They decided that if there was no public announcement about the mistake, no one would know the difference. Then they let Agent S stick around, and they fired the guy that had lied to them."

"So what do we care?" asked Boyd.

"From our intelligence gathering, Agent S is either too brave or too dumb to realize what kind of hornet's nest he kicked over. Either way—brave or dumb—works for me, because he takes on the bad guys. But I'd rather have a definitive answer. The question is: how do we find out what he's made of? I am issuing cigars to the person with the best plan."

"Cubans?" asked Jimmy Magette. Jimmy was a greedy one, but a mover.

"Those are illegal," said Tanglewood.

"Cheap bastard."

"I want pipe tobacco," said Boyd.

"Too bad," said Tanglewood. "Cigars are the only prize I have. Start talking, people."

Katie Spindel, who was already being scrutinized for such unmanly talk as not wanting cigars, glanced at Eastman but said nothing as the wags in the room ransacked their brains for answers.

Eastman said, "Don't we have a behavioral specialist who can answer that question?"

Tanglewood said, "A what?"

"A psychologist?"

"No," he said briskly, "because psychobabble isn't hard proof. C'mon, people, we need a test."

Several suggestions from the group were easily shot down before Boyd joked, "Hire someone to mug him."

Tanglewood pointed to Boyd. "Close, Van Dejong, but no cigar."

"Send him to a bad neighborhood," said Magette.

"I like that. Tell me more."

"Lots of things could happen. Assign S to the highest crime neighborhood in Brooklyn, and put one of our guys in to stir up some trouble."

"How is that different from what I said?" asked Boyd. "—about hiring someone to mug him."

By way of answer, Tanglewood tossed a cigar to the other man, and said, "Get it done, Magette, no fingerprints. Boyd, there's a subtle difference between those two thoughts that I need you to work out for yourself." He meant that Agent S and the rest of the world could never know of the FBI's interfering role in the life of Agent S.

Katie threw a questioning look at Eastman, which prompted him to say to Tanglewood, "I don't like it. It's out of bounds."

"Agent S," said Tanglewood sharply, "is a Fed, very much within our reach, not a civilian, and he's a big boy. Meeting over."

Eastman stayed seated in contemplation for a moment while the rest of the task force rushed out of the sweatbox. He really did want off the case, and very badly so, because he didn't like the potential for collateral damage. Tanglewood was botching it as far as he was concerned. Gaming a fellow Fed the way they were doing—someone who wasn't guilty of any crime—was out of whack, out of line, and just plain outrageous.

Boyd peered at him as though reading his mind, causing Eastman to wonder whether or not he could safely confide in his curly haired desk mate. Maybe he wanted to end this thing too.

Eastman asked, "What are you thinking, Boyd?"

"Hatcho Miso," Boyd told him solemnly.

"What?"

"Season with that stuff and you'll never want deli food again. Laugh now, but you'll thank me in fifty years."

CHAPTER FOURTEEN
Call it a Sample

"To be a real prize fathead, you've got to swallow whole all
the lies you can think to tell yourself."

—The Lady From Shanghai

The last time I saw Marshall Colotine he was talking
animatedly to the assistant manager of Taxpayer Education.
Then Marshall disappeared, by which I mean he never came
to work at the IRS again. I didn't make any connection
between the two events at the time, or for a long while
afterward. So much for the idea of him taking over my work
with Chief Kirliew.

Marshall was about my age, one of my recent
trainees—though he didn't need my help—and he seemed to
drift serenely through a parallel universe that sometimes
intersected ours. He moved with the sort of confidence that
gave the impression he had something going on the side, and
didn't much care what happened in the big room. That's why
I didn't think about him even when the pencil-mustached Ori
Chasen, Assistant Manager of Taxpayer Education,
drummed his long fingers on my shoulder.

For some reason, I followed Ori out of the room when
he beckoned. All of these approaches were authorized, so
why not? Right? He led me to a part of the basement I had
not seen, a section all its own, marked with a Plexiglas sign.
There I met his boss, Ginger Berlin, who called me

"darling," and wrapped me in the kind of embrace usually reserved for a favorite son long absent and sorely missed. At this point I was used to affectionate strangers who had been stalking me. I tried not to think about how much it annoyed me.

"Good to meet you," I said. "What am I doing here?"

"Special offer," she purred. "Join the Taxpayer Education team."

"I already have a job."

"This one's supplemental. It's a great deal. Address the public after hours. No pay, great experience."

"Why me?" Perhaps I was pliable by reputation. In other words, a well-known chump.

She opened her arms. "You earned the bright lights and the big city, babe."

"And if I don't want what I earned, then what?"

Ginger smiled and put her fingertips gently behind my ear to draw it close for a soft aside. "You already belong to us, sweetheart." Apparently "Taxpayer Ed." was tied to the research unit of which I was now a member, which hinted at some obligation. Before I worked at the IRS, I had no idea there was such a unit, a select corps of volunteers who would go out and make speeches at the request of civic groups on whatever topic they chose.

I had heard of the effulgent "Ginny Berlinni," though, and the fact that she shunned her nickname. She wanted to be taken more seriously, and she obviously thought the name made fun of her. That might have been why I liked it. I'd seen the movie *Cabaret*, and Ginny's personality was as vibrant as those in any Berlin nightclub.

"Do you doubt me?" she asked. "Or do you think that a stint with us will be like Walk-In?"

"That small matter had crossed my mind, yes."

Walk-In. I had so far avoided that dreaded zone where taxpayers could haunt us in person. Anyone who had gotten their scars there could tell you that Walk-In was "the worst." In theory, it had an important function where a taxpayer could make a direct payment or physically show you a document for quick resolution of a problem. In reality, that portal was something quite different, more like a pressure valve for those who got fed up with calling us on the phones.

"It's different when they invite us into their community," said Ginny. "And this isn't close to mid-April."

"If you say so." The pressure in Walk-In mounted as we approached each year's April 15th deadline when the visitors grew more numerous and panicky. Even with a thick wall between our sections, you could sometimes hear the screaming arguments from the other side. At one time, I thought the stories about that zone were apocryphal, the sort of gruesome fairy tales used to make German children behave. *Don't want to listen to me? I'd like you to work Walk-In on Monday.*

I soon learned that a greater number of Service employees were fired out of there than anywhere else. Dante Alighieri would have recognized this section of the IRS as the innermost circle of Hell that he wrote about in his *Divine Comedy.* This was Circle Nine, the very bottom of the well, reserved for traitors, where insubordinate TSR's got sent as punishment. I never sent an employee there myself. It was too awful. I once had an intense fear public speaking and considered conquering it a work-in-progress. Crowds of fifty or more still struck me with trepidation. So why was I even considering voluntarily going toe-to-toe with the potentially angry taxpayers?

Well, there was the matter of prestige. I had been selected as an official IRS Spokesperson. That sort of public recognition was actually the flip side of the coin compared to Walk-In, where group managers would disavow any knowledge of your actions. This move was theoretically good for my career. But there was that word "theoretically" again.

Monitoring my indecision, Ginny informed me, "Hector Chavez already agreed to it." Management liked to stir our rivalry. It worked too. They had probably told him the same thing about me.

Ori chimed in, "You can quit at any time." Perhaps they could comfortably offer me that option knowing that "quit" was not in my vocabulary. I hoped that "spokesperson" was not synonymous with "symbol" or "target."

It struck me that this tiny Taxpayer Education department was at the center of a mystery. "Didn't Marshall Colotine work for you? Where is he now?"

Ginny's smile didn't waver, as though she'd anticipated the question. "Briefly, he did. He doesn't work at the IRS anymore."

"Oh? Where *does* he work?" Deflection irritated me.

"Ha. Ha, haa." The two of them laughed as though we all three shared the rollicking secret of his new employment. Now I wondered whether Marshall had that NSA job I'd turned down. Maybe national security was a better career path than I knew. The very thought of it certainly made this pair jolly.

<u>Tuesday, March 11, 1986</u>

For my first Taxpayer Education assignment, I found myself in South Ozone Park at a veteran's hall, where I shared this evening with the community at large. The crowd, all of them African Americans but one, looked uncertain of me, and why shouldn't they be? They wanted tax information, but didn't know what to expect. What was I doing here again? Oh yes, Ginny Berlinni and Ori Chasen inspired confidence. I almost forgot.

Housekeeping first. I tallied the audience as thirty-one people and scratched that data onto the outreach form.

The organizer offered me a microphone, but I shook my head. I introduced myself, thanked them for inviting me, and outlined my talk, pausing only to ask, "Any questions before I begin?"

The only Caucasian in the bunch, a fortyish man with a great square forehead and pointy jaw looked around as though casting for support. Though he didn't find any, he went ahead and challenged, "Why should we trust you? You're the government."

"Only Taxpayer Service and my only job tonight is to explain how to save you money."

"Why would you want us to know that?"

I guessed he was a little paranoid. He wouldn't be the first of his kind. Maybe the better question was: Why did I want to go out and take this abuse? Oh yes, my career, such as it was. There was also the matter of getting in more practice with tougher crowds.

Public speaking had once been my greatest fear and I had set out to turn my weaknesses into strengths. This one had made it to the top of the list. In public school I spent sixth grade through twelfth grade agreeing to participate in school plays and then giving way to the worst forms of stage fright. Triggered by the pressure, I had paralysis and convulsions brought on as a byproduct of neuropathy or nerve damage from "untreated diabetes." That was the diagnosis anyway. I would go as far as the wings of the stage, and find myself physically incapable of going further. That was when I actually made it near the stage rather than running away. In college, I'd taken public speaking courses from the most gifted of professors and finally conquered it after a fashion. I converted my nervousness to performance energy. Hecklers were part of the deal. Instead of slipping backwards to my stage fright days, I had to stop overthinking these things.

I said, "Maybe you should listen to how I'm going to save you money and see if you want to ask that question again at the end." That got a few laughs, maybe nervous ones. I was sure that the community organizers who invited me were embarrassed that there was a conflict before we even began.

"Maybe we should string you up," the heckler persisted. He stood suddenly, kicking his chair back so that it went flying. In a freak accident, the chair hit the legs of the guy behind him, a white-haired gentleman in a World War II flight cap. The people around them gasped, thinking that the old man might be badly hurt. The heckler turned and put up his hands in apology, but the ex-military man decked him on his pointy chin, knocking him cold. Four people each got under a limb and carried the troublemaker outside. The rest of my visit went beautifully.

Winning felt good. Later, I signed up to do another fifty lectures.

WITH THE TAXPAYER Education gig going so well, I went back to work hoping that the night before signaled a change in luck. That day, Marshall Colotine reappeared with a jaunty step rarely seen in Taxpayer Service, and although he took a zig-zagging, high-fiving route, it was clear he was making his way inexorably over to my supervisory station. He wore a slim cut suit over a strong physique, and had a sweep of dark blonde hair with just the right amount of gel.

When he arrived, I said, "Hey Marshall, where've you been?" He had another job obviously.

"I'm working for U.S. Customs."

"As?"

"Boarding ships and finding illicit money, drugs, weapons, and sometimes people."

"I didn't catch your new job title."

"Big ships," he amplified evasively. If a voice could wink, his did. Maybe I was reading too much into it, but it sounded like he'd memorized what the agency does, like he was reciting a cover story. The underlying enthusiasm, however, sounded genuine. He was doing something even more exciting than he could say, and he wanted me to know that.

He said, "Why don't we meet at Junior's later? I have something to tell you. It's my treat."

"I can always go for that."

JUNIOR'S WITH IT'S rich history and even richer menu, was a staple of the growing-waistline crowd. It was right across the street. Best of all, it didn't have the cameras and microphones secreted in our office. Right after work, I found Marshall in a booth with two menus. Once I slid in on the opposite side, I wasted no time.

"What is it you want to talk about?"

"Virgie."

"I doubt that," I replied, picking up a menu. "*Virgie?*"

"Yes."

With my eyes on the sandwich page, I pretended to misunderstand. "You can have her. I'll hook you up."

"It's not like that," he said with exasperation. "I'm talking about your Virgie problem."

I spared him a glance. "What makes you think she has something up her sleeve that I can't handle?"

"If you don't know that, you're in worse trouble than I thought."

After we ordered, we gave me the whole tawdry history of Virgie, meaning her random sleazy affairs, other than the one I already knew about—hers with me. Marshall was just spilling it all out there.

We were interrupted by a server offering coffee refills, caffeinated in one hand, decaf in the other. Marshall tried to chase the man off, but I welcomed the chance to think for a moment, add milk, and stir. The details Marshall was giving me were powerful blackmail information if I ever wanted such a tool.

I studied his face, his naturally narrow eyes that were so hard to read, and his ears that stuck out just far enough to keep him from being insufferably handsome. "How could you know these things?" I asked. "This dirt?"

"This comes out of the vetting process whenever our agent is sleeping with someone." That sort of dossier-building sounded a little high-grade for the Customs Service, but what did I know?

"Why tell me, Marshall? I don't work for your bosses. Does this have something to do with Taxpayer Education? Is it some kind of rabbit hole? Go in there and end up something else?"

A subtle shift in his expression told me I'd hit the mark. It sounded crazy to think that I had been vetted for an agent's position wherever Marshall worked. Based on what?

"I'm trying to help you. Call it a gift. Call it a sample…"

"Would either of those descriptions be correct?"

"It is what you think it is, but you can drop that whole community outreach thing now. Your first outing for them was a set-up, another agency trying to get you in trouble."

"That night? That was just a heckler. I never figured you for another Verna Tucks."

Tossing a four dollar tip on the table, he said, "If that makes you feel better, sure. It may have seemed like nothing,

290

but it could have gotten ugly if he managed to turn people against you."

"I must be too likeable to get into trouble."

"It will get worse," he said. "This isn't about taxpayer education. It's about *your* education. If you're with us, no one can do that to you again because you'll be on the other side of it. How's that sound?"

Us? What it sounded like was CIA bullshit and an offer I couldn't accept. I had a life plan, one I had discussed with Linda, and she liked being consulted. I'd pissed her off enough already. What would she think if we got back together and I suddenly jumped off into a life I could never talk about with her? I wasn't willing to take that chance. "Sounds like fun, Marshall, and thank you, but I'm not interested."

"Look, you turned down our colleagues in the other agency. We thought it was maybe because you were waiting for an offer from us."

"It wasn't that way. I'm just trying not to get sidetracked by every shiny penny on the road."

He tightened up. "Reconsider."

"I don't think I will."

Before we left, he "slipped" and called his outfit the Company, which meant CIA in case I didn't get the point, and said that he would incentivize the offer with a better "present." When I didn't nip at that opportunity, I saw him again just once. And that once would be a doozy.

WHEN EASTMAN AND Boyd got back to their work zone, Boyd said, "You want to hook up with Katie, don't you?" Agent Spindel, he meant.

"No, Boyd, I was thinking about switching desks with her, though. Let's see if she can cope with you better than I can."

Obviously, Boyd had caught Eastman checking out Katie Spindel—either now or one of the many times before—and correctly noted his interest. Disregarding Eastman's answer, Boyd continued, "What I wouldn't do to her. She wouldn't be fit to work for a week."

Eastman mustered a noncommittal grunt. Such was his problem. He didn't talk trashy like his FBI brethren so he kept his mouth shut. More to the point, he had too much respect for Katie and couldn't afford to let it show. Women were making inroads at the FBI, but they were only allowed on an upward trajectory when they were so loaded with testosterone that they were barely thought of as female. Women like Katie faced a bulletproof glass ceiling, as did any of the men who tried to help them. Eastman was tempted every day to make an alliance with her because he was unattached. One day, and one wrong move, though, and he'd be ostracized.

His other obvious route to a relationship—newswomen—tried to cultivate him whenever they found out what he did for a living, but those were the ones he really had no respect for. News was crap. It was lies on top of mistakes. The one time he'd dated a reporter, Cassie Rodgers, she confirmed that perspective for him after he read one of her stories promoting a theory about where consciousness goes when we die. According to her source, Peter Wexler, it goes into the stars.

"I'm proud of myself," she said. "I labeled this Wexler guy as a physicist."

"He wasn't?"

"No, but it added credibility to my story."

"That got past your editor?"

"No problem."

"Your friend Wexler sounds interesting, I'll give him that, but he's probably been dropping acid since the 1960's."

"But what if he's right about consciousness, Monroe? No one will read a story about a drug addicted engineer that has a theory about the cosmos."

"You like shaping the news, don't you?"

That remark set her off. "Packaging it is half the job. There's nothing wrong with that."

"No, I heard you say it. You like deciding which information deserves a better look, and you like it so much that you fix the facts to go the way you want."

"That's not all I can fix."

After that conversation, she had promptly dumped him.

But the final straw that shattered his belief in the printed word was the first time the boss had him put out a cover story that was one hundred percent false for the press to print. And they did. Not their fault, in this case, but news was crap. Katie was real. But how would he ever get near her without ruining both their careers?

"Time to get a drink," said Boyd.

"I don't drink, and I didn't think you did either. Isn't liquor on the list of stuff that 'will kill you' as far as you're concerned?"

"Mostly, but sometimes a drink has to happen. We have things to talk about, if you know what I mean."

Monroe didn't, but he wanted to know what Boyd meant, so he went along. Maybe they were on the same page with the Agent S thing after all.

THE BAR VISIT did not go as he expected. Eastman and Boyd weren't on the same page, or even in the same library. Boyd kept pouring liquor into Eastman's glass and asking if he thought his FBI career was going well or "going down the tubes."

The next day was an ugly one: the type of day that comes with a searing hangover where you have to work, and still face all the things that made you drink the night before.

To top that off, Tanglewood came out and declared, "You and I are having lunch."

Having a hangover and facing the boss caused a feeling of dread all morning, an itch you think you will never endure and still have to. Then the bombshell comes.

When Tanglewood finally got to the point over a plate of chicken alfredo, he said, "The bad neighborhood test fizzled." He meant South Ozone Park.

"Of course it did. It was a bad idea."

"But the Passentino trial is coming up and that gives me a new idea. Our boy is going over—"

"Our boy. You mean S?"

"Yes, that's who we were talking about. Guy's going over to the examination section. What I want, put a mobster in his inventory. Just a low level guy with a big mouth. Someone touchy."

"Another test?" Eastman could barely contain himself at the ongoing deception. "Let me get this straight. You're going to transfer a mobster to his caseload? Have him audit a mobster?"

Tanglewood said, "Just a thought I'm kicking around. Call it tempering the sword. Look, I understand you are not comfortable with this op—"

"Why do you say that?" He caught something in Tanglewood's tone of voice.

"You're 'blown out,' so you said?" He pointed at Eastman with his fork and Alfredo sauce dripped off it. "I guess the pressure of the job is too much for you. I guess you should quit then. Or maybe I should let you go."

Eastman burned. Oh yes, he had used the words "I'm blown out" the night before. To fucking Boyd. Direct quote. Eastman never figured Boyd for a traitor. He could have sworn they were going to talk about Agent S or even Katie. Trying to control his temper, Eastman said, "I had some drinks when I said that. It was Boyd who got me loaded."

"It was still you who said it."

Eastman stood up. "Is this how you run the office?"

It was Tanglewood's turn to flare red. "Sit down."

"Why?"

"Just sit. And pick up your damn napkin."

And he did.

"Look, this Shapiro—excuse me, Agent S—is a just a guy." And the IRS is our tool to do with what we like…to get convictions… or to just use him to kick someone in the teeth. Agent S is perfect because he does the job without asking questions, and if you were really paying attention you would learn that quality from him."

"There are too many moving parts in this investigation over too long a period of time."

"No, there are not. It's simple. If S gets Clarkeson on tax fraud, the Senator goes down. If Clarkeson tries to kill S—"

"Whoa!"

"Which he won't get near, but then we'll get Clarkeson on attempted murder."

"Or S dies in the process, and we get Clarkeson on *actual* murder?"

Tanglewood waved that off.

Eastman said, "If this plan is so good, why don't we let Agent S in on it?"

"Because he's got no imagination."

"You mean all he wants to do is be a Revenue Agent?" Eastman fumed.

"Exactly. He's got a bad case of tunnel vision. He turned down NSA. He turned down CIA, and he's kept himself out of all the useful areas of office politics even though the sand trap nearly wiped him out. Mark my words, S will not play along with any extracurricular career opportunity that comes his way. Not voluntarily."

"Then why do you want him on your team so badly?"

"Because of his extracurriculars."

"What does that mean?"

"He has a girl that he loves—"

"Right, that would be Linda."

"—that would be 'L,'—and meanwhile he humped the psycho bitch 'V,' who's connected up the chain. Because of that entanglement, I *own* the sonuvabitch and he doesn't even know it yet."

"Your hold is that solid?"

"It is to him. He's not so perfect and moral as he thinks he is, or wants other people to see. That's what makes the hold good."

"And having leverage on someone is important," Eastman said bitterly, "because some of what we do here isn't all that kosher."

"See? I told you it was simple. You want to find too many moving parts? Go get yourself a model train set."

CHAPTER FIFTEEN
This is WAR

"Someday a real rain will come and wash this scum off the streets."

—Robert De Niro, *Taxi Driver*

April 7, 1986

Apparently, spring was a wonderful season to break someone's legs with a baseball bat. I thought the IRS was a tough outfit, but the impromptu class in leg breaking was the lesson of the day in the parking lot behind our Brooklyn office.

One of the many enterprising reporters who hung around the courthouse explained that you don't do it in sloppy, ass-backward swings. It's an act of precision, an art. It's called kneecapping, and the less knowledgeable practitioners use a bullet where the kneecap sits on the joint. They aim right for the tender hollow on the side. These amateurs put the slug in every which way with unpredictable results. But if you don't shatter the kneecap itself, you are doing it wrong. True artists keep a harmless-looking bat handy, rather than a traceable gun, and take a single swing, artfully estimating where the knee is under the slacks, and listening for the distinct crunch that is made by no other bone. The fuss is minimal. The lesson lasts a lifetime.

An April kneecapping like the one reported while I was at work was a sure sign that jury selection had begun in the Brooklyn courthouse attached to us. In this case, the main event was the Arlo Passentino trial. Jury selection puts defendants in a bad mood, which could certainly be enough to explain why some obnoxious parking space competitor could earn a surgical procedure like that, but in theory it's also a great way to show potential jurors that there is an easy way to vote and a hard way.

Passentino was not the average taxpayer that I expected to encounter, or wanted to encounter. But it could happen. For those in law enforcement, any information about his world sat in a distant category labeled: Good to Know.

It is important to note that, contrary to news reports that Passentino's man, Salvatore Purisi, did the kneecapping—and news reports are often wrong—this attitude adjustment was proven not to have been carried out by anyone who could be tied to Passentino. It was done by some anonymous person reputed to be in the entourage after they had a brief dispute with a discourteous driver. No charges were pressed. Enough said.

That very same morning, I saw Mr. Passentino when he arrived, and he looked as magnificent as described in all the stories I'd heard, a beaming gentleman dressed and groomed to perfection. He sauntered over from his limo at the park across the street, doing up his jacket as he went. The trees did not have their leaves yet, but I remember that particular celebrity highlight came on a nice day. Spectacle aside, I went about my business thinking that the trial would have nothing to do with me and that these worlds would not collide.

Two days later, the morning of April 9, was less routine, since I was dragged out of the building by a bomb threat. The call came into the courthouse, clearing both the courts and the IRS. Reportedly, Passentino told a friend, "Tell them it's not me. They'll be blaming this one on me."

He was right about how it would play out. The theory went that every bomb threat coincided with when Arlo Passentino wanted to go out for a smoke.

The man who made the call actually claimed he was Arlo Passentino. The FBI later discovered that the culprit was a hospitalized mental patient due for sentencing in court that afternoon for making threats against the President. I counted this as an object lesson for investigations: the obvious connection is not always the right one.

"LET'S TAKE A break and stretch our legs," said Tanglewood.

"Sure." Monroe Eastman was ensconced with his boss in a rare visit to the combined courthouse and IRS building at 35 Tillary Street. Passentino, who was on trial here, was Eastman's other case. In this instance, Eastman was the one pulled in from the sidelines because the task was a big one.

"You think you know what Passentino's defense is up to, huh?" Tanglewood asked as they prowled the hall in the direction of Taxpayer Service.

"Sure I do. They're employing classic Carrot and Stick—the prize versus the threat. We're looking at the 'stick' part now, with that kneecapping."

"What's the carrot then?"

"Once the jury is good and scared, his team will wave a pile of bills in front of them. When scared people see a way out, and have something to compensate them for their trouble, they tend to jump at the opportunity."

They were slowly passing the doorway for Taxpayer Walk-in. Tanglewood peeked inside for curiosity's sake. People shuffled along, papers in hand. No crisis at the moment. "Nothing we can do about it."

"What do you mean there's nothing we can do?" asked Monroe. "We can wire them up before they meet with anyone."

"Wire them? Out of the question. That's jury tampering."

"How?"

"Making them think that Passentino is the kind of guy that needs to bribe someone to get exonerated. No one is supposed to have contact with the jury, including us."

"If we can't help safeguard the trial, then why did you drag me to thirty-five Tillary Street?"

"We're doing what you suggested. Your boy works here." He pointed to the call center doors.

"We're looking after Agent S?"

"Not us. You are. It's a favor to him," said Tanglewood. "I hope he appreciates it."

"What's it entail? I can't surveil him 24/7 all by myself."

"Then you don't love him as much as you think you do."

Eastman sighed. Maybe he didn't.

Tanglewood said, "I wanted you to get familiar with the layout of the place to make it easier. You'll come back whenever there's a threat to him."

"And how will I know when that is?"

"That's your job to figure out. If you're too burned out to see it, then Agent S is in trouble, isn't he?"

Monday, May 5, 1986

I was sitting at a research desk learning the computer system known as WAR so that I could be officially transferred to our sister department, but I was clouded with thoughts of Marshall Colotine in Junior's Restaurant. There was his informal warning about Virgie coupled with his pressure for me to join him at the CIA, which I quickly rejected. He looked very serious when he said, "Reconsider."

While I was casting around for another solution, Mike Soderling yelled through his office doorway, "Shapiro, get in here."

I knew by now not to say anything dumb like, *what did I do?*

He stood up. "On Wednesday, you're in charge." Just like that.

"What does that mean, on Wednesday I'm in charge?"

"It means what it sounds like." He slicked back his brown hair, put on his jacket and shot his cuffs, ignoring his scraggly greying beard. "I have an all-day, out-of-town manager's meeting to go to, so you're in charge of everything that I run."

"Everything that you run?" I said incredulously.

"What are you, a fucking parrot?"

"I'm just surprised. Not that I don't have the confidence in myself, but aren't there people who usually fill in for you?" He might see this as routine, but it was a huge responsibility for me that all the other managers might view as a temporary promotion over their heads. For the sake of one thrilling day, I could take a lot of heat down the line.

"They're all in the same meeting. Yeah, it's pretty dopey to pull everyone out at the same time, but so what? It's not tax season. I didn't complain to the brass because I know you can handle it."

Okay, that was a little better. "Is Patton joining me?"

"He's on vacation."

"And Hector?"

"Hector can kiss my ass. I don't trust him. He reports to you on Wednesday."

I hid my surprise. "You want me to work out of your office?"

"No jackass, you have to cover for everybody. That means you have to be out at one of the group stations where you can monitor the stats. You'll sit at Virgie's desk."

"I'll need her keys."

"She'll *give* you her keys. I have an appointment right now, too. Watch my phone."

This was almost too good to be true. Would Virgie be dumb enough to surrender her keys and leave my personnel file in the drawer where I could get to it? The drawer where she kept all of her blackmail material?

WHEN WEDNESDAY CAME, and I went to Virgie's station to stake my claim, she already knew the deal. It saved me the trouble of having to explain the situation to her. In fact she seemed ready to go. Almost.

As she put her things together to leave, she pointed to her computer and said, "You know how everything works, right?"

I deadpanned, "Do you?"

"Very funny," she said humorlessly.

I enjoyed that, though the rest of her business consisted of tense moments where she loitered nervously, reaching for this or that, at one point nearly dipping into the very drawer I wanted to get at. At the last possible instant as she walked away, Virgie reluctantly pressed her keys into my sweaty palm.

I sat heavily in her chair. It isn't every day you get to destroy a blackmail file. I couldn't jump on it until she was long out of sight so I said a silent prayer that she forgot to remove my personnel file, and that I would have a chance to weed out all the libelous nonsense that polluted it.

There were thirty-five employees tied to seven different stations arrayed around the perimeter. Could I cover for the Branch Chief and all of the Group Managers for the first time ever, and still have time to examine the documents properly? This was the chance of a lifetime, so I would damned well try.

Her chair was still warm when I sat in it. I changed the terminal to split-screen mode so that I could see all the real-time call stats, and forced myself to wait ten minutes in case she doubled back. There were nine keys on her ring, most of them silver and short. I hummed the theme from Final

Jeopardy as I kicked out the two long, gold ones, and examined the rest for wear.

When my self-imposed wait and the game show tune were over, I took the four most used keys and matched each of them against the lock. The third one made it turn. Taking a deep breath, I slid the drawer out, *and bingo.* There was a file with my name on it in thick black marker. Most of the employee files around it looked like they were on a diet, while mine was thick enough to choke a King Cobra. It was awful that she did that, but what a present to fall from Heaven.

I rifled through the papers with growing astonishment. Not only did the file contain copies of my work; it also contained altered copies of my work featuring bad forgeries of my signature. I had no idea of the depths Virgie was willing to sink to.

I took a quick look and found nothing wrong with the legitimate samples of my work, even though they were marked, "erroneous." I wanted to think that she'd left the file behind because she finally realized that she had no career as a forger. I needed that image in order to properly enjoy the moment. But more likely, she'd been given no choice. Even Virgie would not make a mistake like this. Revenge 101 says, Don't hand the victim your revenge material.

Call it a sample. I had a strong feeling that my access to this file was the present that Marshall Colotine had spoken of: that he'd blackmailed her to stop blackmailing me. It was a sample of the kind of power Marshall now had, and of what he was offering if I joined his outfit.

In the middle of my savoring, Hector came up to me and said, "Look, I know I report to you today, and I know you have a lot to do. You could use me for whatever."

"Soderling said you could kiss his ass."

Hector laughed, "I bet he did. You got work for me?"

"I do. Cover for me."

Hector had no qualms about supporting whatever mischief I planned. He immediately trotted over to an employee who was waving frantically.

Rapidly, I made three piles—the first two being that which would stay and that which would go. The third pile was to preserve some samples of the forgeries in case Virgie chose to complain that things were missing. When I was done, the depleted file sagged as if it had undergone radical liposuction. In a way, it had.

At the end of the day, it was normal to visit the shredder. Almost everything from Virgie's file on me went in for destruction. This time I was excited to be shredding. Good ol' rapid-fire, industrial shredding machine. It wasn't particularly huggable unless you wanted to lose an ear.

Now what did I owe Marshall Colotine for this gift? Maybe nothing today, but the CIA liked to think very long term.

June 6, 1986

I was deep in the heart of Brooklyn when I purchased my first car, a 1978 Oldsmobile Delta 88, for $2,700. A good "chunka change," as we used to say in those days. It had the virtue of being shiny and looking clean. I hadn't yet made it out of the neighborhood when the thermostat busted fifteen minutes later, making my baby blue transport steam like a heap of junk. Since this was Brooklyn, and "not a fuckin' charity" as the dealer described his car lot when I went back to him, he insisted we split the cost of a new $15 thermostat. And since he was a great sport, he installed it for free.

Thus reestablished, I went to visit Linda to show off the wheels. I had hoped that a car of my own would raise my status with her, but when I got to the door, she refused to see me. I didn't know if she would ever forgive me for what she'd seen, but I would never give up. We were always on and off but this was going on too long and it was too much my fault. The problem was, I had no idea how we were going to resolve things without having a conversation.

When I got home, I called her again. It rang until the answering machine kicked in, her sweet voice on the tape. The fact that she hadn't changed her number gave me hope. Maybe she was monitoring the call. Even though it wasn't a conversation, maybe I could interview myself while she listened.

When the beep sounded, I said softly, "Hey Linda, I'm really sorry for what you saw with Janis. Nothing happened though. She tried and I stopped her. *Why did I look like a mess?* She... tried hard."

I took a deep breath. I almost gave up while I was behind, but I had to get the story out. "You probably want to know what we were doing in the closet in the first place..." God, that all sounded terrible out loud. "It was to get a drink. There was a stash there." Another deep breath. *"Why were we having a drink?* One of the employees tried to attack her and I fought him off. I thought it was going to be in the papers and you'd read that and forgive me. But I checked all of them. They kept it out of the news."

Suddenly, she picked up and shouted, "You were in the damn closet having a drink with another woman, giving her a chance to do whatever!" Before I could respond, she slammed down the phone.

Good. She was listening. That was a good sign.

To myself I said, "Yeah, when you put it that way, it sounds bad. The car is nice, Linda. Want to go for a drive?"

On Monday, I drove my shiny car to work, finally ready to collect the parking space I was entitled to. The building bent back on itself like a wishbone, forming a courtyard that defined the scope of our precious spots. I flashed my ID at the parking lot attendant and drove on through without noticing his objections.

He chased me down, saying, "Hey, hey, hey, you're not supposed to be in here."

I pulled into a spot as he caught up to me, yelling all the way.

"Since when?" I asked, bringing out my IRS ID again in case he'd missed it. I couldn't remember how many times I had sat in Ladislav Ras' Square Orange Skoda in this very parking lot planning my next moves. I couldn't have been in the wrong place.

"Since I decided to tow your car," he said.

"What's going on here?"

"They expanded the executive ranks, so there's no room for you anymore."

I counted the empty spaces. "Looks like an open field in here to me."

"They come and go as they please. That's up to them. Now get out of here or you'll find your car gone."

I knew something was brewing with this man, and time would tell. Something Crooked This Way Comes. Nevertheless, I didn't want to pay a towing company and I wouldn't get away with breaking his kneecaps. The car purchase was a complete bust. That's how I still ended up taking the train the evening that Brinkman ordered a hit on me. If not for that, I would have driven right by the ambush. If not for that, of course, they probably would have tried to hit me another way. But I'm getting ahead of myself...

CHAPTER SIXTEEN
The Combat Zone

"You get a lot more with a nice word and a gun than with a nice word."

–Al Capone

My next ordeal started when Mike Soderling said he wanted Wayne Patton and me in his office immediately, as in "do not pass GO and do not collect $200." We didn't hear from Soderling very often, so his bellowing sounded serious.

Once we had assembled in his office, he said in a more reasonable tone, "I have a little job for you boys." Patton and I looked at each other.

Soderling continued, "It's a thing between me and my old rival in Boston. A bet."

"Yes, sir," I said to stave off the anticipation.

"I need you to go to a full-time training class in Boston. It's a tough one but you both qualify."

"What's the bet?" asked Patton.

"I told that rat bastard who runs the Boston office that each of my guys would get perfect scores on each and every test taken in his district."

"But how—?"

"—You figure out how. If I lose this bet, you'll both pay dearly for it."

Even though none of the three movie versions of Captain Bligh had a beard, Soderling at that moment looked as though he would gleefully keelhaul someone if he didn't get his way. With his marching orders memorized, we cleared out of his office.

"Mike yelled at us," said Patton with his head low. "We're in trouble."

"He did not yell at us. I was in the same meeting with you at the same time and I perceived it very differently. Mike just wants us to do well."

"Or what?"

"Wayne, don't worry about it. We'll do fine."

"Fine is not a hundred percent."

How did Wayne make it this far in the IRS? I wondered. Well, he was ten years older than me after all. I guess slow and steady works too.

My old manager, Lucinda Dwyer—who no longer liked me—was coordinating the trip. With a perky smile, she recommended the Lafayette Hotel, and very strongly suggested that nothing else would do. Brand new, she said. Everyone is going there, she said. Did I want to be the only fool who went somewhere else? I did not.

What she didn't tell me was that it straddled the area affectionately known in Old Boston as the Combat Zone. If you walked out one exit, you were marginally in the safe neighborhood, if you walked out the other, you were in Sleaze Town, the high crime area. And wasn't this the sort of thing Marshall Colotine was warning me about?

I checked into the giant, dark obelisk they called the Lafayette Hotel and immediately secured my traveler's checks in their office safe. That is to say I handed them over to a tightly-buttoned concierge named Helmut, a middle aged man with a crisp German accent. I made a point of saying that these checks were what I would use to pay the bill when it came due.

Returning from the box area, the Helmut said, "I must have an imprint of your credit card."

"You understand that I'm not paying by credit card, right?"

"Yes, we know that. It's just a precaution"

"I want you to make a note that I have a $500 limit on this card, so if you try to put the whole hotel bill on it, you'll find that impossible." I spoke slowly to get my point across. I still didn't trust him, and not because of the language barrier. The instruction was simply too important to get wrong when I had bigger things to worry about in Boston. And maybe I sensed something in his too-eager desire to collect everything I had of value.

"Yes, we understand. You are paying by traveler's check. We just have to have an imprint, which we will return to you when you leave. Please."

"Here it is. I don't want any misunderstandings."

"There won't be," he said.

But, oh boy, there *would* be.

I DIDN'T SEE Wayne Patton outside of class. He was staying at the Holiday Inn, and he had brought his wife and kids with him, the only way to keep peace. Sherona would be damned if her Wayne went on a "vacation" without her. That would complicate things for him considering we both needed time to study. For my part, I did not want a taste of that family dynamic.

Class was challenging, the tax issues brand new to me, but I was determined to take my own advice and pretend that Soderling was not going to tie us to the keel of his ship if we were less than perfect. I would get the best results by keeping my stress levels down. As the instructor told us how the IRS calculated corporate barter transactions, I sat in class contemplating leisure activities, and thankfully they let us go early on the first day.

While the sunlight held, I sat in Boston Common and sketched scenes in charcoal: the gazebo, the passersby, the ducks on bended wing. At night I got a few hours of studying in, and things were going well. Considering that my usual pattern was to work all day and study tax at night, training in Boston without any other responsibilities was relatively easy.

On the third day, however, it seemed I'd caught a local bug and it was rapidly wrestling me to the ground. My heavy limbs barely got me back to the hotel. I needed to go right to bed. When I went upstairs with my key card, though, I got a row of red lights on the security box instead of green.

I sighed and dragged myself to the lobby to find the concierge.

"You are being silly," Helmut said after I explained what had just happened. He made a point of tamping down his precisely calibrated moustache, swiping at it with his thumb in two alternating strokes from the middle outward. "Of course your key works. Many people are confused by these new electronic cards. The maid has just gone in there and everything is fine."

"I tried it four times."

"Go back upstairs and try again," he said.

Though I was now running a fever, I trotted upstairs again and got another flash of red lights. At this point it was obvious to me that they had changed the lock. This time I spent a few minutes splashing cold water on my face in the lobby bathroom, and then demanded to see the manager.

The manager, Sigrid Lutter, was a six-foot-three female weightlifter with a heavier German accent than that of her subordinate.

"Why am I locked out of my room?" I asked her. "And why do your people play this game where they don't admit what happened?"

"It was your card." *It vas,* the way she said it, but in a tone that dripped with contempt.

"What about my card? You mean my Visa card?"

"Visa card, yes."

"You mean the Visa card that the hotel was just taking an imprint of? The one you weren't supposed to use because I was paying by traveler's checks? Traveler's checks that are in your custody?"

"Yes, that card."

"What happened with that card?"

"You don't have enough money to pay for your stay on that card."

My ears felt hot before and now they were blazing. "Yes, it was not a secret. I said that several times when I checked in."

"You don't have enough money to pay."

"I do and you're holding it. What is the concern? I've only been here three days, I don't owe that much."

"You pay the whole two weeks now, or stay locked out."

"You have my money in your safe. Let me get it for you." I was trying to hold myself steady, leaving open the possibility that reason could win out.

"We can't let you go to the safe."

"If you don't like me, I'll gladly go to another hotel, but you have my bags."

"Yes, we keep the bags until you pay."

"But I can't pay unless you give me my money."

"Give us a different credit card." Round and round we go.

"As I told Helmut in the first place, I don't have any other card."

"Then we keep your bags and your traveler's checks and you sleep in the street."

"My credit is backed by the federal government."

"Government employees have been known to be deadbeats too. Now you need to leave the building before security throws you out."

By now the blood was pounding on my eardrums and my fever was burning behind my eyelids. I had to find a place to lay down. I followed her pointing finger, and exited onto a street that looked unfamiliar. I tried to get my bearings. Where were the gazebos, and the couples strolling arm-in-arm? Where was the red line of the Freedom Trail with its cobblestones, lanterns and window boxes? Or the big gleaming glass buildings of Boston's downtown? I would take any of those sides of the city. But here trash littered the street, graffiti scarred the walls, and worse yet, some thuggish young men were straggling out of the bar across the street and making their way towards me. I froze. Of course. This was the Combat Zone. Backing up, I leaned into the exit door's panic bar.

Wrong side. Emergency levers were only installed on the insides of doors. I would have to turn around and grab the handle, and there was no way to do that inconspicuously.

The group headed towards me was definitely together and keenly interested in me. I began to cough. I doubled over, making as if I needed to hold onto the door handle for support, and tried to pull it towards me, and then push it. It was locked up tight, not even a rattle. To get another moment to think, I turned around and kept coughing as though I was about to discharge a lung. It wasn't too far from the truth of how I felt. When they drew close, I stood up straight, turned around, and forced a smile. With two fingers pushing through the material in my jacket, I pretended I had a gun and would enjoy using it. If this didn't work...

The gang's leader did a double take. He steered his crew around me, and the bunch kept walking as though they had another destination in mind.

I'd used that trick before in the bad old Brooklyn neighborhoods. It was touch and go every time, though the evil smile sealed it. Now I traced my way to the other side of the building, and I was really pissed off. To me, this shakedown by the hotel manager, this Sigrid Lutter, looked like a federal crime, as were all criminal offenses against a federal employee. I had passed the FBI Building earlier, so I went to find it again. It seemed like a good idea at the moment.

The two agents I met with were tall, fit, "all-American" types, which meant they looked Swedish. They were friendly enough as they immediately explained that there was nothing they could do about my situation. "It isn't in our jurisdiction."

I wasn't so sure about that, but I couldn't press the point with them. My head was throbbing and I was ready to curl up on a cardboard box, but the taller one kept talking. "My advice to you is to keep in mind that you are in the IRS."

"Oh. Right."

"Got it?"

"No. I'm going to need more to go on than that."

"There are certain things you can do, certain powers you may wish to exercise to immediately bring government contractors in line. If I were you, that's what I'd do."

I still didn't get it. It sounded like generic advice. The clue finally hit me as I was shambling out. Creds. Using my creds and asserting the power behind them was something I would never do if I had any other options, yet this was the time for it if there ever was one. If that's what I was going to do, though, I would really have to sell it hard after seeing like such a wimp. I had an idea. With renewed energy, I hurried back to the hotel via the safe route.

"Get Sigrid Lutter down here." The staff heard my tone and moved quickly to get her.

"Yes? Why have you come back?" The big woman held her back even more stiffly this time, and I didn't know that was possible.

I flipped my badge wallet open and swung it in a slow arc to let everyone study my credentials. In a voice that sung to the rafters, I announced, "Boys and girls, let me reintroduce myself. I am a federal agent, just off the phone with the IRS District Director, in conference with the Treasury Department's District Council." I paused to let them imagine what all that might mean. "I've been instructed that if you do not at this moment release my room key and my traveler's checks, and cease attempting to bill my credit card, then I am to revoke your privileges as a government contractor."

That got Sigrid's attention. "What does zat mean?" Her accent was getting worse.

"It means I will commence immediate evacuation of all Federal employees from this building." I gambled that there were a lot of them. I said it loudly and officiously while claiming the receiver of their house phone, which had a broadcast button on it for the loudspeaker. "And when I'm done here," I told her, "you won't even be allowed to rent a broom closet to anyone who ever worked for the government." Even if nothing happened, I was feeling fifty percent better already.

Perhaps being a foreigner made her unfamiliar with our ways. Or perhaps she was afraid of the German owners of this French-named American hotel. I'll never know.

"Helmut," she said to the frightened concierge. "Give this man a new key and open the safe. Immediately."

Once I had my property restored, I put my creds away, released their phone, and hauled myself up to my room. There I fell asleep fully dressed, face down on the bed.

There was a newspaper and flowers on my doorstep the next morning.

Meanwhile, both Wayne Patton and I toiled like mad men in hopes of scoring the requisite one hundred percent on every test. In the process, we met the "rat bastard" who ran the Boston office, Callum Dawkins III. His hair was a fine silver comb, his suit some kind of vicuña and silk blend with all the right creases. With a thumb in his vest pocket, he said, "You're Soderling's people, aren't you?"

"We are," I confirmed. No sense denying it.

"And did your boss call me a snobby, old money, Boston son of a bitch?"

Patton was aghast. He whispered to me, "You don't insult people with roman numerals in their name."

"Quiet." To Mr. Dawkins, I replied, "He didn't elaborate to that extent, but it sounds like something our Branch Chief might say."

"I do enjoy trouncing him and any sap he sends over."

"You wouldn't really take his attitude out on us, would you?" Patton asked.

"Hmm, how might I put this in Mike Soderling's terms?" he asked, tapping his chin. "Ah yes, I hope that

Soderling, and both of you, choke. I'll double my bet with him and take his house." He sounded delighted with himself.

His smugness was enough incentive for Patton and me. I was still sick, and both of us were sweating tears, but miraculously, we squeaked it out. Three tests. Perfect scores for each. When I think back, I can still recall the strong scent of Callum Dawkins III's tobacco as the pipe fell out of his mouth.

On my last day in Boston, my newspaper and flowers from the hotel came with a handwritten, albeit perfunctory note of apology, and an explanation that the IRS would not have to pay for any part of my stay. I crumpled the note in my hand. While the lodging being free may have saved the government a few bucks, it did nothing to make up for Lutter driving me out with a fever to "sleep in the street."

When I got back to Brooklyn District, I discussed the hotel matter with the appropriate authorities within the IRS. Now I had a real conference with the District Director.

"You did the right thing," he said on the phone.

"I did?"

"Yes. This extortion racket of theirs has been reported several times in the past couple of weeks. We've just gathered the data from various agencies."

In fact, he elaborated, a few government workers had been kicked right into the Combat Zone when they were thrown out of the place, as had been done to me. Those who came up with more credit were all overcharged, and the rest had yet to be able to reclaim their valuables. Suspiciously, most of them had fallen ill just before they were locked out of their rooms and set upon by the locals. One man was in the hospital with serious injuries. I wondered if Lucinda knew about that, or if her suggestion to use this very special place came from elsewhere. Possibly another test for me by someone with a pay stub that didn't say, "Treasury Department."

"What do we do?" I asked.

"We do what you promised them you'd do. Minus the evacuation."

As a relatively new hotel with no positive history to draw from, their incident with me was judged to be the last straw. The District Director had me write up one of my famous detailed reports, and we blocked the Lafayette Hotel from getting any more federal contracts. It turned out that agencies like ours were forty percent of their business. Sigrid was smart to be afraid, but had wised up too late.

Test or no test, that action helped restore my faith that the government possibly cared for its employees, and was willing to include me in that number. I believed I was doing the sort of good in the world that would make Linda proud.

This reminder soured my gut, because here I was doing it without Linda.

September 1, 1986

Summer was flying by, as summers do, and I was at the office suffering from Linda withdrawal, replaying in my mind every mistake I'd made with her since we'd met. I had a pile of paperwork in front of me and I just stared at it.

Of course, I was magnifying minor things that I probably shouldn't have even remembered. Some days are just bad days, but none of my accomplishments felt right without her. I couldn't stand to be in my own skin. If I had owned a cat-o-nine-tails, I would have applied it to my back.

Tammy noticed my mood and said, "There's nothing you can do but fight."

"How?" I asked in confusion.

"Make sure you get into Examinations Division this time."

Oh my job, right. For a second, I thought she was talking about Linda. Tammy was trying to prepare me for the interview, and I'd completely forgotten that this was the big day. Trying to show her that I had my mind straight, I opened my mouth and nothing came out.

She said, "Look, whatever is going on, you better get out of that blue funk that you're in, and get yourself this job."

So much toughness in Tammy's little frame. If words like that could pass her lips, I could certainly man up to equal them.

Those were the circumstances under which I found myself in another Revenue Agent interview. Once again I faced three interrogators simultaneously in a stripped-bare room with a shaky folding chair. This time, however, they managed to do the honors without the anti-Semitic overtones. As a TSS, I was already classified as a tax examiner, which had to be a solid plus.

This time, my oblivion kept me calm as a rock no matter what they asked. The idea that I might finally get this job and not be with Linda when it happened left me stone-faced, cynical, and combative. That combination of traits must have been everything they were looking for in an IRS agent because I got a quick "yes."

A yes! I asked them if anyone with Roman numerals in their name put in a good word for me, but they let that remark go by.

The way had been blocked and now it was open. Inexplicably, it all felt so sudden. I had a feeling that my days at the hotel and my perfect scores in spite of Ms. Lutter's interference had something to do with this change of fortune. Victories counted for something in our chain of command, both inside and outside of the classroom.

Blue funk or not, I was about to be a Revenue Agent.

SO IT HAD taken me a couple of years after all. *Everything moves slowly in the Federal Government.* Now I would experience a career transition from Taxpayer Service to the Examinations Division, the fruit of Linda's original advice. Original Sin? I had a lot of goodbyes to say.

Hector came to me with his usual flawless timing. Looking sad, he held out his hand for me to shake it, and when I did, it seemed as though we weren't going to say anything. Then he said, "Congratulations," pulled me in by the hand, and bumped shoulders. Good enough for me. I understood.

"Thank you," I said as we backed off. "We'll see each other around."

"I know we will," he said, regaining his usual confidence.

In my next meeting with Margo, she stood up behind her desk and said, "No one is happier for you than I am that you got the Revenue Agent position you've been fighting for."

I wanted to know how she managed to be so happy while looking and sounding not-at-all happy, but I didn't pursue the question. I knew there was a "but" coming, whether I asked for it or not.

She said, "But we need you here in Taxpayer Service."

My gut revolted immediately. "No—"

"And so I'm authorized to offer you... an official promotion to group manager."

"Well, that's—"

"Wait. The only catch is that there isn't any opening." She took a deep breath. "We thought Virgie was out, but she's not."

"Ah, now I remember where I am."

That earned me a half-smile. "Not to worry. We're going to create a job for you."

"How is that possible, Margo?" It wasn't that long ago that they were trying to push me to another division.

"There's so much work in Research to catch up on that we could use another shift and a night manager to run it. Overnight, this place would be all yours."

"Nine p.m. to six a.m.?"

"That's right. You and your team would get special pay to make up for it."

Become group manager of a Research unit and give up on my dream? Likely stay in Taxpayer Service forever? "Margo," I said, "I can only promise you I'll think about it." But in the space of those few seconds, I had already thought about it. Even aside from the crazy hours, I could never handle the technical end. I wasn't fit to shine Janis's shoes, let alone be her equal. I would've needed years more experience in WAR. But there was no use telling my number one fan that I couldn't do it; she would only see that as false modesty.

"Can you offer me the same position in the phone unit? That's something I could really think about."

"No," she said sadly. "That's not my branch."

I took a deep breath. "Then I have to say no."

That's how I came to turn the management spot down and put myself in harm's path in the Examination Division. Such was my tunnel vision. No NSA hacking, no CIA with Marshall Colotine, no Taxpayer Service management. Somewhere in the dark sky above me, where Fate had momentarily taken a coffee break, a heavenly clock was ticking towards an unknown deadline.

CHAPTER SEVENTEEN
Revenue Agent

"Thirty seconds after you're born, you have a past. Sixty seconds after that, you're denying it."

—The Brood

September 29, 1986

On this day, at 8 am, in a courtroom full of fresh faces, I faced the flag, raised my right hand, and took the oath of office as an Internal Revenue Agent. Was there any such thing as an *External* Revenue Agent? I had no idea. It was just one of the musings that tumbled through my head. Another was the fact that he last time I'd raised my hand to take an oath, I was a Boy Scout. This was where fourteen years had taken me. The outfit might have changed, but my penchant for being a straight arrow never would.

Even as I enjoyed the bittersweet moment, I sighed inwardly at the thought of another lengthy training period to come. Two years had passed since Linda had warned me that the process could take a long time. *You've done the right thing. I have faith in you.* What she didn't tell me was that long before the process was over, there would be no Linda. But hey, I might eventually admit that was my own fault.

Before my training even began, I had an audience with the Examination Division Chief. If one of the Roman emperors was Spanish—and for all I know there might have been one—this man was what he would have looked like. He had the imperial manner, the gravitas, and the haircut you see on the statues. I was there with two guys from out of town, and the chief had us stand in a straight line in the military stance known as "attention" when he addressed us.

"You three were selected as the top candidates for Revenue Agent, ranked one, two, and three nationally. I won't say what order."

We all smiled and glanced at each other, trying not to break formation. To be honest, not knowing what order we were in irked me to the point of nearly forgetting the honor itself. The IRS had always provided job rankings. Now they couldn't?

"You are going into a training group," he continued, as he paced in front of us, "but starting from your first day on the job, you are in no way to be considered, or treated, as trainees. If anyone gives you any trouble, they will answer to me."

So I really wouldn't be joining another endless training run? Now he was speaking my language. If this Roman emperor said he could make such a thing happen, who was I to argue? I let that fantasy run its course for five minutes. In actuality, I assumed that everything I'd just heard was all too good to be true.

We went straight from the emperor's office to our first non-training class, joining all those who were officially trainees on Varick Street. These classes, which covered tax law again from a new perspective that included case law and general investigation techniques, all went by in a blur until the very last installment. Stress Management was the module that caught my attention. The IRS made the reasonable assumption that each of their agents would be under a great deal of strain. They even provided a lengthy self-evaluation quiz to show you why you were so depressed, or soon would be. All-in-all, it seemed they were trying to remind you that factors outside of the IRS were most of the problem, as opposed to low pay and office politics.

The day-long class in stress counseling was the IRS's preventive medicine, the parting shot before they set us loose on the world. Our stress councilor, Gwynn Murphy, had one piece of advice, and only one: "When you feel stressed out, beat up someone smaller than you. I always do."

Ms. Murphy did nothing that might have revealed she was less than entirely serious about this counsel. No smile, no qualifier. Did she mean that we should physically beat someone up? Or did she mean it in the sense that the IRS beats up on taxpayers? Either way, it sounded irresponsible and vicious to me. One of my fellow trainees quit that day. I advised him to stick it out and be one of the good guys, as I was going to do, but he said, "the place makes my stomach churn."

Once I was back at my post of duty—same building, top floor—I discovered that we had obviously misjudged Ms. Murphy. My new training manager, Simon Rusterholtz, who reminded me of my used car dealer, asked each of us into his office for a few words with him.

When it was my turn, I brought up the stress councilor's instruction to beat up someone smaller than you, and asked him, "What do you make of that?"

He said, "She's wrong. Don't wait until you're stressed out. Beat up someone smaller than you every day." There wasn't a shadow of humor in him.

Fortunately, Rusterholtz was not some slick sociopath with charm to fool everyone. He came off as a dumbass slob who fooled no one. Even his clothing choices were terrible. I myself had adopted a flamboyant medium blue dress shirt with a white collar, but he carried the 1980s too far, wearing mismatched slacks and jacket, and shirts with paisley designs when everyone else wore solids.

It would have been too easy to call him Simple Simon. There were no doors hinged onto our thin cubicle walls. He didn't care who overheard his drivel. That first day, he spewed a whole variety of equally identifiable nonsense such as, "Don't worry about proving your case. Taxpayers don't know what you're talking about anyway."

The worse news was that the Roman Emperor told the new crop of agents who had come in off the street that I had already spent two years at the IRS, and that I was at the top of the national ranking. Since Rusterholtz did not inspire confidence, they looked up to me and sought my advice rather than their group manager when they had questions. This pissed off Rusterholtz no end. He didn't know what to say about it, so he just handed me my caseload and yelled, "Mind your own business."

Nothing better exemplified life under Rusterholtz and his minions than my pizzeria case. The logistics of such an audit were a mystery to me, and the Examination Division OJI's notoriously taught very little. That day my OJI, Mickey Wogan, sat out of sight on the other side of a flimsy room divider. My section was a collection of cubes aligned like railroad cars, with me in the first car. I ran around to see

Wogan because I felt entirely unequipped to proceed. We walked into another area before hashing out the problem.

"I don't know anything about running a pizzeria," I told him desperately.

"So what?"

"I have no idea how to tell if the taxpayer is cheating, and I want to do this right."

"That's okay." Mickey's eyes gleamed with mischief. He looked like the famous photo of Franklin Roosevelt going for a car ride, cigarette holder in his smiling teeth, his prominent chin high. "Give him... a hard time."

The official excuse for keeping us in the dark was that they didn't want everyone in a cookie-cutter mold. That non-advice scared the crap out of me. I had no intention of giving someone a hard time just on principle. And then what? Make some random adjustments? I didn't know what other people were doing, but there had to be a difference between the Wild West shows they staged in office audit and what we higher professionals were supposed to do.

On my first day speaking with the store owner, I fell back on valuable generalized rules such as, *Get what they have before you tell them what you know.* Then I stayed up all night reading the manual before our next appointment. The manual, fortunately, knew all about pizzerias. There was a completely scientific way to figure out what was going on. I told Mickey Wogan he was finished coaching me.

To my surprise, he agreed, saying, "It's Rusterholtz who didn't want you to have any help, so he'll like this just fine." So I was flying solo in the auditing business.

That was when our Bonnie and Clyde Revenue Agents showed up again. It seemed that Rusterholtz, who was about to leave on temporary assignment, had invited them to visit our group in the hopes that some of their charisma and popularity would rub off on him. It worked. At least with the fourteen trainees. Through the skinny walls and open doorways, I could hear how everyone was thrilled to stop work and congratulate the celebrity pair. The Bonnie and Clyde arrest record for bribery cases had grown more disproportionate than ever, and I wondered if anyone but me was suspicious about that.

As a result of their success, all the post-training agents were coming under a lot of pressure to report bribes. When they explained that no one was trying to bribe them, they were accused of keeping the money offered to them. Soon I would be in a position to find out which party was telling the truth.

When the boss brought the Cunnings around to me, he wanted me to get a full dose of their charm too. Through a smile, he said, "Danny, this is Mitzi and Noel Cunning."

Mitzi was really playing into her role these days with a form-fitting 1930s-style dress over her slinky form, chewing and popping gum as Noel did all the talking in his dark blue pinstripes. I took in their costumes with a skeptical eye, and said without enthusiasm, "Yes, we've met."

Noel looked at me and said, "Oh yeah. So you made it into the Big Show after all. That's why people keep asking me if I know Shapiro. You're supposed to be a hot-shot. But you're never going to do what we do."

I said, "That's okay. Maybe no one should."

LIFE IN THE Examinations Division was entirely different from what I knew in Taxpayer Service. The calendar on my desk was an audit schedule filled with appointments. The calendar on the wall was a "locator," informing management of where I would be that day. According to Rusterholtz, the early days were mandatory office work, but this was the one area where I asserted the emperor's exception for me.

Among my cases, I'd already seen a nail salon owner who tried to deduct hundred dollar dinners with everyone she knew, a limo service owner with a book of fake repair receipts, a pharmacy owner who listed eight cats as "children," and a trial lawyer who burst into tears and confessed to stealing all of his client's escrow money before the audit even began. The computer had picked them all out as likely cheaters, and I would get a sheet telling me which areas were initially suspect. We'd known nothing about the lawyer and his escrow money until he told me. Now I had a magazine owner with a zero circulation. Another easy one, I imagined.

Gerhard Skeans, the publisher of *Leisure Fountain*, was an older man who had been getting away with a tax dodge for nearly three decades. Simply put, his magazine never attempted to sell the copies it printed. Skeans was not in business to provide a service, but to live the life his glitzy magazine portrayed. Other taxpayers were obliged to subsidize Skeans' never-ending vacations, the trips he took to produce content for articles that no one read. Then he went a step further and claimed a complete loss every year so that he didn't pay taxes on his full-time job. By the 1980's, the IRS thought it was about time to curtail this sort of abuse, and pulled Skeans in for an audit, tasking me with proving the case. At the inception, I thought wrapping it up would go as smoothly as my previous cases.

Things rarely go the way they look at the outset. When Skeans sauntered into my cubicle, he glanced behind him and called out, "Bring it in, boys." Four moving men filed in after him and began to fill my small office with twelve dollies stacked to the brim with magazines he had printed over the years.

"Don't let the movers go anywhere," I warned him. He ran a nervous hand through his thick white bristle of hair as I took a few magazines off the stack and thumbed through them. The layouts looked professional. "Good enough. Now haul them all out."

"But—"

"I'm done with them, so that's that." I was five or six months into this "field" agent work. Except for my visit to the cat children, it hadn't taken me into the field very often. Staying in saved time, but I was still falling way behind because I'd been asked to treat each and every one of my cases very seriously. The arduous part was the paperwork, where I put in a tremendous amount of detail for the reviewers and internal spies to read. Now that I had the job, I wasn't sure how I felt about it. When I met people who were trying to intimidate me, I began to wonder whether Rusterholtz had a point about how to handle our natural advantage in the balance of power.

No, I quickly decided, the IRS should only be turning the screws on people who proved to merit that treatment. With guys like Skeans, being firm was enough. In any case,

Rusterholtz was on extended assignment in Texas and the legendary Perry Topaz was filling in for him. I knew that old Perry would back me up because he was a famous expert in business expenses. Perry the Legend, we called him. In fact, I'd read a few of his redacted case files in order to prepare for Skeans. I didn't want any more pizzeria surprises where I was relying on help that would never come.

"I've been in for an audit before," Skeans explained like a pedantic teacher. "Twenty-five years ago, I proved to the other auditor that I ran a genuine business, and he made no adjustment."

"I agree. That was a long time ago."

He waved his hand dismissively. "It's already established that these magazines have legitimate content, and I showed you the proof again just now. You have to let me go."

"No, I don't." He registered surprise, so I continued, "Writing and printing up all these issues means that you're not a complete fraud. I'll give you that. But there's the separate matter of never having shown a profit in the twenty-five years since your last visit here."

He shrugged. "If no one feels like buying my magazine, it's not my problem. I do the work."

"I looked at your records to find thirty straight years of losses, and I find that thirty years of a failed business makes it a pastime."

"So what?"

"So your fellow citizens are no longer going to pay for your hobby."

"Outrageous. I want to see your superior."

"That's not a problem."

"No, forget about your superior," he said with a dramatic finger in the air. "I want to see the original auditor."

"The original? Alexander Hamilton left here in seventeen ninety-five." That made him blink. I pulled out the paperwork to close the audit. "You can't ask to see a previous auditor anyway."

"I'm not asking. I *demand* to see him. My guy was Perry Topaz. I consider him a very good friend of mine."

The name hit me like cold water. I hadn't expected to find a file on Gerhard Skeans in Topaz' case files so I'd never looked for it. Could the very person who I thought would surely back me up, actually be biased in favor of this taxpayer?

It didn't matter. I'd followed all the rules, and if an audit subject wanted to see a man who just happened to be my manager, that was fine.

"You're in luck, Mr. Skeans. Mr. Topaz is three yards away and he probably heard everything."

Skeans looked more shocked than I was, but he let me sit him down while I went to talk with Perry. Perry had a hearing problem so I was sure that he had heard nothing.

The old man wore Converse sneakers to the office and typically planted them on the edge of his desk to help him tip back in his chair. I didn't begrudge him his foot problems, but the only thing worse than seeing those sneakers on the desk was when he took them off. He had them off now, and the socks too, as he used a sandpaper nail file on a wart that had formed over his bunion. The smell was awful and he sawed at the base of his big toe as we spoke. Perry the Legend had tremendous latitude at the IRS.

"Yes?" He glanced at me and continued his sawing, spreading flakes on the desk top.

"I have a Gerhard Skeans here that says he needs to speak to you... He says he considers you a good friend of his... Just so you know, I'm auditing him"

Topaz was trying to work out what I was saying, or he may have been concentrating on the bunion, but he finally looked up and concluded, "I don't know anyone by that name."

"He says you do, that you audited him a long time ago. *Leisure Fountain Magazine?*"

"Hmm. What's he want?" Uh oh. Did Topaz really remember him?

"He's not happy with my decision. He claims that your previous decision overrides it."

I had Topaz's full attention. "And what's your decision based on?"

"Your favorite. The Three-out-of-Five Rule. In this case, it's thirty out of five, a lifetime of losses."

"All right. Bring him in."

"Sir?"

"What?"

"Your feet."

"Oh." He pulled an old argyle sock over the foot with the bunion and the bulge popped right out of a hole in the fabric. "Hm. I guess I'd better put my shoes on too."

I knew that I was right about Mr. Skeans' weak position, and I wasn't going to back down under any circumstances. That made me far more relaxed than I would have been in my earlier years at the IRS, but considerably less relaxed than a guy who sawed at bunions while at work.

Skeans came in, and I heard cordial words exchanged between them as I went out. I sat down and dug into my backlog of paperwork. Before long, they were arguing at an increasing volume, indicating that maybe they weren't such good friends after all. They gradually grew louder until I could easily hear how Perry put it to an end:

"You're wrong, Skeans, and Shapiro is right. You did thirty out of five. I don't want to hear you question him again. You're lucky you're not in jail."

Perry was all right in my book. More importantly, even though I didn't know it yet, I was getting fortified for the audit of my life.

THERE IS AN entire profession that engages in the business of representing taxpayers in IRS audits. While they can be a tremendous help on technical issues, sometimes the people who do this job are totally incompetent or even crooked. They might threaten, call for endless appointment cancellations, falsify information, or even, yes, offer bribes to agents like Mitzi and Noel. If the "rep" comes off as slimy, though, the taxpayer that employs them usually suffers for it. Ward Riley Turlingame was both incompetent and crooked, and he represented my upcoming audit subject.

I caught this investigation as part of a project called CREEPS, the Commercial Real Estate Projects. I strongly objected to the acronym (and its extra "E") because that word implied that the people under scrutiny were guilty until proven innocent. On the other hand, if I'd been asked whether taxpayer's reps could be described as creeps, I'd be far more likely to agree.

As Turlingame surveyed his surroundings—the small desk my office, the moveable walls, and the red and orange unmatched guest chairs—a smug grin registered on his face.

"Why don't you have a seat?" I said, hoping to forestall the sarcasm I usually heard from his kind. The prospect of a seat didn't satisfy him. Maybe he wouldn't be comfortable in our chairs, I reflected. He was an unusually big-hipped man, shaped overall like a bowling pin.

"Nice place you have here, son. You could use a few pictures on the wall." Oh-so-innocently, he added, "Is it *possible* to hang something on a cubicle wall?" He knew it wasn't. In those days, the corporate world was handing out real offices with real doors to all of their management-level employees. To people like Turlingame, we government types looked a little foolish in comparison.

I ignored him and picked up a pencil to signal that I wanted to get down to business, but Turlingame wasn't finished.

"The government-issued pencil, huh? Did they give you a sharpener, son? You really should get yourself a mechanical pencil. I'd give you one of mine, but I don't want to be accused of bribery."

Briskly, I replied, "First, I am not your son. You will refer to me as Mr. Shapiro. And you will keep your comments about this office to yourself. Thank you."

Turlingame chuckled, pleased to get a reaction. Out came the gold cigarette case and the inevitable gold lighter.

"There is no smoking in my office," I informed him.

Turlingame looked surprised, the sort of theatrical high eyebrow surprise that must have played well elsewhere. He scrutinized the cigarette as though trying to figure out what could be offensive about it.

I looked at him pointedly. "You can hold it in your hand if you like, but do not light it."

"Sure kid." He actually put the cigarette and the lighter down in surprise. "So what's going on here? What kind of adjustment are you looking to make?"

"That's better. I'll just make a copy of your power of attorney and we can get down to business."

"Hey," he held his empty hands wide. "I don't need a power of attorney to come in here."

"You know better than that. I can accept information from you, but I can't give you any information. You asked me a question that it would be illegal to answer."

"C'mon. Be a good friend to me. I just have a few things I want to know."

"Which you can ask next time, when you have authorization. Now if that's all you came here for—"

"Which items are you adjusting?"

"Turn around," I told him slowly. "And go home."

He did. And I could have considered the matter dormant, but whoever he was representing was getting a raw deal, and I felt bad about that. The idea of CREEPS was to trace the money that went into the investor's buildings back to the original source to find out if the first property was obtained with legal or illegal cash. If there were a lot of "flips" you would have to go through the whole chain of transactions. But the lady who was targeted by the investigation, Marilyn Kopple, was in residential real estate, not commercial. So she shouldn't have been swept up in the project. Now she had hired this boob who was getting her into trouble before the audit even began. I sat down and created a worksheet that would get to the bottom of whether any suspicion against her was warranted. But I needed information from the taxpayer that I didn't yet have.

Turlingame returned empty-handed again the next week. I couldn't imagine why he would do that. All he needed to do was get a signed power of attorney from the person he was representing. Unless he was up to something else.

Our third appointment was over just as quickly as the first time I had met with him. As I shooed him out, he sighed, "Oh crud. Why do you have to make it so hard?"

"If you don't like coming in for nothing, fax the paperwork to me and call to see if you're cleared."

He made a snarling noise.

I said, "Sorry, the law hasn't changed," and he reached out and snatched the audit file from me.

Now I knew his plan. I yanked it back before he could read anything and I called security, which set off flashing red lights in the corridor and a repeating buzzer that sounded very different from the fire alarm. Turlingame suddenly sat down on his enormous rump and tried to look innocent, examining his manicure.

I went to peek into the hallway to watch for our men in uniform. Perry Topaz came out to ask if someone had hit the alarm, and I said I did. Looking at the ostentatious light show that went with the buzzer, he said, "Aw, you don't have to do that."

"Yes, I do," I shouted over the noise. "This is the third time Turlingame showed up without a Power of Attorney. He has no authorization and he's demanding to see confidential taxpayer information."

"What's his angle?"

I looked over his shoulder to make sure Turlingame was staying put. "He's been trying to trap me in a disclosure violation to get his client off the hook. This time he grabbed the file out of my hands."

Perry's eyes widened with realization. "That's a bad one, you're right. But the guy is friends with Rusterholtz and he's coming back from vacation, you know." Funny that Turlingame would be friends with Rusterholtz. I wondered how that combination had happened.

"Too late to worry about that now," I said, as the guards came in. I explained the situation to them, and said, "Please take this man's picture for our wall and then escort him out, or do what you see fit." They were excited by this rare opportunity and obviously hoped that Turlingame would try to give them some trouble. When he saw the heat I brought down, he hunched up sheepishly as they each took an arm. The guards sneered their distaste at him as he went without a fight.

I thought this wild rep must be a man with nothing to lose to act as he did and then leave without any trouble. But no, it turned out that Turlingame was credentialed as an Enrolled Agent, which was a sort of contract with the IRS that got him through the door in the first place. As Rusterholtz's friend, he must have thought he was immune to consequences. He gambled, and I went ahead and got him disbarred, which meant that he could not enter an IRS office again without being arrested. He was no longer an Enrolled Agent, and that was a tough perk to reclaim. The boss would be angry, but I was right so I didn't worry about it.

Now the taxpayer had to come in to see me herself, and she did.

Marilyn Kopple wore mink. Diamonds and gold glistened from her ears to her fingertips. People stared as she walked down the halls and through the aisles. Obviously, she was still taking some of Turlingame's bad advice to navigate the audit with one stunt after another. There was a school of thought that said you must remind the IRS that you are rich and therefore do not need to steal money. In fact, that was the worst possible course of action because on the surface there was no way to tell if the money on display came from an honest or dishonest source. Fortunately for her, I went by evidence, not appearances.

Marilyn made no secret of the fact that she was greatly distressed to be there. "This is beyond inconvenient," she remarked to people she passed in the hall.

But I got her to cooperate nonetheless, giving me all the records I needed, which consisted of the closing documents on every one of her real estate purchases and sales. Given the verified numbers, I traced her cash flow all the way back to her original small investment and found that her money was clean. I cheerfully gave her the good news and told her to be careful who she hires.

As predicted, Rusterholtz, fresh from his Texas assignment, was supremely unhappy with me when I turned in these results. He demanded that I reverse my decision and find Marilyn Kopple criminally guilty. He even brought the branch chief down on me for added pressure. I refused and invoked the rule that management could not interfere in an agent's final judgement. I was making new enemies fast.

Luckily, my time was up in the Rusterholtz group. But his retaliation was to let Mitzi and Noel Cunning take over the Kopple case—the only case that anyone cared to grab from my inventory. Mitzi stared at me like a zoo visitor and popped gum, and Noel said, "You had your chance, Shapiro."

It wasn't legal for them to re-open the years that I'd covered. Their loophole was to pick the one remaining year where the statute of limitations had not expired. As usual, the couple worked together and wore wires. And like everyone else they dealt with, they somehow got Marilyn on tape offering them a bribe, after which they accused her of fraud and threatened her with a prison stretch.

So now this woman who had definitely *not* been cheating on her taxes was arrested and off to trial despite all of my work to keep an innocent taxpayer out of trouble. Damn Bonnie and Clyde. I knew they were bad apples, and wondered where their little reign of terror would end.

CHAPTER EIGHTEEN
House Legend

"Round up the usual suspects."

—*Casablanca*

Tuesday, March 17, 1987

Treasury does not hand you the agent commission until the training period is officially over, and it had been over since Friday. On Tuesday, while I had my nose deep in paperwork, Zelda, our elderly receptionist, shuffled into my cubicle and put the official document in my hand with a short, "Congratulations." To my complete surprise, she pulled out a coiled paper party horn, put her mouth on the orange plastic mouthpiece, and blew into it, making a sound halfway between a duck honk and a rude raspberry. "That makes it official," she concluded with a straight face.

I smiled sadly, remembered to make an effort to laugh, and thanked her as she left me to muse over the thick, laminated card in the leather case. Way overdue—as I saw it—on the old schedule, the dream I had with Linda, years earlier, when there was still a Linda.

I bit my lip hard as I thought about my situation. Though it wasn't that private in my office, I didn't care. I had tried calling her every time something new happened, and when I lifted the phone this time it was my longest one-way call. I remember saying, "I got my agent commission. I could never have done it without you." I was fairly certain that she listened to my messages, so I pictured her reactions

344

along with my own. In my imagination, she felt joy, wonder and admiration for me, all of which were reluctant emotions, but maybe enough to chip away at our differences in the long run. If she had said anything in reaction, I was sure it would be noncommittal, her emotional cards held close to her vest. *You made it? Wow, good luck.*

It actually cheered me up a little. I looked again and saw the humor in the situation. The "creds" carried by Examination Division, at the time, did not include a badge *per se*, the only shiny part being the lamination. Rather they consisted of the IRS logo, my picture, and a wordy explanation, as you would expect of the Treasury Department:

> "Daniel J. Shapiro, whose signature and picture appear above, is duly commissioned as an Internal Revenue Agent and has authority to perform all duties conferred upon such officers under the laws and regulations administered by the Internal Revenue Service, including the authority to investigate, and to require and receive information, as to all matters relating to such laws and regulations."

> —By the authority of the Commissioner of Internal Revenue

I memorized it as though it might go up in flames. It actually looked similar to my old ID, only larger, to make room for the "legend," as they called it. So now those who wanted to read it, those who wanted to challenge me—and I would meet such people— could verify the authority under which I was acting.

Of course, since this was the IRS, even the commission itself was identified by a form number. An IRS "badge" is Form 4689 D.

In any case, the new creds meant I no longer had to deal with Rusterholtz. I had a new manager, and faced a new beginning.

Wednesday, March 18, 1987

Tanglewood was in a bad mood and had his office door closed as he worked on the department budget. The word from on high was that there was going to be a Federal government shutdown this year and likely pay freezes any day now to prevent an even-earlier shutdown. That would impact operations at the FBI as much as every other federal agency. He wasn't taking calls, but this one came through on an internal line, and the FBI was the first place to have caller ID, at least by department. He had a pretty good idea what the call might be about.

"Cameron Tanglewood?" the caller asked.

He grunted.

"I need a verbal confirmation of who I'm speaking to."

"Yes!" he yelled. "It's Ron!" He didn't like to acknowledge his first name. He always thought it should be Gregory, like Gregory Peck. If it had to be a "C" name, it could have been Carey, as in Grant. A celebrity name would not have been an ironic choice for him. He took pride in his roguish good looks. Ladies said he resembled a "handsome wolf." But he'd gotten stuck with the name Cameron, which a lot of people pronounced in an unflattering way—Came-ron—so he told people his name was Ron.

"So noted, Mr. Tanglewood. You left instructions that interagency information be released only to you."

"Go ahead."

"I have an IRS alert in front of me regarding Senator Clarkeson's tax matters. His refund check is in suspension and his theft deduction has been flagged for audit. Treasury's investigation has been assigned to someone listed as... Agent S."

Perfect. "Okay, make sure they send Clarkeson the check."

"Did you say *send* him the check?"

"Yes, release the hold on his refund, but make sure that his audit notification reaches him in the same mail delivery." Though Tanglewood wasn't a lawyer, he knew that it always made for a more solid presentation at trial if the perp cashed the refund check, especially if they also knew that the origin of that money was under investigation.

"Should I notify the agent in charge on your end? Monroe Eastman?"

"No, I'll tell him." Maybe he would. Actually, no, not likely.

"Anything else?"

Tanglewood thought about it a little further. "Yes. Monitor 911 calls in Felton and Brooklyn, and let me know if any case-related names pop up."

"Will do, sir."

They both hung up, and he leaned back and folded his arms behind his head. Now Ron Tanglewood was in a better mood. A much better mood.

Friday, March 20, 1987

Once I had my credentials in hand, John Aberdeen was officially in charge of me even though my instructions were not to report to him until the end of the week. He was from Montana, a cowboy type, tall and lean, and a real gentleman.

When we met, I smiled and said, "Big Sky Country," recalling a Montana license plate I'd seen a few years earlier. He was happy enough to hear it, but correctly deduced that I knew no more than that about his home state, so he spared me the quiz.

"I won't kid you," he said in his crisp Western accent. "You've got a lot of crap here." Aberdeen was talking about my Phase I cases. He was running the standard case review done when anyone joins a new group. It was especially important when going from training to the permanent group. "You can't bring those through my door."

I let him know, "The Division Chief asked me to treat those cases as Phase II."

"Then he shouldn't have saddled you with this load of crap. Hell, he shouldn't have even given you a full inventory of Phase II cases while you've still got the others." He was right. Treasury's Roman Emperor must have had a screw loose. Maybe the whole agency had a screw loose. Aberdeen sat down and beckoned me over to his side of the desk. "Here, take a look at some of these with me. Everyone in these folders are blatantly cheating on their taxes, but they're small and they're going to eat up time you need for the next batch, the more challenging stuff. Do you know the answer to that problem?"

"Get rid of them?"

"You're smart." From anyone else in that office that reply might have been meant as an insult, but the man didn't have a sarcastic bone in his body. He was a straight shooter.

"Maybe not as smart as you think," I said. "How do I do it without getting in trouble?"

"I'll cover you. Just get them in and out of here quick. It's the taxpayer's lucky day."

"Close them without adjustments?"

"Not that lucky. Settle for something, for anything. Shortcuts and agreements. But don't let any of the cheaters go for free. I call it Aberdeen's Rule."

I wasn't entirely sure how I felt about this rule, but I would have called it benevolent pragmatism. Given the situation I found myself in, it was the only way to go. "And after that?"

"After that, you're going to have some real bad guys to catch."

"Is my new inventory ready?"

"Hell yeah. The first file is top priority. It came in from the FBI."

"They can send us cases?"

"Those are the best ones, although some of your peers think they're the worst. In management circles, they call you the Bulldog. You're a house legend." He smiled broadly, showing me a nice set of teeth. "I want to see the Bulldog come out."

Aberdeen introduced me to Yoffe so I could learn how the paperwork went. Yoffe was a nice guy with lots of homespun advice, but he was no Hector. He also wasn't a bulldog and I supposed that's why they needed me. I didn't know about this new nickname but at least it wasn't Creds. Either way, I was determined to live up to everyone's expectations. I thought I was Superman.

But as smart as I imagined myself to be with my new commission in hand, I made a boneheaded mistake the very same night. I went to celebrate at Patrick's Pub with a young lady named Melody Persky whom I'd met at a singles dance. Patrick's Pub would become our regular place.

Melody was a woman of limited imagination—my nice way of thinking she was not very bright—so as I saw it, we had no future. But she was beauty incarnate, and that helped me rationalize our linkage at the time. Melody, who would become Linda's rival, and she who would indirectly set events into motion that could not be stopped...

Saturday, March 21, 1987

The senator had gotten up at 9 AM—his Saturday compromise to wake up late, do some personal business, and then enjoy the weekend. He got ready with a cold shower on the "needle" setting and did a twenty-minute workout routine on the bike and punching bag before going into his home office for a half-day's work. At a few minutes after ten, as he was going over a list of local residents in trouble who he might be able to "do business" with, Alma knocked on the door and brought in the mail, as he expected she would do.

"Lock the door on your way out, Alma."

"Yes, sir."

Clarkeson enjoyed the mail that came to his home. Some of his more ambitious constituents, who were looking for special treatment, put installments of cash directly in the envelopes with no explanation at all. These were the people he favored, and this pile was the best he'd seen in a long time. One of these envelope-fillers had a company that was too small for the city job it was hired for. Now it needed loan guarantees to get the job done. For the right price, Clarkeson would put the city of Felton on the hook to pay off the loan if the contractor defaulted. With the latest envelope, the company reached the threshold of "contributions" at which the senator was willing to guarantee the loan.

Now Clarkeson saw the refund check from the Treasury Department with its multi-colored hues showing through the envelope window. He kissed it even before opening it and used his antique brass letter opener, the one shaped like a dagger, to slit the edge. And, yes, the check was made out for the exact amount he requested.

Then he saw the other letter from Treasury, the very last piece of mail in the pile. This one didn't have a plastic window showing a check. The logo was in black. This item he tore open raggedly by hand, and stared at its contents, dumfounded. It seemed to be a summons for an audit of his tax return.

351

For the same year where he just got his refund a moment earlier. A summons for this coming Friday. "What the fuck?"

Did it really say Blaine Clarkeson on it?

Yes, it did. Senator Blaine Clarkeson.

He took his dagger letter opener by its handle and stabbed it right into the desk. Then he dragged over the phone and dialed Brinkman, who took a little too long to pick up.

The lawyer had to override his voicemail. Then he said, "Okay, we're good now. What's up, boss?"

"I'm being audited!"

"By who?"

"The Internal Revenue Service."

"For what year?"

"The year I just filed. I just got the damn refund check. How could that happen?"

"It's strange, but it's possible. When are they calling you in?"

"Not me! It's gonna be you. Friday the twenty-seventh. It says bring all records. How the hell am I being audited in the Brooklyn District IRS Offices?"

"It's that love nest you bought in Manhattan. You took business expenses on it."

"Still, why is it Brooklyn?"

"Brooklyn District covers the whole metro area. But the twenty-seventh is no good for me. I can get a postponement."

"No postponement. Clear your schedule and get there. I want this over with."

"Whose name is on the letter as the auditor?"

"It says… Daniel Shapiro, Revenue Agent. Who the hell cares?"

"Wait, what unit is Shapiro in? It's in the upper right hand corner."

"It says Unit five two seven, why?"

"Nothing to worry about. That's a training unit. It's nothing. Shapiro won't figure anything out. Even the police didn't get it."

"I don't give a damn. Whoever he is, he can still cause trouble. Listen to me. Wake the fuck up, if you haven't already. Do not handle this piece of business the way you handled Junior. I want the problem gone fast."

"It will be."

"No, that's not good enough. I want you to have a back-up plan in place for that same night in case he doesn't listen to reason."

"Trainee or not, he's a federal agent," Brinkman reminded him with what sounded like a measure of concern.

"There are ways to do it where it won't come back on us. No more discussion. By the morning after that audit, I want to hear good news."

Clarkeson slammed down the phone and made two more decisions: On Monday, he would cash his refund check. Then he would fire Alma, for handing him that shock.

Friday, March 27, 1987

Although I was behind in my work, it couldn't be helped that I had a taxpayer's representative named

Brinkman scheduled to come to my office in a few minutes. The audit file in front of me was simply labeled, "Blaine Clarkeson," and the address had him in upstate New York, which seemed very unusual to me. I was about to look him up in our WAR system to get some background, but at the last moment, my finger hesitated over the "send" key. The name sounded familiar, like someone who had been mentioned in the news. I pulled out the tax return in question and flipped to the signature page.

Sure enough, his occupation was identified as, "Senator," though I knew that he wasn't part of the elite club known as the U.S. Senate where there were just two from each state. Clarkeson was part of our local senate, a body of over sixty members. Even little Connecticut had over thirty local senators, so there had to be thousands of them in the country. Did the prohibition on looking up politicians apply at his level? Was I free to look him up if he was my audit subject or did that require permission? The topic hadn't been covered in revenue agent training, probably because revenue agents were not trained in WAR. If they wanted anything from the database, they had to put in a request to a user of that system and wait to see if the request was accepted. I decided not to chance a SWAT team response. I felt sure I should be able to handle this audit with the information in front of me.

Anyway, time was up. The burly rep who showed up at my office for the audit clamped his paw onto my hand in a vise grip to show me he was a workout king, but I knew that trick already. If you didn't meet pressure for pressure at the outset, you'd get your bones crushed. I poured it on to match. I may have puffed myself up with more confidence than I felt, but this part I could handle. This was my first really big case.

"You picked the wrong guy to audit," warned Curt Brinkman. "You have no idea who you're dealing with."

He was referring to State Senator Clarkeson, but I believed he meant that I should fear him as well. Brinkman's suit wasn't quite a thousand-dollar job, but it was marvelously tailored to accommodate his weightlifter's shoulders. I could read the word, "Rolex" on his watch. With his diamond cuff links, two gold wrist chains, tie chain, and stick pin there was not one accessory he didn't have, or feel the need to adjust in front of me. Best of all was the Harvard ring he rotated on his index finger. He glanced at our surroundings contemptuously, fabric walls stretched on metal frames to form my six-by-six cube. I was waiting for him to say, *I earned all my money eating people like you for breakfast, lunch, and dinner.*

It was a good act for a mob lawyer, but not the deportment I expected from the representative of an elected official, as he was supposed to be. By this time in my career, I'd already seen that when dishonest people are powerful enough, they make the rest of us pay their taxes. I said, "That's a smooth opening line, Mr. Brinkman. However, I think we'll just take it step by step today." I winked in order to irritate him the way he was trying to irritate me.

He dropped his jaw and stared wordlessly in a classic courthouse antic—the best show I'd seen since Turlingame.

"I know, I know, Mr. Brinkman, you're deeply offended. Have a seat." We sat simultaneously.

"How long have you been doing this?" he said in an effort to know his enemy, and open a wound if I were sensitive about being a novice among my fellow agents.

"Since the Carter administration," I lied without any compunction. Two years, seven, or fifty, it was none of his business.

"I thought this was an area for recent trainees," he said in a voice sluggish with disappointment.

"You thought wrong."

"But the letter…"

"The letter was wrong. There are trainees in this group, but I'm not one of them." This part, according to my Division Chief, was entirely correct from the start. "Will that be a problem for you?"

"Ah, no, it doesn't matter," he said, digging into his oversized valise to fish out a power of attorney and hand it to me.

"Thank you."

He waited quietly for me to read it and put it away before asking, "Do you realize that this is a *Senator* that you're auditing?"

"A New York *State* Senator, yes I know."

"I've been in this business for over twenty years. You're not going to get anywhere on this and you'll ruin yourself in the process." He casually dug deeper in his valise to show he was unconcerned with my fate.

I smiled. "Let's give it a try, Mr. Brinkman."

"What triggered this audit?" he asked.

"They don't tell us that. The returns get assigned to us without comment."

"I see." What he saw was that I was playing it close.

"I will be happy to tell you what areas I would like to examine. I'll even let you choose what you are prepared to go over first. Is that fair?"

"If you would be so kind." No more sophomoric nonsense. Brinkman was knocked down to an ordinary lawyer for the moment.

"We'll do contributions and casualty," I informed him. "What's your poison?"

"Charitable contributions first."

"I'll need to see the canceled checks." *Aberdeen's Rules of the road: Get what they have before you show them what you know.*

"Right here." Brinkman produced a folder that turned out to contain canceled checks with a schedule tied into the tax return.

Now I could afford to be nice. I said, "This is a well-prepared schedule, Mr. Brinkman."

"Thank you." He sounded genuinely relieved.

I was able to breeze down his neat list, observing, "There is indeed a canceled check for each item claimed on the tax return. The only problem is this $2,000 contribution to Friends of Old Bailey."

"What's wrong with it?" He sat forward with lawyerly concern.

"Friends of Old Bailey is not a 501(c)(3) organization." Meaning that it did not have the federal government's EP/EO seal of approval that would legally allow for a deduction.

"That's your contention."

I laughed. "There's a book right here on my desk." I put my hand flat on the thick volume the way witnesses prepare

357

to swear on a Bible. "It's the first and last word on the subject. If an organization is not in that book, contributions to that entity are not deductible. Would you like to see it?"

"No." Looking disconcerted and a bit angry, he took a deep breath. "Look, Mr. Shapiro, Senator Clarkeson wants this over with. It seems that you've got the adjustment you were after. Let's sign off on this unpleasant business so I can get out of here."

Ignoring him a moment to glance at the documents, I said, "Now we'll talk about casualty."

Brinkman's eyes widened perceptibly, betraying... something. "You want to continue? What is this you're talking about now?"

"On the Senator's Schedule A—in his itemized deductions—he shows a very large deduction for theft."

"His home was burglarized. There's a list of the items that were stolen. It's attached to the tax return. Do you have that?"

"Yes, I do."

"Then what else could you possibly want to see?"

"Start by telling me the circumstances."

He was ready, and fairly well rehearsed. "It transpired during the Senator's vacation. The thieves got into his basement where all of the family heirlooms were stored. It was a very professional job. They cut the telephone lines first."

"Anyone hurt?"

"Nobody home. They cut the lines just in case."

"Uh huh." Mine was a skeptical uh-huh that made him avoid gilding the lily any further.

He said, "The deduction is actually very conservative. Many of the items stolen were one-of-a-kind antiques that were difficult to price, if not priceless."

"What kind of insurance did he have?" If his insurance company covered it, there would be no loss.

"His mother had just died and left him this inheritance. These items came out of storage facilities and safety deposit boxes so they could be appraised. They were still in the valuation stage." I liked this kind of information since it implied the existence of more documentary evidence. For instance, I could verify part of his tale by finding out if his mother had really just died. And if she hadn't, why would he place all of his valuables in jeopardy? In any case, why would he pull everything out of storage at once?

"No losses recouped through insurance then?"

"The homeowners gave him something. He reduced his tax deduction by the recovery."

I made a note. "It's still a sizable deduction, Mr. Brinkman. Did Clarkeson, excuse me, *Senator* Clarkeson, file a police report?"

"Yes, he did." Brinkman had this file at his fingertips too. The report had a photocopy of a handwritten list of the missing items attached. In part, they included some remarkable antiques:

    c. 1920 Set of 4 Kozma Lajos Dining Chairs. $2,950

    c. 1910 Crown Milano Blown-out Art Glass Biscuit Jar
       $855

    c. 1830 Empire Mahogany Portico Clock with Ormolu
       Mounts $1,702

c. 1890 R J Horner carved quartered oak server $5,220

c. 1830 Ring, Regency Emerald in 15K gold Vernatille setting $3,117

19th cent. French girandole, Baccarat, incomplete, $300 (sentimental value)

c. 1840 Edgar Lowe Clock in walnut case. Working condition. $2,745

c. 1830 English Rosewood Daybed $1,675

c. 1900 Oak sewing rocker with tapestry seat back $279

1909 Pietra Dura cufflinks with art deco swan design $325

1890 Drop Arm Fainting Couch $1,560

1861 Silver cast caddy spoon by Martin Hall & Co. w/ diamond reg. mark. $684

1865 Birds Eye Maple Serpentine Chest of Drawers Dresser $985

c. 1880 French Majolica Porcelain Bear $392

The list went on for several pages. I glanced up at him as I read the report. The confidence he hoped to project was belied by his habit of running a finger under his right wrist chain. While I was up in Boston I'd picked up a book on how to tell if someone was lying. They talked about things like micro-expressions, fleeting and contradictory facial changes, which I looked for now, and found. Something was absolutely wrong here for a mega-powered and highly experienced rep to be so ill at ease. What was he hiding?

While reading the list, I said, "It sounds like that was some beautiful stuff. I love antiques."

"Yes," he said blandly, "it's a tragedy."

"They must have used a truck to haul it all away."

"Yes, they must have. Are we almost done?"

"Well, this report confirms exactly what you've told me, sir."

"It does." Brinkman was pleased.

"And the valuation does look conservative. Not everyone has a police report to back up their tax claims." *Put them off guard.*

"The Senator is highly scrupulous in every area of his life."

"Was your client ever robbed before?" *Look for a pattern of fraud.*

"Yes, he was. Two years earlier. Look, I know what you're getting at. The Senator was fortunate enough to come from old money. That neighborhood is a target for everyone who wants to get their hands on it. After one theft is successful, they smell blood and come back. The police know how common that pattern is. They investigated both times so there's nothing for you to find."

"Nevertheless, I'll have to take a look at the older tax return. Do you happen to have a copy of that one with you?"

His shoulders rose. "What kind of piss poor training do you have? You find nothing here, and yet you expand the audit to another year?"

"From what you've told me, there should be nothing to be concerned about. Let me look at the prior year return, put all suspicions to rest."

He got to his feet. "You miserable little paper pusher."

"Can I expect your cooperation?"

"Where's your manager? I'll have your job by the end of the day." *Absolutely hiding something.*

"No problem." I was doing it all by the book and had nothing to fear. Looking at both years' returns was standard procedure in a casualty case. I walked him into Aberdeen's office, and the two of them went into the ring. Brinkman lost. Then he demanded to see my manager's manager, which was fine too.

All the way up the line, Brinkman was told there could be no interference with my investigation. If he did not like the results, he could exercise his rights of appeal when it was all over. Management smelled his fear as well as I did. Probably more so.

Back in my cubicle, Brinkman tossed the state senator's prior year tax return at my desk like it was tiresome garbage. I went straight to the part I needed, and again I asked for the police report. That paperwork also showed a robbery with an itemized handwritten list of stolen items, and there it was: I suddenly knew why this accessorized gorilla had fought so hard to keep this information from me. The police had not compared the two lists very carefully, or they would have seen the problem themselves.

"Where is his 1040X?" I asked calmly.

"I don't follow you," said Brinkman.

"An amended return after the first year of the senator's break-in?"

"I know what an amended return is," Brinkman said testily. "There was none. Nothing to amend."

"Senator Clarkeson must have filed a 1040X at some time to reverse his earlier claim when the police recovered the items stolen in the first robbery."

Brinkman turned red. "What the hell is the matter with you? He never recovered anything. Nothing more to report.

He got robbed twice and the police never found who did it and never found any of the items."

I could see how defendants in court could be scared shitless of this giant bruiser. I couldn't be intimidated though, since I knew where this was going.

I said, "Is that your testimony, Mr. Brinkman?" Like a court of law, the statements made by either a taxpayer or his rep in an audit were known as testimony. I studied him for a moment, noting how quiet and apprehensive he suddenly became, and then picked up my notes. "Let's read back the record to be sure. You stated that in 1984, Senator Clarkeson's home was burglarized and a number of family heirlooms were stolen."

He said, "That's correct." No wisecracks from Brinkman now.

Checking my reference I proceeded, "According to the most recent tax return, and the police report, this included a 1910 Crown Milano Blown-out Art Glass Biscuit Jar valued at $855."

"If that's what it says, yes."

"Well, he must have had two of those jars because he also had a 1910 Crown Milano Blown-out Art Glass Biscuit Jar stolen in 1982, then valued at $792."

Brinkman adjusted his class ring nervously this time. Harvard wasn't helping him very much. "Inflation. Could have been in different condition. Could have been anything."

"Fair enough," I allowed, "but then the state senator also had two sets of 1909 Pietra Dura cufflinks with art deco swan designs, *two* 1830 Empire Mahogany Portico Clocks with Ormolu Mounts, and two 1880 French Majolica

Porcelain Bears. Each stolen one at a time, two years apart. What are the odds of that?"

Brinkman was squirming in his seat, looking for the exit. "I don't know."

"In fact," I continued, "twelve out of fourteen of his most distinctive family heirlooms peppered throughout these lists appear to have been stolen in 1982 and again in 1984. Yet you say that the items stolen from the first break in were never recovered. And you said that Clarkeson's mother had just died in 1984. So where did it all come from in 1982? Would you like to re-think your position, counselor?" I paused to let him change his statement, but mostly to watch his eyes narrow.

Brinkman startled me by slamming a beefy hand down on my desk. "You just made the biggest fucking mistake of your life." Then he leaned in and spat in a whisper, "You're dead."

At the time, his words didn't mean much to me. When Curt Brinkman made that promise, I was too young to know a real threat from schoolyard trash talk.

I met his gaze. "I'll mail you the paperwork that your boss has to sign. Meanwhile, show yourself out."

Brinkman steamed past the wall clock, working his big shoulders like the wheel rods on an old locomotive. It was six PM on the nose. I thought he was going to blow a horn.

Since I was weeks behind in paperwork, and it was late already, writing up the adjustment for the state senator would have to wait. I packed my briefcase slowly to give Brinkman some leeway—wouldn't want to meet someone like that in a dark hallway—and then lifted my jacket from the seat back and took off for home.

The wind whistling through the empty cubicles I passed along the way didn't surprise me. My peers were mostly marathoners on the way to their pensions while I was still the sprinter I had been in high school: young and dumb and full of… idealism. I had noticed that the IRS sometimes bowed before rich and powerful cheaters who had the wherewithal to fight like demons, while the poorly represented, such as small homeowners, nurses, and manicurists, took the brunt of it. To me, people like state senator Clarkeson were the reason that policemen, firefighters, and teachers didn't get paid as they should, and why the whole federal government was in bankruptcy for that matter.

I ran for the D train to keep up my exercise, and for that same reason, I didn't mind lugging twenty extra pounds of files. In fact, I'd kept Clarkeson's file with me so that it didn't conveniently disappear from my desk at work. Mr. Brinkman seemed like the sort who might pay off the cleaning staff for some midnight skullduggery.

Allowing the crowd to cram me into the boxcar, I watched the rubber edges of the doors attempt to meet and then separate, and join again after the overflow commuters wedged in. None of them cared how many times they stopped the train. When there were no inconsiderate stragglers left to glare at, I made a fanfold of the Wall Street Journal and began my ritual of selecting the shares of stock I hoped to be able to afford one day. It was a bit like fantasy football. I was loading up on General Motors when the train squealed to a halt and the lights went out. I made sure I could feel the briefcase pressed between my knees, but I also stayed alert for a gentle pressure on the bottom of my wallet, with pickpockets being the more likely danger. Just regular New York stuff.

The conductor said, "We have a tree on the tracks at Prospect Park. We are sorry for the delay." I could hear the collective groan of my fellow passengers. One of those noises was probably from me. The Prospect Park tree-fall happened too often. From that point, we travelers heard not another word for half an hour. I didn't worry too much since in these cases, no further explanation was ever forthcoming. In due time, the lights blazed, the train lurched back to life, and the passengers cheered. I joined them in this noise too.

The crisp and salty autumn air at my Brighton Beach destination disarmed me the rest of the way. Galloping down the station stairs, I planned the rest of my evening: dinner on the stove and a call to Linda. No one expects to die on a beautiful night.

At Brighton 10th Street, however, darkness reigned. That was where all the lights had been smashed and the ambush was staged. I was ready for a karate fight, if necessary, but not ready for the pick-up truck with the wicked iron cowcatcher. Now it chased me down the block and angled toward me on the sidewalk. It wasn't going to be a mugging.

Belatedly, I figured out that Brinkman actually meant *dead* when he plainly said I would be dead. If I'd been inclined to look up Clarkeson in the WAR system, maybe I would have seen a clue in his background. I should have postponed the whole thing and completed the research.

That was when the salt air washed over me. I thought about the beginning of life, and childhood memories of being overwhelmed by the tide. I thought about Linda. Childhood was forever out of reach, and now so was she.

CHAPTER NINETEEN
The Senator

"Being right is not a bullet proof vest."

—Ray Liotta, *Cop Land*

I sucked in air through my teeth, anticipating the pick-up truck slamming into my back. But it didn't. Not quite yet. There were no other people or cars in sight, and therefore no help. There was a six-foot high wooden fence along the properties to my left with the other side of the wide street too far away to cross past the speeding vehicle. I knew there was a short wire fence at the corner house on the next block. That became my objective and I ran flat out for it.

I saw the car lights veer left in alignment with me just before I heard the tires thud on the curb, one after the other. The sound of the engine drilled in my ears, and the headlights were directly at my back, throwing their long shadows ahead. Instead of losing my briefcase full of confidential information to the would-be killers, I clutched it to my chest and leaned forward to sprint, my speed buying another second or two.

The pick-up was slightly hampered when it tried to get all four wheels on the sidewalk and found out the hard way that it was too wide. The driver must have hit the brake too late. The passenger side mirror was clipped off and went spinning past me as the truck backed up. Quick peeks showed me what was going on. The truck, once back in forward gear, had to veer into the gutter again to avoid a darkened light pole before re-taking the sidewalk, and bumping down again at the next crossing.

All the while my legs pumped furiously.

I made it across the street to the wire fence, leaping into the air to try to surmount the top edge in one bound. I would have cleared it except that the cuff of my suit pants caught on the tie wires, causing me to pivot face first toward the grass. The edge of my briefcase clocked me on the chin. The wash of the headlights was everywhere and I could swear I felt the heat of the engine. My cuff tore away, dumping me flat. I scrambled up and forward, hearing the pick-up crash into the heavy corner post, uprooting a block of concrete, vibrating the wire links down their length.

Without knowing whether the small truck could advance further or if anyone had gotten out, I leaped toward the yellow light of someone's den. Through the small window, it looked like a soft shag rug carpet lined the floor. I thought I could look forward to a soft landing, but I would have to extend my briefcase in front of me to clear the glass.

I raised my case while in the air, and it hit something more solid than a window, and then flew out of my hands. In rapid succession, my head hit whatever was left of that object. Something snapped and momentum took me halfway into the window frame. I can still see in sharp detail the glass in the air and the astonished faces of a family diverted from their evening television.

It was at that moment that someone from behind yanked my legs and pulled me until the window frame hit one of my armpits. I thanked my broad shoulders and kicked out, making that someone howl. Then I pushed against the wall, slid the rest of the way in and finally hit that soft rug. At least most of me did.

Someone in the street called out, "Is our friend hurt? Can we come in?"

I raised my head and warned the family, "They're not my friends." Then I saw that the briefcase had made it inside, whereupon I muttered something to my new hosts about please calling the police and then allowed myself to pass out with my face pressed up against a rusty burglar bar that had snapped off the window frame.

"UNDER NO CIRCUMSTANCES will you speak to Agent S while you're there," Tanglewood warned him.

Eastman had been called in after hours for a face-to-face with his boss, and he was pissed off about once again getting a belated read-in on the Clarkeson case, which was now shut down. Police in Brooklyn had picked up Agent S on a Clarkeson-related 911 call.

"Why not?" Eastman asked. "S's job is done, right?"

"Yes, he's done, and we stay invisible. S doesn't know our hand in this, and he never needs to know."

Eastman sizzled. "Our hand in this, as you call it, is the fact that we screwed up and he's lucky to be alive."

Tanglewood smiled insufferably. "Once again, all I want from you is to go to the Sixtieth Precinct in Brooklyn and speak only to the captain there. Go any higher and you'll attract attention."

"You want me to settle the cops down with a cover story."

"I like the way I said it better. If I have to spell it out, yes, I want you to shut them up. Then you'll have the pleasure of picking up Clarkeson tomorrow. Right now, find Katie and take her with you."

Eastman pressed his lips together. He could see by the sparkle in Tanglewood's eyes that he'd thrown in the team-up with Katie to pacify him. Eastman hated to admit it, but that tactic worked. At least for now.

I SPENT SOME quality time in a private room at the Sixtieth Precinct with police who were highly skeptical that an upstate senator's audit could explain what happened to me in Brighton Beach. I didn't ask for a lawyer or pay much attention to the questioning since I was not fully there. I was irritated at the start because the police interrogated me as if I might have been the thug. *All we know is you broke someone's window, tried to get in.*

"Yes, I broke the window with my briefcase and my head, coming home from work. The perfect crime."

At that point they threatened to charge me with attempted burglary, but I think that was just to counter my sour attitude. I reminded myself that these accusations were routine. It was their job to wonder about who did what.

After a while, a sergeant came into the room and took the detective aside for a private conversation. I heard him murmur, "FBI," and thought I heard, "cover story."

"They want to speak to him?"

"No."

Suddenly, the detective came back and told me I was a hero. I had no idea what had changed.

"You caught the guys?" I asked.

"No, but we will," he smiled. "We have parts of their vehicle now as evidence. Because of you, the whole neighborhood will be safer."

"Because of me not getting killed, you mean? That's all I did."

"Mm, the way you handled the mugging."

"Wait, you're treating this as a mugging?"

He looked at his shoes. "That's up to the district attorney."

By then we were a few hours in, and two of the CID guys from my IRS office joined them as guests. They were plainclothes agents, but wore jackets and ties. Nothing flashy, just browns and grays like any other detectives. CID wanted me to themselves and had their own questions that were a lot closer to the mark than what I'd been hearing so far. The one with the red tie asked, "Why didn't you report the threat to us before someone tried to kill you?"

"I thought it could wait."

"But it couldn't, could it?"

I took four aspirin at that point, and they asked if I felt like going to the hospital. Flippantly, I said, "No I got some wonderful sleep when I passed out."

My head still hurt, which probably limited my cooperation, so I ignored them all and went home to finally get some real sleep. I was determined to be a tough guy with a concussion.

Freud said that half of dreaming is what you fear and the rest is what you wish for. This evening I had both. I dreamt that another assassin had come to follow-up on me in my home, the gun muzzle making a cold, hard imprint in the small of my back. I was apprehensive and at the same time comforted that I was dealing with an amateur; I knew precisely where the gun was. From my karate training, I knew that I could rotate left, narrowing his target while executing a lower block. The lower block would sweep the gun away, leaving my assailant open to a palm heel to his nose, all of which I would execute in one smooth maneuver. My left hand would be in a position to secure the wrist that held the gun. The assailant would be disabled if not killed and the gun would be released. In the process, I could prevent a fatal shot and take a bullet in a non-vital area or preferably none at all.

In my dream, I made the moves I was taught, and it all worked out, up until a point. I rotated and pushed his gun arm sideways with a left block while beginning to lash out with my right hand. But the bullet proved faster than the motion of my arm and the shock of it entering my fleshy left side stunned me well enough to give the attacker the opening to put a second round in my chest...

I awoke in a heart-pounding, head-aching sweat thinking how incredibly realistic that scenario was. When I practiced my karate, I never let myself think about how easy it was to fail. Wouldn't a bullet always win? What if that was the sort of attack I faced next time? Would the senator's people be stupid enough to come after me again? Our CID guys had said that if they don't find a connection between the senator and that truck, they were going to wire me up for my next meeting. I almost welcomed a wire at this point.

"What about the FBI?" I asked, recalling the hushed conversation.

They glanced at each other before answering. "What about them?"

"Are they running their own investigation?"

"Don't you have work tomorrow?"

IT WAS MY habit to watch the morning news as I dressed, and today was no exception. It tended to calm me. After splashing some cold water on my face, noticing all the cuts and treating them, I turned on the television. One news cycle ended and the next began. As I looped my tie, I heard a reporter say, "A New York State Senator has been indicted." I let the tie drop, and turned up the sound.

"You are watching footage of New York State Senator Blaine Clarkeson being led away in handcuffs by FBI agents on the steps of the capitol building in Albany, a spectacle that..."

Blaine Clarkeson was the state senator I was auditing, Brinkman's boss. Indicted for what, I didn't know. I was too stunned to catch it. All I knew was that this development was too quick to be about me. I made sure I still had his file and headed off to work in shock.

AT THE OFFICE, my telephone was ringing away as I came in. It stopped by the time I put my hand on it, but it rang again moments later. The caller was Brinkman. I wanted to ask if he was calling as the senator's rep this time or the senator's enforcer. By now I knew that the police might have questioned him rather sharply. The press certainly would have hunted him down for a comment, and our own door-kicking CID guys may have reached him; early risers the lot of them.

If anything like that had happened, Brinkman had nothing to say about it. Instead he sniffed, "Send me your adjustments. I'll sign anything you have."

Here was a man who had quickly lost his appetite for trouble. That wouldn't stop me, though, for recommending Clarkeson for fraud charges. Even if it wound up Brinkman all over again.

I found out later that Clarkeson had been indicted for corruption, "a scheme and artifice to defraud the citizens of Felton, New York," at the top of the list of bribery and kickback charges. The FBI had been watching him for a long time. They were obviously not so anxious to publicize my situation, which some could argue, they precipitated.

Friday April 3, 1987

The next time I saw Yoffe at the office, he said, "How does it feel to be the survivor of an assassination attempt?" He had a giddy smile, but he actually wanted to know.

"Somewhere between relieved and never-the-same-again. Sweaty palms, head on a swivel. You walk down every street expecting to be targeted. You walk out of this building thinking that's the moment when you're going to die. If I were the President of the United States, I could say, well, my security team will catch it earlier next time."

"…but you don't have a security team," he reminded me softly.

"None who will run interference for me until after something happens, anyway. So I have to take precautions of my own."

"What can you do?"

"I intend to do lots of things to keep me busy, like crawling on my hands and knees looking under the car for bombs and making sure I'm not backed into corners."

"You need to get out of here for a mental adjustment. Go far away to the wilderness where the threat is animal, not human. Arrange that as soon as you can."

Aberdeen overheard us and said, "I have a better idea. Maybe you should carry a gun. There's an immediate opening in CID. I could get you in there next week."

"I don't know about that." I wasn't particularly a fan or an enemy of guns. I'd used them on the firing range, and like my father before me, I was an extraordinarily good shot. Carrying a gun every day and looking after it was an entirely different story.

"Decide fast. You'd have to apply today."

"Then I have to say no. I like the option of going away on a camping trip better." Although my friend Bobby Bowman wasn't ideal company, I knew he would want to join me if we went to Montana. Yellowstone Park would be great this time of year.

"Someone can still gun you down when you get home," said Aberdeen, "but suit yourself."

Sunday, April 26, 1987

Before I could go on that camping trip, I had what would turn out to be one last date with Melody Persky. The Limelight was a popular nightclub in New York City because it was built from an enormous old gothic church. I loved everything about the place from the alternative music to the dark, hidden alcoves on every level.

I had climbed down from the second floor because Melody wanted me to buy her a drink. Our romance had been going well and I was becoming fond of her. I'd made her a painting of yellow flowers, walked with her in Flushing Park, and went bike riding the following week. I needed to be with someone to get over the pain of losing Linda. But in these weeks after my near-death experience, I'd begun to worry less about myself, and more about possible revenge on people close to me. After all, some of the senator's crew, including his lawyer, Brinkman, were still at large. That was why I tried to keep such a close eye on Melody. From where I was standing in the center of the club, I could see Melody up on the balcony where I'd left her. We waved cheerfully at each other. I ordered the drinks and took them in my hands.

To my shock, the next time I looked up, I could see Linda standing right next to Melody on the balcony, engaging her in a somewhat animated conversation. Neither of them looked down. Knowing Linda as I did, there could only be one purpose in that—the greatest love of my life was sabotaging my relationship with my girlfriend. My heart soared.

I gave them a little time and when I came back with the drinks, Linda had left.

"I thought I saw you talking to someone up here," I said, disappointed that Linda was gone.

"Just some woman I bumped into."

"Interesting conversation?"

"No," she said in a hurry.

Whatever Linda might have said to discourage Melody, it did not work. Or maybe Melody did not have the mental wherewithal to comprehend it. I would have to break up with her myself.

It was a painful breakup for both of us the next day. I couldn't stand seeing her so sad. Our talk went on for hours as I tried to talk her out of the idea of "us," and she sobbed uncontrollably. We were seated on her doorstep because I didn't think it was a good idea to go inside even one more time. I wondered several times if I should relent. I mean, I had to be crazy to still be in love with Linda, right? Maybe I only imagined her up on that balcony. And why was I breaking up with Melody when I didn't really know where Linda and I stood?

Finally, I said to Melody, "I had no idea you liked me that much."

"I don't. It's okay. I know that now." The red in her eyes hadn't gone away. "I just don't want Linda to win, and I don't know why you want her to win."

What now? "Linda?"

"You did see me talking to her at The Limelight. It wasn't the first time I met her."

"Is that how she knew we'd be there?"

"I told her we'd be there."

"Why?"

"I wanted her to see us together. I thought it would break her down, but it didn't. She's been telling me all along that I'm not right for you."

Good ol' Linda. The last time she'd done a thing like this, we'd found ourselves back together.

I took my leave of Melody, got in my car and drove to the nearest park. There I found a good bench without too much bird poop on it and sat down. Instinctively, I knew the road ahead with Linda would be hard. Yet this was the way it was meant to be. I was sure of it. Of course, she was a little nuts, but that was part of why I loved her. To all outward appearances, I led a charmed life; I had an outstanding, model career in terms of my track record and advancement; I intended to claim the woman I loved and keep her forever; I was a man without a problem. And of course, that picture of my life wasn't true.

My problem was this notion of being superman. Not the character Superman, *per se*; I wanted to be the only super being on this Earth. It seemed to me I could accomplish something akin to that in the world of work at least. Here I was, smarter than most people, working harder, and applying excellent work habits. There were times when I studied all night and planned the next steps all weekend, resulting in unique or record-breaking achievements. Extrapolate that scenario and you could stride the world like a colossus.

Yeah, right. The hubris of the young. The problem was, there is no such thing as a superman. Human beings like me have to have a balance, a personal life with some degree of stability. Otherwise, you burn out and accomplish nothing, become nothing. Unfortunately for me, time and again, I

379

balanced it all by having a personal life in which I was the opposite of superman.

So now I had this vacation, during which I could clear my mind, and I'd come back and give it another try with Linda. Because I had to admit it was only a try.

<u>Monday, June 22, 1987</u>

The moment I got back from my camping trip, the phone rang. It was Linda. My hands started shaking. I didn't know if I could speak, but somehow a few words or sounds trickled out.

"You want to get together?" she asked. "As friends?"

"Yes! What are we doing?"

"Playing some volleyball," she said. "We need one more player."

After her joust with Melody, I didn't know if she intended to reel me in or blow me up. We were not in the habit of playing volleyball together. Knowing her as I did, though, this excuse meant that she'd tacitly forgiven me for my closet time with Janis, and I was determined to never let her down again. I said, "Sure. I know how to be one more player."

That day I was thin, bearded, unevenly sunburned, my uncut hair wild, my eyes bloodshot. I looked in the mirror and laughed—hysterically, I suppose—and took a picture for posterity.

Showering took care of my scent, but didn't help me much in the appearance department. Maybe it would earn me some sympathy. One more glance in the mirror and I had to go.

I caught up with Linda in her white top and beige shorts, and said, "Where's the gang?" There was no gang.

Taking one look at my scorched face and tangle of hair, Linda said, "Just what kind of vacation did you have with Bobby Bowman?"

"You don't like the look?"

"No."

"The vacation was challenging. Things got a little... crazy."

"Crazy?"

"We fought. Got lost in the woods. Face to face with a bear. Things like that."

In fact, all those things had actually happened. The bear left after I let him claim some of our food. Bobby, however, wouldn't let up on pestering me with the question of whether he could date Linda. That's why he was done.

"I want to hear all about it," she said distractedly. "You're seeing someone, aren't you?" I supposed she had been bursting to say that.

"Other than Bowman?" I laughed. "Just a date or two that went well. Why? You and I aren't on a date now, are we?" I didn't know whether she knew that I broke up with Melody.

"No," she denied quickly.

"Then that's kind of a sharp tone to take, don't you think?" I teased.

"Oh... oh no, I was just asking. No it's good that you're seeing someone."

"Why?"

"I don't care about it. We shouldn't talk about it."

"Right. It's not like you brought it up or anything. And you and me, we're not…"

"No, of course we're not." She turned to hide her smile.

Sensing victory, I grabbed her and spun her to face me.

She gripped my collar with one hand and reached behind my head with the other to pull my face close. The desperate strength in her hands aroused me. She pressed us together so hard that my teeth were cutting my lips. She forced her tongue in my mouth like a battering ram. I couldn't believe how exciting it was to have the woman I loved want me that much. She ground her hips against me in a demonstration of the pleasure that could be mine.

Finally, she released me and backed off. "No," she concluded with a smirk, "we're not dating. I feel nothing but friendship for you."

"I'm glad we cleared that up," I gasped before she grabbed me again.

Dumb as I am, I couldn't stop thinking she hadn't explicitly forgiven me. In a pause, I said, "Really, nothing happened with Janis."

"I know," she said under a bright flush, "but we've never going to mention that or bring up her name again."

"Good deal," I replied as we came in for more.

At one point she said, "But I am going to need for you to shave."

"Sure thing," I smiled. "Volleyball has been great so far."

That afternoon and evening, Linda and I had sex for a second time, a third time, and a fourth time. I was happy. My life would be different now.

CHAPTER TWENTY
A Perfect Shot

"I'm not going to hurt you; I just want to bash your fucking brains in."

—Jack Nicholson, *The Shining*

Wednesday, August 12, 1987

And then life went on, and as far as work was concerned, it was not so different as I thought. After yet another round of training, and a few days where I signed out for field work, Aberdeen said, "By the way, you're an Expert Witness."

"Expert witness for what?"

"You'll be called upon to testify for the government at Tax Court trials."

"How did this happen? And why?"

"I put you in for it. You were accepted as a fraud specialist." No surprise on the specialty. I was someone who knew the IRS's definition of fraud, and I had already advised on whether cases should be prosecuted or not. Great for the resume if I left, and great too if I stayed. I was used to these quick mini-promotions at the IRS. For a moment, I thought about the old me, who would have asked, "Aren't witnesses the first ones killed?"

"By the way," said Aberdeen, "you have a trial coming up."

"Of course I do." I held out my hand and he slapped a heavy file into it. It was one of those giant accordion files that lawyers use, and I had to quickly secure it with my other arm before it hit the floor.

I camped out late in the office to study the new assignment, looking for the earmarks of fraud. The taxpayer's business was remodeling, with a specialty in concrete. The IRS looked at him hard after the taxpayer offered to put the first investigator under the paving stones. The allegations concerning both the pattern of hiding income and the threats to the revenue agent were all documented in front of me. It probably represented a mere fraction of the crimes committed. As I knew by now, we didn't usually get serious threats unless there was major criminality hiding behind it.

When I finally flipped my way through to the end of the paperwork, I found a bright orange sticky note on the reverse side of the last file folder. It said not to schedule any on-site meeting with the taxpayer without informing CID of the appointment. I'd already met that crew. They were the guys who were supposed to protect Treasury agents from threats on their lives. Or mop up afterward. Theirs was the job I would have been doing if I'd taken Aberdeen up on his offer to carry a gun. Technically, I should have called them the minute Brinkman threatened me.

I noticed that some of the pen marks on the sticky note went all the way to the edges and some of the letters were cut off and didn't continue onto the surface behind the note. Based on something I remembered from the start of the file, I lifted the square and relocated it. I was able to align the pen lines on the edges of the note with some stray marks I'd seen on the very first page. Once the message was in its proper place, the letters were complete. That told me that the orange square had been written in one place and then moved to another.

The presence of the warning and the fact that it had been shuffled to the back of the file was mildly unsettling, as though someone did not want me to find it easily. I wouldn't have found it on this evening if I weren't so thorough. Now I had the office to myself, an uncomfortably darkened space with a lot of passages where an intruder could hide. Breathing rather quickly, I realized I should have asked Aberdeen which agency originated the file. There was nothing inside to indicate that, but I suspected that something like this must come from the FBI. To settle my fears, I called Linda at home to make sure she was okay, but I got no answer.

I needed background information on the taxpayer, so I looked him up on our WAR system. There was plenty of evidence of prior collection activity, and I took copious notes. In the encoded history record, I found my answer. The file had previously been worked in Rusterholtz' group. My old group manager was the one who had transferred this file to me. There was no actual control name, but his group number was an unmistakable match for the transfer-in code.

If I didn't know WAR—and most revenue agents didn't—I would not have found out. What was a case like this doing in his training group in the first place? I resolved to ask Aberdeen in the morning.

At 6 PM exactly, I decided to shut the system off and go to Linda's even though she wasn't expecting me. When I reached for the switch, my screen suddenly cleared and replaced the words I was looking at with the message, "LOOK BEHIND YOU." I turned around, and the zipper, our in-house news system, blinked to life with a series of animations. It lit up with flags, flashes, fireworks, and then a message in all caps. No one there to see it but me. I itched with dread. Why would it come on now?

It said: YOU KNOW IT'S BULLSHIT, RIGHT?

Hector. That was his signature phrase. He knew how to run WAR, but how the hell did he get into my new department and program the zipper?

The same message ran three times in case I didn't catch it at first, the repetition telling me that he was serious, not pranking the division.

New message: YOU KNOW WHERE TO MEET ME... This ran only once.

I did know where to meet him. I locked up the file, and went there without delay.

It was dark in the Dungeon, lit only by display lights behind the cafeteria counters, but Hector's suit and shape were unmistakable as he emerged from behind a pillar. I was somewhat relieved it was him, but not by a longshot was I lowering my guard.

I said, "How is it necessary to meet like this?"

"I don't know about you, but I wonder who monitors the hidden microphones upstairs at this hour. They'd have to be pretty hard core." He was his usual green-clad self, but being more direct and sounding more serious than I'd ever heard him be.

"What about the zipper?"

"Deleted the program, cleared the cache. It doesn't keep a record of the operator." And his broadcast looked like a prank anyway.

"So what is this about?"

"Your new case."

"I got it from Aberdeen. He's one of the good guys."

"That's what they wanted you to focus on, and that's why they waited to filter that file through him. First they gave you the senator, and now you have this dangerous fraud case?"

"There's always going to be a tough case."

"Don't you know what case laundering is? Use your head for once. Someone is trying to get rid of you."

He was Hector, so I didn't ask how he knew about my case, but I did ask, "Who would be out to get me?"

"I have a five-page list. Do you want me to read it to you from the top down or the bottom up?"

I knew that he could be right. Hell, this was the wise old owl. When had he ever been wrong? The audit that had landed on my desk was suspicious. Someone had been hoping that I didn't notice the orange note right away, but they didn't want to be so obvious as to remove it entirely. That might have raised uncomfortable questions later.

"What do you think I should do?"

Hector came closer and said, "Refuse it."

"You don't know Aberdeen." I meant that Aberdeen would never jam me up.

"I don't doubt he's a good guy, but drop it before it's too late."

That was when Hell expanded to swallow us whole. In rapid succession, two muzzle blasts lit the place up. Hector went down and rolled away.

"Hector!" I shouted. No response. In the barely-lit room I couldn't see if there was any blood trail. Hoping he was only taking cover and not hurt, I ducked behind a pole. A dark figure loped away with an awkward gait. I couldn't see any more movement, but when I replayed the unusual motion in my mind, I realized there were two figures stuck together as though the larger one were dragging the smaller. I felt like I'd been punched in the throat.

A man with a grating voice called out, "I'm sorry I missed you. Now we need to do this the hard way."

"Do what?" I asked.

"I have to kill your smartass girlfriend if you don't come out."

Smartass? I didn't want to believe he meant Linda, but he couldn't have meant Melody. How would anyone have found out so quickly that we had gotten back together?

A woman I couldn't see cried out, "I'm sorry, Danny. Melody left me a message saying she wasn't giving you up, and that she was coming here to see you. That's why I came—"

Linda! My crazy, impulsive Linda had come to defend her man. This was worse than any of her earlier stunts. But she couldn't have known what she'd face in this basement. Given the timing, I wondered if someone had forced Melody to make that call.

"Now that you know which girlfriend I mean," yelled the stranger, "you can make the right decision."

Though I didn't recognize the voice, this person had done a scary amount of homework on me. I didn't need any time to think about whether or not I wanted to save Linda. I would give my life for her. I started to step out of the shadows to face him, and another shot rang out.

I ran forward, and too late heard a new voice warn, "Stay back!" The man holding Linda was shot and slumping, still clutching her close as a shield, only now he had a clear shot at me. He took the opportunity to blast away and the bullet tore into my kneecap. As I went down, the pain lit up my head brighter than the zipper.

Once my mind cleared a bit, I recognized the man. Salvatore Purisi. I'd seen him daily as part of the Passentino entourage when they arrived each day for the trial. Apparently, he specialized in kneecap destruction by gun as well as bat. If anyone needed a second opinion on the subject, I could confirm now that he was accurate in at least one method.

His coming after me did not come out of nowhere, though. I'd heard from a reporter friend that Purisi had left the Passentino family's employ and started working for Clarkeson. Big step down, in my opinion, but he wasn't taking resumé advice from me.

Salvatore took one more shot and he missed because I made a flat target on the floor. Hector must have crawled clear because he was nowhere in sight.

A man who looked like an FBI type took his second shot at the assailant but only clipped his ear. Salvatore was in front of a light, and I saw the blood splash. A third shot from the good guys' side would turn out to belong to a female FBI agent, who was being even more careful and got even less of a result.

That distraction and the next round of suppressive fire, however, was enough for Linda to break loose and come running towards me. A bad idea. Her escape would surely not be enough to keep Salvatore from shooting her, or the FBI from shooting her by accident. I shouted for Linda to get down, and pretended there was a gun in my hand too. Salvatore saw my motion and moved toward cover, whereupon Linda turned back to him and completely surprised him by chopping at the crook of his elbow. Hitting him in that soft spot must have surprised him even more when she relieved him of his gun and started to run for it. He grabbed her around the waist and she threw the gun towards me.

My mind was working fast but not fast enough for that turn of events. I hoped there would come a day when I could ask Linda, "How did you do that, and what were you thinking?"

Trying to catch a gun is really not the great idea that it seems like in the movies. Not catching a gun, and losing possession of it, is even worse. Maybe all couples should practice throwing guns to each other, should one or the other ever be held at gunpoint and need to make a daring escape.

Because my reflexes had always been great, I couldn't miss the objective entirely. My hand went up to meet the pistol, tried to close on some part, and only deflected it. I may have struck the trigger. In any case, it went off.

Couples trying gunplay should also throw one another hearing protectors of the kind they use at gun ranges. I didn't have mine when the weapon went bang. My fear for Linda's safety made it seem the loudest sound I'd ever heard.

I didn't know if the stray shot hit anyone, but the next thing I knew, Salvatore came up with a backup gun and fired off a round to cover his tactical retreat. Since I didn't hear that many footsteps, I was sure he remained somewhere in the half-lit room, still in the game.

Linda had wriggled loose and thrown herself flat. Good girl, though I didn't know if her move made it more likely, or less, that the accidental discharge had struck her. She was holding very still.

Now I peered into the darkness for Salvatore's first gun, began crawling with outstretched hands, and a chunk of metal came sliding towards me and into my wet palm. It was the gun I was looking for. Had to be. And that move could only have come from Hector, I told myself. I checked the safety and the magazine. A couple of bullets were missing from the clip. But not all were unaccounted for because one of them was in my knee.

I'd heard that knee injuries are among the most painful experiences you can have, and doubted it, but I was beginning to get the idea through experience even before the tsunami of pain had done its worst. Instead of my eyes adjusting to the dark, everything seemed to be getting dimmer, which was a bad sign. My Boy Scout training told me that a tourniquet might be in order, and I remembered that I carried a fancy one around my neck. I think that's why ties were invented.

Still no movement or word from Linda. I wasn't going to be any use to her if I passed out, so I had to at least try to reduce the bleeding. I whipped the tie off my neck, my every movement causing my knee to scream. Flags, flashes, and fireworks in my head made a beautiful contrast in the dark. I rolled my pants up above my knee to make a base, wrapped the tie from top to bottom and top again, making an overhand knot as tight as I could manage.

Technically, this was not a tourniquet, though it made a serviceable distraction. To make a real one, all I had to do was use the gun to make a torsion stick. Then I just needed to be lucky enough that my twirling it would make the weapon go off by accident again and this time shoot the bad guy dead wherever he was hiding. Then I'd be all set. But if there was a better plan to get us out of this alive, I didn't have one.

"Linda!" I hissed.

"I'm fine," she replied in similar *sotto voce*.

It was such a relief to hear her speak that I nearly passed out. It embarrassed me that I was having such a hard time staying conscious. First I had conked out by bashing my head into glass and burglar bars. Now I was doing the same from a bullet in the knee, and feeling teary eyed that Linda was unhurt. What a wuss I was turning into. What I really needed was for all the other shooters to circle around and kill each other while I napped.

Something nudged me in the ribs, bringing me alert again.

"Hector?"

He rasped, "I saw which way he went."

"You saw Salvatore? Are you badly hurt?"

In labored breaths, he said, "Don't worry about me. I saw you get hit too. Salvatore is making his way over to the back door, but it's locked after hours. He'll circle around the edges looking for another way out, and when he can't find it, he'll shoot his way out. You know he will."

As if hearing his cue, Sal did start shooting again. I heard a loud clang as the shots hit metal, and the remaining lights went dark except for the exit signs.

"Who else is here with us, Hector?"

"Feebies."

"The FBI?"

"Two of their best. Monroe Eastman and Katie Spindel." The man knew *everything*.

"Do you work for them, Hector?"

"You don't know that, and I can't say."

"You passed me that gun because it was an extra. You're already armed, aren't you?"

"Help me sit up," was all he said.

I did, and told him, "I'm going over to help Linda."

"Do that. Pick her up and then move left until you hit the counters. That will be as far out of the line of fire as possible."

Though I could see virtually nothing, I was able to orient myself by the direction of the exit signs. From that bearing, I crawled toward where I last saw Linda, sweeping my arms to make sure I didn't miss her in the dark. My right leg dragged like dead weight. Two arms and a left leg had to be enough to get me wherever I needed to go. With my martial arts training, I repeated to myself, "No pain, no pain, no pain."

Then I whispered, "Linda?"

"Here."

"One more time."

"Over here."

"I got you."

When I was close enough, she found my mouth with hers. "Clever move," I said.

"Nothing to it, Danny. We've been together in the dark before."

"Have I mentioned that I love aggressive women?"

"I made a decision. You don't have to worry about my par—"

I hoped she was going to say that she changed her mind about listening to her parents, but a bang and a muzzle flash spoiled the moment, and whatever she was going to tell me.

"Come on," I said. "We have to keep going."

We started to follow the route Hector had mapped out for us, and a wave of agony hit me. Now I said it out loud, even more urgently, "No pain, no pain, no pain!" We kept going.

My second mantra should have been, "No shock, no shock, no shock."

"You're hurt," said Linda.

"We can make it," I said before I banged my head on the counters. "Okay, we're here." I hugged her close and kissed her again.

"I have her," Sal yelled. "Don't come near me."

If he'd grabbed a woman, it had to be Agent Spindel because I still had Linda in my arms.

After that, things happened fast.

Eastman got one bank of the main lights on. Sal saw who he had grabbed, pushed Katie away from him, and dashed out the exit. So one of the doors was unlocked.

Hector was wrong for once and I was grateful for it because it meant Purisi didn't have to run past us shooting.

Eastman ran to Katie, helped her up and held her close for a moment. She kissed him quickly and then pushed the door back open, at which point they both ran the way Sal had gone, and I lost sight of them.

Simon Rusterholtz came in through the other door. No jacket or tie. Just his bad-taste in shirts. From the revulsion on his face, he did not look like he was with us good guys. Then again I never thought he was. He saw that all of us were down on the floor and he laughed. I wished that those two FBI agents would hurry up and get back.

Rusterholtz wasn't venturing any closer than his five yards but he also wasn't waiting. He said to me, "Sal is worthless with his kneecap bullshit, and you three pieces of crap have been a lot of trouble to me." He reached behind him into his waistband and Linda gasped. I was faster on the draw. Simon took my bullet in his stomach.

Or maybe not *my* bullet. Marshall Colotine had jumped out from behind a nearby column. He, Hector, and I, had all fired at the same time. More interagency cooperation. I wondered what that service would cost me.

LINDA AND I got married the next year, and Eastman and Katie came to our wedding. Linda's parents did not. My former friend Bowman wasn't invited.

Without financial backing, our nuptials were an intimate affair. Ginny Berlini did the entertainment. Hector was my best man. Melody Persky was Linda's bridesmaid. Just kidding. Of course she wasn't.

Thankfully, Hector wore a tuxedo instead of his usual green suit. His breathing was still impaired from the bullet in his side, though he was expected to make a full recovery. To ease the pain, he drank a lot. I think he liked saying, "Mazeltov." I was hoping he would drop a clue about his connection to other agencies, but after the toasts, a few more drinks made him taciturn. I'd have better luck later.

Right after the ceremony, Eastman came up to us and revealed, "We came here from an operation." Katie was on his arm, holding a dazzling smile.

I tried to wave them off. "Please. No shop talk today."

"You're going to want to hear this one. Katie and I busted Bonnie and Clyde."

"Mitzi and Noel?"

"They're in jail awaiting trial."

"What? How?"

"We wired up a taxpayer, and got the Cunnings on tape making empty threats about a fake assessment, and demanding a bribe in exchange for not ruining the man's life. It's entrapment."

"Is that something you can prosecute?"

"The charges against them are creative and some of them might not stick. But their careers at the IRS are over."

"How come that never came up before?"

"Because they would always tell the taxpayer to take some time and think about their response until the next meeting. They also warned them never to say whose idea it was, or the audit would come back every year. Now all of their past cases are under review. The "CREEPS" Kopple case was overturned immediately under the authority of Perry Topaz."

"That's fantastic." Whatever the senator had done, it was great to see the IRS get its own house in order even if we needed an outside agency to do it. Even if it removed some of the flavor of old-time movies I had come to expect in our shop.

I had begun to think that no power on Earth was going to stop our Bonnie and Clyde, but they were much like the originals after all, finished in their mid-twenties while the rest of us were just getting started.

We broke out the champagne, and Linda said, "Maybe we should have done a Bonnie and Clyde theme for our wedding. Bullet hole cake, mmm."

"Or not," I countered, thinking of how I had to fire at Rusterholtz.

"The music is playing," she said with a twirl. "It's time to dance."

"I can't," I said, glancing down at my damaged legs.

She pretended to misunderstand. "Sure you can. You put your hands here and here." She situated my left hand at ten o'clock on her shoulder and raised my right hand to two o'clock just like a steering wheel. "And then you get moving."

Hiding an initial twinge of pain under a genuine smile of joy, I said, "You're right. It does work."

After a kneecapping, you never walk right again and dancing is limited to the Quasimodo Shuffle. I was no exception. Yet dancing with Linda, that day and every day, was more than worth it.

~ fin ~

**To share your comments, visit our <u>CREDS</u>: the IRS Adventure Page on Facebook.
www.facebook.com/credsbook**

<u>Creds Glossary</u>

Disclosure The intentional or unintentional revealing of taxpayer information to someone outside of the IRS, or even within the IRS who is not working on the case in question. Technically, it also included instances where no one saw the information, but could potentially have seen it because the file was in an unlocked drawer. Sharing information with outsiders should occur only when a qualified representative presents a duly executed power of attorney. Committing an act of disclosure at the IRS in the 1980s was like walking out of a nuclear power plant with an unacceptable dose of radiation, as depicted in the movie *Silkwood*. The voices raised in a disclosure investigation were as loud as any emergency alarm, and the "scrubdown" was intensive.

Flashing Your Creds Showing your credentials as a federal agent.

In the Service Working for the Internal Revenue Service.

ITP Illegal Tax Protestor. The term does not refer to illegal taxes. It refers to people protesting existing tax law in an illegal manner, such as not filing due to a philosophy that challenges the legitimacy of government. An additional facet often involves advocating the physical destruction of the government or its personnel.

PDT Potentially Dangerous Taxpayer. Both a designation and the name of a program under the Office of Employee Protection.

POD Post of Duty, the designation for an employee's official home base—a phrase that was used every day, verbally and on paperwork, although few knew what the letters meant.

PRP Problem Resolutions Program, the specially trained arm who dealt with persistent problems that taxpayers encountered in getting their issues resolved with the IRS.

R/A's Revenue Agents, the prime movers of the Examinations Division, as opposed to R/O, a Revenue Officers, the key players in the Collections Division.

Rep Short for Taxpayer's Representative (not to be confused with TSR), someone with power of attorney, who could be a lawyer, an accountant, an enrolled agent, or even an uncredentialed tax preparer. Usually the empowered rep would show up without the taxpayer. Sometimes the whole point of this arrangement was to avoid any unpleasantness.

Research A section within Taxpayer Service where advanced informational requests from the general public are fulfilled.

TSR Taxpayer Service Representative, the equivalent of a corporation's customer service representative.

TSS Taxpayer Service Specialist, a rare promotion within Taxpayer Service that is comparable to the power of those in the Examinations Division in that it empowers the specialist to actually increase or decrease a taxpayer's tax burden rather than simply making a referral to other departments.

Technical A small section of elite scholars who field technical questions referred to them. These were primarily inquiries that depended on an expert knowing how our computer system coded the history of a problem. "Elite," by the way, didn't necessarily mean better paid. The technical section were people who were smarter and worked harder, and often had better experience independent of their time-in-grade.

WAR Stands for Write and Respond, the encrypted operating system for the country's master tax history database. This is a fictional term for a system too confidential to identify.

Ben Parris

ACKNOWLEDGEMENTS

Creds: The IRS Adventure was the labor of decades, most of it drafted from my daily journal when I worked at the IRS in the mid-1980's. As a novel, it picked up speed in recent years, especially with the help of many discerning readers starting with Ken Altabef (Alaana's Way), who looked at my rough outlines and notes, and called for the spicy scenes.

My amazing first-draft readers were Madelyn Fisichella, Lauren Freund, and Megan Prokott. Thanks to Nancy Zhang and Danielle Howe, as well, for their helpful comments on the first pages.

My extraordinary second draft readers were Hannah Wyborski (remarkable attention to detail), Michelle Shin, Elizabet Cabrera, and Maggie Auffarth.

Third draft readers Janelle Hart (seeker of balance) and Nicole Kosar (finder of things what were way-too-sketchy) did a wonderful job of telling me what was left to address. Special thanks to Kirsten Kim for adding one last look at the proof stage, and for her promotional efforts.

Any mistakes that remain were the result of my pig-headed refusal to listen to their good advice.